GW00660105

The Centre
of the Labyrinth

The Centre
of the Labyrinth

Philip Lloyd-Bostock

QUARTET BOOKS

First published by Quartet Books Limited 1993
A member of the Namara Group
27/29 Goodge Street, London W1P 1FD

The extract on p.109 from *The Sixteen Satires* (Satire II, lines 13–18) by Juvenal, translated by Peter Green (Penguin Classics 1967, revised edition 1974), copyright © Peter Green 1967, 1974, is reproduced by permission of Penguin Books Limited

The Ezra Pound quotation on p.169 from *Collected Shorter Poems, Personae* (New Directions), is by permission of Faber & Faber Limited

Lyrics from *My Fair Lady* on p.468 are quoted by permission of International Music Publications Limited

A catalogue record for this title is available from the British Library

ISBN 0 7043 7030 2

Typeset by The Electronic Book Factory Ltd, Fife, Scotland
Printed and bound in Great Britain by
Bookcraft Ltd, Midsomer Norton, Avon

Contents

PREFACE

Philip Lloyd-Bostock was still working on this book when he died, soon after his fortieth birthday. Had time not run out on him so cruelly he would no doubt have revised it, correcting inconsistencies and reconciling the narrative's two endings. Rather than guess at his intentions, the publishers have judged it best to present the text as he left it. The work necessary to transform it from a fragmented, largely handwritten manuscript into a connected, legible book has been done, but nothing has been added and only a few repetitive or obscure passages have been taken away.

Part One

1

In Memory of Those Yet to Die

An old lady paced around the metal room. She seemed grim and preoccupied, and the grey shift she wore looked oddly uncomplicated beneath the frozen puckered tension of her face.

She walked methodically, though without apparent purpose. It was an effort for her to move at all, for her body was old and stiff. After a while, the rhythm of her walk became less regular. She allowed herself to amble loosely, as if the emotional pressure of her earlier mood had relaxed. It was not surprising that she appeared so self-absorbed. There was nothing in the room to engage her attention.

Under a window too high to see out of there stood a tall cabinet, made from the same metal as the walls of the room. It had no catches or fastener, no visible means of discovering its contents. The floor of the room was curiously springy, giving a slight bounce to her arthritic pace. No light-source could be detected, no ventilator, door or heating system. Apart from the cabinet, the room was bare of furniture.

Suddenly the woman stopped and remained motionless a few moments, as if transfixed by an insuperable block in her thoughts. Her face showed apprehension, a kind of nervous anxiety. Whether the cause related to the past or the future was impossible to determine. Her skin bore the crevices of suffering, on which was imposed a more complex map to accommodate the added weight of emotion. Yet her face bore the vestiges of past beauty; her bearing was that of a woman who once possessed a sense of her own elegance.

Her old green eyes, faded and rheumy, gazed at the metal ceiling almost in accusation.

From beneath the shift rose a frail and tremulous wrist. For all the world, it apparently took on an attitude of benediction. She held the arm up vertically and looked intently at its thin erect column. Then, drawing her other hand from under the material she brought it across to meet the other's veined back. Lightly caressing, she drew her five fingers back towards the fleshless area of the elbow. In the cold glare of the intense, uniform light, she stood and clasped herself.

A momentary jolt of her head broke this immobility. Her eyes stared more intently, starting out of their sockets. At that precise moment the cabinet opened – a synchronized double movement from the inside outwards – to reveal its interior. It seemed some kind of psycho-telekinesis had operated at her behest: a willed transference of thought taking the place of ordinary mechanical control. No doubt the whole thing would have been clear, even banal, to contemporary witnesses of the event in the year 2020; but to this prophetic narrator it was – is – extraordinary, and this pseudo-historical narrative of the event was in fact based on the shaky foundations of speculation about the future of science, as of everything (as indeed was the 'was' in that sentence, or the 'was' in that parenthesis, and so on *ad infinitum*).

The cabinet was empty save for a pile of exercise books in the middle of the central shelf. The books looked forlorn and anachronistic in the midst of so much uncompromising modernity. Their edges were rough and thumbed and they were arranged, not higgledy-piggledy, but definitely out of alignment.

The woman walked forward again reverently and with gentle, tremulous hands removed the top book from the pile. Evidently things were not yet so far advanced as to allow her to spirit objects from place to place; and there was something rather satisfying in her motion and attitude, as if she had been a penitent recovering an ex-voto endowed with magical properties.

Seated on the floor, her head inclined to one side against the icy metal, she placed the unopened book on her lap and scanned its gaudy cover. Although it was a child's writing-book, the design was curiously at odds with its function. It portrayed a sophisticated circus poster, on which a wasp-waisted siren, draped in scarlet velvet with leg-of-mutton sleeves, a pair of elaborate lyred wings sprouting from her blonde hair, pointed vampishly, simperingly, to the roll of events. It was evident that the woman knew the description with pleasurable familiarity – or perhaps, rather, that she was a backward reader (or had reading become outdated?) or even that she simply enjoyed the labial and plosive contortions of Italian (which was it?) – because her lips moved noiselessly as she read:

GRANDE
ARENA
MILANO
STAGIONE ESTIVA 1897
DAL 17 GIUGNO AL 15 SETTEMBRE
STRAORDINARI SPETTACOLI
GRANDIOSI BALLI
CARLO IL GUASTATORE
BRAHMA
ATTRAZIONI DI VARIETÀ
PALAZZO DI CRISTALLO
CINEMATOGRAFO. CALEIDOSCOPIO
BERSAGLI. PATTINAGGIO. FESTIVAL
GIOSTRE. ALTALENE. AREOSTATI
FUOCHI ARTIFICIALI
ILLUMINAZIONI ED ALTRI DIVERTIMENTI
SERVIZIO DI CAFFÉ E BIRRARIA DI PRIMO ORDINE
BUVETTES. BARS. GELATERIE

———

L'ARENA E APERTA TUTTI I GIORNI dalle 14 alle 24

Why had she read with such attention? Another would merely have glanced at it, and registered it instantaneously for what it was: an announcement, a telegraphic signal, a kind of emblem, like a winged tyre representing speed; not have systematically scrutinized its every detail. Yet something in her concentration revealed the cause. So rapt an expression flooded her face, so imperceptible an upturn appeared at the corners of her mouth, that it was clear her heart was entirely engaged, that the reading, line by line, word by word, syllable by syllable, letter by letter, was filled with some spiritual flush of meaning and the omission of any one element would have destroyed the spell of a much-repeated ceremony – as if a priest had inadvertently passed over the 'Agnus Dei'.

Once she had made out the minuscule capitals of the last line – SERVIZIO DI TRAMWAYS ELETTRICI LIREA DI PORTA TERRAGLIA – she let her eyes flick upwards again to the picture of the sickly-yellow theatre, framed in a myriad light-bulbs and naphtha-flares, the huge throng jostling inside its iron-work supports only discernible by a few crudely sketched hats, gaudy buttonholes and banked heads and moustaches. Did the picture itself mean something to her? Was her imagination transported to such a scene, from her own past perhaps? Whatever her reaction, it lasted only a moment, may, indeed, have been a mere reflex, an element of the prescribed pattern of reading the picture; perhaps even a superstition comparable with the fear of rearranging domestic objects in an unfamiliar order.

Her delay in opening the book was short-lived. And now the furrowing of her brow became even more intense, the careful support of the book more firm, held, as it was, between her stiffened hands as she read:

'But we live now in such an age, that the deserts of any thing, are the meanes and occasions of not obtaining it.'

This story was written for myself and for two other people. I have made no concessions to anyone else. The allusions are not explained. The thicket of the narrative has not been cut down with the machete of vulgarization. I am not unconscious of the dangers of over-literariness, but I believe them to be outweighed by the demands of truthfulness. In my case, truthfulness is pretty Byzantine; and my writing mirrors that inescapable fact.

That last statement may not be entirely true. I am no longer sure. Things are difficult now. As St Isidore said,

'*Fabulas poetae a* fando *nominverunt, quia non sunt* res factae *sed tantum loquendo* fictae.'

I wish it to remain confusing. I hate clarity. I believe reading should be difficult, because life is difficult.

This story does not speak to the blood. It is a labyrinth of words interposing itself between those who read and my own defensive self. I am the Minotaur, the *Homo daedalus*. I let the Word do its work.

It has been agony to write, a kind of constipation. The words came out in hard pellets; but then they inexplicably joined themselves together in a swimming morass of *post-facto* dysentery.

I don't know what is happening to my brain. We only have our brain with which to understand our brain; and the cord has been broken.

It is difficult to live, but even more difficult to explain one's life.

There were many things she hadn't quite understood, although her face had, for the most part, worn an expression of bland recognition, indulgence and sentiment as of one who read to have her prejudices confirmed, not her world turned upside-down. This complacency had, though, been punctuated by signs of confusion, scepticism, even disbelief. Occasionally she reread passages that had made no sense on first reading, her papery forehead crumpled and furrowed by the effort of understanding; and, when the strain became too great, she tossed the book aside, pursing her lips in a bleak line of contempt or impatience. But in the end she still persevered, moved more by curiosity about herself than by any higher form of engagement.

Much in her manner of reading showed this was not the first time she'd embarked on the story. The way she held the book had something of the familiar devotion of a priest with his breviary, or of a child engrossed in a protectively clutched fairy-tale, whose excitement was the more intense for the number of chantable retellings. Even her outbursts against the sections she found preposterous lacked spontaneity. It seemed probable that the dimensions of her life had shrunk to an endless rereading of this book.

The text made no proper sense unless it was being read by her; for she alone understood it, its truth and its aberrations and the mysteries which explained those aberrations. She was inseparable from the book, had no meaning outside it. Like Don Quixote, the moment she strayed from the pages and wandered about in the public domain with a pretend autonomy, she needed to be recaptured at once, rescued from enchanters and falsifiers, corrected by the true narrative. It was her present condition that was the lie, the fabrication. The truth lay in the words that gushed from Jerome's dying brain, scarred across with lesions and clouded with neural fluff, clinging to the receding vision.

2

A Child Born, a Son Given

'You must take my child,' she said, *'and protect him for me.'*

No other words issued from the prone body, exhausted by birth-pangs and the effort of guilty sacrifice. Gradually she subsided into a low spasmodic shuddering and turned away to face a wall whose surface, uniform and untainted by discoloration, seemed like a further reproach and caused her to shut her eyes. Only the anxious presence of the other woman threatened her hermetic insulation from the panic of life, from the quick, new life of the child just removed from her awkward, despairing grasp by the nurse.

The silence of the hospital room seemed like a suspension of matter, so white and empty was its noiselessness.

Venetia waited for the moment to pass. She hoped in vain that Adelaida might suddenly turn back and speak again, so dissipating the blur of embarrassment and confusion that hung between them. She sat, hands clasped in her lap, staring at the obviousness, the thingness of the clambering sweetheart-ivy she'd brought for Adelaida and to which alone truth could be assigned. Feeling she ought to be considering the consequences of the peremptory command – the inferred disruption of her own freedom, the psychological consequences of the mother's abandonment of the son, the sudden vertiginous changes in both their lives – she found she could only concentrate on the minimal details of the room. Was this her defence against Adelaida's imposition of duty and transference of guilt: a kind of motor paralysis in which all sensory faculties were reduced to a single stressless seeing bereft of meaning and reference? It was the kind of question she would ask herself years later, when, deserted by language, she tried to understand.

'OK,' she said at length. It was characteristic of her to speak in a way that an uninformed observer might interpret as monstrous insensitivity, a baffling miscalculation of other people's states of mind or an amazing use of a register and idiom sharply at odds with circumstance. The manner was, however, merely an indication of a desire to defuse the situation, a cautious, nervous wish to treat Adelaida's decision as of little consequence in the greater scheme of things.

The nurse returned and fussed around Adelaida's bed, unfazed by her elephantine torpor. Unheedful too of the irritation felt by both women at her intrusion, she rearranged the objects on the stainless-steel cabinet – books, fruit, a small Spanish madonna with swords pointing at her heart – as if a fresh domestic order might eradicate the malaise she herself sensed in an odd confrontation.

The room was all right-angles and straight lines. Each item in it was self-contained, yet part of a concerted whole. The hard edges of the panic-button box and the squared-off castors of the medicine trolley mirrored the clean angularity of the tubular lighting as it cast its headachy glare like a pristine tent.

When she had finished, the nurse turned to Venetia and gestured towards Adelaida. 'Is she asleep now?'

'I don't think so. But we should let her rest. May I see the child again?'

'Yes, of course. Come with me.'

Venetia rose and looked towards Adelaida as she gathered up her things. She wanted to rouse her gently, cradle her body in her arms and overwhelm her with compassion; in the midst of so much sorrow, to show her an action that obeyed a higher morality, one that the world might misconstrue but which was the only one she could sensibly enforce. Why on earth had Adelaida never discussed her intention to abandon her child with her? It was understandable, if questionable, that she should have refused an abortion. But the determination to proceed with the birth, assuming that Venetia would shoulder responsibility for the child, only confirmed the disorder of Adelaida's mind. Yet might it not be true that the boy's interests would be best served by separation from a mother who could never love him? Adelaida would never be able to absorb a son into the maelstrom of her political radicalism; not just from a practical point of view, but because she could not calculate or see those ordinary, generic demands of life, those bonds and needs which orchestrate the world. Ordinary people suffer and struggle in the preordained framework of their lives and need the reassurance of seeing others in the same predicaments. So far had Adelaida strayed from this model that Venetia – and, indeed, Adelaida herself – recognized how her understanding had shrunk and contracted, moving ever further away from a normality of vision into the systematic madness of revolutionary fervour. Her mind now was an intricate confection of stratagems and expediencies, manifestoes, placards and abstractions, universals divorced from their specific inspiration. Where would a nappy fit in, what peculiar interstices would a rocking-horse inhabit? How could you kiss a grazed knee when your head was full of *poujadisme*?

And here was she, Venetia, full of unplumbed love, ill at ease with her own birth and lot, cast adrift in an ocean of loose tides, longing for sight of land. A mother in spirit, as adoring as only the untrammelled can be, tractable and eager, one step away from motherhood. Surely she could do it?

Adelaida's back gave off no such potential. It lay fixed and guarded, the heavy contours of the body pregnant again, this time with stoic immutability. The process of excision was already complete for Adelaida. A simple moral argument and the exercise of extreme pragmatism had served to carry out a kind of full-term abortion, one in which the child's real life, though spared, sprang from some anonymous other womb. The instincts and desires of motherhood had succumbed, in advance of the baby's arrival, to Adelaida's awareness of her unforgiving duty. She could allow no encumbrances, and repeated this to herself in the infrequent lapses during her pregnancy when the kicking of her child caused her resolve to falter. Her feelings about Venetia as a surrogate may be surmised only vaguely.

Probably she saw her as no more than a willing and docile wet-nurse who would complete the clinical removal of the child, vacuum it up into a frustrated embrace.

As she walked out of the room, Venetia glanced back, but her gaze took in everything except Adelaida, just the apparatus of health and life, the symbols of regeneration. At one level she was conscious of the need to record what she saw, freeze-frame it in perpetuity so that, when the time came to analyse and seek its meaning, she could revivify its static imagery and feel again its emotional impact. Somehow she could – would have to – obliterate from her mind that icon of cast-off love in its unnatural posture of slouched nonchalance. It was as if she had already assumed the role of mother, and was herself just risen from that clinical bed to visit her own first-born, leaving behind only some dark negative of herself. Closing the door with a tense movement of her hand, she felt herself sloughing off the fetters that had tied her to Adelaida and moving resolutely into a new world of light, colour and joy. The door slammed harder than she had intended. She strode along the corridor behind the nurse. Supreme in purpose, her majestic frame disappeared into the nursery.

3

Soul Meeting

The past no longer mattered. It had become an indistinct relief of barely perceived figures, buildings and landscapes, undifferentiated even by the smallest prominences or salients. So vehemently had she dissociated herself from its force that it had subsided, hardened and rendered itself innocuous, molten lava turned to grey and friable Pompeian ash.

Whenever she considered her origins, Venetia was amazed at how puny an influence they had exerted over her evolving self. Conditioning, nurture, inculcation, behaviourism – all seemed like meaningless terms in an unread textbook to a strange waif who stood out like a cut-out advertisement hoarding for Self-Determination.

A more detached perspective might have shown how certain concrete things could not but have moulded her, whether or not she recognized their strength. The death of both her parents – snapped, mangled and burned in a car accident; the enormous financial settlement made over to her as a result; the books given to her for intellectual guidance by a single sympathetic nun. In retrospect, she could never understand why she had ever even tried to jeopardize the efforts of the creators of her unheard-of freedom by experimenting with the dull routine and assumptions of a girl of her class.

'I suppose I'd noticed that thing that little girls have of actually *wanting* to wear the same dress as all the others. At twenty, at Ascot, it turns into every girl's nightmare. And God knows, they drop that lunacy pretty fast; but I must have been infected with a *mite* of conformism. I remember buying a Hermès headscarf once. As soon as I came out of the shop I realized what an idiot I'd been, and tried to give it to a girl in the street. She was absolutely amazed and looked at it as if it was a primed hand-grenade, muttering something disconnected in, I think, Polish . . . She couldn't wear it any more than I could. I realized then the futility of trying to acquire or assume the semiotic *charge* that clothes and things have.'

'You were always contrasuggestible,' said her elegant aunt. 'You don't need to justify anything to me. I've always been amused by your progress. You chose the path of rebellion. I only hope it's as fruitful as the narrow conformism on which I've made *my* fortune.'

Venetia's career had been a confusing mixture of failures, abandoned projects and effortless success. The convent where it began had been so extraordinary as to seem, in later life, like the frantic dream of a spiritual reformer who had conceived the cloister as the oubliette of a medieval donjon. In fact she remembered its rigorous discipline as something which might possibly have happened to her, but was more probably the experience of someone four hundred years her senior.

She recorded her religious scepticism in ways which could only infuriate the nuns, sworn, as they were, to patient resignation. After hearing an especially credulous sister, elevated on a nimbus of faith, narrating the story of the miraculous aerial transportation of Our Lady's house from Asia Minor to Italy, Venetia, using an artful collage of American comics and Irish sacred pictures, had composed a cartoon that she stuck on the notice-board. It showed the citizens of Gotham City staring open-mouthed at the sky, with random captions declaiming, 'Is it a bird? Is it a plane? No, it's the Flying House of Loreto!'

The severity of her punishment was equal to the scale of retribution visited on Martin Luther for nailing his ninety-five theses to the door of the Schlosskirche at Wittenberg. She prayed for forgiveness and rededicated herself to God: 'Oh Jesus, wounded on the Cross for me, help me to become crucified to self for love of Thee!'

Roaming miserably the long high corridors, she stared out at the snowy landscape through windows from which the glass had been deliberately removed. Perpendicular windows, their apices gaped with crumbled mortar and plaster which threatened to fall inwards. Standing beside the embrasure, you could gauge the variable force of the air as it blew in: spirals of wispy chill curling round the edges themselves, powerful, direct gusts through the centre of the aperture, and sometimes a freak change of direction and strength as a disturbance from the Lettish steppes insinuated itself into an isobaric drop over Banff and ploughed up all the air before it.

Late for lessons, late for benediction, late for bed, she compared life inside the convent to a perpetual running for a departing train. She felt more love for the icy, hoary mountains outside than for the colder hearts of the vengeful Scottish nuns. They punished, hectored, screamed and browbeat, demanded from her something called a 'firm purpose of amendment' which her innocent mind couldn't yet understand. They roared odd things at her about sin, the Devil and Our Lady, strange skeins of words: Resisting the Known Truth, Sins Against the Holy Ghost, the Sin that Cries Out to Heaven for Vengeance, Wilful Pleasure in the Irregular Motions of the Flesh, Blessed is the Fruit of thy Womb . . .

What seemed to excite them especially was the convent's peculiar bathing ceremony. Sitting in a chipped enamel bath equipped with rusting plungers and levers, whose trails of brown stains looked like Italian provinces, Venetia had acquiesced while a nun placed a wooden 'modesty' board over the bath, thus concealing the lower half of her body from her own sight. Goose-pimples covered the whole expanse of exposed skin by the time the nun began to scrub her with carbolic-reddened hands, singing a gruff and dirge-like 'Salve Regina', as fulfilled as Philomena, the nightingale of God's creation.

Gradually Venetia's bewilderment solidified, passing through rebellion into a sullen loneliness, alleviated only by private enthusiasms. Despising her friends for their cowed obedience, she found constant sources of offence in their crassness; and tried proudly to justify her growing solitude.

'I feel different,' she confided in her aunt. 'They're all stupid, they ought to be thumping those beastly nuns, not smiling and obeying the rules and saying, "Yes, Reverend Mother, no, Reverend Mother, in eternity, Reverend Mother".'

She took refuge in a passion for clothes and dreamed at night – and during the day – of Balenciaga, Poiret and Worth, only spasmodically flirting with mini-skirts, Courrèges, plastic kinky-boots and bat-wing sweaters. Her ideas were almost always incorrigibly up-market, banishing the vulgarities of current fashion to the realms of kitsch or the historical accident.

When, therefore, she found herself sitting in an attitude of upright correctness, translating Sallust's harsh Numidian battle-scenes, parsing and construing, or reciting passages of Shelley memorized to the last semicolon, she was in fact under the influence of powerful escapist forces.

> Yellow, and black, and pale, and hectic red,
> Pestilence-stricken multitudes . . .

(The rainbow-palette of those arrogant Royal College of Art students; already she preferred the muted colours of Missoni and Saint-Laurent.)

> . . . there are spread
> On the blue surface of thine aëry surge,
> Like the bright hair uplifted from the head

> Of some fierce Maenad . . .

(Back-combing à la Dusty Springfield, sticking a wodge of *tignasse* into your peroxide stack and sculpting the result into a fibreglass meringue whirl so breakable that it hurt your teeth to look at it.)

> Lulled by the coil of his crystàlline streams . . .

16

(No, that really *wasn't* a Catholic thought.)

> Cleave themselves into chasms, while far below
> The sea-blooms and the oozy woods which wear
> The sapless foliage of the ocean . . .

(Sexy, emerald-green, diaphanous material from which one breast might accidentally burst out and trail in your midnight zabaglione.)

But these were pubescent reveries, and were gradually ousted by a more vertical, more comprehensive imagination – still wild, still defiant, but finding pleasure in the text itself, not the bent tangents that brushed past it. She read and read: with a torch under her bedclothes, behind the confessional, in smoky railway-carriages (missing connections as she did so), during dancing classes (conveniently cushioning the impact of her unpopularity as a partner), in front of the television, listening to quiz programmes on the wireless, curled up in a mass of grey tunics with the close friends she was at last cultivating. She took piano lessons only so as to be able to sneak novels concealed between sheets of music into the practice rooms; whenever footsteps approached down the corridor, she would resume her spastic rendition of 'The Merry Farrier' and drop the book inside the piano mechanism. During the short exercises after lunch, she would walk round the edge of the convent garden, under the wasted larches and their dusty fall-out, her head not moving from the magnetic sentences of the novel in her hands. Whenever *real* exercise threatened, she would crawl into the capacious cloakroom locker and curl up among the hockey-sticks, galoshes and bundled school cloaks to hide from the monitors and perpetuate her second-remove life.

In a headspin of isolation, she cultivated her sensibility and became fashionably lachrymose, shedding tears over the plight of Bolivian tin-miners, earthquake victims in Iran and the overwhelming nameless tragedy of life (following Heraclitus, not Democritus). The more distanced from herself

17

these catastrophes and inequalities were, the more poignantly they wounded her. Yet the moods were so alterable that she swung between tenderness and indifference, terror and impregnability, passion and ataraxia. All kinds of fervour overtook her.

During a stormy formal parting from the Mother Superior, who accused her of squandering her ability and straying from the certain path of truth and happiness, she felt her adolescence sliding away from her. Her retaliation was firm, a warning of the pugnacity that later came to dominate her character:

'I'm grateful to you and the sisters for teaching me, for including me among the children they think worthy of education. But I'll find it hard to forgive your neglect of my emotional life. Couldn't you see what was happening to me? I don't think any of you really cared about my feelings, except for Sister Aloysius. It's strange, that. You'd have thought that nuns would have seized on the opportunity to smother an orphan with love and protection. I suppose I haven't been very lovable.'

She looked sadly at her feet.

The Mother Superior had become silent, not wishing to equivocate or lie.

Venetia went to Paris. Partly out of a desire to shake off the grey dust of the cloister, partly longing to escape from the stifling South Kensington fostering aunt who took titular care of her, partly because she loved Paris even before she'd been there. Subsequently her version of events was that she was bored, disappointed and inactive, a disaffected sluggard at the Sorbonne.

'I couldn't bear the idea of a country whose spirit was defined by the fact that the highest praise was expressed by a sentence like, "C'est normal." If normality is perfection, then I'm just not interested.'

She went to Barcelona, Vienna, Beirut, collecting languages like specimens. On her return to London, she had discovered that art was more important to her than the abstractions and ambiguities of literature.

'I thought I could combine the two things anyway in

this art-history degree at the Courtauld. I was completely spare and consumed with cynicism about the social life I was supposed to lead,' she explained to Jerome.

She had met him after a public lecture on the 'Toilet of Venus' – (well, not *on* the 'Toilet', *about* the 'Toilet', *diciamo*) – at the National Gallery. He had been sitting behind her, transfixed by the eloquence of her back as it registered in turn assent, disagreement, sympathy, impatience – mostly impatience – and admiration. The sophistication of her mind and the liberal tolerance of her spirit seemed equally visible, extruding through the surface of her inventively contrived, but not altogether successful, apparel. For Jerome (a youth of expectation) this onrush – or backrush – of instinctual sympathy was as powerful as the surge of feline pheromones. It was as if Venetia had walked towards him, then reversed, tail erect, and bumped her hindquarters, charged with rich deposits of *amicizia*, against his shins.

Jerome had the look of a gilded archangel with a high sleaze factor. They spoke shyly and exploratorily, testing out their inkling of friendship and overlaying it with signs of their credentials.

'I once did some photographs for a monograph on Velázquez,' he said. He spoke in a kind of unstressed growl. 'In Spain. I had to spend days in the Prado badgering officials to get them. They were all frightful old crones, each one more grotesque than the last; like the really bulbous Menina. But in the end I got very excited by the technique of his late paintings, those incredibly unrestrained slashes of colour, no *carefulness*, rather like *tachisme avant la lettre*. So unacademic. I'd love to know what those pretty infantas and inquisitors thought of them. The infantas were pretty, I mean, not the inquisitors . . .'

Venetia liked the looseness of his chatter, its lapses into diffidence and self-deprecation combined with a willingness – apparently not unpainful – to speak out. A different, less curious mind might have felt it was being addressed either as a public meeting or as a distinct unequal. To Venetia it was magic.

Above all, there was an astonishing mirror-effect in what they said to one another. Had she been asked to discourse on the same subject, her aesthetic criteria might perhaps have differed – *would* have differed – but the phrasing and register would have been almost identical. She had longed to know someone like this. How providential that they should meet at an event which, by providing them with a subject of mutual enthusiasm, allowed them both to parade their feathers to such good effect!

'I'm going to a private view of the Covent Garden costumes for *Fedora* next week. Such a thrilling opera, all those Russian anarchists in Switzerland at the turn of the century. What a chance for a designer! Lots of huge astrakhan overcoats, silver-topped canes, magnificent bearded anarchists, sulky-filly exiled princesses; even the bombs should be pretty. Would you like to come? A friend of mine did the designs, I think you'd like him.'

Perhaps that was a bit unsubtle. From the beginning, she never was in any doubt about his homosexuality; and this sally had converted a direct invitation into a mixture of an indirect inquiry and a publication of her *courant* knowingness about sexual conduct. Just so long as he knew what the terms of their friendship were likely to be, that she had no predatory designs and wished him to be as he was.

'Yes, I'd love that.' It had worked. The probable inference of her suggestion struck home; and he was relieved that it fell short of implying he was any the less attractive to her. At this period of his life, Jerome still clung to a vague illusion that his homosexuality was probably developmental, the result of a protracted adolescence; and he had not yet subjected this assumption to the scrupulous analysis which eventually dispelled it. It was still important for him to interest women, to test out his power over them, at whatever level. The subsequent loss of his ability to attract them was to cause him a certain pain and sense of deprivation (though it seemed a necessary consequence of his honest leap into certainty). But that self-ghettoization lay in the future. Even had he been able to foretell its imminence, he would never have guessed that this odd girl would become the prop he used to counteract it, like a frail sapling precariously stretched from the shore.

Venetia's attention was meanwhile diverted from the card

indexes, photographic files and cut-down xeroxes which seemed such a dreary framework to her passion for neo-classicism. Jerome fascinated her and she knew he would never bore her. For *taedium vitae* was already setting in. The absence of *struggle* in her life, the Greek *agonia* which ennobled and vitalized, had left her fearful that the activities she devised for herself, unprompted by material need or serious conviction, were crushing her spirit, the spirit which longed like an Athenian for adventure and newness.

Friends – a difficult, immiscible collection – warned her that she was betraying symptoms of spoiledness and probably heading for membership of the International Art Trash network. She would end up an art queen, a gallery-haunting spectre for whom Art transcended Life. She would be left stranded, unloved, passed by, never knowing who were friends and who bloodsuckers – those that leech on to you, and you shake them off, and more and more of them cling on, with purplish blobs forming on the skin all around; you sweep them off with a hand, salt their backs like herrings to make them crack and blister, prise them off agonizingly, they've grown claws . . .

But no one could properly believe she would fall victim to the luxurious drudgery and torment of the Poor Little Rich Girl. Her determination (seen in the firm placing of her feet, one heel pointing decisively back at the instep of the other rock-solid foot), her eccentricity (seen already in too many details of appearance, behaviour and conversation to be thought of as anything but an ingrained and regular irregularity) and her good nature, spirited laughter, unobtrusive concern for others and passion for discovery (or perhaps only *re*discovery, since it was necessary for her finds to have a historical dimension to be of interest to her) all diverted her from the arranged marriage with Mammon that the less perspicacious foresaw.

And she was beautiful. Not winsome or (lose some, lissome) flimsy. Out of all women, maybe, she was most *un*like Claudette Colbert (whom, paradoxically, she adored, the saucer-eyed wanton of the crap movies, the pretend-child Cleopatra who simpered: 'Queens do not hiccough . . . Queens only talk of the stars.' How jealous Jerome became of that, how he longed for some general guidelines of that kind!)

On alternate days she had green, then grey, eyes. This pleased her enormously. It lent her unpredictability of a kind. In other respects, too, she resembled an odd-eyed cat. There was a lazy, stretchy quality about her movements, though they lacked the efficient, streamlined purposiveness which characterizes a cat's self-grooming. The bone structure, both of her body and face, was heavy and pronounced, so that when her gestures were prompted by ill-temper one could say she appeared solid, even lumbering. But since her nature was generically sweet, this was not often the case. One was struck rather by the fine, firm-jawed oval of her face with its translucent skin, a delicate, virginal mask drawn exactly over her features. Indeed, her skin was so white and her eyes darted with such fire that Jerome unearthed a baroque conceit to describe her: she 'made Norway torrid with two suns and Ethiopia white with two hands'. The flush of blood seemed to have been channelled with careful precision into the cheeks and the sensual mouth, leaving the rest of the face drained to an arsenical pallor. Her ears, under the heavy sweep of hair, lifted back and upwards with more determination than those of other people. Their fine points were lost in the enveloping corona of glossy coils, but their lobes – or rather the psychic absence of lobes – could be clearly seen. Jerome ascribed mystical, mediumistic qualities to her on the strength of these ears.

Her body was less distinguished, at least to her own critical eye. No protests could persuade her that she was anything other than too fat. The developed, trained eye with which she appraised the proportions of the human form in Italian art deserted her when turned on her own intractable body. She had besides a tendency, born of nervousness and arrogance, to incline one shoulder slightly forward, giving an irregular slant to her whole torso. This apart, her breasts and robust rib-cage rose and fell with healthy strength; and her hips, though ample, were not fat, not padded as she insisted like an infanta's farthingale. Her height counteracted any impression of excess volume, and the weight was redisposed by the gentleness of her movements and gestures. Seeing her for the first time, a purse-lipped art historian had burst into an altogether unexpected labial flowering as he exclaimed: 'It's as if the Habsburg dynasty had finally produced a beautiful scion!'

Why, then, did she become so obsessed with Jerome? It was quite simple, at least when you measured the complexity of the obsession against that of their two individual personalities. Singling out one characteristic that she detected over and over again in him, she decided it was vulnerability alone which defined him – nothing else, no subsidiary, lesser or even greater facet; more than his literary madness, his mystic detachment, his beauty. He was helpless, lost; a soul driven by buffeting winds, condemned to find himself within himself and never even to figure out the terms of the theorem, let alone its solution.

One day she watched him caught in the terrible riddle. No fly had ever been rendered so defenceless by a spider's web, no shrew by a patting cat. A *grande dame* Bloomsbury relic had him on one side, a Conservative backbencher on the other. He had upset the first by not asking her any questions and outraged the other by asking too many. He sat between them, rashly balancing a drink which was already, even then, multiplying the molecules of the hepatitis-B virus in his liver, trying to undo the damage caused by his involuntary tactlessness. In effect, the two old bats had already recovered from the slights and were beginning to speak to one another across him in a conversation which, for them, obeyed the rules. Jerome, however, smarting and still clumsily embarrassed, tried to recover lost ground. He interjected pointless mollifiers which reaffirmed, he thought, his intelligence, umpiring between two contestants who weren't even in competition. Their tough self-regard had hardened long since but he persisted in his futile act of contrition, until eventually the MP rose up and walked round to sit on the other side of the old lady, freeing himself from this irritating and unplaceable gadfly. Jerome drank, grasping the glass in both hands, gulping with relief not unmixed with shame, and smiled nervously across the room at Venetia.

The homosexuality was never a problem. Even before

meeting Jerome, Venetia was convinced of the indispensability of homosexuals in a world such as hers. They were decorative, they turned everything, she felt, even the most unpromising material, into a party. They didn't mind taking over in the kitchen. They criticized your frocks knowledgeably and constructively. They understood your vulnerabilities and listened on terms of sympathetic equality. They adored children and played with them with unembarrassed gusto. They could explain the plots of operas and the superiority of one mezzo over another. They didn't shout at you or make you feel subordinate. Above all, they seemed to have the secret of triumphing over adversity.

It was difficult, indeed, for either of them to conceive of homosexuality in moral terms, let alone condemn it (except perhaps in jest, a parody of the grimmer Catholic or Calvinist denunciations). Venetia saw it primarily as the simple preference for one orifice over another. This impression was not to last, although the laid-back tolerance prompting it was never shaken by later revelations which stripped the scales from her eyes.

Jerome, it was true, tried harder to wrestle with its Catholic infrastructure: God, it seemed, using us as tennis-balls. But increasingly he dismissed the idea that it could be lumped in some mad category merely by naming it the Sin that Cried out to Heaven for Vengeance. What help was that, where did you go from there? Logically, surely, Heaven should answer that cry and smite the homosexuals in some biblical cataclysm? Perhaps that was what AIDS was? If so, it seemed pretty dull beside the Flood and the death-throes of Sodom.

What, then, if you considered homosexuality as no more than a variety of lust? That, conversely, seemed to Jerome to devalue and falsify it. And, at all events, as he himself experienced it, it was so innocuous a diversion that it couldn't properly be classified in the big league of envy or anger (although in his case, perhaps, it was not uncontaminated with sloth). The lust of two libertines met frontally. No one engaged in it unwillingly; no one lost decency. Most of the pastiche storm-troopers turned out to be social workers or schoolteachers trying for the most part, with unnatural effort, to regain the respectability denied them and withheld, yet given as a birthright to the conforming majority. The only envy as such seemed to infect those who were less successful at it than others.

At most, in his perception, gayness could be regarded as an occasional social embarrassment equivalent to, say, a regional accent. When he tried seriously to establish the kinds of moral aberration it involved, he could find only three: a playful, defiant sort of pride (which blindly derogated heterosexuality to the level of obviousness), a more or less slothful attitude to all other kinds of recreation (save those, like weightlifting, which bore heavily on vanity) and an unserious – and by no means universal – deceitfulness which was integral to the theatricality of things.

All in all, it was very agreeable and accommodated itself faultlessly to the demands of Venetia and Jerome's attachment.

Their lives had not converged and locked together immediately. Both still clung to a sense of individual identity, and to the need for experimentation with that identity, seen *in toto* and therefore in isolation.

Venetia's experiments were more extreme than Jerome's. She toyed, in a spectacularly uncommitted way, with what Jerome contemptuously called *Hochleben*, even with the idea of marriage. Not, eventually, to an Englishman of her own background, so firm was her resolution, given the backsliding of her career from its promising origins, never to demean herself by struggling to rejoin that fossilized caste. The South American she chose – for the choice was hers, whatever he felt and said about it – succumbed passionately to her initial rejection of him as he followed her round the Crush Bar at Covent Garden. Venetia, defiantly alone, read her programme three times – there was something talismanic in that, the warding off of importunate evil spirits – glancing up and dodging periodically behind pillars until she found his persistence too difficult to resist – even, in the end, rather appealingly boyish – and allowed herself to be approached.

Six months later the drawing-rooms of Buenos Aires were snorting and sedately recovering their equilibrium, dusting down their ruffled dignity; and Venetia was back in Notting

Hill, angrily playing the piano and weeping through the night. Jerome held her hand and hugged her while she cried, racked with disappointment, not so much at the failure of the affair as at the realization of being unmarriageable.

His efforts to console her were skilful beyond measure, though her awareness of his technical aptitude was somewhat clouded by her helpless gratitude. Together they decided that she needed to recover alone, in a climate less oppressive than London's, one in which she could look inside her heart (as the nuns had taught her) and make dispassionate, unadulterated decisions about her future.

Although in retrospect they both laughed at the misfiring of this careful plan, at the time they sorrowfully believed that Venetia was lost to the world. For they chose Sikkim; and Venetia, too demanding to be content with the incomplete vision of a sixties dropout (befuddled and partisan by virtue of the status of an outsider), became a novice in a Buddhist convent.

It was fortunate – for Jerome, at least – that she found it impossible to suppress her natural characteristics in the cause of this new servitude. The nuns reminded her too much of Scotland (and her own spirituality had not progressed far beyond her early religious training). She never found the necessary humility not to be irritated by their illiteracy. She was so befuddled and zombified by the droning of 'OM, mani padme hum' that she had to be excused from circumambulating the monastery and scrambling her brain even further. She hated saffron. Her butter-lamp smoked irrepressibly. She was kept awake by barking dogs. The mandalas all went wrong. Her arithmetic let her down at the prayer-wheel. The altitude made her empty-headed. And she longed for men.

There were other false starts, although their potential for catastrophe was not so marked. Passing through Bayreuth she so entranced the *Intendant* of the Festspielhaus that he asked her to work there as a foreign press and liaison officer. But this promising start was aborted by her reservations about Wagner. A festal shrine dedicated to a composer who at best she found over-stated and windy was a tawdry kind of sacrilege. Inside her head there was still a *guerre des bouffons* being waged between Italian and German opera and the Northerners were losing ground to Verdi as she began to detect in Wagner more and more anti-Semitism, misogyny, egocentricity and other bleak philosophical shortcomings not likely to appeal to her unNietzschean mind. So she left.

Back in London with Jerome, she embarked on desultory literary enterprises, but gave up when her interminable book on follies started to threaten her sanity. Jerome was furious. He had done the photographs for it, and he accused her of selfishness and capriciousness when she refused to submit it for publication. He'd had to slave-drive her during the writing, standing over her while she weepingly scribbled, rescuing her notes from the various places she deposited them (a laundry-basket, a visiting groceries van, the compartment under the spare tyre in her car, a frying pan – 'Is that what they call cooking the books?'); and he was obliged to rewrite most of her frantic, breath-less draft.

Henceforth they decided that work should be for her no more than a diversion from idleness, for she was unlikely to commit herself to any single career which, by definition, blotted out the possibility of all others. It was this resolution that underlay the structure of her whole life and its restless refusal to shut doors which might open on to adventure and knowledge. It was not a point of view to hold any appeal for the secretary of her trustees.

'You don't seem to be able to sustain anything, my dear,' the secretary barked, her battleship-grey chignon a visible reminder of her inflexibility. 'Your father was such a believer in *productive* wealth. And now you seem all set to fritter it away without even thinking about the future. Has it anything to do with that friend of yours?'

'I don't know who you mean, and I wouldn't answer you if I did,' Venetia replied, aghast at an impertinence that seemed to imply a hyper-efficient and clandestine system of social espionage. 'I'm still uncertain about what I want to do. And I think that's an honest self-appraisal and the only progress report I can offer. Thank you for your concern.' Get out of my hair, you diesel-dyke. God, I can feel the jealousy in you. What wouldn't you do to have my freedom? And a hopeless old bag like you could sure do with a homosexual or two in *your* life!

She was granted the financial independence which so exactly mirrored and complemented her escape from other constraints. It was just as well, for when her field of vision included figures or financial analyses – the insurance hints, say, of the tabloids – the words tended to clot and congeal into blobs of greyish sago porridge even more intractable than those victuals at her convent that had needed no teeth.

The one remaining check was her indissoluble attachment to Jerome. Yet the links were in practice so loose, so deliberately unbinding – given the impossibility of their total forging – that Venetia thought of them as unseriously as Jerome was later to think of the chains and bonds of sado-masochism; and she regarded their friendship as a further means of achieving a state in which she – they – would float like tangling and untangling algae in the sea of life. He certainly shared her optimism, and described their future to her as graphically as he could, using a great deal of the *ekphrasis* he so admired in Lucian of Sanosata.

'There's a species of butterfly called monarchs which originate in North America. They're enormously ambitious in their migratory habits and travel south as far as Peru, so their lives consist of an endless peregrination filled only with feeding and courtship. You find them fluttering down the Mississippi, buffeted by cross-winds, swooping over Mayan ball-courts in Yucatán or dodging lepidopterists in Bogotá. Soaring, drifting, struggling, existing. But however energetic they may be, they never reach their point of origin. Essentially they're liberated from the baseness of *beginnings* and so just enjoy this fantastically mobile, stressless migration. And they're very tough, highly coloured, exotic creatures unsuited to anything pedestrian or sedentary. Couldn't we give it a go? In zoology it's called euroky. The ability to live under variable environmental conditions.'

Venetia was game. She already found herself in a shifting, unpredictable world in which the old formulas – the *grands récits* – were beginning to look unbearably rickety. Her days were so random that she was sometimes driven to compare her 'adventuress' behaviour with the Catholic prescriptions for conduct she so vehemently denounced. With increasing deliberation she was propelling herself out of a predestined world, feeling, like the heretic Pelagius, that free will outweighed the forces of preordination (divine or otherwise) and that her life must prove how effectively that free will could be exploited. It was impossible, moreover, to ignore the fact that there was a symmetrical reciprocity in the enthusiasm with which she herself was being *expelled*, frozen out of society. (It must have been like this, she thought triumphantly, for Louise, Duchess of Portsmouth. Some role-model, huh?)

It could not be done without Jerome. His stimulus to the enterprise and his amazing fellow-feeling made him indispensable. His would be the silken thread that led her through and out of the Labyrinth. Anyway, it was too *exciting* being with him. His intelligence, his sensitivity, his sometimes maddening elusiveness, that edge of mystery and the all-important boundary beyond which neither would ever stray, poach or question. And it was workable, she believed, just so long as she recognized the need never to swamp him – *Vénus toute entière à sa proie attachée* – or to dispel the illusion that he too was in control of his own life. When she thought seriously about it (which wasn't often, she was so impetuous and reckless) she clearly understood the risk she ran of ostracism and the accusation of freakish perversity. And then, as a stern reminder to be lodged in her memory, she wrote down on a piece of paper the admonitory advice of that clear-sighted Japanese courtier of the tenth century, Lady Murasaki Shikibu: 'If one gives free rein to one's emotions even under the most inappropriate circumstances, if one has to sample each interesting thing that comes along, people are bound to regard one as frivolous. *And how can things turn out well for such a woman?'*

It was very propitious for Jerome as well. His career as a photographer was only middlingly successful, yet based on solid foundations of technique and imagination which made his eventual triumph probable. It was essential for him to have a companion to egg him on to further achievement and make the effort worth while. It had to be a woman, since his sexual experience led him to categorize men as either ephemeral toys or militant straights who feared and despised him.

There was already something distinctly hard-headed and pragmatic in his view of homosexuality. The stability of his passion for Venetia was unlikely to be threatened by affairs with men (on either side, it appeared). Not that he had always been so sensible. Obsessed once with a seductive steelworker, he'd driven from London to Consett at dead of night and circled mooningly, in the low red glare of the blast-furnaces, around a concrete tower-block whose address he'd happily discovered on a scrap of paper in his back pocket. Such infatuations, however, bore within them the seeds of their own destruction, like kamikaze dandelions. He succumbed to them less and less, aware of making a compromise, admittedly, but also that none of the modern gay alternatives held any attraction for him. He knew there was nothing much to hold gays together – except for clamped sphincters and the ambivalent bond of a shared interest in promiscuity. He was simultaneously avoiding the complacent fragile monogamy or alienating promiscuity of homosexuality, the tears and confusion of bisexuality and the deadening surrender of heterosexuality. In some ways their relationship resembled a homosexual one, only one in which the first, passionate sexual stage had been omitted entirely and replaced with a tight but independent camaraderie.

What was their life to be? The banner would bear a succinct lemma: PEREGRINATIO MUNDI. It would have the intensity and arbitrariness of dreams. All would be left to chance. They would plunge head-first into the deviant category of 'vagabondage' in which Lanbroso, that loopy psychological taxonomist, had lumped Byron, Tasso, Goldsmith, Petrarch, Cellini and Cervantes. Venetia thought it would be like a French movie, irresponsible, dynamic and peripatetic, with an intense literary core analogous to – but a bit more fluent than – the captions of Jean-Luc Godard. Both of them were bored by the simplicity of the merely picaresque. The Kerouac prescription was too sinewy and virile, too much a battle, and the word 'cool' made Venetia go hot all over. Their longing was for things that were remote, strange and untried. They would assume new characters, change like chameleons, defy their own fates. It would be a matter of radical experiments, not a mere repetition of the same old selves in different guises in different drawing-rooms. Their life, their alternative, had to be entirely new, self-generated, a tapestry of paradoxes and adventures consonant with the inexplicable conjunction of their destinies. For most people the highest adventure was that one day, they might find themselves sitting in a room opposite the person destined to become their husband or wife. This was too modest for Venetia and Jerome. They would constantly be arriving in places where they knew nobody and could act on impulse alone. Surprises would lurk behind strange doors and hit them in the face like pleasurable muggings. Always they would be alien. It would take energy. As Venetia said, 'You can't stand back, you gotta step up 'n go.'

The important thing was to live in the present, exposing themselves to whatever arrived, unpalatable and testing as it might be; to abandon the past, seductive and languorous, while its literarized memories continued to beckon their literary minds. And they should dismiss the future as a mere hazardous version of the present, yet to be faced. It could be dispatched and discharged without making dull provision in advance.

Jerome, having no past, found it easy to carry out that part, but he couldn't reconcile it all with the supreme notion of controlling one's own destiny. This latter idea surely demanded a less extemporizing approach, a clearer sense of purpose and of one's own potential? His compulsive sexuality, that pricking demon, had already begun to wreak havoc, nurturing his fears of self-destruction; and he wanted to get on with things. But there was no inner guidance; and he was too selfish to listen to anyone else's advice, being unable to see that the experience of another might have some relevance in his case. So the harnessing with Venetia, their double yoking, gave him the illusion of pursuing a single course, a wayward one fraught with danger and perversity, in parallel with a collaborator whose waywardness was even more manufactured than his own. There would be no sacrifice of his independence, and yet his thirst – and gift – for loving friendship would be satisfied.

Venetia, endowed with the anarchy and the special fears of the rich, held a more rackety view of things, a *Weltanschauung* of incipient decomposition according to which one's sense of fulfilment increased in direct proportion to the invisibility of one's aims. She preferred a disaster, *any* disaster, to anodyne placidity. Reading that Queen Christina of Sweden had written to Cardinal Mazarin, 'I love the storm and fear the calm,' she had experienced a shock of recognition and repeated the sentence over and over again in a mock-Garbo accent.

Whereas some people, most people, found reassurance in adopting ideas handed down infallibly to them from the heights of tradition – or actually adopted them without being aware of, or concerned for, their provenance in any degree whatever – Venetia was a natural image-smasher, goaded by her own scepticism to dismantle all the safe, cautious, sanctified idols.

She was neither easy-going nor predictable. Jerome accused her of being like an unexploded bomb. Monotony would kill her more surely than a tidal wave. The more phenomena and accidental events that could be festooned along the thread of life, the more it enticed her rococo appetite. Her mind was all incrustations, excrescences, curlicues, unforeseen curves and volte-faces. She wanted to walk along, plucking at ribbons and swags disposed at irregular intervals to dangle before her, sometimes leading her into enlightenment and happiness, sometimes snaring her, girdling her with error, sometimes barring her even from reaching a glittering target.

'I don't really understand sex, anyway,' she said to Jerome with a smile of self-deprecating honesty. 'I think I'm one of those people who don't really need it. I can just about understand how it's so important to you. It seems so volcanic, so inescapable, a compulsion like any other – and yet it's also so laughable, such an idiotic posturing, all for the sake of a few seconds' lost consciousness. Quite frankly I'd rather forgo it. Anyway I'm *better* at other things.' This statement was as near as she got to self-analysis on the subject.

There was something faintly ridiculous about them as a pair, as they both acknowledged. Common sense should have driven them into marriage and gradual sexual compatibility. It might have done in an earlier age. Neither, ironically, had any belief in the efficacy – or even existence – of common sense. Venetia, in particular, thought of it as a dim eighteenth-century Scottish invention designed to justify a narrow Presbyterian world-picture.

Their friendship was nevertheless tantamount to marriage. The only obstacle to its consummation was Jerome's sexuality, more strong and straightforward than Venetia's self-denial, which demonically impelled him to nourish it, destroy it, placate it, stimulate it, heed it, ignore it. Venetia, with her over-simplified view of homosexuality, never quite fathomed the compulsive workings of the demon that so often, suddenly and unannounced, seemed to inhabit Jerome and then, as brusquely, to abandon him.

In a maze of financial arrangements she could barely retain in memory, Venetia set up a trust for David and invested the residue so as to release a regular, moderate income for herself and Jerome. She had forgotten how much of the balance had gone to charities, friends and the abortive projects of people she admired. Jerome, though approaching the problem from a different point of view, shared her determination to avoid the unhappiness of the rich; their insecurity about the motives of others, their defensiveness, their access to instant panaceas which left them less fulfilled than ever. But it was difficult to control the flow of money in such a way as to place them – however artificially – among the ranks of the needy. Whenever the credit built up, Venetia disposed of it: sometimes sensibly, sometimes with intemperate abandon – but never with the effect of increasing her resources. The most frequent recourse was to travel, since by moving they could simultaneously spend the excess, remind themselves of their insecurity and impoverish themselves. There were times when the irregular cycle threatened actually to destroy the capital foundation. At such moments Venetia panicked and came to understand Jerome's position (for he insisted on maintaining a certain economic independence from her; and anyway could have no legal claim over her).

Jerome was unembarrassed about his dependence. It was a simple matter of one person helping another and deriving enormous satisfaction from doing so. When he felt a little guilty at his own parasitism, he reminded himself to behave like Gertrude Bell, who, on discovering in conversation with the Aga Khan III that to him £2,000 was as sixpence to others, leaned closer and asked if he might therefore change a shilling. There was the aplomb of the poor for you.

A sense of purpose survived only in their determination to remain purposeless. Neither had any knowledge, understanding or love of ambition, and they felt thus ideally equipped for life in the late 1970s and 1980s. Because of this complacency, there were many stringent aspects of modern life they would never need to confront. They would never have to learn Basic or take dinner with business wives. Committed technophobes, they were delighted to inhabit a world in which a knowledge of microelectronics was actively superfluous. It was inevitable, their friends believed, that they would understand little about the intricacies of ordinary life; they had so distanced themselves from its adherents. Jerome, in particular, was aware, too, that since they had chosen not to join the world, there were immense tracts of experience which, paradoxically (given their omnivorous intent), would elude them entirely. They would probably never, except in the pages of novels, confront the question of power.

One of the drawbacks to their peripatetic life was that she missed the consistent intellectual stimulus of her friends, scattered as they were in New York, London, San Francisco, Buenos Aires, Paris, everywhere she had alighted. Yet Jerome's service in this role was so competent that she came to see him as a sort of mobile brain, a roving book, rather like the moving court of humanist scholars whom Mary of Hungary uprooted from Buda and took with her as her carolling entourage when she retired to Brussels.

Their love necessarily transcended its own limits. Their progressive discovery of one another was apparently infinite and each characteristic or quirk, hidden in some recess of character and manifested in some new incident, seemed only to confirm their earlier judgement, the unreserved love that needed no compromises or sacrifices. There was, perhaps, more calculation, more deliberateness in Jerome's love for

Venetia than in hers for him. In his heart he found it hard to believe that he deserved such profound and unqualified love. Nothing that he did or felt seemed to his own critical judgement to qualify him for its constant renewal. And yet he knew that it was essential to Venetia that her love should indeed be without reservation, so peculiar was its genesis, and that she asked nothing in return.

In this way Jerome sought to escape from the leprous taint of homosexuality and benefit from his security with Venetia. The twin worlds of male and female would be balanced in a slightly distorted mirror-image of the norm, with Venetia acting as the constant while his vagaries and forays all savoured of male sweat. He was able, too, to capitalize on his unBritishness, not repress it or apologize for it. This new life would proclaim his homosexuality triumphantly (or, rather, his love for women and sexual lust for men); his Catholic mind, his polyglot culture, his lack of humour about himself, his love of cats. He did nasty contraventional things like pulling down the window-shades against the sun on aeroplanes, cutting his meat before eating it right-handedly with a fork, talking over-volubly. He was, he was assured, one of life's day boys. Sometimes his manner would be terminally sophisticated; at others a kind of corrupt adolescence.

Venetia meanwhile went so far beyond the pale of the world that, the more extreme the option presented to her, the more natural it seemed. Irredeemably harnessed to Jerome, hugely disdainful of the perpetrators of disdain, swamped by a passion that looked for no slaking, she willed herself onward. They were launched on their mutual commitment, a kind of marriage, a love-affair such as even the Jacobean dramatists had never imagined. They were, against all odds, closer in defying probability than if they'd been a brother and sister, clasping one another for protection lost in a foreign city. The more they loved each other, the more they had the impression of prising apart, with their joint strength, the walls of a tunnel that threatened to crush them.

Each was capable of living the accidental life of a rich *objet d'art*, one which changed in all its aspects, undergoing vicissitudes, causing human love and despair, constantly displaced, re-evaluated, condemned, applauded. An uncut ruby would serve as their lodestar. The one they had in mind had caused Pedro the Cruel to murder his guest, Abu Said of Granada, in the precinct of the Alcázar of Seville; then it was presented to the Black Prince in 1367, the year of the Battle of Nájera; then won by great Henry V at Agincourt; and now reddens the imperial Crown of Great Britain. Or – and this identification had a special appeal for Jerome – like the white marble Christ by Cellini given to Philip II by the Grand Duke of Tuscany and carried aloft on men's shoulders on the journey from Barcelona to El Escorial.

Venetia was immensely happy. 'What care I if they put me on the wing-shaft,' she murmured, 'just so long as he's on the fuselage?'

4

En Famille

The arrival of Adelaida's child had been the firmest cementation that could have been devised for this brittle *mariage blanc.*

'We *must* take him on,' Venetia insisted, with an unnecessary urgency that belied the fact she could already depend on Jerome's agreement. 'He's the sweetest child. And God knows what would happen to him if we didn't. She's absolutely determined to abandon him. Watching her lie there, all angry and alienated, no one could doubt she intended to destroy him. In the middle of it all I suddenly saw a ghost, a kind of spectre hanging over her. At first I thought it was some sort of funereal, death-like thing. But gradually I recognized it was more specific, it was those pictures of the Jonestown massacre, buckets of Kool-Aid cordial being spooned down the infants, Herod revivified, a dreadful, dreadful nightmare threatening the poor child. I'm sure she would kill him if we allowed her. It's amazing she didn't have an abortion, I suppose it's part of her ingrained Catholic mania. But we *must* look after him.'

Jerome was staring at her and trying to work out the sincerity of what she said. Finally he was satisfied.

'The whole thing depends on you,' he said. 'You know I adore children and I'd be thrilled if we could bring him up with us. I guess he's in for a pretty rough ride, though. Let's hope he was born with his mother's resilience. I don't suppose we'll ever know who his father was?'

'Not a chance. She's so far gone now, I'd be surprised if

she ever spoke again. The whole crisis has made her even more impenetrable. She looked like a dugong washed up on the shore. She must be *really* disturbed now. Can you imagine her wanting to abandon her baby as soon as it's born? And, even worse, giving it over to *me*, a member of a class she's dedicated to overthrowing? Well, not exactly overthrow, more like re-educate, I suppose. It's not my money she rejects, it's the way I obstinately refuse to believe in oligarchies, natural supremacy, the duty of the intelligentsia to support political initiatives, endless, endless objections. God, when I think of all those rows we had – not just the ideological bickering but the interminable arguments about Pattie Hearst and the proper use of inherited wealth, the futile circularity of it all, *yak, yak, yak*. Sometimes I thought I was arguing with myself because I came to know her point of view with such numbing familiarity that it almost seemed my own. I could have done it in my sleep. Come to think of it, I often have.

'Anyway, since neither of us is scared of genetic throw-backs, I don't think we should hold his parentage against him. And he's adorable, helpless, like you were when I first met you.'

'Great. That settles it. I like the idea of an emotional clone of myself. And I've never believed in eugenics since I heard about all those bad boys in the Old Testament born to such virtuous parents, like Cain to Adam and Noah's kids.' He took a slug of blue curaçao. 'God, it looks hot down there.'

'Hundred and ten, maybe. I really don't think we'll be spending much time outside. My days of over-exposure to ultra-violet are long since past. Who wants to end up all creased and withered? To tell the truth, I think we've got quite enough crocodile handbags.'

'I don't see why anything should change much. We can still whizz around and share looking after him. But right from the start we've got to get him used to a slightly unusual schedule. God, what would happen if he turned out to be a rugger heavy or a racist bigot or something?'

'Come on, that's a risk everyone takes,' she answered. 'And in his case, if he goes to the bad, it's likely to be in a rather more spectacular way. This isn't exactly the formula for parenthood you'd find posted on the walls of the ante-natal. What shall we call him? Adelaida said something about honouring some half-baked fascist called Onesimo somebody-or-other, but I think it's a terrible mouthful and they don't like Hispanics much here. Anyway, I've always hated anapaests.'

She looked out of the window, pleased with her affectation. She'd adored it when the loudspeakers at the Notting Hill carnival had blasted *Hot, hot, hot* at her in the same rhythm. The desert landscape seemed to smile up at her in approval. By the time they got to Phoenix they'd be parents.

Jerome turned to her and swore as he caught his sleeve in the arm-rest.

'I think maybe we should leave problems like that till last.' He put his arm tenderly around her shoulders, moved by the idea of this extra closeness in their lives, and followed her gaze out of the window. They were silent for a moment. 'Let's just not talk. Let's think about it, really think about it, OK?' There was a spaciousness around them, a lull of calm and happiness. Almost a loss of consciousness for, had it been less than that, one or other of them would have given voice to an idea.

America – its heartland etherized and spread upon the operating-table below – was beginning to envelop them now, and threatened to eat away at their migratory resolution. Even the landscape of Arizona, alien, barren and tormented, didn't so much inspire feelings of fire and drought and rifts as the realization that the USA was for them a vast continuum, the Western desert an appendage of the lush orchards of California.

The Americans, anxious that people and things should actually be what they seemed, completely misread their exteriors and misunderstood their social origins. They could not, there, be the beneficiary victims of snobbery since no one had a clue who they were or might have been.

No other American city was quite as congenial for them as San Francisco. New York upset their notions of success and the measurability of people's worth; Venetia, in particular, felt claustrophobic and weighed down by the need for air-conditioning, badges of achievement and night-energy. Houston gave them a gradual cranial migraine from the unbridgeability of its horizontal and vertical axes; a scattering of fabulous buildings was no reason for dizzying yourself like that in the desert. Los Angeles mobbed and cloyed, demanded too much self-articulation . . . But their experimental settlements, apparently as random as crows on a telegraphic line, were expansive and flattening. They were dragged up by America, thrust in front of ordeals and truths, scraped past alternatives that hurt and educated, puffed up with their apparent capacity to shoulder any new material.

They had flirted with South America but had been defeated by its irritants, each one as minor as a mosquito-bite but enough in totality to make the whole organism swell up in hives. Ecuador had seemed the ultimate in alluring hot-houses; but soon proved impossible. Their books rotted in the humidity and had to be painted with a diluted creosote solution. Nor had they been able to resist acquiring a menagerie of apes, parrots and suckling-cats which had threatened their resolute impermanence.

A shrinkage was affecting their mobility, born from the awareness that most of what they wanted was to be found here in this unlikely continent: mystery, ingenuousness, cities throbbing with height, lunacy, seriousness, fear, pandemonium. They were beginning to forget their old, rotted Europeanness, the vertebral core which had seemed so inseparable from their passions. Here anything went; and like the gaskets on Jerome's cars, it usually did. There was no point in expecting strange events. As soon as they'd happened they began to seem normal. The whole idea of America was so bizarre. No wonder the Spanish *conquistadores* had thought they might find mermaids there, or even Judas taking his annual vacation from Hell (Jerome got to meet him several times).

'Mightn't it be better,' Jerome said eventually, 'to forgo this child and make the leap into a straight marriage? And have our own child?'

This was devil's advocate stuff. Anyone could see the psycho-sexual biology precluded *that*.

'I feel I can love this boy more than any blood-child I could produce.' She smiled, as if a comic bravery could mask her awareness of possibilities infinitely abandoned. 'This is all so serious. I've got to be utterly honest about my feelings.'

'I've never yet known you capable of duplicity.'

'Sometimes I pretend, and the pretence gets a grip. I pretended I loved Sergio because I wanted to experience love. But this actually involves a real responsibility for the very first time. Do you think he'll be OK with us? What on earth will he make of us?'

'I guess we'll just have to *be* there all the time, contrive some kind of security. It reminds me,' Jerome began a characteristic digression, 'of Madame Butterfly's poor little son just hanging around for ever while she scans the horizon for her beastly husband and witters on about whether the robins are nesting in the USA. Meanwhile the husband's been off shacking up with the second Mrs Pinkerton, some American broad with big tits. And *then*, can you beat it, Madame Butterfly makes the boy play solo blind man's buff while she commits ji-gai and showers her carotid behind a lacquer screen. Is that sadistic or is it not?'

'I don't think we need worry about that. Please be serious.'

'We're both really trying to find reasons *not* to adopt him. I don't think that's a very positive approach,' he said, his face now assuming a conventional almost pedagogic gravity. 'We both love children. We're utterly committed to each other. I for one am willing to make the necessary compromises to be a decent dad. I don't quite know what that means, except for stinky diapers and sleepless nights, but it makes me no different from any other prospective father.'

'I think you'd be brilliant,' she enthused. 'And as for me, I've got to admit the one reservation I've always felt about the commitment we've made to each other is that it must be barren. It would serve its own ends admirably, but there'd never be a final purpose to it, a sort of prize. Let's face it, this is the most fantastic chance. If I were back in my Buddhist phase, I'd be gabbing on about karma. In a way I think I actually *do* believe that my friendship with Adelaida was all destined to lead to this child. While it was going on, it was so odd and inexplicable, apparently based on zero in common. But now it all makes sense. She was a kind of child-bringer, a miraculous creature who confers fulfilment, like something in a Norse myth.'

'We'll do it. We'll have him as our own child,' he said decisively and hugged her towards him. 'We'll face all the problems as they arise. We've never listened to convention in the past. Why on earth should we start now? I think you're absolutely right, it *is* some kind of providential gift.'

'And he'd have no future without us. Adelaida will never relent.'

A bumpy area of turbulence interrupted her, and cut short what promised to be an exhaustive speculative survey of Adelaida's future character. They looked nervously out of the window and saw, close at hand, the grid and strips and gas stations of Phoenix. David was now their child.

To all outward appearances theirs was to be a conventional family; and yet between man and wife there was no sexual bond, between child and parents no shared blood.

5

San Francisco

It began again. At least he knew what he was in for. Deliquescent memories and chimeras clustered in his febrile brain. Had the familiar torpor abandoned him to leave him prey again to all those anarchic, meandering sensations he tried so hard to keep at bay? In an access of grave exertion, he considered the random passivity of much of his conscious experience. A quarter of an hour before he had stood transfixed at the cable-car junction on Russian Hill, listening intently, beyond mere caprice, to the *perpetuum mobile* of the humming electric wire: a low, metallic whine which could have been a malfunctioning siren, so unstrident was its failed urgency. How unlike the aleatory oscillations of his own thoughts, this manifestation of the constant sameness emanating from the bowels of the seismic rock! So limited was his own will, so constrained by a variable metabolic rate and by his shifting self-awareness, that he knew he could never aspire to this salutary line of fixity. He must remain forever supine, liable to the caprices of his everyday fate, subject to the dizzying alternations of energy and inertia, impressionableness and impermeability, day and night. There could be no prospect of ordering the sequence by interposing some kind of self-regulating machinery, some triumph of the will that might programme his moods in advance. It would always be like this. God, he was lazy! If only he were able, like the Comte de Saint-Simon, to order his valet to wake him up in the morning with the exhortation, 'Get up, Monsieur le Comte! Remember you have great things to do!' Perhaps he could train David to perform this service.

The present now seemed like a re-entry into some disturbed and murky atmosphere. His brain-shuttle was leaving behind the safe clarity of the Sea of Unconsciousness to find itself again in the swimming, gaseous layers where monstrous images lurked and ambushed, ensnaring his drifting shell. Failure and Disillusion, Giant Anxiety and Pigmy Hope reared in front of him like dinosaurs flexing in a hologram. The neuroses all crystallized. He could no longer slump over in slothful ease. If this continued, he'd have to go back on mianserin.

It was time for the infallible remedy: surrender to his amphibious nature, submersion in the enveloping reassurance of the deep and wide claw-footed Victorian bath.

The serenity of the eddying pools of water – they looked like reactivated ammonites – overcame the disquieting *crise de nerfs*. He started slowly massaging his calves with a sisal glove, upwards from the ankle to stimulate the circulation and make his heart thump pleasurably. Small rivulets of sweat began to slither down his forehead. The dead scales of skin slicked around the edge of the bath as he mercilessly flayed his Golden Fleece. He cut his toe-nails, murmuring caressingly to himself about their superlative cuticles, their nacreous keratin that burst with calcium, *perlas de Oriente. Amboina 'aljofares de Timur!* All future shock seemed to be swallowed up in the sluicing, wooshing temple of Hygena.

His cat Bonaventure crouched on the marble slab, watching him with something like indulgent malice. 'Can we talk?' he asked. He loved his cat with a passion bordering on Egyptian idolatry. Only a slight drawing forward of its ears and the trembling antennae told of involvement. It was as static as he was splashingly restless, yet the contours of its spine, haunches and ruffed neck all seemed on the point of spreading into a sympathetic languorous writhing stretch. They yawned and blinked slowly, very slowly, at each other in mutual reassurance.

'Had an exhausting day, have you? OD'd on ox-heart? All that eating, must be so tiring.'

This cat was celebrated as a local hero and vigilante. Its

affectionate and trusting nature, combined with extreme hunger caused by Jerome's desertion of it on a two-night stand, had led it to make such importunate overtures to an increasingly exasperated burglar that it was eventually flung through the window with such vehemence that a neighbour had reported the incident and the intruder been caught.

His couchant attitude and uptilted mask gave Bonaventure the imperious air of a Trafalgar Square lion. How sad, Jerome reflected, that cats couldn't enjoy and share this sensuous aquatic pampering so akin to their own luxuriance! He remembered Venetia telling him a story about some swimming cats she'd once seen. Crossing Lake Van in eastern Turkey on a steamer, she'd leant over the rail and stared in disbelief at flocks of cats, one eye green, the other eye blue, over-arming their way through the ship's wake. A shoal of crawlers, Duncan Goodmews, more eager than bulge-eyed porpoises, more intelligent than whales, as lissome as eels. What can they have looked like on dry land, their wet fur all pinched into shiny spikes, as scrawny as punk gerbils? So unlike the present shimmering gloss of his own body, swept by cross-currents of heavy water, sleek and stroked, the hairs all curlingly disposed in black arabesques. He squirmed and looked down as his Caravaggesque thighs pressed against the slimy enamel, their strength visible in the heated sinews rising hard and solid against the fluidity of the water.

He pictured to himself his own fourteen-year-old body in the long-past days at school as it splashed dionysiacally in the cavernous and greasy communal bathroom. Instead of sitting sedately in the zinc baths by the hot-water pipes that ran round the edge of the room, he and his friends had filled the entire tiled space with scalding hot water and floated the fragile craft on the surface. Gingerly edging himself into the tub, each child had paddled around, armed only with a twisted wet towel with which to belabour his neighbour, trying to topple him from the safety of the bath and plunge him into the thrashing, boiling water – no easy task, since each child was nearly invisible to all the others through the billows of steam. Precocious classical scholars that they were, they had imagined themselves at the sea-battles of Salamis or Syracuse, and had yelled, 'Thalassa! Thalassa!' at each other.

(Their discovery by the matron then brought about the most classical of punishments, the composition of a Horatian ode on the tactics of battles.) What had happened to his brain since then? He knew the answer so well, but could not easily recognize that the mess of his present life which had replaced that galling discipline had alone engendered this decline.

The vapour in his brain was like a cerebral sauna, removing the debris of the threatened crisis. Immobilized and blank, he allowed his gaze to stray in a disengaged kind of way over the physical objects around him: a glass shelf of stephanotis plants, a tiled dado of Edward Lear limericks, a huge mahogany wardrobe the door of which had swung slightly ajar to reveal an empty interior. The light was filtered sulphurously through a yellow blind covered in some sort of bulrushes. Someone had written in lipstick on the mirror: 'Make this the year you lick dieting.' The moulded ceiling-rose was lacking one of its fleurs-de-lys, the cornice interrupted at intervals by flakes and cracks like river tributaries. Glistening with gold thread, an embroidered *mantilla de Filipinas* draped its heavy folds over a wicker screen, which stood, tall and dominant, beside a tiny round table covered with miniature dolls' plates and dishes – plaster marzipan cakes, *salade niçoise*, *boeuf en daube*, rainbow trout, fish and chips nestling in the *Daily Star*, *crudités*, a tureen of vichyssoise, buttered parsnips, crayfish standing in crisp lettuce, truffles and pralines. Nothing New World, all the objects and features uprooted and transplanted from cloying Europe.

A huge billboard hanging on the opposite wall now began to fill his placated consciousness. On its pitted surface a farouche and falcon-eyed Moroccan potentate announced: 'Prince Kar-Mi Presenting Mysteries of the Spirit World and Demonstrations of Occult Powers by a Series of Astounding Feats that have no Counterparts on Earth'. Its maleness and strength set it apart from the feminine clutter of the rest. A declaration of independent sensuality infused with a mystic aura. This would be his talisman for the night's prowling, the ransacking of the streets for maybe-this-time. All the sexual anticipation was mirrored in the Oriental horoscope: an allegory of destiny in the parallels of spirit and sperm, ectoplasm and orgasm. He resolved to glower like a Saharan Zouave, savagely emanating irresistible magnetism to subdue his cowering enemy-lover. Only tonight the conquest would be sealed by a volcanic sexual consummation with the enemy Uhlan, a trapped fetish surrendering his masculinity in a climax of lust.

But literary premonitions of this kind could never ever materialize. He knew ruefully that he would have to revert to the lowest common denominator and take refuge in unchallenging banality and conformity to the dull and repetitious pattern, the ritualized manoeuvres of cruising and seducing compliant men. The sponge squeezed out the hyssop of gall, the bitter need for compromise and realism.

'Jerome, it's now three days since you called.' The shrill register of the voice echoed the squally ringing of the telephone which had announced it. 'Am I so unimportant? So easily cast aside? What are you trying to do to me?'

'I tried several times, but it seemed like you were tied up on the telephone.'

'Sounds like one of your more extreme fantasies. You know I go crazy if we stop communicating. I thought this was supposed to be the difference between me and your one-night stands. Didn't we agree that we had no sexual barriers to contend with, only the limited liability of friendship? How do I get your attention? Do I have to put on a leather harness and a foraging cap? Or is it stetsons and spurs this week? Maybe I should go the whole way and fly off to Casablanca for a hydraulic penis-transplant?'

The string of questions and reproaches was characteristic. Venetia's unserious wish to inhabit the homosexual part of his multi-faceted life always seemed like the final gesture of a sexual cripple. Couldn't he be allowed to retain at least the imaginative aspects of his sexuality without these facetious onslaughts and aborted invasions?

'You only had to call. No need for surgery. All this strutting and fretting.' He fingered his appendix scar and glanced down at it nervously. 'I miss you so badly. I'd come down to LA to see you if I didn't hate it there so much. How *is* life among the smoggy Platinum Palms airheads? Met anyone whose brains haven't turned to scrambled eggs?'

'I feel as if I'm drowning in royal jelly. If anyone else shows any interest in the interface between my aggression and my sisterhood I'll scream. And the Infant Phenomenon is going crazy, all the other kids either whimper like computers on the blink or yell out orders at him like marine drill sergeants. If you don't come down here and rescue us, I'm coming up to San Francisco to foul up your sex life. Sorry, darling, I don't mean that. But I really must see you soon.'

Jerome didn't really mind Venetia getting caught up in the summery sediment of Los Angeles. He felt it was probably good for her to absorb the sleek, gorged mediocrity that he'd long ago rejected. She was living in a 'senseless-killing' neighbourhood. She slept beside a refrigerated fur-closet; or was it a fur-lined refrigerator, she'd never quite worked it out. Her days were long and easy. Like an Angeleno caricature, she drove a hundred miles of freeway and surface to assemble the fifteen ingredients for supper. She was more susceptible to novelty than he was, more adaptable, readier to give things a chance. But David was another matter. A vulnerable baby, wrenched from the arms of his crazy Spanish mother and deposited in the enveloping adoptive embrace of the adoring Venetia, he needed protection from her untidy life, alternatives to its frantic, prodigious quest. Wild and directionless as he was too, Jerome felt able to give David the props and balance of a real father. He often took his own virtues for granted. And the more time they spent together, the more Jerome was able to reduce the chances of Venetia severing her paradoxical, contra-suggestible commitment to him, the one linear constant in his fragmented life.

'Wow, that's some ultimatum. You've got me cornered,' he answered. 'OK, come on up.' It sounded as if she were downstairs waiting for him in a hotel lobby. The fact that she was four hundred miles away and yet could be addressed so closely somehow summed up the simultaneous distance and proximity of their lives.

He'd got out of the bath by now and was standing naked beside the window, lifting up the blind to look at the ashen bulk of Alcatraz emerging from a drifting layer of fog. He shivered and goose-pimples began to form on his skin.

'Sweetheart, let me get back into my bath. You'd never forgive yourself if I caught gay pneumonia. All because you yack on on the telephone like Lou Reed on heat. See you tomorrow. Bring me something special from Life's a Beach. I'll probably never wear it, but it'll liven up the closet. And clear your head of Angeleno fumes before you get here. I suggest a Quaalude on the flight and *read something* European. It's time for the cultural gear-change. I love you, honey; but I'd love you even more if you could come on like the Duchess of Sanseverina.'

'Jesus, why do we have to carry all these books around in our heads? It makes me feel like one of those Arcimboldi portraits. A head all made out of dusty nineteenth-century novels. Or like someone looking at life down a freeway tunnel covered in graffiti saying "Voltaire says . . . Kant suggests . . . Coleridge says". I don't think I've ever *had* an original thought.'

'Well, darling, *Simon says* GET OFF THE LINE.' He pulled a towel one-handedly around his loins and thought treasonously about the twenty-four hours' grace he was being granted. Time for another chapter of real-life picaresque novel. He looked reproachfully at the cat staring up at him. 'Mmmm . . . Yes,' he breathed. 'His Serene *Catness* and *Fatness*. What are you staring at me like that for? No, don't tell me, I know, a cat can look at a queen.' He was already inspecting his groin for chancres as Venetia grudgingly rang off.

6

The Way Out

Jerome was sunken in hydrophic slumber, Endymion forever sleeping to stave off the fear of old age. Conflict and pain had ceased. It all went hideously wrong as the blankness hardened into the edges of a terror-bound nightmare. He found himself in the midst of a jolly, laughing crowd of friends: straight, balanced friends from his past. They were gathered around the entrance of a night-club, exchanging banter in a natural, spontaneous celebration of happiness. As if propelled by their enjoyment they descended the stairs and reached an immense area surrounded by divided compartments. In each of these a scene of sexual fantasy was being acted out. Many of them were heterosexual, but all involved the infliction of pain. Jerome passed quickly by the straight ones (both during the dream and in his recollection of it) and finally stood spellbound before a scene of amazing violence in which gigantic leather-clad men whipped and strangled, scraped and tore at one another, their faces contorted with hatred, the passionate cries they uttered eerily silenced by the heavy, studded door through which he watched.

By now he had split away from his friends, who were drinking bright cocktails and chattering about what they had seen and the seamy sexual ideas with which they'd been uncomplicatedly inspired. Jerome felt leaden, marked down by his obsession, a solid object no lightness of wind could touch.

Then the visit began gradually to pall for his companions.

There was an exit door, and some of them drifted out through it with the marks of satiety on their faces. Inexplicably, they then reappeared in the room and seemed not to have gone out at all.

There was a growing but still restrained panic. It seemed it was not in fact possible to leave. Some, however, were succeeding, and the numbers in the place began slowly to diminish. Those who remained looked increasingly desperate as their attempts to leave repeatedly failed. Jerome, who till now had stood intelligently aside, refusing to join in the momentum of the puzzled herd, began to believe that he alone could magically understand the secret of escape. He listened at the door as people went out and heard a series of banging sounds after each one left. He felt sure there was some kind of numerical code involved, a magic Pythagorean formula which released the prisoners. It was, he decided, a simple matter of adding one stroke to the total of one's predecessor.

Gliding through the door, he found himself in an enclosed corridor, matt black like the inside of a camera. Beyond it he sensed that the staircase rose majestically to freedom. He knocked carefully on the end-wall, one more tap than the double tap of the girl who'd gone before. An invisible door opened at once and he stepped through with relief.

He was back in the room. The simple formula was incorrect. He walked slowly around to calm himself and caught a fleeting glance of the glistening leather torture-chamber and its mute screams. Somehow there was a link between this tableau and the failure of his theory.

He leaned disconsolately against a wall, looking at everything as little as possible. More and more people were leaving now and not reappearing; only small pockets of men and women, their eyes registering a glassy hysteria, remained behind. There *must* be a pattern, some fatally obvious 'Open Sesame' eluding his grasp.

After long reflection he knew the answer. It was an answer that had been impressing itself tentatively on his mind, but which he'd been unwilling to accept. Only those who'd managed to accept, control, understand or exorcize their sexuality were able to leave.

Jerome summoned up some false courage to test the hypothesis he knew to be true. Pausing in the outer corridor to knock desultorily, losing count of the number he knew anyway to be ineffectual, he again re-emerged into the prison-room. There were even fewer people by now, but he recognized a girl who had once told him of her admiration for the brave and inventive sexuality, the *Zusammenheit*, of men together. Her eyes showed that she too now knew the answer. She, as much as Jerome, was a no-hoper; but her circular progresses through the corridor and back would be less infinite than his. He was on some eternal Infernal revolving cornice-platform (the image now actually metamorphosed in his dream), all *speranza lasciata*. He was bound with fetters like the men behind the doors (a further image which now hypostatized); the backs of his hands pressed impotently against the wall behind him as in a fairground Rotorama, and the floor falling away beneath him, doors flying open, round and round in the maelstrom of the Norwegian sea, sucked into infinity . . .

7

Post Coitus

The policeman buckled on his holster and leaned down to snort the line of cocaine proffered by the still-somnolent Jerome. Underneath his uniform tunic a leather harness creaked and strained, pulling pleasurably on his drained testicles. He tied Jerome's bandanna, carefully co-ordinating the movements of his gloved fingers with the white anaesthetizing rushes. Jerome watched his nightstick protruding imperiously as the huge moustache moved closer and came to rest against Jerome's head, as tousled by fitful sleep as his haircut permitted. Serge and leather and metallic flashes; buffed, milk-fed Californian skin, dark olive under the braggadocio stubble. Authority vanquished, the collapse of order and routine through the irrational power of sex; the *miles gloriosus* changed into a ministering Helot. Phew, some kind of sex! Hours of pounding acid, every nerve-ending racing with momentum, so many times had they approached orgasm, then rescued each other from near-trance. The policeman's kisses had turned Jerome inside out, their tongues pressed and cleaving until the climactic mutual acquiescence. *Zaebos, anum meum aperies . . . Leonard, asperge me spermate tuo et inquinabor.*

'You're a hot man, you know that? You British sure do know how to keep a cop happy.'

'I just wish we had more practice,' murmured Jerome wistfully.

'Stick around and fix yourself some breakfast.'

His gaze fell on the policeman's wallet, which bore the

legend 'Yoko Ono, Dakota, New York'. A hard man, he thought. It would be counterproductive to expect any further contact with him. Even that last detail could not undermine his fetishistic precision and convert him into a sentient creature aware of things going on outside his own sexual cybernetics.

But then surely the mere act of sleeping with Jerome had been a betrayal? Could any predetermined fetish ever remain intact after it had been realized? All fantasy fulfilment had in the end to contain that one crucial ingredient of self-parody, the weak point at which one person surrendered to another and recognized their tenuous mutual conspiracy.

Happily the policeman's departure prevented any further sleepy erosion of Jerome's basking complacency. He'd been memorable for his intact authenticity, or was it his authentic intactness? Not one homosexual signal had interrupted their homosexual embraces. This was something the world would never understand.

Jerome lay back in a drowsy euphoria, eviscerated, pillowed eternally. Soon he would have to get up and slog on down to the Welfare Center. He did voluntary work there, scrubbing the vast steel *bains-marie* in a kitchen full of roaring blacks all higher than the drunks they were feeding. The drudgery was a boost for his novelistic imagination – a kind of slice of Zolaesque low-life – as well as a sop to his conscience. Each time he entered the slimy kitchen he felt good as he recalled Allen Ginsberg's 'America I'm putting my queer shoulder to the wheel.'

Jerome lay back *à la grande horizontale* and tried to feel the sensation in each limb in turn. An immense contusion throbbed perfectly on his inner left thigh and he could feel a chain of yellowish-black circles forming on his neck and shoulder. The battle-scars made him smile secretively. Thrusting his arms under the pillow, he lay on his stomach starfished in an exhausted X, and started counting backwards: Frank, Manfred, Adam, Edward, Bob, Robert, Michael, Elliott, Javier, Yannis, Joseph, Wolfgang, Joachim, Gerhart, Mark, Said, Abdullah, Mehmet, Giorgio, Henry, Angel, Sebastian, Philip Paul, Andrew – all the saints in the calendar, all the devils in the demonology, dead angels. All now in sexual aspic. Like the casket the Duc de Morny kept beside his bed, filled with photographs of his conquests, flowers decorating their pudenda. The list reminded him of the man he knew who always yelled out 'Jose!', 'Mark!' or 'John!', whatever it might be, at the moment of orgasm, largely to show he remembered the name. It was OK with the monosyllables, fine, a neat idea, but 'Sebastian!' or 'Belisario!' must have presented some problems, more with synchronization than memory. Jerome's catalogue was his alternative to counting sheep; reciting the incantatory litany of past lovers, dwelling on the strange conjunction of so many lives, their mysterious devolution on to his own. Did he really possess this centripetal force? Just now, in the morning light, with his tightened under-eyelids, a distinctly centrifugal one was asserting itself, creaking into lazy action as he sought half-heartedly but deliberately to expel the policeman from his orbit and consign him to that same sanctuary of dead memory. In this way their guaranteed estrangement from this point could be made to appear as the result of Jerome's harsh and manly rejection, his purposeful cult of non-alignment. The *post coitum tristitia*, the deflation and the evanescent triumph could all thus be resolved. He felt abandoned, like Ariadne on the Naxos shore by the faithless Theseus, and abandoned too like a wanton, calling queen cat on heat.

'*J'aimerais ce pays si je n'étais captif.*' How San Francisco had enslaved him! He turned over to flick on the wireless. 'The ultimate opera movie: Bellini!' it yelled at him. 'The bickering, the broads, the *bel canto* and now the block-buster biopic!'

8

Thesaurus Regina

Words, words, words, words! His inner cry rang out as despairingly as Lear's howl on the heath (blasted). *Howl, howl, howl, howl!* There was no escape from his obsession with words; their form, their origin, their synonyms, antonyms, semantic field, adequacy, variants. No sooner had he heard a new or striking word than he set to analysing it, parsing its components, translating it into as many languages as he knew or didn't know, forming outlandish derivatives from scraps of morphological and phonological information. Often the substance of what was said to him was entirely submerged in this train of thought, and on the strength of this inner digressiveness he acquired a reputation as a thinker and a good listener. 'Jerome is so patient, so sympathetic and intuitive,' Venetia boasted, only gradually realizing that those qualities masked an inordinate and private self-indulgence. Their discussions took on the form of an obtuse angle in geometry, ever widening from its point of common origin.

'I have a vague *angst* this morning, something to do with that rebuff last night. Or perhaps it's a kind of fear of failure mixed up with remorse. Isn't it odd that I *know* that tomorrow I shan't even be able to remember the grimness of this morning, let alone make sense of it.' Her prose maundered relentlessly through the ramifications of feeling; but Jerome was lost, stuck and foundered at the single word *angst*, which had prompted an associative journey through the reasons why foreign philosophical loan-words were generally German, the oddness of the conjunction of four consonants, the difficult phoneme of the German 'a' and finally coming to rest in an absurd anagrammatic cloud of gnats. But his capacity for recovery was considerable; and he was able to answer Venetia in the appropriate vein and the linguistic flashes got lost in some kind of useless mnemonic log-jam.

Sometimes he felt that this was a considerable handicap. Particularly when he *knew* that his view of other people was unfairly coloured by his reactions to their use of language. One of his more promising liaisons had, like so many others, foundered on the rocks of linguistics. Irresistibly *gamin* as he'd been, the guy's iterative use of 'So he turned round and said to me', illustrating every incident and anecdote, had conjured up so headache-making a picture of humanity perpetually spinning on its axis that Jerome broke off the affair.

Often he wanted to tear the brain out of his head. Just to stop the constant whizzing inside, the darting from synapse to synapse, the neurons firing, the dizzy interchanges between sense and nerve-end, cortex and memory. Perhaps his relentless sexual activity was an attempt to prove to himself that he had a body as well, that he was not all brain, like a disembodied cauliflower. It was only in orgasm and sleep that it seemed to stop. Then the skeins of words could snap – but only to be messily reassembled later when his frantic consciousness returned. Walking, driving, eating, seeing, he was tormented by sentences, strangled in their subordinate clauses, clotted with parentheses, sub-paragraphs, whole dictionary entries. At any one time his mind could embrace every hedge and corner of a labyrinthine maze, knowing everything and nothing, incapable of controlling the intersections of the facts. At each junction there was a grey patch like the optical illusion of a child's puzzle.

What most disturbed him was the interference this caused in his work. Not only did his visual faculties seem to be waning under the attack from these intensely verbal flights, but he appeared also to be trying to *subject* his sight and the material of his photographs to a pointless linguistic analysis. A bridge was no longer a simple construct of girders and supports; it was all bridges; London Bridge in the Arizona desert, the Golden Gate with its suicides, strung-out, Blackfriars Bridge with God's banker dangling underneath, the Bridge of Sighs with a scurrying conspirator, the bridge with the frozen figures on a willow-pattern plate, the bridge of a boxer's nose, fetish bridge played by old ladies in rubber, brig, Brig, brigadier, brigantine. He could almost no longer *see*. The connection between object and describer was lost, everything become utterances which related only to other utterances, just as books so often spoke of other books.

One of his favourite – and most tiring – *reductiones ad absurdum* of this propensity was to construct circular sequences fashioned like dragons consuming their own tails. It was important that they should stray as far as possible from sense as the world conceived it, the links so tenuous that they snapped under any analysis other than the one appropriate to his own. They were like *culs de sac* (was that the French for colostomy bag?). Thus the idea of 'decimals' didn't, as perhaps it should have done, remind him of his inadequacy at arithmetic. It prompted a kind of headspin analogous to the merry thought processes so characteristic of marijuana: decimals, decimate (decim-eight, 10–8); Decimus Burton (at last a *visual* image of villas in Tunbridge Wells); Latin ordinals as forenames, Quintus Gaius Flaccus; was Gaius the Latin for gay? *Le gai-savoir* and the Provençal troubadours; *gai-savoir-faire*, was that what he lacked? John Lackland, lacklustre, ah, that was it, *lustrum*, five years in Latin and back to decimals.

He was like a bemused lexicographer wandering in a sea of slang and private languages. Rather like Gary Cooper in *Ball of Fire*, compiling an encyclopaedia but out of touch until Miss Sugarpuss O'Shea, in the dazzling shape of Barbara Stanwyck, drops in to explain the higher mysteries of jive talk.

Toying with a lens-filter for one of his cameras, he had again veered off into the madness of erudition and words. Filter, *café-filtre*; Melitta, the Roman settlement of Malta; pederasty and sodomy among the Knights of Malta suppressed by Philip the Fair of France; Philip von Eulenburg,

Count Moltke and the sexual scandals that had rocked Berlin; Berlin, Marlene Dietrich murmuring 'Darling'; Darlington, the station for the Bowes Museum; the bows of a ship, its stern; Laurence Sterne and Tristram Shandy; *Tristan und Isolde*, yes, Isolde on the bows of a ship (what a back-formation!) *and* the love-potion, the *philtre*. He often woke up sweating from nightmares in which these circles endlessly elongated themselves, hideous ellipses in which every word refused to be finite and sowed further words in its wake, dragon's teeth that reared up and again sowed their own progeny.

Like Hofmannsthal's Lord Chandos, Jerome was beginning to lose faith in the organic connection between words and things. It was as if, with only the barest knowledge of structuralism, he had intuitively groped towards the position of an extreme minimalist and found himself in the middle of an obscure medieval philosophical disputation . . .

It was not just a matter of losing faith in an organic link between words and things. He compounded this process with a secret desire that such a link should be dissolved. Nothing could be duller than simple equations in which x = y; far better to qualify, modify and allow that equation to fluctuate so that . . . = y provided that y = . . . etc. *ad infinitum.*

In this way language could become an entirely self-referring code, so intricately – but loosely – connected with objectivity that its pieces seemed to assemble themselves at random. If you were very clever you could divorce the words wholly from pedestrian meaning. Jerome felt an early tingle of excitement when he read a sentence in Ivy Compton-Burnett's *Dolores*: 'From toil for her bread, unfitted for her tenderness, he had taken her to comfort unbought of weariness' (= in taxpayer's lingo, he had married a girl otherwise obliged to work for her living). He was even more delighted to read of Lycophron of Chalcis – whose *Alexandra* was so hard to understand, a sixth of the words used in it to be found nowhere else, characters appearing under the names of animals or indicated by riddling allusions, Zeus meaning Agamemnon and vice versa. This was wonderful, almost as divorce-like a severance of language from reality as you could invent.

His obsession with language as its own sign-system led him to reject ordinary communication, common sense and the notion of a direct relationship between appearances and reality. Unable to throw off this handicap, he constantly sought esoteric inner meanings, symbolic quantities and allegories, arcane cryptographies, qualifications and ambiguities. Simple one-to-one references seemed of no account, debasing, as they did, the rich complexity of association that words should carry. In this respect – though in no other – he felt some affinity with those fierce Moravian Anabaptists who took to burning their own Bibles, fearing that the literal, the letter of the text, would obscure its spirit, the words seducing one's eyes and understanding to stay on them alone instead of passing through to the true meaning. Mallarmé had surely been right to hold that to name an object was to destroy its suggestiveness. Words, descriptions, pointers, should instead be somewhat frayed around the edges, pregnant with imprecision.

Thus the world became increasingly meaningless for him. Its phenomena were dismantled, and reassembled in some gigantic Meccano construction at the mercy of a hyperactive child. Each piece became infinitely elongated; each had its own indistinct moon of words circling around it. He was a polyglot of the kind you read about only in Victorian encyclopaedias. He could slip effortlessly into any language while most of his compatriots' acquaintance with French was confined to learning how to pronounce Simon Le Bon.

None of the terms of this perception had direction or purpose. Its very futility was why he longed for it to stop while at the same time it made any cessation impossible. Unlike even the function of a literary conceit, in which the disparity of the two basic premises unexpectedly pointed to and illuminated a third, his wild analogies and disjunctions led nowhere, devoured their own tails. And, unlike the leaps of the metaphysical mind, his petty jumps were banal, incommunicable, uncontrolled, like the gambollings of a naturally earthbound lamb.

The hardest part to reconcile himself to was the fact that despite, or more probably because of this frantic inner logorrhoea, human discourse was a faculty which substantially eluded him. Words separated from their useful function like detached retinae; and his interest in them was that of a collector of brightly coloured objects, a Nabokovian lepidopterist rather than the utilitarian who strings them together to inform, question, articulate, persuade. Speech was, for him, an act of self-sacrifice. Every sentence involved so painful a suppression of the possibilities of each word that it was easier to keep silent. If language was indeed generative, how much better to leave it unused, the pregnancy of each morpheme and phoneme utterly undisturbed.

He became more and more aphasic. Words seemed pointless. What did it matter anyway if the whole world was soon to be reduced to communicating in dot matrix or hip-hop rhyming couplets! Only with Venetia was he able to tease out sentences as elaborate as the towering galleons of Marie-Antoinette's coiffure. Their shared self-consciousness made this possible, as well as their determination constantly to renovate their relationship in serious discussion.

Language presented the most formidable difficulties. His phenomenal memory meant that he had merely to see a word in any language, in order to associate it with its meaning and store it in infinity. Thus whenever an idea or image occurred to him and was accompanied with a seemingly interminable series of alternative names, it was impossible to think in one language without simultaneously thinking in all others. This was the first factor that rendered him speechless.

Although technically polyglot, Jerome had little facility for the mechanical use of languages. Their use left him inexplicably flustered and tongue-tied, the expression of his ideas died on his lips. He excused and justified this by reflecting that others who were necessarily good linguists – interpreters, international white-trash socialites, bus operators, Popes – were competent only because they used a restricted and dull corpus of ideas in their practical exchanges. Those, like Jerome, whose ideas were more fluid, more diffident and experimental, could hardly rely on the same pragmatic efficiency.

The second factor was that his antipathy to imitation was so ingrained that he could scarcely bring himself to use a form once it had been used and lodged in his memory. Every sentence constructed, every idiom uttered led him to seek not to reuse it in its appropriate context but to consign it to the scrapheap of useless recall.

He did not, in any case, adhere to the necessary systems of language to compensate for this reverse amnesia. His memory ousted all individual items and particularities, ousted the abstractions necessary to make sense of them. Grammar was for him not so much generative of infinite permutations as a dead-handed tyrant binding words with fierce bonds as they struggled to lift themselves off the page and fly around in untrammelled autonomy, richly ambiguous and pregnant with suggestivity. Acts of syntax, the conception of a predicate or the subordination of a clause, repelled him to an extent where he preferred to allow the words their Saturn-rings of potential meaning rather than harness them severely to the rotted skeletons of received thought.

But it was not only these hateful words which distressed him. That aspect was child's play compared with the constant argumentative thinking, most of it unproductive and aimless, which robbed him of tranquillity, simplicity and sleep.

'I just long for a period of utter blankness,' he sighed to Venetia. 'Just drifting around with none of that dreadful whirring inside. What I need is some magic lever I can pull to make all the cogwheels and flywheels grind to a halt. It would be amazing if my brain could be like some kind of machinery you shut down for the night and cover over with a tarpaulin. All ready to burst into action again at the flick of a switch; but temporarily out of operation. God, what would I give for that, OUT OF OPERATION.

'This morning I spent three-quarters of an hour thinking about how I'd sulked with that creepy Fernando guy who thought I was rich. But it was worse than that, because I was thinking about the fact that I was thinking about it, knowing full well how pointless it was – I don't even want to see him again, let alone understand what made us act so viciously towards each other. It's all such a terrible waste, and a fearful strain.'

'It's exactly this that California's supposed to counteract,'

Venetia said. 'You learn how to control your thoughts so that they're only channelled into fruitful analysis, and the rest gets obliterated. I've always known that your brain's a kind of curse, like periods, only it lasts all the time. Mine isn't that great at switching off either; but at least I know what I'm *supposed* to do to control it. Drugs help.'

'Like hell they do. I only have to have the mildest hit of grass to career off into some idiotic racetrack that ends up in terminal paranoia.'

9

Good Old England

'Voulez-vous triompher des Belles? Pas exactement.'

In the middle of their experimental passage through the world, they were sometimes rudely brought back to the lives the past would have prescribed for them. These reminders of lost opportunity served their purpose, after they had taken place, in showing them that they had indeed rejected only the pointless, the stultifying, the blank mapped-out debris of experience.

This would be Venetia's destiny: swimming against the tide, womanfully cleaving her course through the billows of convention.

Venetia and Jerome both received invitations from a woman they had never met to spend the weekend for a large dance. In self-defence they agreed to drive together to Leicestershire, fearful of the social exposure neither of them had learnt to control to advantage. Although they both partially inhabited a microcosmic orbit to which they had been born and accustomed, their several idiosyncrasies left them ill-equipped to conform to its unshakeable patterns and expectations. Jerome felt marginalized by his sexuality – despite the universal lip-service acceptance of it – and Venetia found herself floored by her own intelligence and her consciousness of the materialistic considerations which underlay her movements within that milieu.

The house was small but grand, a William and Mary manor surrounded by undulating hills and rich pasture.

The late-afternoon summer light suffused the landscape with green and gold reflections. Oak trees and box hedges spread luxuriantly despite the gasping desiccation of the June drought. Venetia was hot and apprehensive, Jerome more composed, fitfully calm, beatified by the rushing air and dappled foliage. Neither of them had any real appreciation of landscape and, like the Verdurins at La Raspelière, had often turned their backs on celebrated panoramas to engage in abstract conversation. Yet Jerome enjoyed his cursory forays into the English countryside, a temporary *paysagiste*, secure in his indestructible urban roots, as fixed in his characteristic inner metropolis as these trees in their Horatian rusticity. Venetia really *needed* the city and the sensation it gave her of immediate involvement. Even the strict delimitations of their weekend expedition left her with a Johnsonian malaise. 'Where was the wit in bleating and lowing?' No *Nouvelle Héloïse*, she understood nature only as a strange diversion from the real business of living, a force that left other people inexplicably affected and subject to unreal imaginings.

'You must be Jerome and Venetia. Do come in.' They were already linked by God knew what secret negotiations, some hurried conclave of hostesses. The woman was secateuring flowers from an already manicured bed, and carried a wicker trug. As they got out of the car, she stood up and brandished a trowel in greeting, her shellac smile directing a steely lance at Venetia's involuntary enmity. No aspect of her demeanour betrayed any affinity with the exiled *Wandervogel*. Every detail seemed assembled by a computerized precision tool, the careful wash of countrifiedness hardly concealing her true familiarity with the red and white citadels of Cadogan Square: a life circumscribed by the tetrahedron of Market Harborough, Peter Jones, the soda fountain at Fortnum's and a dismal grouse-moor in Perthshire. Jerome could have ridden her blinkered along its perimeter, safe in the knowledge that her silk headscarf would have fluttered contentedly along the hoof-indented track. Her greeting was as practised as a child's *Für Elise*, and only the most sensitive would have detected her dissimulated terror at the prospect of entertaining two well-known anti-conformist intellectuals. Lady

Saxmundham had been peculiarly persistent in imposing the two *exotiques* on Lady Clanboise. Their social claims to hospitality had indeed been clouded by disquieting stories about their rejection of the innate values of their class. But Lady Saxmundham had cleverly emphasized their urban chic, alluding also to the *bien-pensant* circles they sporadically frequented in London and Paris, subtly understressing their moral ambiguity. Lady Clanboise was ready for a change in any case; her most recent one had been the menopause.

Jerome's effusions were more articulate than Venetia's, though his deep-throated caution kept them within the bounds of propriety.

'How do you do? It's so kind of you to have us to stay. What a marvellous place. Venetia and I have had the most thrilling drive' (that 'thrilling' a little too 1930s camp, too E.F. Benson for complete heterosexuality). 'You're so lucky to have all these wonderful colours all around, it's made me feel so grey and drab in our urban haunts.'

'Do you think so?' She made a mental note of this useful indicator of a conversational topic for dinner. 'I'm so pleased you could come. We're quite a small party, but I expect you'll know some of the others.'

There was numbing array of Land-Rovers and shooting-brakes in the drive. Venetia's inner nostrils scented cartridges and labradors, over-subsidized underwriters and Barbadian retreats. She was grateful that they entered the house through a back door, edging through *toile de Jouy* corridors cluttered with the paraphernalia of wellington boots, billiard cues, gymkhana rosettes, croquet mallets and monogrammed hairbrushes. No incongruity, everything predetermined by decree. A grave Portuguese carried their bags.

'John, I wonder if you'd mind going over to Rising later and rescuing Lady Henrietta, her car's broken down; and take some jump-leads, a tow-rope and a warning-triangle.'

Alien João dreamed of a girl leaning backwards over a boat of the sardine fleet, naked except for the fishing net draped across her breasts. Bewildered by these mysterious instructions, he assented to their general drift. Meanwhile he led Jerome and Venetia meekly up a mahogany staircase to their pretty bedrooms – asphyxiating with pot-pourri and over-pollenated flowers, a comprehensive allergy syndrome testing-ground; cocooning them in oligarchic security, the feminine chrysalis of a patriarchal genus of slave-owning imperialists.

At dinner Venetia felt as if she were cruising in the Sargasso Sea as she listened to Lord Clanboise's well-rehearsed conversational sallies. He in turn was astonished and embarrassed by her unexpected treatment of his hardy perennials. He pushed up a social daisy and she turned it into a frangipani, his tea roses metamorphosed into waxy tuberoses. She had quite forgotten how people spoke to one another; she herself only spoke to David and Jerome, both of whom served as eccentric paradigms.

'Yes, I do live in London, but my adopted son and I are absolutely compulsive travellers. In fact we've just come back from Mount Athos. I managed to get in dressed as an Anglican curate, but I suspect that the *very* susceptible monk was less gullible than he pretended. It was so exciting to see the blinding austerity of the Eastern cenobites. Do you think they can – or indeed *ought* to – sustain their sexual chauvinism?'

Lord Clanboise speculated hard and settled on blandness. 'My dear, who am I to say? I'm sure they have their own reasons. I went to Turkey once, couldn't get over the memories of Gallipoli.'

'Jerome and I have just seen a wonderful Australian film about the Gallipoli campaign. It was just perfect for Australians to recapture its atmosphere. They caught that extraordinary male bonding of the soldiers. I could almost understand all that *Tell England* romanticization, the complete superfluity of women. No wonder Emmeline Pankhurst had such a hard time.'

She hated herself for littering her conversation with diffuse semiotic signals, alienating plums of over-literacy, polysyllabic padding. But Lord Clanboise had obviously been forewarned by his superficially intelligent wife; and Venetia owed it to herself to fulfil his well-grounded fears.

'There's the story about a Greek shipowner,' Lord Clanboise

began one of his ancedotes, 'who peppered a group of
industrialists by shooting across the line of guns. They lay
there wounded and yelling until someone fetched the police.
When the host explained that the man was an important guest
and the finest shot in Greece, the local bobby just said: "No
wonder. The way he shoots he must be the only one left."'

She felt afraid that he might suddenly expect her to answer
him on his own terms, perhaps ask her what she'd shot and
out she would come with that old joke about the *mallard
imaginaire*.

The equine man on her right, prematurely middle-aged
with his protruding veins and crêpey neck and called George,
offered no prospect of relief. He had clearly categorized her
as *hors-concours*, a symbol of that uncomfortable end of
the female spectrum which could never be squared with
prep-school matrons and strident touchline *vocalistes*. He
remained silent and apparently unembarrassed. At all events,
his other neighbour was making all the running.

'He drove all the way to Fort William from the Mallaig ferry,
and James was sick, he threw up all over the place, probably
too much whisky at the Skye Ball. The sick hurtled all over the
car, so we stopped and an *extraordinary* Scotsman came along
the road, he was *dancing*, can you imagine, at eleven o'clock
in the morning! Just wandering along doing the "Duke of
Perth" all by himself. I thought I was seeing things. James
wanted to take him on to Fort Augustus, so we put him in
the back with the dogs. I think he smelled worse than they
did, the poor darlings.'

Her pearly lobes reddened with excitement. Flaccid George,
his head filled with investment portfolios and claret fumes,
stared ahead, grateful for this gushing flood which so effectively
counteracted Venetia's alarming presence.

Indeed, Venetia's performance was on schedule. Jerome,
glancing apprehensively at her from the far end of the table,
silently implored her to suppress the relentless cultural
Hippocrene and to engage in the rules of the game. By now,
however, she believed that Lord Clanboise's rugged Bastille
had been stormed and that she was licensed to excavate the
foundations of his world-view.

'How extraordinary your life has been, Venetia. It must

make us all seem frightfully narrow. How did you come to adopt a child when you're not married?'

She was right. His curiosity and humanity had surfaced. It was as if an iceberg had rolled over to reveal huge volumes of igneous rock beneath, quick to take fire, its dormant volatility made naked and plain. His broad, flushed features, the stippled veins around his Wellingtonian nose, the clenched muscles at his temple had all softened perceptibly during Venetia's energetic discourse. After dinner he sent word to his wife that the ladies should not withdraw, and chose not to register her raised eyebrows.

None of this process escaped Jerome's aquiline gaze, and he was forced to concede that Venetia had succeeded in defrosting the contemptuous, tunnel-visioned aristocrat. He, for his part, had established a kind of elevated platform between Lady Clanboise and himself on which they danced an elegant conversational paso doble, never once acknowledging their dislike for one another. The effective aperient had been Jerome's charming *politesse*, his absorption of the unyielding code which the Guermantes had unspokenly laid down for peripheral socialites: the slender division between modesty and self-effacement. At no stage did he exaggerate his claim for attention or suggest that the values of the Bohemian, the artist, the homosexual or even the itinerant preacher might equal in importance the monolith of the English lower upper classes. Lady Clanboise, relieved if a little disappointed, prattled angularly about uncontroversial playwrights and annual general meetings, seizing on his up-front feedlines as if they'd been seedling magnolias thirsting for her nitrogenous fertilization.

In a lull in the conversation, he inwardly heard his own rehearsal for a conversation with George. '*What does it feel like to be a capitalist usurer, kidding yourself and the rest of the world that you provide an essential service, when in fact you're lending money to corrupt Third World governments and perpetuating the appalling cycle in which they can't even afford repayment of the interest let alone the capital itself while millions of people get dragged into the spiral of national debt so that people like you and this ninny beside you can afford your indispensable trifles . . .*' The tirade was inexhaustible, yet he knew he lacked the courage, energy or seriousness to go ahead with it.

Two hours later, Jerome and Venetia, vowed to the inseparability of Castor and Pollux, were languidly acquiescing to a stream of protestations of familiarity, reserving their strength for the social Himalayas in the interior of Revelstoke. Their progress along the peaks was adroit, oiled by the security they had discovered at the Clanboises'; only momentarily did it falter when a tiara seemed just a little too aggressively fender-like or an Ypresque poker-back failed to detumesce. The talk was of bloodstock and fatstock, cousins, vermin and winter sales. Venetia clasped a coeval duchess with relief, assured of the social mobility that their closeness would lend her, albeit praying hard for the continued absence of the duke. The young duchess, always responsive to Venetia's fluttering, panting intimacy, drew her aside to an *oeil-de-boeuf* through which they could girlishly stare and dissect while sustaining their own reciprocated affection. In the middle of an animated update on Venetia's San Francisco experiences Jane clutched her arm peremptorily to draw attention to a squawking duo of feathered punks, bobbing and swaying excitedly near an endangered jardinière.

'Do look, aren't they adorable? I suppose you know that Marcus has been playing Iachimo in *Cymbeline* at the Royal Court? Apparently when he comes out of the trunk in Imogen's bedroom he has to brandish an immense phallus the size of a Corinthian column. I do wish he'd brought it with him. But then I don't suppose anyone would notice it in this room. It's so dreadful, his brother just died. He drowned in his bath and they found he was simply bursting with heroin. God, I don't know how we cope with all these junkies dying.'

'It's like an epidemic, where you expect people to succumb. It's almost worse for our generation,' Venetia said, 'than for all these old fogies in St James's, you know, the ones whose fingers start to tremble and their palms go clammy as they get nearer the obituary column in *The Times*.'

The duchess had prematurely sacrificed her coltish curiosity for a *mariage de convenance* designed principally to bale out her embittered grace-and-favour mother. In consequence her dialogue with Venetia was designed to show that she had lost none of her *outré* scale of values and her contact with the world of counter-cultures and artistic heterodoxy. She hoped, in this way, that her husband might be seen merely as a sensibly submerged appendage, necessary for the maintenance of her highly mobile but irredeemably pointless life; so conscious was she of the unflattering light in which her alliance could be seen, especially by those whose fluidity and indefinable social position separated them from the grooved ruts of élite conformism. Venetia, for her part, was grateful for the hierarchical cushioning which Jane could provide, and enjoyed in an uncomplicated way the self-apologetic confusion of so grand a *grande dame*, respected beyond her tender age yet anxious to spread her cultural tentacles. She was disengaging herself now from Lucretia, an old enemy turned bosom confidante; and Jerome, observing them, thought with satisfaction how ironic it was that it should be the phonetic sound of Esher, *suburbia maxima*, the Surrey with the dirge on top, the epitome of everything they contemned that welded together the two girls' names and social class.

Passing Jerome in mid-discourse and patting his arm in mock-condescension, Venetia went to an upstairs lavatory, more to sedate her nerves than to piss. One look at the women in the ante-room was enough to confirm her miscalculation. While some stood in attitudes of theatrical self-examination, primping their slubbed heads as if they'd been the Beardsleyesque cascades of which they dreamed, others bent reverentially before unstructured lines of cocaine laid out on porcelain surfaces and plastic hand-mirrors. One stood inert against a sabled coat-rack, willing upon herself the strength to confront again her heartless lover. Beside her a compassionless trio disjointedly recalled their separate experiences of a single seducer through an Algerian haze of opiates. 'Don't be dumb, he never liked clinging women, no wonder he ditched you' – 'I just got so exhausted listening to all his crap that I passed out under the bed' – 'You mean you didn't know he got the clap at Elaine?' Only exclamations seemed to unlock their jaws from the clenched delivery of their class.

Mortified (and sickened till she reminded herself of a parallel scene when Virginia Woolf, already deranged, was sickened by the 'soulless yap' of two girls in a lavatory discussing their boy friends, and that had been only a month before her suicide), Venetia turned, intrigued, to watch an elderly ball of tulle as it planted itself magisterially on the threshold. Background and breeding conquering nervousness, it tottered forward to relieve its nephritic bladder, with nostrils pinched more to exclude the hateful human dregs than the death-dealing fumes of narcosia. None of the younger women was deterred by the doom-laden countenance; its presence served rather to focus their comfortable modernity, their defiance of the rules of conduct embodied in the very fabric of the pedimented windows and the frigid flagstones. The matron's stately exit, redolent of handbags and pancaked dignity, went unobserved.

Inwardly taking sides with the outraged reject, Venetia thrust aside one of the giggling harpies and knew that her and their lives would never re-converge. More and more had she experienced that same certainty and taken to a kind of resigned sadness, knowing, as her personality hardened and grew less malleable, that whole colonies of humanity would scatter like lemmings before her daunting presence. It seemed the capsule she inhabited had an impenetrable glycerine coating against which even the well-disposed slithered and bounced. Mostly, however, like these empty and septum-seared girls, they simply fled. Still, it had to be admitted that each flight and each slide consolidated her sense of identity in a way that contrasted with Jerome's endless re-examination of his own values. She wasn't forced, as he was, to reassess her performance and modify its extremes in order to capture some cheap acclaim. It was this widening distinction which allowed her to feel unguiltily protective towards him.

At that very moment he was balancing a plate of cold roast beef and salad in front of an admiring – and envious – dowager. His appetite, unslaked even by Lady Clanboise's starchy cuisine, grew as the night advanced and his miracu-lous brown fat invisibly devoured the adipose tissue. His accomplished forking in no way interfered with the stream of subordinate clauses and periodic sentences. In answer to a question about the nature of his work he replied:

'At the moment I'm engaged on a photographic survey of the baroque influence on English architecture; the extent to which native Palladianism withstood the onslaught of Vanbrugh and Hawksmoor. I'm hoping that eventually, if it turns out to be as comprehensive as I hope it will, it'll be possible to turn it into a television series. The main problem is how far I can personally be involved in the production – as opposed to merely submitting a set of beautifully composed shots. But I'm anxious about participating too much. I'm not sure whether the use of my voice-over might give the series too mandarin a feel, like the Spanish programmes on the Prado. I thought they suffered really heavily from the narrator's pompous and stilted presentation.'

The dowager, reflecting ponderously on the message underlying this unfamiliar medium, decided on admiration tempered with a defensive promotion of her social superiority. Her chins hung like stalactites. Although her thinking day began with the 5.40 p.m. 'News' and ended with the 'Epilogue', the idle telephoning and issuing of commissions that filled the remaining hours conferred on her a clear sense of her own elevation above those who merely acted and did, pitifully constrained by responsibility for their own sustenance.

'How simply marvellous. I'm sure we shall all enjoy that. It must be fascinating to see so many houses from your workmanlike point of view. I'm afraid I sometimes think I must be virtually blind. Especially when it comes to architecture. Once, when I was staying in Tuscany, I got lost on a walk and went into the wrong house. I'd mistaken it for Montegufoni.'

Why toady to these creeps? He stood to gain nothing, materially or intellectually. The only sensible conclusion was that his politeness was now so ingrained, so automatic that he'd actually lost control of it and had forgotten even how to exploit its obverse.

The dowager introduced Jerome to a younger, less benevolent *consoeur*, whose glance of acknowledgement missed Jerome's by several yards, as if a rivetingly interesting parrot had rocketed backwards from his left shoulder. Jerome, trapped in a triple airlock, gasped for an oxygenating response, but gasped in vain and left the two women free to embark on a dialogue that seemed to have begun some time before his birth. The drawing-room, with its hectares of Lelys and carved swags and cornucopias, its intricately indented cornice and its Aubusson tapestries, appeared to be viciously conspiring with his two erstwhile companions to instil a sense of unease, an emphatic pronouncement that his erratic conduct disqualified him for ever from their static grandeur. Everyone in his immediate vicinity seemed to inhabit a uniform physical and spiritual landscape, their safe utterances confirming their inalienable privileges.

He summoned up the necessary social reserves to excuse himself in a position of semi-power, a Congress of Vienna delegate outmanoeuvred by an unsubtle Metternich but retaining – precariously – his country's territorial integrity. He would have liked now to have been on an upper floor so that he might descend the lily-hung double staircase with Anglo-Hollywood éclat. As it was, he ascended it slowly, conscious of the regularity of his movements, an exactness which shielded him from the after-effects of his ambivalent encounter. Much the same consciousness lay behind his assumption of an over-syntactic speech and delivery in which the gnarled syntagmata tried vainly to assert his respectability but succeeded only in confusing and discomfiting his audience. He had no other defences to fall back on, no firm credentials, and his social adaptability and conversational freedom suffered accordingly. He needed Venetia. Only Venetia, his spiritual seer-sucker-succour, removed the brittle glasshouse frame around his bruised mental foliage. He stopped to watch her as she leant pensively – and unmistakably dismissively – over the balustrade, perched like a *trompe-l'oeil* Tiepolo over the contemptible throng.

As he left, a drunken old queen lurched up to him and asked, 'Why is it that the youngest sons of marquesses are always gay? You're not the youngest son of a marquess are you, by any chance?'

'No such luck,' Jerome replied coldly. 'Sorry to disappoint

you. Maybe it's because the heat's off them to produce brats and so they swing totally to the opposite pole.'

'What? Er . . . yes, of course.' Jerome savoured the amazement in the sottish face; for his question had, of course, been rhetorical and effetist, scarcely anticipating so exhaustive an answer.

Venetia and Jerome embraced and updated.

'I've been talking to old Lady S. She must be ninety-three in the shade. They were all banging on about a bat they'd seen in the auditorium at Glyndebourne – bat as in vampires, not Lady S. It was unbelievable how much mileage they got out of that story. Apparently the bat had flown around and glinted rather prettily in the lights, and all of them felt the need to say something boring about it – one girl was frightened it might get caught in her hair, another one said something about enhancing the magic of the opera, a terrible creep said he wondered if they released bats from a box like dry ice. Yawn, yawn. And imagine, the story must have gone the rounds already during the interval; hundreds of idiots talking about a bat while they ate their picnics. Sometimes I wonder just how the English upper classes get by intellectually; I wouldn't give them an 0-level between them.'

Agreeing that things were little more than routine, they decided to go into a bedroom and do some drugs. Jerome dropped a fructose tab before snorting the cocaine and enjoyed the clinical transparency of the glass tube. Then they rolled some Maui Wowie into a joint and lay close beside one another like figures on a Tudor tomb. They looked upwards at the *chinoiserie* rotunda of the bed. 'You are the sunshine of my life,' one of them said with real affection, and Venetia moved her metallic pumps around in a rhythmic dance.

'I like your new cowboy boots,' said Jerome.

'They kill tarantulas and they're good for climbing chain-link fences.'

'Sometimes I think D.H. Lawrence was right when he called England a bouquet of vomit.'

Jerome arranged the folds of her dress into a shape suggestive of a Mannerist *linea serpentinatra*.

'You'll always have the advantage over me, you bloody slit. It's just like driving offences – you can wield your femininity and get the cop to tear up the ticket. If I wield mine, I get had up for immoral importuning.'

'Why not give it a whirl with Lord Saxmundham? I'm sure his *vice* is not just *anglais*. This dance needs a little theatre. Nothing overstated. Just snake your pelvis around a bit, use your wrists, and pour unctuous honey into his ear. And try and make it in front of the Lord-Lieutenant . . .'

Jerome, while savouring the image of this *coup de théâtre*, knew he would never do it. He could never bring himself to be the catalyst for a social collapse, however bored and contemptuous he'd become.

'I've been talking to Francesca Martínez,' he told her. 'She was surrounded by men like a cluster of King Charles's spaniels. It was extraordinary – and rather flattering. She singled me out and freed herself from the mobsters as if they'd been so many fronds of pondweed. I think there's something about the fragility of her position in England which makes her take sanctuary in other marginal allies. It's odd how, in spite of her *succès fou*, infiltrating the stuffiest and most dismissive circuit, she's retained a sense of herself as being still a tentative outsider. And she always keeps a reserve of distance. It never allows her to commit herself totally to social mountaineering. There must be something very extraordinary in the Argentine system of child-rearing – something to do with all that anachronistic concern with dead English values, Hurlingham, St George's, Harrods, polo, all that shit – which actually qualifies a girl for our fragments of historical survival better than their own offspring. What do you think?'

Venetia squirmed like a cat, mildly jealous of this Argentine invasion that recalled her own historic débâcle in Buenos Aires.

'I suppose,' she answered, 'that for a start I should be more interested in all of this English jamboree if I'd arrived from some wind-blown *estancia* where there was nothing to look forward to but over-polished *latinos* playing with lariats and status-enhancing *palermitanas*. In both *our* lives, after all, the stress has been on rejecting the values we've been presented with. As if nothing ready-made – whether it's a TV dinner or a social framework – could meet with anything but outraged dismissal. *I*, for one, have always felt the need to construct my own life; at least then you *know* that the mistakes and the catastrophes are your own responsibility and can't ever be attributed to some sort of mass fallibility. I don't think anyone could ever *discredit* us in the way that, say, a logical positivist might discredit Catholicism or a Swift political chicanery. Our values – especially your acceptance of, quasi-*belief* in, homosexuality, and my renunciation of orthodoxies and adoption of David – *could* become the new orthodoxy. In which case any number of critics could lambast us into the gutter. I guess all rebellious spirits lay themselves open to that kind of paradoxical backlash; just as if an army of moralists retreated immediately after advancing, so that an entire battlefield of alternative opinions could be annihilated. Like those dragon's teeth in the Argonaut legend. What I *most* feel, though, is that we've both listened to the heart and acted in accordance with its contradictory impulses. So the coldness of reason not only eludes us but seems like a terrible negative force which constrains and torments other people's lives.'

What *was* she on about? Had reason really deserted her? Had drugs rushed in where reason feared to tread? Although Jerome was lost, he knew that in fact he understood. She was looking at him intently as she continued.

'The Argentine girl is presumably as lost as we are. Or alternatively, perhaps, she's discovered here a sort of miraculous concretization of the values she's been acquiring all her life, only oddly in a distant and inappropriate hemisphere. But I think her gesture towards you means she still feels a little bit ambivalent, frightened perhaps to give up the successes of her triumphal progress but needing to understand and acknowledge the self-doubt of other partial misfits. What did you talk about?'

'We talked about the modern Argentine novel and the decomposition of all the literary coteries in Buenos Aires. She was very convincing about the ways the novel can no longer be used as a weapon for political change. That role's been usurped by the torturers. So it's forced into increasingly peripheral areas; dealing with obsessions, irrealism, dreams, moral failure, headgames, with the reading public

77

withdrawing further and further into a neurotic literacy, increasingly at odds with the factual Gradgrind news-devouring masses. Maybe it's just the same old death-of-the-novel controversy we've already thrashed out in Europe. Only I suppose that its connection with political tyranny makes it more interesting. At all events, I could see that Francesca was sticking to her esoteric guns *in order to* widen the gap between her besiegers and herself; and every word she said made them visibly reassess their claims on her attention. A kind of electric current moving nervously between them and her. She continued pushing further into matters beyond their knowledge or interest, while at the same time maintaining their interest in her discussion of these, for them, dead issues. They were all dangling like unhappy resistors on a circuit; unable to reciprocate her statements or even to make their physical position more tenable, so effectively had she plunged them into intellectual and social darkness. Dazzling.'

Jerome paused and heard a muffled semi-musical sound coming through the window from a distant wing of the house. After a while he identified it as the ecstatic chorus of mainline heavies, frazzled and heaving, eyes closed in oblivion as they sang along in ragged unison to 'Hi Ho Silver Lining' in the discotheque. There would be an overwhelming sense of corporate jollity, the artistocracy celebrating its enfranchised state to the strains of a proletarian rant. Soon the bread-rolls would start to fly and huge teeth would be bared in a mass asinine rictus. Sweaty girls in pearls would elbow their way to the champagne as if stranded on the poop deck of the *Titanic*. An unspoken agreement formed osmotically between Jerome and Venetia that they would renege on their contemporaries and explore the milder virtues of the aged. They embraced like gladiators and Jerome ran his tongue inside the delicate mollusc of his lover's ear.

'Try not to stand too near any stars,' he said. 'We don't want you being eclipsed, or as they say in San Francisco, don't park by a fire-hydrant.'

Triumphantly they cocained their way to the great staircase. This time their appearance would be *echt* DeMille;

Camille and Alfred, the élan of Valmont and Mme de
Merteuil crossed with the *pudeur* of Cécile and Dancény.

> A party next of glittering dames
> From round the purlieux of St James'.

Their attention was arrested in mid-descent by a miniature class-conflict. A Marxist parable? Three elderly ladies,
ruched and rinsed, stood lending their conversation artificial emphasis with clamorous gestures and conspiratorial
wrist-clutching. Their closeness seemed indivisible, as if
any attempt to prise them apart might have demolished the
entire English class-structure. Indeed, when this happened
– more by accident than design – Jerome and Venetia
believed themselves to be watching a significant incident.
Two junkies, spilling their debris of silver paper and plastic
straws, emerged from behind a brocade curtain and thrust
their snickering bodies through the colloquy of shocked
ladies. All that they stood for – the inherited correctness,
the despairing courage before England's imminent demise,
the correlation of breeding with virtue – foundered in their
ball-gowned discomfiture. Their assailants, unaware of the
devastation in their wake, forged forward to other Round
Ponds they might convert into tidal waves. The ladies
steadied one another in their majestic collapse and found
themselves unable to articulate a single or a collective
response. Taking refuge in reciprocal looks of outrage, they
moved graciously away from their corner, now become a
tainted cell as yet one more psoriatic layer flaked off the
crust of Empire.

The great hall meanwhile was pulsating with adultery.
Assembled to celebrate the induction of a young virgin into
their army, the society horde strove now to dismantle its own
morality in a temporary concession of licence.

Jerome, separated again from Venetia (as often seemed so
necessary during their short-lived experiments in reality),
leant seductively against a garlanded pilaster. At these
moments of alienation, he was often absorbed with remembered and imagined visions of uniformed thugs in peniten-
tiaries rearing up from iron-framed beds or abusing one

another and rutting like brutish animals. As he tried to concentrate on the febrile romp of the dance, his thoughts turned
to drug-dark cellars and construction workers coupling and
uncoupling like locomotives and fenders. Could this be the
same planet?

10

Fives

An anxiety which recurrently attacked Venetia was the fear that her life was being led at too low an intensity; that the extraordinary insights and profundities characterizing other people's lives were something altogether eluding her. She believed in the existence of a different, companion dimension of heightened experience into which the perceptive (and gifted) regularly stumbled without impairing the ordinary conduct of things. For her part, this awareness only made her regret that she had spasmodically glimpsed such a dimension, prompted by stimuli as diverse as a musical phrase, a bitter unhappiness, an access of sentiment. Gradually, as she grew older, she came to realize that she exaggerated the gap between others and herself in this respect. Experience showed her that their responses were as humdrum as her own, that they, too, had recourse to drugs to up the ante. However firmly the revelation established itself in her, however, she was still prey to the longing for hi-fi digital Truth, the urge to scale and descend the full moraine, the ringing clangorous sensation of a raw reality perceived head-on and uncluttered.

Overcome with melancholia, she crossed into the hall and spun the globe in its mahogany frame. It squeaked slightly, its cycle hindered at each revolution by a flaw in the mechanism. Russia, the United States, Australia – the names of the larger countries became distinguishable first as the momentum gradually slowed. Then, rather at random, Colombia, Saudi Arabia, India and Spain, as the colours separated out from their kaleidoscopic blur; and she tried to work out the logic for each country's pigmentation – green for the emeralds of Colombia, orange for the vitamin-packed health of Sweden, yellow for the jaundiced corruption of the Philippines, crimson for the blood of the British Empire. And the deep cobalt sea enveloped all the colours so that they jostled and pressed together like multiple foetuses afloat in amniotic fluid. It became impossible to concentrate on the geography, to equate the chromatic chequerboard with countries, cities, landscapes, physiognomies, emblematic snapshots even, in her memory, of a glimpsed pavement or a dead creature. Unlike Jerome's, her faculty of sight often rested on the surface and failed to pass through to the meaning of things. Looking idly at the globe, she felt a kind of disturbance at this visual superficiality; reflected how her knowledge of the world, despite the resolutions they had both made at the outset, was shrinking and becoming reduced to a formulaic outer shell of half-pursued imaginings. She lay for hours, memorizing the layout of the Palazzo Schifouaia from the *Guide Bleu*: each fresco of the Salone dei Mesi. She looked at street-plans of Warsaw and tried to summon from memory what the intersection where the Lodz and Cracow highroads diverged looked like. Was it the bridge in Avignon which led nowhere? And did that put it in the same league of futility as the arch at St Louis? There was no way of telling how wrong her conjurations might be, since she was now too lazy to confirm them. She really must try and uproot herself from her cosy slough, if only to renew the vigour of her sight.

It was tempting to blame David for this immobility, yet she refused to do so. Instead, she reminded herself of his extraordinary adaptability, a quality that removed from him all the restraining limits which tied down mother and child. He travelled with the ease and aplomb of a Bedouin, unencumbered by nostalgia. No, the fault lay with her and with Jerome, who seemed by now to have slumped into an oasis of self-indulgence and West Coast *laissez-faire*. Even though he tried conscientiously to include Venetia and David into his life, organizing expeditions, expending energy on their happiness (essential to his own), his sexual craving rooted him progressively to that fertile soil. Thus were both he with his lustful stake and Venetia with her new placidity conspiring to defeat their jointly declared aim. It was a peculiarly insidious kind of Californization.

As if to remind Venetia of this, David followed her into the hall and, slapping forcefully with his pudgy fingers, set the globe spinning and squeaking once more. His action showed how modern a child he was, a creature of self-assertion and arbitrariness wholly unlike a Victorian infant, docilely stroking his hoop. Venetia loved this trait in him and tended, by telescoping his age, to lump him with her cinematic idols – Gary Cooper, Jack Lemmon, Pier Paolo Pasolini – for their shared twentieth-centuriness.

As the globe returned to rest, David drew back his arm and studied intently the five fingers of his right hand.

'Why is Jerome going away?' he asked.

'What do you mean, darling? He's not going away, don't be silly.'

'No,' he said: though whether the 'no' confirmed Venetia's reassurance or flatly denied her version was unclear.

The strange exchange soon forgotten, he snuggled up close to her and stayed silent while she looked idly though a curious volume of symbolic engravings. They were smudged and indistinct, a badly printed set of pictures from the sixteenth century, pictures which didn't so much reproduce nature or tell a story as reveal some obscure, didactic truth. She stopped at one that represented a sleeping child, sturdy and angelic like David, who dreamed he ascended a staircase to Heaven and that, as he climbed, the steps fell away behind him. These consecutive actions were telescoped into an emblematic and impossible simultaneity, as in a squashed cartoon comic.

What did it mean? Venetia had reacted correctly to the cryptic image, speculating about its purpose, confused by its imagery. The author gave the clue in his explanation. It was an investigation of the nature of dreams. They were not to be interpreted literally since they were only signs or confused accounts of reality, caused by the absence of the sun and the cloudy vapours to the brain. Dreams, then, only have value in so far as they transmit true information, information significant outside the dream. So the only thing to be learnt from this dream was that we should always be determined not to fall back from the preordained path of virtue leading to Salvation.

'Mmm,' she thought, 'what a feeble morality. I wonder if David has dreams like this.' Who could tell what went on in his bright head? His inescapable *otherness*, the fact that he had never lived in her womb, sustained by her vital juices, drip-fed by her umbilicus, meant she could only ever approximately guess at his thoughts. He *seemed* to have some strange gift: but its nature and origin eluded her.

She smiled secretively. In the warm presence of her child, she lapsed into a dream, a dreamy dream, not at all like the harsh parable just deciphered. In her dream Jerome kept surfacing and telling her of his love. Even his voice smiled.

She wondered about the enigmatic picture the three of them must present to the world. It certainly could not be one of a complacent, solid family group, the posed brood of a Victorian burgher. It must look fairly peculiar. An analogy occurred to her as she thought of the endless flux and open-endedness of their lives and the way it might be interpreted. She remembered how, as a child, she had been fascinated by the stray families that seemed to wander eternally around the world. They belonged to the wrong nationality for the route they were travelling, apparently lost on the international air-circuit. A Greek family travelled from Warsaw to Madrid, a soft-spoken Brazilian one from Adelaide to Djakarta. Were they permanently displaced, stateless refugees, butterflies with no feet, who shuttled around without ever landing, or sleeping in transit lounges, secure only in their joint identity as a family?

Jerome, meanwhile, was lying on his stomach on a bed in another room, kicking his heels up in the air and poring over a pornographic magazine. After studying a photographic strip in which an all-American boy was subjected to extraordinary humiliations by his scar-faced slave-master, he came to the classified ads with their wild metalanguage and codified cries of ecstasy.

SLAVE RANCH
Has hard labor for sons and slaves
3+ hours from LA. Unusual amenities
include underground dungeon . . .
Dads and Masters can put your sons/
slaves to hard work and rewards.
Bottoms solicit me for arrangements.
Surveying tops and bottoms for ideas,
equipment preferences. No fats, fems, alcoholics,
drugs. Not interested in phonies
or play acting. Box 3177.

— BREECHES AND BOOTS —
Seeking lean submissive partner who
wears riding clothing and has a fetish
for tall, tight, polished boots. I am
booted and breeched too, white, 50, 6ft.,
165 pounds. Into leather, light S and M,
motorcycling, boot worship uniforms.
French active and Greek passive. Your
nude photo gets mine. POB 935.

NAKED, CHAINED, SHAVED
Duluth W/s. f/f.

Gradually the erotic images fell away, their charge dulled
by the irony that undermined them. His eyelids drooping
with fatigue, Jerome surrendered to the insidious embrace
of sleep, more satisfying to him than any of the tumultuous
mirrors of savage sexual release that now fell from his
fingers. Approaching death, the shadows of mortality, his
mind evacuated the pictures that attached him so firmly
to the physicality, the bodiliness of things. Sliding, falling,
floating, he allowed an airiness to fill in the interstices left
behind. Clouds of dreamy abstraction drifted unhurriedly
into the spaces. He was attaining his characteristic domain,
the mysterious regions in which man was at his most
naked and vulnerable, unarmed against the unforeseen,
unforeseeable adventures that would buffet his vacated
mind. Reason couldn't prevail, experience would tell one

nothing. A delicious helplessness would sweep over him, all his relentlessly over-active faculties suspended, abased before this powerful god.

The dream that assailed him didn't seem memorable even while it was happening. Its elements were too surreal, a flimsy kind of fiction, its coherence only of the most exploded kind. The sequence had something to do with an angel dropping out of the sky bearing a tattered cloak, was it? Or a dead animal? And then a child walked out of a prison wearing the name-tag of an evacuee and ran in triumph through the streets of a deserted town waving five plastic soup-plates it announced it had won in some unnamed competition. A ball of light bearing, somehow, the marks of a tiger rolled clumsily behind the child in desultory pursuit.

Piecing together the remnants of the dream afterwards, Jerome almost abandoned the attempt as a fruitless exercise. Nothing of a symbolic or Jungian nature seemed to have survived it. And yet, while he strained to reconstruct the fast-disappearing strands, he clutched tenaciously at a thread, the silken cord of the labyrinth, which seemed to hold the clue to all the other amorphous and inconsequential pieces. The number five seemed to have recurred with some insistence. There had been not only the child's five trophies, but after (before?) there had been a stockade, a medieval heraldic palisade made with five lances thrust into the ground. A cache of alchemical retorts, emblazoned, he thought with the same device as the pennants fluttering from the lances, was arranged on five levels so that liquid and vapour passed between them in complex scientific processes of rarefaction and crystallization. And there had been the five gaping wounds which, when the descending angel turned against the livid sky, had flamed and cicatrized in his unclothed torso.

Loth as he was to receive instruction from other people, suspicious and dismissive of their ideas and sense of reality, Jerome was peculiarly ready to look for information in his own dreams. It was as if through a veil of obscurity they could penetrate to the core of truth that eluded him in his own waking consciousness. He struggled hard to discover things, often complicating them and rendering them even less tangible with his infuriatingly rational mind. But dreams, those involuntary messengers, could alone perhaps deliver the message, the Pythian oracle.

What was the importance of five, why the clusters of images in fives? What particular significance did the phantasmagoric number have for him? No idea, no sudden revelation swam out of the blue to illuminate his puzzlement. He would have laboriously to investigate the matter and pursue it in the capacious library.

Venetia was still there, reading aloud to David and ruffling his hair with more enjoyment than she seemed to be deriving from her text. Jerome smiled at them but decided against asking Venetia's advice. This research was a secret pleasure, devoid of meaning or interest to anyone else; and the triumph of discovery could come only from his own labours.

Passing rapidly over the small section devoted to David's books – although *Five Go to Smugglers' Top* beckoned with false promise – he arrived at a shelf of re-editions of ancient Renaissance texts which reflected Venetia's now abandoned interest in the esoteric and hermetic background of iconography. Quite why she had hung on to them was a mystery which, despite her expertise in mysteries, she could never adequately explain. But for Jerome, during his present search, they held out the prospect of strange, crabbed interpretations of magic and symbolism. There would be paragraphs of lost formulas, catalogues of miracles arranged into species and genus, natural history arrived at by erudite guesswork. A fertile ground for his purpose.

After a few false starts – an obscure *Cosmographia*, a *Speculum humanitatis*, the *Enneads* of Plotinus, a *De omni scibile*, a huge compendium of Valerius's *Maxims* – he hit on something of apparent significance. With a scholar's reverence he lingered over the pregnant title: *The Garden of Cyrus, Or, The Quincuncial, Lozenge, or Net-Work Plantations of the Ancients, Artificially, Naturally, Mystically Considered*, by Sir Thos. Browne. Phew, there can't have been many editors around in those days insisting on snappy titles. He found, buried in the ramifications of this apparently shapeless ragbag, short, unexplained references to numerology, a science the author seemed utterly to accept as proven. Numbers appeared to be transcribed on to seals which communicated mystic intelligibilia. Five, it seemed, was the seal of the archetypal feminine cosmic force, the generative BINAH, the mother of life and the fountain of souls. How, through the burgeoning rhetoric, could that be made to relate to Jerome's quest for his identity? There was something relevant, maybe, in the feminine angle, the idea perhaps that his homosexuality conferred on him the magic status of hermaphrodite, the sanctified mingling of animus and anima? But surely it was cancelled, or counteracted, by the stress on generation and fertility, for barrenness was the lot of Jerome's confrères.

Other allusions added little to dispel the mystery, but only succeeded in complicating the question further, pointing up blind alleys into yet more recondite areas of scientific inquiry. In the *Timaeus*, the fifth whore of the universe was Venus – did it have a sexual import? The five books of Moses symbolized the Law. OK. There were the five senses and the five ages of the world before Christ. Isidore of Seville, Bede, everyone seemed to have something to say on the subject. St Columba, the gentle founder of the community of Iona, had gone into ecstatic seizures in chronicling the various meanings of the number:

> It also embraces all things that are and seem to be . . . This number designates at once all things in the higher and lower realms. There is the Supreme God; then Mind sprung from Him, in which the patterns of things are contained; there is the World-Soul, which is the fount of all souls; there are the celestial realms extending down to us; and last, the terrestrial realms; thus the number five marks the sum total of the universe.

It was altogether too general, too comprehensive to mean very much unless you had a vested interest in Christian cosmology. But here, here was something. It took as its starting-point that idea about the feminine principle underlying five. In some way it indicated the truth of marriage, the mystic joining of souls in sacramental union. But behind this was an insistence on the notion of generation, fruitfulness and continuity. In cabbalistic theory, five was the letter *He*, the fifth in the alphabet, and, as Browne warned, 'If Abram had not had this letter added unto his Name he had remained fruitlesse, and without the power of generation.'

So that was it. The true application of this numerology lay in a premonition of Jerome's sterility, the wasting of his seed in sexual congress without issue. The number five served as a reminder of his powerlessness to procreate, the ending of his line, his tribal nullity. And, of course, that association of five would remain indelible. Each time he encountered it, it would rise up to tell him mercilessly of his core of deadness. His life would end with his own life, no posterity would survive his extinction. He wished he hadn't bothered. It seemed he'd allowed himself idly to drift into another blind alley from which there was no exit into enlightenment. The whole search had led only to the uncomfortable confirmation of something he already knew, and he smarted with the frustration of it.

11

Heavy Leather

Jerome didn't have a problem with paedophilia. He was well out of it, he felt, and rejoiced that the New Gay had evolved an insurpassably egalitarian version of sex in which your masculinity was confirmed by the mirror-image hunk of masculinity with which it was consummated. Nobody counted under the age of twenty-one and one could almost feel sorry for the devastatingly beautiful teenage rent-boys who hung out on Polk Street, their Apollonian features distorted by the resentment they felt as life and its clients passed them by, together with the march of sexual fashion. No wonder they cultivated nostalgia for the 1960s, when they'd have been prime cuts in velvet and scalloped ringlets.

The new cloned virility did have a kind of empiricist logic. If you weren't attracted to women, why on earth go for pretty boys who looked like girls? An immense reservoir of Men stretched all around, glistening with pre-packaged Ur-homosexuals, all of whom sought nothing more taxing than clones of themselves to be hooked up in an everlasting daisy-chain whose links could be joined or separated *ad infinitum* like the segments of a worm. Men with men; it seemed both natural and highly perverse. Jerome appreciated it not just as the visible hypostatization of his own preconceived ideas, but as a sensible revolution, which, while it reversed the normal terms of reference, was still hugely workable and efficient. And it so spectacularly overturned the old prejudices about homosexuals chasing surrogate girls. In achieving this, the modern gay went a long way towards securing the most absolute overthrow of the tarnished stereotypes of sex.

Jerome was delighted, also, to find literary confirmation in Donne. In *Ignatius his Conclave*, he discovered a passage where the poet thundered against just such a monstrous perversity. Describing how a cardinal, a son of Pope Paul III, had raped a bishop, Donne speculated about the crazed appetites that prompted this bestial act: 'His stomacke was not towards beardlesse boyes, nor such green fruit: for he did not thinke, that hee went farre inough from the right sex, except hee had a manly, a reverend, and a bearded Venus. Neither staied he there; but his witty lust proceeded yet further . . . that his Venus might bee the more monstrous, he would have her in a Mitre.' It had everything: originality, wit, perversity. Catholicism, fetishism, extremism. (Mmm – that 'have her in a Mitre'. Everything Jerome held most dear. His admiration for the contrary view to Donne's was only partially tempered by his puzzlement at the story being told in a sermon. In a *sermon*, for Christ's sake! Imagine Father O'Malley telling that to the assembled pious ladies, bricklayers and au pair girls at Our Lady Star of the Sea, Notting Hill.

Jerome didn't have many preconceived sexual desires; but he did know that the more he absorbed himself in contemporary sexuality, the wilder became the extremism of sexual fulfilment. The men he spoke to about sex – and they often spoke to him about sex, less out of intellectual curiosity than with the purpose of exciting either him or themselves, a verbal equivalent to masturbatory foreplay – seemed to have left ordinary 'vanilla' sex far behind, as distant a memory as water-wings in a swimming-pool or alphabet elephants and zebras in a reading-book.

Nobody did these any longer:

1. Delicate, exploratory stimulation, kissing, gentle neck-biting, etc.
2. Playing with your lover's cock and erogenous zones, and sucking them.

3. Wondering whether the moment had come for the Big One.
4. Preparing for the Big One with lubricants.
5. Anal penetration.
6. The problem of how to bring the passive partner to orgasm when you'd just had such a good time and needed to lie flat on your back.
7. Rousing yourself to do (6) somehow.
8. Resting.

All this might have been the sequence in a yellowing 1961 rule-book. Today it had the appeal of industrial archaeology; and any betrayal of adherence to its guidelines blew you apart as just not 'going with the flow', a hopelessly nostalgic romantic or a dinosaur cleaving to the Pleistocene slimes of prehistory. Everything was subject to the most uncompromising *jusqu'au-boutisme*.

Now, if he was to examine the possibilities – or necessities – open to the modern gay, he would come up with the fantasies his friends had pantingly expressed (and even more pantingly realized). They, too, were standardized; but the world and her husband were even less likely to summon up much fellow-feeling for them. They included:

1. Being strapped on to a St Andrew's cross with leather restraints around the wrists and serrated iron clamps gripping the ankles.
2. Being burned all over with a soldering-iron, the nipples frazzled and their aureoles scorched.
3. Being dressed in cotton-wool from head to foot (like the White Rabbit) and yelled at by a soldier (this from an avowed infantilist).
4. Being put into an executioner's hood and penetrated over cold steel by a blond, bearded giant.
5. Being kicked to the ground, crawling around in a forest of jackboots; then clasping two sturdy, gleaming boots like the portals of a temple while your ass is breached over and over again until it feels wide as a drainpipe and sore as hell.

6. Being made to whimper like a spaniel and to lick or eat out of trash-cans, wallowing in recycled beer.
7. Being pushed into a bath and lying slumped there, encircled by huge muscular guys in leather, as you murmur, 'Yessir you gotta piss on me; I disobeyed your orders, you're gonna run me outa the army, gimme all that punishment, all you got, down my lying, cheating throat, over my tits, piss it all on down, hot steaming piss, I want you to give it to me . . .'
8. Being stretched naked on the ground, handcuffed and bound and spattered with hot wax and come.
9. Doing one, or some, or all of these to someone else.

Together with these it was necessary to take one or more of the following:

> ACID
> ECSTASY
> WINDOWPANE
> REDS
> AIRPLANE
> SULPHATE
> MDA
> CRYSTAL
> MAGIC MUSHROOMS
> MESCALIN
> ANGEL DUST
> AMYL NITRITE
> COCAINE (well, perhaps)

Lacking these ingredients, sexual experiences could be dismissed as half-measures, coy and timid *pis-allers* that bore the same relationship to the REAL THING as plankton to oceans, marmalade pussy-cats to prowling tigers.

Sometimes you couldn't stop. You had sex for days on end, with one partner, with ten. It was a kind of fever. The lust just seemed to go on haemorrhaging, an unstaunchable leak. Once the first conquest was out of the way, under your belt, it was easy. Perhaps the smell of spilt semen aroused the pack sniffing the air around you. The only limit was a man's capacity for multiple orgasm, and that could be arranged somehow: feigned orgasm, passivity, megadoses of vitamin E, damiana, zinc, Siberian ginseng. Rising from one crumpled bed, or straightening up from the cold metal of a car bonnet, the brain refused to succumb to common sense and instruct the sex-glands to cool out. Rather they boiled over again and sought further release while the torrid mood was on them.

It was an astonishing kind of sexual extremism, presumably born of the defiance innate in a minority already oppressed.

Jerome was more than nonplussed by this state of affairs, despite his eager espousal of post-liberation homosexuality. There were difficulties even with the central act. He was inclined to feel, with Shelley, that sodomy was an 'operose and diabolical machination' (not that that made it any the less alluring), and he recoiled intellectually from the grosser manifestations of pain and suffering. Shelley had, indeed, expressed this all with such fastidious delicacy in his commentary on Plato: 'It is impossible that a lover could usually have subjected the object of his attachment to so detestable a violation or have consented to associate his own remembrance in the beloved mind with images of pain and horror.'

And yet Jerome's own remembrance skulked darkly in black torture-chambers and cellars, behind caged palisades and the screams of the voluntary damned. Sex was the defining force of his life. Perverse and peevish! What a slave is Man! To let his itching flesh thus get the better of him!

Around him in America he saw a scene of devastation wrought by the new sexuality. So compulsive had the heavy sex become that amazing changes in fortune resulted from it, lives were reversed and reconstituted, extraordinary journeyings undertaken. Intellectual masochists, whose former dreams were all of constriction and humiliation, had assumed the mantle of celibacy, the robes, even, of holy orders, after those dreams had fractured in their realization. Their libidos – already contorted and convoluted in their cerebral imaginings – were battered into irreality by their real-life tormentors; intensified, of course, in direct ratio to the degree of their sufferings, yet necessarily repressed as their very survival demanded.

A paterfamilias had eloped with his son.

A fawn-like boy, sitting disconsolately on a South London banquette, his greased hair flopping over one eye as if to disguise the torpor of his gaze, was to be found, some fourteen hours later, staring excitedly out of the window of Concorde as he winged his way to a new-found land at the behest of a benefactor, hawk-eyed and predatory as a lepidopterist, whose *nostalgie de la boue* outweighed even his credit-rating.

Multiply qualified professionals, doctors, lawyers, teachers, had abandoned their work and become plumbers and dispatch riders, telephone engineers and grease monkeys, driven by the irresistible sexual cachet of manual labour, not content with the mere assumption of working-class brutality for finite ends but impelled to adopt it with manic literalness. No longer did these men periodically abandon their routine to enact the rituals of the brothel. The brothel was now where they lived, and they carried it around with them, like snails their shells.

These were, Jerome believed, instances of Life imitating Art far more extraordinary than those nineteenth-century neurasthenic decadents who sidled sullenly away from prosaic *mondanités* to cultivate their aesthetic sensibilities in silver Latin poets and nuances of scent, the effluvia of angel-water and vervain.

He discussed this odd phenomenon with a professor of microbiology as they sat side by side, gripping cans of Budweiser, in a combat-jeep *inside* a Houston bar.

'It's one thing to act out a persona alien to one's own; but quite another to *become* that persona. I really hate to see people make that mistake. Their whole lives end in ruin, they're trashed by the time they're thirty,' said the professor, pushing aside some camouflage-netting that had fallen over his drinking-arm.

'I often think that when AIDS finally hits us, we're going to see an amazing explosion of creative talent. Do you ever wonder why there no longer seem to be any young gay writers like there were in previous generations? It's because they're too busy dissipating their energies on sex; it's just the most accessible way of expressing yourself and in many ways the best.'

Jerome vaguely conjured a memory of Venetia saying much the same thing: 'You gays ought to be sure-fire novelists if you could only get out of each other's pants.'

'I just can't imagine what it must be like to look at yourself and realize the unbelievable craziness of what you've done,' he said. 'When you stare at the hammer and toolbox, the rubber plunger you've traded for the gilt-edged securities of middle-class success. Especially *Americans*. You're supposed to be so ambitious, so clear-headed about what you want to be.'

'That reminds me of a great joke. You see, there were these three faggots hanging out and discussing what they'd like to be. The first one says: "I'd like to be a butterfly, so I could fly around and suck all the juice out of the flowers." The second one says: "I'd rather be a flower so that all the butterflies could come around and suck out all my juice." And the third one says: "I'd really like to be an ambulance." And the other two think, Christ, what's he on about, an *ambulance*, for God's sake, and he says: "That way I could experience the sensation of an entire man being shoved up my behind."'

Jerome laughed out loud, then stopped immediately, realizing he was breaking the rules of the joint. You weren't supposed to be seen enjoying yourself. The butch mask would crack and all the others would think you were a sissy. My God, he thought, I could be a Bateman cartoon, 'The Man Who Laughed Out Loud in a Leather Bar'.

After a moment's recovery he became serious again.

'But what is it that lets us turn our lives upside down like this? How do we let it happen? This extraordinary upheaval?'

'You sure do have a British guilt-complex. It's not a matter of letting anything happen. We Americans have learned to *make* things happen, the way *we* like them. Being gay is just an accident of fate, and it's up to you to look at it positively. And be *proud* of it.'

'How can you be proud of something you didn't do? You can't take the credit for it as if it was some kind of achievement.' Jerome looked down at his can of beer, moody again.

'It *is* an achievement if you make it come out good. Anyone can be a misery queen, weeping around when he should be sleeping around, making everyone else unhappy. The hard thing is to do it with style, to bounce up again when they put you down. Anyway, a good screw does wonders for the morale. And there's a great feeling of solidarity. We're all in the same boat.'

'Boat's a bit of an understatement. More like the *Titanic*. But you're so sane, I know you're right. If only I could just divest myself of the great big suitcase I carry around full of guilty questions. Just get on with it in the simple way it comes across to the world. But I can never quite decide whether I want to be guilty or not. In a way it's so uninteresting to be guiltless. I think I need the material for all that inner moral wrangling. You see, I just can't look at it your way. The gulf between our two cultures is just too immense. I'm plugged into a million circuits that fan out and swarm all over the heap of Western culture like flies on a putrefying tip. And anyway, I'm so *serious*. I once overheard someone say, "I am not a serious person" – and I *longed* to be able to say that without hypocrisy.'

'Yeah, I think you *could* work on that a little. I guess we Americans just aren't so tormented and wired-up. Do they teach you to talk like that in school?'

'No, you learn it by yourself. As a defunct-mechanism. We get a lot of practice . . .'

His bleak sentences were drowned out by the sound of a cement-mixer, part of the industrial surplus décor, which began churning around and emitting electronically programmed male grunts. Jerome took the opportunity to go over to the bar and order more beers. The barman was busy arranging for a discount flight to San Juan for his dog and himself. He raised his eyebrows at Jerome and slowly wound up the deal. The wait was quite a relief, though; and it was a hell of a lot calmer than those places in New York where you got screwed while you were leaning over the bar waiting for your change.

'Thanks, sweetheart,' said the professor, 'I really appreciate talking to you. We get a touch self-absorbed down here in Houston and we need to expand our horizons a little.'

'That's one of the good things about being gay; you get to meet all kinds of different people, you stay fluid while all the straights atrophy in their marriage-prisons. Sometimes I really believe all that liberation stuff about gays being naturally democratic and egalitarian. Though you'd never believe it if you saw this place in London. It's a vast discotheque where the poor, pretty street-boys are let in free to dance as bait for the rich queers who sit around up above toying with their champagne and looking down through regulation-issue binoculars. It's a kind of subliminal brothel, a huge monument to capitalist exploitation. All masquerading under the pretence of glam street-cred, ghastly self-congratulation, a kind of false American promise of upward mobility. All it does is reinforce the immovable class system, the *haute bourgeoisie* using the terminally poor as their plaything, cat and mouse, Jesus it makes me so angry.'

'I never met an Englishman who could keep off the subject of class for long. We Americans would see that place as part of the New Dawn, where all the struggling underdogs would be saying to themselves, "One day if I worked hard – or even, if I danced like Rita Moreno and moved my ass like in *Flashdance* – I could end up one of those rich guys up at the top of the heap. Isn't that a healthier way of looking at it? I just don't get all that *envy* shit in Europe. It's real hard for a Texan to identify with.'

'You're dead right. And I didn't come to the Lone Star State to talk about sexual politics. It's been great talking to you. You know we English, we Eurotrash run the risk when we get to the States of going wild and just squeezing in as much sex as we possibly can. Lots of us don't even get to talk to the guys we fuck with.'

'Don't worry,' said the professor, 'most of us Americans go through the same thing. Half the guys who think they're real liberated don't bother about conversation, they express themselves *entirely* through their dick, so that twenty min-utes of sex is the total focus of their entire day. Everything's sacrificed to it, the day's like a planned anticipation, prepara-tion, for an event which is interchangeable with hundreds of others before and after. It's a little unbalanced, yeah.'

'I didn't know you Texans went in for understatement.'

'Sure do,' answered the professor, and he put on his black felt dude Stetson (XXX with pleated-feather band). 'I'm organizing a cowboys' cook-off next week, Tuesday, late, at Branded in Montross. Hope you can make it, we like a bit of European meat.'

How on earth was this American, shrewd as he might be, to fathom the layers of Jerome's identity? Because Jerome looked the way he did and had a vaguely foreign accent, most bourgeois Americans tended to accept appearances and assume he was probably an authentic Canadian lumberjack. The swirls of concealment, irony, self-referral and parody entirely eluded them. How could he be fancy or smart with such a downbeat image? *Nostalgie de la boue* was not a thing many Americans felt; and, as John Wayne so unanswerably speculated in *Brannigan*: 'Why would a *bona fide* lord wanna be a cop?'

Two American regular guys walked past, so healthy that even though they were smoking, they seemed to be expelling only gusts of vaporized glucose. While intellectually clinging to the notion of personal liberty, Jerome really hated smoking. Or rather he despised it. He couldn't understand why grown men should, by smoking, publicize their indifference to the world as well as their own insecurity. There were places – Greece, he remembered – where you couldn't go *outside* for fear of contracting passive cancer. (Inside, you might as well just hand over your lumps for autopsy.) The Greeks sat in clumsy circles smoking with one hand and twisting keys or worry-beads in the other, a perpetual dancing fidget of nervous excess. In love with the easeless death of lung disease, oblivious to the car-crashes they caused as they fumbled with lighters or the mass stampedes they unleashed from the football stadiums they so carelessly set alight. And yet he recognized that the cigarette was an integral prop of the inveterate cruiser. And he was forced to admire the supreme self-confidence in their conviction that they would still be found irresistible despite their stinking handicap. Fastidiousness never had been, or would be, macho. Marlboro Country didn't welcome careful aesthetes.

'That reminds me,' Jerome said, 'of the time I was taken to a male brothel in Cádiz by the owner of a sherry firm. We arrived at this perfectly ordinary, rather grim block of flats and went up in a lift to the fifth floor. There was a spy-hole in the door which was opened by a fantastically ugly woman – at least, I think it was a woman – wearing a very greasy mantilla. We hovered around in the hall while Segismundo made polite conversation with her. Then we were ushered into a large *salon* where there were five sofas placed against the walls, and on each sofa there were three guys dressed in identical fetishistic uniforms – three choirboys in surplices, three bullfighters, three soldiers, three leather queens and three cowboys (or, at least, a very peculiar Spanish version of cowboys, a long way from Oklahoma). So that whatever your particular fetish, you had three guys to choose from. It felt really peculiar standing there holding a tiny glass of marsala and eyeing those guys. They looked so solemn just sitting there in their threesomes, not talking, just waiting to be chosen. I took a cowboy, he looked so awkward pretending to be cool and at ease, chewing some highly scented Spanish gum – cinnamon, was it? It looked like his red neckerchief was strangling him and he was just longing to go home to his wife and kids. We had great sex. I think it was something to do with the fact he'd been singled out from fifteen, some obscure kind of competitive machismo. But just imagine, the *elaborateness* of setting the whole thing up like that, so precise in its calculations, so theatrical with all those costumes.'

Often he longed for some physical affliction – obesity, pockmarks, baldness, palsy, even infibulation – which could allow him to get on with life by blocking the yellow-brick road along which he danced in sexual conquest. Perhaps he should emulate St Christopher Cynocephalos, so apprehensive that his astonishing physical beauty might prove too tempting for both women and men that he prayed to God for a transformation and was rewarded by the discovery that his peerless body was now surmounted by the head of a dog. As things were, whenever he was bored or needed reassurance, he got laid: but the operation was never so percussive and crisp as the term implied, involving as it did a sequence of ritualistic preparations, elaborate courtship dances with his quarry, fairly intense narcotic boosts and hours wasted in a post-coital euphoria that progressively dissolved into the nondescript boredom which had itself given rise to the whole fatuous cycle. Meanwhile, others were rehearsing operas, designing satellites, giving birth, altering wills, correcting homework, circumnavigating the world, lancing boils, righting wrongs, transplanting hearts! Where did that leave him? Was he anything more than a dick-struck clown pulled mercilessly this way and that by facile lust? Of course, what *he* was doing was demonstrably more fun and aroused universal envy (usually disguised as contempt). But it had to be admitted that it was not unrepetitive, that it was more and more and more of the same thing; and that it denied him spiritual companionship and dampened the fires of his intellect. It was a long time since he had talked about anything he was interested in with anyone other than his cat.

Early in their friendship he'd asked Venetia how he might deal with this pansexual obsession, other than with bromide or aversion therapy.

'Must you bang on like this? It's like some medieval knight jabbering on about his *bonne renommée*.'

'I'll never be able to work properly. It's all so compulsive. It's hard for me even to *think* about doing other things.'

He'd caught her in a bilious mood and she snapped back, only half in jest: 'I don't know why you're so worried about work and stuff. As long as they have sidewalks you've got a job.'

'No, I really mean it. And anyway, at least as a photographer I *could* theoretically be a success and a homosexual all at once. Lots of gay people just can't afford to be ambitious. There simply aren't any professions where they can get anywhere. Television, maybe, teaching (if you're careful and still half inside the closet), all those dreary old clichés, theatre, ballet, opera.

'In some ways I'd really like to be a journalist. But I

get quite out of control when I think of the staggering anti-gay lobby, especially in Fleet Street. They *really* don't like queens. And they're supposed to be open-minded liberals. In fact it's like the stuffiest regimental mess; only, of course, all the other aberrations – drunks and things – are tolerated with a knowing smile. The satirical magazines are the worst; like giggling prefects singling out originality and smearing it with all their dingy smut . . .'

Venetia recognized the sound of grinding axes, or was it the clatter of hobby-horses being ridden to death?

'But politician, lawyer, civil servant, industrialist – forget it. You might as well not put your foot on the first rung of a ladder which is going to break a few steps up. I charge thee, fling away ambition. By that sin fell the angels. And I can't believe talented homosexuals aren't embittered by that. They certainly should be. Titus Oates has a lot to answer for.

'I'd just like to make some kind of mark, leave something behind. It looks like it's not going to be a baby.'

'I can't understand this obsession with fame and posterity. Remember that American politician's advice: "Don't get caught in bed with a dead woman or a live man." It's just impossible to be a Significant Person – if you make a public pronouncement on any issue and claim some kind of credibility, all the world does is turn around and ask, "Who does she think *she* is?" Just imagine, as an example, the Emperor Hadrian, who completely reformed the Imperial system and conferred extraordinary benefits on Rome, and also just happened to like boys. Do you think every time he went into the Senate with his lover Antinous they all minced to their feet in unison, stuck one hand on their hip and flapped the other wrist and shrieked: "Cooh, look at *her*. Silly old queen"? You should have a more relaxed view of it all. There was a person called the Marchese Frangipani – I promise you – and the only thing he's remembered for is having invented a special scent just for gloves. I think that's terrific, really memorable. And what about Nicanor of Alexandria, whose only claim to fame was a textbook on punctuation? Who cares about posterity anyway? I think it's really overrated. Fame's when you become material for schizophrenics.'

'Don't you take *anything* seriously?'

'In the immortal words of Wally Faye in *Mildred Pierce*: "With me being smart's a disease."'

12

Aire and Angels

A luminous, loose-clouded day of blue glass, the 'thirties
blocks on Russian Hill pointing upwards through air of
an astonishing transparency. The brilliance of the blue was
so peculiar that there might have been some substance to
the eighteenth-century Salamancan theologians' squabbling
over whether the sky was made of a wine-like fluid or of bell
metal. A Zeppelin floated over and across, in an irregular
zigzag, its flabby haunches spreading a puff of complacency.
In the distance Mount Tamalpais was satisfyingly massive
beyond the flying, spindly whizz of the Golden Gate Bridge;
and the city and bay seemed warmly swathed in the green,
rustic embrace of the hillsides. All of this was trapped outside
a window-frame, as her pale face stared wearily out from
the drawing-room. She had never mastered the art of sitting
alone, staring into infinity, utterly inward, like Garbo with
only a guttering candle for company.

Venetia had begun to find David vaguely trying. Ordinary
toys met only with a sophisticated frown; extraordinary ones
– like Gay Bob, perhaps, the doll with lumberjack, soldier,
motorcyclist and cowboy outfits (and equipped with a
special closet to come out of) – paled in the presence
of a superior reality, the Real Thing, Jerome the Ultimate
Mannequin. She always found children embarrassing and
worried deeply about their reaction to her, as indicative
and damning, she thought, as those of domestic animals.
After performing some ineffectual hand-silhouettes against
the wall, she decided to dress David in a bale of moiré silk.

As she made her way to the wardrobe, a better idea struck her. Opening the drawer, she took out a pristine yellow duster with a luxuriant nap. Her mouth crammed with safety-pins, she inexpertly cocooned the child in the velvety material, wrapping and winding clumsily like an apprentice mummifier. The baby was appreciative but puzzled, and watched Venetia's face as if it might somehow provide the clue to the meaning of this strange operation, so like and yet so unlike her ordinary ministrations. The wrapping over, Venetia tied a triumphant granny-knot and sat the child at a short distance from where she stood, not even having to feign her smile of satisfaction.

'There now, who's Venetia's little human duster? Don't we just *love* that jaundiced look? Who's going to grow up like Jerome and have *nice* hepatitis?'

David's evident pleasure was further heightened when Venetia attached a leather leash to the protruding safety-pin. His throat gave out a subdued squeak as she began to pull him slowly across the polished beechwood floor. Wishing to prolong the exciting experience, she left him there as she went to the fridge, took out a slice of iced carrot-cake and sat on the floor, a spent dirigible leaning slumped against the fridge-door, hyperventilating and cramming in large mouthfuls. The child seemed apprehensive and disappointed at the brusque interruption of their game. To pre-empt the impending screams, Venetia crawled towards him, too idle, too taken with her own seal-like movements to rise to her feet. This time she removed the leash and, clasping the child strongly with both arms, launched him forcefully across the floor. Spinning and shrieking, he came to rest a few yards from the prominent door-jamb, leaving an irregular but glistening track in his wake. This was clearly going to be a success, she thought; he likes it, I like it, the floor likes it. But how to achieve a regular coverage?

She had no alternative but to reattach the leash and, using wide sweeping movements, describe semi-circles with the helpless infant. But David's soul was that of an anarchist (Adelaida's pregnancy had been highly disturbed), and he baulked at the formal pattern of this new variation. Venetia's acute antennae received his signals of frustration and she reverted to the improvisatory violence of the previous game. Slamming his shoulder against the base of an Ionic pilaster, he screamed with pleasure; and, pushing with his wriggling, pneumatic legs, vainly tried to prolong the momentum. Dashing in response, she swung him around and around on an axis, like a roulette-wheel, never calculating on the delicate equilibrium of so volatile a child. His cushioned bottom revolved deliriously, his rounded limbs spasmodically stretched and contracted in an ecstatic transport.

'This is easy,' she thought. No need to dredge her pedestrian imagination for shiny charades and embarrassing feints. The monotonous rain struck the windows like the interstices of a sieve and she felt comforted by the revelation of her secret power.

Jerome came in from the elevator and gazed at the now inert ochre infant. His relationship with David was close and physical, but he had never achieved the tranquillizing effect of Venetia's miraculous game. As she explained its simple rules, he lifted the child in his arms and stroked the slightly soiled duster.

'Our experiment in parenthood is bearing fruit,' he said. 'Adelaida will not be pleased. She was so determined that David should hate us. I think that was the only way she could rationalize her actions.'

'Well, I think he's fabulous, Jerome, and I want one of my very own.'

'Hard to reconcile with your present life-style. Parthenogenesis?'

'You don't understand. The only difference between you and me is that I just don't have whole streets of establishments to cater for my every sexual caprice. The expense of spirit . . . Only in the case of you guys it doesn't seem like it's too expensive, just the outlay on a few Budweisers and half an ounce of Humboldt County.' She flashed her teeth nastily.

'Don't attack me now. I'm in a state of high paranoid shock.'

He sat down and made her do the same. She was clearly in for some soul-baring. What had happened was this.

* * *

Jerome accommodated his ass to the rodeo-post and thrust his groin into space. Another compulsory, compulsive session of standing in wait. *Hier stehe ich, Ich kann nichts anders.* Stand by your man. His leather chaps creaked and glistened as he savoured the *mauvaise foi* that separated his delicate sensibility from its macho carapace. Maybe his external façade could never carry as much conviction as Sartre's municipal dignitaries *inhabiting* their contrived apparel in *La Nausée.* But there *had* been something peculiarly majestic in the shy but assured manner of his walk down Polk Street in this *bourgeois-épatant* costume (assuming there were any *bourgeois* left to *épater*). It was impossible for him ever to make the two polarities of his act coalesce: the brutal assumed *déclassé* and the cerebral aesthete. But the act was enough in itself, the ritualized performance of a theatrical charade in which all the actors understood the rules but conspired to ignore them. Authenticity had importance only in the climate of a Lacanian laboratory. What relative importance could it have beside the arrogant blackness of those swivelling and drug-dilated pupils, overflowing with sexual security, of the cowboy beside him? 'A Malibu and two Cape Cods.' It sounded like an up-market real-estate barter in a game of Monopoly. Its dull real meaning was transcended by the beauty of the man ordering the drinks. Jerome – who, like many beautiful men, and unlike so many others, had never quite believed in his own beauty – reacted sorely; if I looked that good it wouldn't be *me* buying the drinks. Was there any point in pursuing it? He obviously wasn't alone. On closer inspection, Jerome detected signs of wastage or wrinkling of the eyes denoting suppressed terror rather than humour. He drank his St Pauli Girl straight from the bottle.

He reached for an extra quarter in the recesses of his tight clothes and eventually found one wedged under a small phial of emergency spot lotion. There was a sudden stench of old socks; two of his neighbours, blest pair of sirens, had broken an ampoule of amyl nitrite, seeking to enliven their flagging conversation with chemical laughter. Their temporary loss of control was so complete that one of them touched Jerome suggestively, his helpless eyes raised in supplication through an idiot grimace. Came like Tarquin, ghastly with infernal lust.

Although momentarily disconcerted, it was easy for Jerome to release the constriction of his tensed-up and displayed body after a while: a natural shift into the passive awareness of the guttural and demonstrative men all around, whose glances darted sporadically in every direction without interrupting the continuity of their weird exchanges. The instructions on the shampoo-bottle he'd clutched in the YMCA steamroom had become an ironic prophecy: 'Should eye-contact occur, flush with clear water.' The focus now of multiple eye-contact, he found himself at the intersection of a grid of laser-stares as regular as the Place de l'Étoile.

> Our eye-beames twisted, and did thread
> Our eyes, upon one double string . . .

> . . . let her rave,
> And feed deep, deep upon her peerless eyes.

Still, as Mae West had said, one would rather be looked over than overlooked.

The inescapable, *de rigueur* appearance which Jerome cultivated was the closest possible approximation to a First World War army captain, the kind you saw in sepia photographs. *En masse* the clones looked like a consignment of troops waiting to entrain for Flanders. Slight variations on this strict model were permissible – a Zapata rather than a cavalry moustache (or even a thin Argentine pencil), highlighted blond streaks (a pointless venture in those whose convict haircuts frequently came under the Devil's Island scissors), the omission or the application of moustache wax (on sale next to the action lubricants and eight-strapped erection-sustainers). The moustache, at all events, was the supreme semiotic feature. The target of its immensity was pursued with great determination and with little regard to its relation to the rest of the face. Many could only have been justified by features as massive as Stalin's: and yet they graced faces as pinched and fretful as those of master of ferrets. The body, too, was subjected to punishing rituals in pursuit of a uniform ideal. It was impossible for the shoulders to be too broad or the waist too thin, the thighs too powerful or the legs too long. Elaborate inquisitorial racks and pulleys had been devised to help produce these characteristics for those inadequates who veered towards either the ectomorphic wimp or the endormorphic great white whale (your dick might be moby, but that was no excuse). All of which was bad news for those with small pricks, for the custom-packed structural frame only emphasized this frailty; and size queens were one thing that *had* lasted through the 'seventies.

Jerome in the early days had been reluctant to sacrifice his blond mane *à la* West German intravenous drug addict. But it had inevitably fallen to the floor around him as the faggot Delilah crimper whispered words of practised reassurance. The hair *had* to be short. Juvenal in the second century AD had foreseen this all in his *Satires* and mockingly described the pseudo-masculine philosophers:

Your shaggy limbs and the bristling hair on your forearms
Suggest a fierce male virtue; but the surgeon called in
To lance your swollen piles dissolves in laughter
At the sight of that well-smoothed passage. Such creatures talk
In a clipped laconic style, and crop their hair crew-cut
    fashion,
As short as their eyebrows.

It had been more painful, in fact, to get used to the idea of not being thin. His delicate bones and elegant Procrustean string-bean height had captivated, in an earlier, less hidebound era, a delighted public which almost feared for its astigmatic vision on seeing such elongation. Jerome was a little diffident and noncommittal about muscles culture. He saw it as a life sentence: once you began you couldn't stop for fear that the whole quilted card-castle would sooner or later come tumbling down and turn into a spreading pat of lard covered over with slack lizard skin. 'Incredible vascularity!' they gasped, while he worried about his veined skin turning into a road-map. But he surrendered, and gradually roundels of muscle began to bulge from predetermined points and the neon-lit mirror revealed a stretching of the skin under strain which he prayed was not reversible. Venetia occasionally tried to suggest, obliquely, that enough was enough, that she far preferred Greco to Rubens, Giacometti to Cocteau; but this was one of those areas in which she had tacitly agreed to concede his autonomy. His body was a maquette in plasticine, living sculpture to be altered and remodelled entirely at his will. And one got used to anything.

In the prevailing climate, Jerome had in fact no alternative but to render himself a clone. To resist the fashion was to make too strong a revolutionary statement; and it would have been a self-denying ordinance, for his prospects of sexual fulfilment would have diminished in proportion to each feature he renounced. Surely, his straight friends tutted, Jerome is too clued-up and bright not to see through the whole thing? It must, they concluded, be some extreme form of self-parody.

Clothes were more of a problem. Essentially they, too, were governed by a rigid code. Venetia compared the tight prescriptions he was subject to with the sumptuary laws issued by Philip IV which tried to regulate Spanish dress. In some ways it was an apt comparison. In the stringent economic climate of the 1690s, Philip tried to restrain the excesses of ruffs and Brussels lace collars, the outrageous status conferred by bales of silk. In the affluence of California, the unspoken pact of homosexuals decreed a prohibition on the fripperies of camp in favour of an uncompromising adherence to clothes born of cowhide. Out went the velvets, coral, sparklers and platforms of the death-throes of 1968. With them, the baby with the bathwater, went the notions of self-adornment, androgyny and love. In marched an abrasive army in leather and chains, discharged berets: construction workers laden with triple belts that clung to their swivel hips, innocent of hammers or picks, sub-Olympic decathletes, cultivating the art of street-urchins and using launderettes only for bleaching, cowboys far, far from the range.

This uniform was a badge of identity throughout the world. Although it was primarily an English, German and American creation – fitting, as it was, for an aesthete Aryanism – it could be found in furtive small-town bars in Italy or Greece. It meant a life dedicated primarily to sexual gratification. It meant a sophisticated repertoire of sexual techniques, a relaxed but self-controlled view of drugs, an underlying narcissism. Above all, it allowed one to fuck oneself, without resorting to masturbation. Any number of mirror-images could be conjured to your orgy-mat, a Versailles of silvered lovers, infinitely multiplying.

Jerome was a perfect mirror, giving an illusion he sustained by virtue of his modesty, that despite his beauty his partners were as well-formed as he. Yet they were not intimidated by him; they could become momentarily as beautiful. In this way the clone – the reduplicated army captain sitting helplessly on his conveyor belt – climbed up to the semi-divine status of mega-clone, the paragon more beautiful even than the look permitted, who burst asunder its constriction: the one into whom all the others hoped to metamorphose by the insertion of his magic prick. The phallus was the object of all their veneration. They worshipped it with an idolatrous fervour that would have shamed the frenzy of the professed devotees of the ancient god Priapus at Lampsacus on the Hellespont.

He knew what it was to be one of these clones. How could he not? Like it or not, he had joined their number. They measured and assessed one another according to some notional optimum. You got points for outstanding features that corresponded to the ideal; other points were knocked off for supposed or real deficiencies. When clones met, subtle and complex arithmetical calculations were set in motion. If, say, you had a great body but the face was only so-so, then a certain number of points were deducted; but in a place like a disco, where the body's vaunted importance was supreme, you could regain those lost points and *soar* above the guy with the Adonis features and the diabolical bum. Each clone mentally slotted himself into a league division and gauged his prospects according to a clear-eyed valuation. In many ways (and this was a source of consolation) it was better not to be in the premier division. Then you scared off more contenders than you attracted and you ended up like a virginal exhibit in a pristine sculpture gallery. Belonging to the first rank of the second division, however, qualified you to rescue these premier division beauties from their isolation and granted *carte blanche* to pick off some pathetically grateful and eccentrically appealing no-hoper from lower down the league.

The bar counter jutted into the centre like the spit on which San Francisco itself was built, and swelled grossly at its tip in a shameless imitation of an exposed glans. Striplights ran down its length as regularly as arteries; as if a rampant prick had been strapped down to the floor and was straining to resurrect itself and flap gratefully back against the stomach of the ceiling. This phallic suggestion fell short of itself, though. The motifs of the locale seemed to be a hard-edged, high-tech functionality, far from the lush or organic, with hidden light-sources trained on its regular and brusque features. A chain-link fence divided the bar from a separate, nameless area and was hung about with men in studied postures suggesting electrocution – elegant electrocution, but electrocution none the less – against the wire of Buchenwald. The front of a motor-cycle fiercer than a maharajah's tiger protruded from the wall and a dehumanized leather fetishist lounged stroking its useless throttle. Jerome imagined his perineum pierced by the protruding brake-handle. Up a few steps a pool table was bathed in a spectral light that illuminated no further than the rectangle spreading from its ceiling source. Grateful for its provision of a focal point, if only as spectators of a non-existent game, the men and boys stood around looking inwards with sad eyes over the recipient half-smiles adapted to give a foretaste of the full smiles of kittenish surrender they'd become were another to take the plunge.

There was a lot of wood everywhere: redwood, a reminder to those guilty American moral renegades that they were still American in a land of pioneers and ranchers. That they could always swing an axe and football a log-jam instead of scoring a million tilts at homosexual pinball. The walls were hung with impossible icons of masculinity: yellow hardhats and photographs of super-aerated, iron-pumped bullies in attitudes of hostile challenge. Their perfection (according to the collective ideal) ironically only served to emphasize the comparatively puny physique and imperfect bone-structure of their emulators below. One picture had slipped to an oblique angle with the effect that an unsmiling pastiche Nazi with a U-boat-launching jawline now looked sadly subservient and resentful beside his correctly aligned neighbour, a cheeky, cowlicked boy whose tee-shirt was more rags than material and who might, in another city, have seemed incongruously compliant. There were no chairs, for these would perhaps have concealed assets of height or handicaps of short stature; the merchandise had to be pitilessly visible. In their place a wooden rail ran around the wall, polished by a thousand anxious arses perched cowboyishly on its questionable ease. The bar staff, chosen apparently for size of moustache, moved noiselessly with the grace of castrated lions; the repose of their faces and the dilation of their pupils betrayed an inner high, as if their ears, cruelly exposed, sucked in only the high wattage of the music, *mouillé* by the honeyed propositions that accompanied the selling of each beer. Jerome resolved to try and imitate their inviolability.

Like everything else in the gay world, the bar breathed a smooth aerodynamic freemasonry. It was a supremely efficient machine with each greased jack and piston of its mechanism in perfect co-ordination, a machine for cruising. Entering alone meant becoming part of the power input. The initiate was processed into the oiled circuit to emerge refreshed and twinned, his ego reinforced and his groin and prostate gland pulsing in anticipation of the next consummative stage. Sometimes, though, the machine broke down. A queen had hysterics. A rebuffed lover yelled bitter reproaches. A pep trip turned murderous or lachrymose. Yet these breakdowns aside, nothing could have been better customized for its avowed purpose. The concept, of course, had been made possible by the heroic struggle of Gay Liberation a decade before; though the bland cynicism of this modern beneficiary was partially at odds with its idealistic progenitor. It was like the ghost train at Battersea funfair. You embarked on a hazardous journey in your frail and imperfect bark. Passing through frissons and ordeals, you emerged into the light.

To broach the apparently self-contained integrity of the

smiling men required an effort of will. Jerome's timidity was, he knew, most manifest in his struggle with language. He suspected that the authentic, successful Don Juans – hadn't a Spanish intellectual once claimed that all Don Juans were fundamentally homosexual – were able to dispose a sequence of adaptable, flexible words by which to mould themselves to every contingency and unexpected zigzag in the court-ship dialogue. Even if the projected lover turned out to be obsessed with baseball, NASA or mice, or was Finnish, or understood only words beginning with the letter 'k', or spoke only in riddles or rhetorical questions, the Don Juan could never be fazed and reduced to the dull silence which affected Jerome even before his first foray. Their words must be like elastic balloons, expanding and contracting loosely but filled with a helium charge to lead them inexorably to their sexual target after passing through an infinite realm of parries, off which they triumphantly bounced.

For Jerome each word was a landmine. He could, God knew he could, decide the first overture in the space of time during which the nervous cast of his body, displaying its début, strengthened to the point where it radiated strength and lust. But every utterance (every phoneme and morpheme) could go wrong. Behind each syllable lurked all the contempt, ridicule and irony which the other could water-cannon back on to you. The sexual bond could be shattered with a single damning revelation. Each sentence identified you further, left you trapped in an increasingly intricate spider's web of com-posite personality, any strand of which could lead you to the irrevocable rejection. A strategy as complex as the logistics of Austerlitz was needed so that when your left flank was knocked out by an unforeseen cannonade, reinforcements could rush to close the gap even as an alternative offensive was launched by another, invincible detachment. Jerome, whose only dim connection with Napoleon was his name, the name of the Emperor's brother, the nocturnal King of Naples, shrank from a battlefield in which, like Fabrice del Dongo, he was more likely to get lost in a cloud of gunsmoke, perhaps not even knowing which battle he was attending, than to carry off the victor's laurel.

Against this he knew that conversation developed loosely,

like an amorphous uncurling. His own silence began to seem very loud. As its inner din increased, he recognized it would become harder and harder to venture any utterance at all (however uncontroversial). The hubbub of the bar diminished until it was no more than a fluttering and unconvincing stage *rhubarb*, or so it seemed to him as his own dumbness started to clang hectically against the bone-frame of his brain. Worse than any pitiable mute on a Spanish railway train, worse than the entry of a provincial *ingénu* into the salon of Princess Mathilde Bonaparte, as fearsome a disability as the fibromas of the Elephant Man, his mute handicap shone around him, lighting up his co-intrigants with the glare of St Elmo's fire. Best convince himself of his power of devastation, recall the triumphs, summon forth from the endless glory-strewn path of the past and base his confidence in that supremely empirical foundation.

The crucial thing was to keep disappointment and fear out of your eyes. And to be careful what tune you hummed to yourself. He had once caught himself lipsynching to a jukebox, 'Don't you want me, baby?' *telling* the world, subliminally, of his insecurity. Self-doubt, hesitancy, inner thought of any kind, never ever won fair *man*. The best thing was to plunge into conversation, sexual overture or not, so that animation renewed the dead face and registered an easy, rangy *désinvolture* that bleeped into every television channel. You couldn't smile on your own, otherwise everyone thought you were an alienated crazy or out of your head on drugs and probably a dead loss sexually. Anyway, the rule was: on your own, hard and uncompromising, cobra-primed and stripped for action; in the company of others, free-spirited and gay (in its outmoded sense). Nobody could ever quite decide which worked best.

With time he had come to see how these trivial fears of rejection and humiliation masked a greater, deeper fear. He was afraid that one of these flirtations might develop into a passion so strong as to destroy his love for Venetia and David. In the past he had undergone a small number of infatuations and his susceptibilities had been torn. Yet he had always known that he could resist involvement because he had not wished for it, and he was used to only bringing his wishes to fruition and the converse. He had felt great pity for those who came here to seek love. He could see how their lives were fields of infinite solitude, despoiled of laughter and permanence by sudden rages and terror. The nominally guiltless promiscuity was a treadmill for rats whose complicity in their own torment made his pity irrevelant.

He got such a heavy eyeballing that he nervously hid his face with his glass and swallowed an ice-cube that then sat and throbbed painfully in the recesses of his chest. One of the problems about being a clone was that, unlike the Bowie queens or the modern *stylistes*, you didn't have any hair to hide under.

He was, after all, a *neues Gesicht*. It seemed necessary to assess them all simultaneously so as to avoid commitment to the threatening bearded angel of darkness with the Hilliard ear-drop while keeping open the option of the over-pectoralized bruiser with the Joan Crawford shoulders. Maybe the latter was a lesbian anyway, you never could tell: a denizen of the automotive sweatshops south of Market, all sexual identity lost amid the oily rags and dead compressors. Jerome, at the apex of an isosceles triangle of stares, could expect a pincer-Panzer assault from either angle or both. But his own momentary hesitation and the shy aversion of his gaze allowed the two wooing contenders to register each other's presence and cut him briskly out of their calculations.

His heart fluttered and he felt girlish and shy, wondering if he dared disrupt the universe. Did he dare to earth a peach? God, sometimes he thought he must be the worst cruiser since the *General Belgrano*. At times like this he needed to flash in on his mental self-instruction: THINK CAT, sleek and self-sufficient, streamlined beyond the dreams of a Swedish designer. He could manage it when he was tired; in fact it then became natural and effortless. But now, in active wakefulness, there was too much highly-strung trapeze wariness, self-consciousness degenerating into remorseful timidity.

He would never, he feared, be a tumultuously popular faggot; the kind everyone went mad for, killed for, died for.

His mind went back to the story of Thessalonica in 390, where the most admired charioteer of the day lusted publicly and lewdly after a boy slave. Murders were committed, jealous riots ensued; and the Emperor Theodosius I imprisoned the citizens in the circus, barred the exits and slaughtered them all. Three hours of carnage, 7,000 dead, all because of one little boy slave. Now, *that* had been pulling power.

Jesus, why couldn't they have a kind of plebiscite on one another? When they were all assembled, each queen would write on a slip his judgements of the physical appeal of the others on a scale from 1 to 10. Or alternatively, as each man entered the bar, the others could hold up a score-card: 5.8, 5.9, 5.7, like Torville and Dean. Or better still, the hunky barman would blow a whistle and they'd all put down their drinks and get on with it. Or get into a delicious huddle at the outset and agree on a placing. Or perhaps they could emulate the Babylonian wife-auctions Herodotus describes:

All the girls of marriageable age were collected together in one place, while the men stood round them in a circle; an auctioneer then called each one in turn to stand up and offered her for sale, beginning with the best-looking and going on to the second best as soon as the first had been sold for a good price. The rich men who wanted wives bid against each other for the prettiest girls, while the humbler folk, who had no use for good looks in a wife, were actually paid to take the ugly ones, for when the auctioneer had got though all the pretty girls he would call upon the plainest, or even perhaps a crippled one, to stand up, and then ask who was willing to take the least money to marry her and she was knocked down to whoever accepted the smaller sum.

Of course, it couldn't work here among these bruisable egos. And the problem was that most of the bidders were also potential wives. They would in effect be both buying and selling themselves.

Maybe if he just went home and set the *whole* operation in motion again *ab ovo*. He resolved to re-rehearse his earlier ritual of preparation. After a simple metamorphosis he would

117

reappear: twinned in splendour, glittering siblings. Their sex could be a flash of mirror-incest, front to back to front, and there would be no eclipses . . .

For the next few minutes, during which no one spoke to Jerome, he planned an unobtrusive exit. *Mundus senescit*, and me with it. Steal home, wash, brush his hair, possibly change.

> Fluttering spread thy purple pinions,
> Gentle Cupid, o'er my heart;
> I, a slave in my dominion;
> Nature must give way to art.

As the lull threatened to become an embarrassing freeze-out, Jerome was rescued from commiseration when he suddenly caught sight of a pad of paper which had been thrust in front of his face. He bent to look at it closely and read: 'I THINK YOU'RE REAL NICE. I'D LIKE TO BE YOUR FRIEND.'

What the fuck was he supposed to do about that? The owner of the pad stood with no trace of shyness in his bearing and his eager smiling face. Jerome looked away nervously, and glancing back, saw him tear off the page and rapidly write on the next one: 'I'M DEAF AND DUMB. DON'T BE AFRAID TO WRITE THINGS DOWN FOR ME. DO YOU LIKE ME?'

He proffered the pad with one hand and a pencil with the other, and stood back, wearing the same expression of stultifying keenness. Jerome panicked and smiled with an aloof elegance.

'ARE YOU TURNED ON BY SHORTS? HOW DO YOU FEEL ABOUT MINE?'

This was written down by El Sordomudo's sidekick. Jerome looked down from the great height conferred on him by both nature and the power of speech. He saw a pair of frictional red spandex briefs so tight that the genitals looked as if they'd been dropped in as an afterthought, like marbles. 'UP TO A POINT,' he wrote, and moved away.

Another of the candidates was gradually winning, thrust forward with the irresistible force of Queen Charlotte's birthday cake. The rigid visor of his peaked leather cap exactly reproduced the angle of his nose; the luxuriant, almost Elizabethan, sable moustache continued the regularity of an impassive mask of totemic fixedness. The cap was fearsome and authoritative. It seemed, too, to counterbalance the huge bulk of the body, a bulk which otherwise might have shrunk the head to a microcephalous extreme, to a lighthouse look-out instead of the anonymous, forceful, arrogant mask it now was. Its shiny chain and visor intensified the drilling, boring luminosity of the eyes they half-concealed. The line which ran from the nose to the corner of the mouth, on one side of the face only, was a deep gash of cruelty, almost a Prussian scar, though it had probably been engendered by humour. The memory of a failed encounter with a Los Angeles cop with a similar streamlined surface spurred Jerome into reciprocating the veiled signals. He was so extraordinarily depersonalized. (Why *did* the Emporium on Market Street advertise *personalized* leather goods? Surely they were missing the point?)

Surely this guy was too beautiful even for Jerome? *Domine, non sum dignus et intres sub tectum meum,* he thought, miserably. But let's give it a whirl. He swung his eyes. Purposively. And then the idea transposed itself into nineteenth-century furbelows as his memory switched to Eugénie Grandet's despairing, terminal: *'Je ne suis pas assez belle pour lui. Il ne fera pas attention à moi.'*

> I can give not what men call love
> But wilt thou accept not
> The worship the heart lifts above
> And the heavens reject not,
> The desire of the moth for the star
> Of the night for the morrow,
> The devotion to something afar
> From the sphere of our sorrow?

'So who are you?'

This was it. There could be no way of answering that didn't reveal his hopeless otherness. Best to take advantage of the San Franciscan curiosity and just rattle on.

'I'm Jerome. I'm visiting from London. Hanging around.'

'Do you like what you see?'

Always the innuendo, the narcissistic manipulation of ordinary ideas.

'I like it a lot. But I find problems relating to American guys. I think I'm getting acclimatized' – (Oh God, too long a word, too redolent of quadrangles and dusty libraries. Or perhaps it was OK, Californian argot?) – 'although I could never live here.'

'Yeah, it's easy and hard all at once. I'm from here, so I don't have to go through the traumas of these guys who arrive from Des Moines, Iowa, and wonder if they should be back on the farm.'

That was all right. Sensitive but unpretentious. In control of language. A Platon Kuratáev whose words sprang organically from his life without passing through a deadening filter of style. The story continues in the version Jerome relayed to Venetia, in which he made allowances for her morbid curiosity and appreciation of the bizarre.

'So we had a few beers and talked about his life as a theology student at Edinburgh. I hadn't met too many seminarists who looked like that. But he said his studies had left him with a permanent Christian faith. The Scottish were just outlandish, the accent of the dockworkers at Leith was so exotic, so macho. Eventually, though, he'd felt frozen out by the gregarious complacency of the Scots.

'I got a bit tired and lost interest in what he was saying, although he still radiated a magnetic animalism. It seemed like a good idea to cut off the dialogue, so I started messing around with his dick and suggested leaving. He seemed kind of relieved and pleased, with a big boyish smile. And he got excited in the car. Not just sexually excited, but somehow revitalized all over. He swerved across the street to show me a Technicolor Queen Anne. His own house on Duboce was self-consciously Victorian. All the details were accurately reproduced and yet it seemed factitious, the effect destroyed by loads of Americana: ionizers and juice-extractors, tracklights and facial saunas, symbols of what Jane Austen calls a "finer self-cherishing". He squeezed some orange juice, turned head-on towards the work-surface, incongruously domestic in all that leather. He'd become totally human now; the leather – his second skin – encased a bundle of ordinary feelings. Another guy came in in a pretentious dressing-gown and I had the distinct impression he was checking me out as a possibility for later on that night. I was a bit nervous and resented his interest; or rather I'd have preferred him to have been really, honestly interested, visibly excited. As it was, he was just nonchalant and presented an uncomfortable distraction, disrupted Tom's developing intimacy with me. Anyway he pissed off, thank God, pretending to have come down for a copy of the *National Geographic. At four in the morning?*

'Tom gave me a joint and a hit of crystal, warning me in my English naïveté that all these things were just like *so* strong, strictly for the bedroom. He was right – as we both know – and it hit me just as I was talking about what I liked to do sexually, and I felt, can I carry on? Shall I just chuck in the whole idea of making sense? Is this getting in the way of the action? I began to lose the sequence anyway and decided to press up against his ass and play with his cock. It was a good decision; he gave a kind of electric jolt and spilled the juice. The orange juice, I mean, sweetheart, don't get me wrong. Then we went upstairs through endless attic corridors. I saw a whole series of rooms without furniture, kind of Chiricoesque, a sense of desolate vacuum, like your worst dreams. There was an orgy-room at the end – you know, a leather sling on chains hanging from the ceiling, a black leather mat on the floor strewn with dildoes, tit-clamps, ankle-restraints, poppers, harnesses – and signs of recent use. I was feeling pretty stoned, and I was really glad that he led me to the shower and guided the special proctoscope kind of nozzle to clean the shit out of my ass. I'd never have made it alone.

We started on some real heavy sex. It went on for hours. Do I really have to tell you about it, you've heard it all before? . . . Phew, you're a wonder, I was really dreading having to go through all that stuff. It was violent, nasty and very, very long: I felt we were enacting Swift's idea about "most sorts of diversion in men, children and other animals, are in imitation of fighting". We tried just about every variation you could think of. I guess the only thing

121

we didn't get round to was Danae and the shower of gold. I must say, I've never really understood the mechanics of that one anyway. Do you just lie back with your legs open? Fun as it must be to entertain a divine metamorphosis, I can't help feeling it'd be a little uncomfortable, all those freezing cold coins dropping in. Somehow with Europa and the bull or Leda and the swan you can get a *rough* idea of what actually went on. But a shower of gold? Is there something I haven't been told?'

'I'll show you some pictures, if that'd help. Titian and Rembrandt had a go at it.'

'Anyway, the important thing is what happened afterwards. When it was over, I went through a series of terrible confusing traumas. I felt that the weight of my head, which was lolling upside down in a post-orgasmic stupor, was beginning to force the breath out of my throat, and that the combination of this and the scar-tissue on my heart from the amyl might be leading to trouble. You know how we queens are always thinking about death. Getting up from the sling, I unhooked my legs from the chains and landed heavily on the floor. Perhaps my movements were too quick. The percussive shock to my head and kidneys was instantaneous. I stood there blankly, surfacing from the oblivion of the *petite mort*; but only momentarily. Straight away I felt my body quivering uncontrollably, with my head in a kind of swimming fluxion, a circular orbit spinning in space. I looked at Tom but didn't have a clue who he was, what he was doing there and where in Hell we both were. Distinctly *Huis clos*. Characteristically, though, as you'd expect, my vertigo was counteracted by an immediate reflex action: a refusal to let him see my loss of defences, an iron will to try and conceal the humiliating symptoms. That's always been one of my greatest fears, the idea of coming across as an amateur queen. It all has to be so slick and mechanical, no chinks of vulnerability. But it was hopeless. I've no idea how long it lasted, although he told me later (perhaps to reassure me) that I just stood completely rigid, immobilized for a few seconds. It was somehow even more frightening to regain full consciousness. I couldn't be sure enough of his concern for me and I needed to be looked after. All we'd established between us was a fierce exchange of lust. But I'd lost the power to calculate, so I just hugged him and shook quietly, telling him that I was scared. "Just hold me and look after me. It'll be over soon. I don't know what's happening." He responded beautifully and made a big capacious embrace for me to take refuge in.

'We showered in the usual Californian-Hockney way, prolonging the orgasm in a soapy clinch, and he obviously took pride in the sensuous pressure of his massaging fingers stroking and prying drenched in aloe juice. Then we had a drink and the paranoia hit as I realized I was expected to leave. The closeness I'd imagined we'd established was an illusion. I was going to have to stumble across back to Russian Hill. And not just crash out, curled up with that all-important protective arm hooked over my body. A clapped-out faggot, dragging his abused body and mind back through the early-morning fog. It reminded me of those extraordinary bits in the *Pillow Book* where the Japanese lady lays down the endless rules of protocol about how a love-affair should be conducted. Apparently the lover mustn't be discovered and has to leave in the morning, even in their promiscuous society; but he has to conceal the fact by spinning some idiotically elaborate story to the mistress: "It causes me infinite pain to abandon the delicate cloud on which you float, so serene to my vision; yet the beauty of this morning is such that I must rise and gaze on the dew as it hangs on the cherry-bough." Something like that. Meanwhile the slag knows all along that it's a jumbo lie, but has to reply in like vein, trying to restrain him, flattering him, you know. So neither of them believes a *word* of what they're saying. But if it isn't said, they're suicidal with remorse. If he does something in the wrong *order*, even, she thinks she's been subtly trashed. So in comparison with *that*, I suppose I got off pretty lightly . . .

'But God, it felt awful; and the depression was suddenly fed by an even greater fear. I remembered how he'd taken Polaroids of me in the foreplay. The memory kept reasserting itself while I feebly tried to piece together the events of the last four hours and gather the strength to leave. We exchanged addresses and telephone numbers without much enthusiasm; and then, a minor solace, he said he'd drive me home, that he'd intended to all along, and the only reason I couldn't stay was because all those bedrooms had been stripped of furniture. It was apparently one of those households where people don't actually sleep with each other. Wow, that little explanation did more than anything to speed up my recovery. At least I hadn't been just another clingfilm-wrapped phallus bought on a conveyor belt at Cola Foods.

'On the way home I tried to minimize the dizziness in my chlorinated brain, to say things that were half-way sensible yet not too obvious. It seemed to go all right, and he made long and eloquent claims about the success of our sex. But my surreptitious and guarded entry into the apartment (did you hear me come in?) and my attempt at muffled face-splashing somehow turned me in on myself again. I didn't feel I could talk to you about it; you looked so calm and beatific lying there beside David. As soon as I was horizontal, a serious wave of paranoia gushed over me. Little fragments of experience reassembled themselves. Everything conspired to make me believe that I was the projected victim of a blackmail attempt. Those shots of my self-satisfied face gazing down at a purple blood-engorged prick would be just perfect incorporated into a photomontage cover of *Crazed Honchos* or *Uncut and Heavy*. A few strategically mailed issues to my employer, instant rewriting of my contract. It was all I could do to sustain the train of thought which I was simultaneously trying to expel and replace with neutral and anodyne details. I tried flowers and San Francisco, dangling garlands of roses, Arcadian nymphs, Et in Arcadia Ego, ego-trip, LSD, sex, yes, that was it, BLACKMAIL. A soaring concrete canyon, the Transamerica Pyramid, Masonic-Egyptian sets of the *Magic Flute*, the unsmiling room-mate's copy of the *National Geographic*, dentists' waiting-rooms, abscessed teeth, medical insurance, money, rent. All-American Boy, BLACKMAIL. Ernö Laszlo cosmetics, the Duchess of Windsor, Diana Mosley, Unity Mitford with a vegetable brain, Berchtesgaden, art treasures in salt-mines, saline drips, wimps, BLACKMAIL. All the sequences ended the same way. They were like a fantastic hydra. Each time I tried to focus on the innocuous heads, the evil and baleful ones kept rearing up, arching backwards to strike with *more* force, with *more* conviction. *And* I'd left my surname, so easily traceable. The best thing seemed to be to try and persuade myself it was just not true. Like in the texts of the seventeenth-century Spanish probabilists, I was allowing myself to be swayed by insufficient and circumstantial evidence that I was emotionally predisposed to believe – even in the face of the obvious weight of the real truth. Hadn't he said in the Eagle that he was still a *believer*? There was some feeble security in that conventional Christianity, alien as it might have been to me. Christians just aren't blackmailers (unless you count the Jesuits). He'd talked to me in a loose and friendly way. He'd asked me whether I minded my head being in the pictures, laughingly saying that some guys wouldn't allow that. But what if it had all been an elaborate performance, a bravura *tour de force* of deception learnt over years of practice? He didn't work. Maybe all his income came from blackmail, a catalogue of victims like me. But then again, surely no one could sustain the charade, the dialogue so natural and infinitely predictable. His guard must surely have dropped momentarily and shown glimpses of the steely plan beneath. In a frantic attempt to reassure myself, I dragged myself out of my Valium saturation to re-examine the cards that Tom and his room-mate had given me. Maybe in confirmation of the Christianity theory, they would turn out to be reliable and unformidable things, like vets or social workers. Total failure: both cards bore just the name and address, and a sinister additional feature – a mailing address, a PO box number. Doubtless the collecting-point for a vast international nexus of blackmail contributions. I had no alternative but to drop a Tuinal, bury my head face downwards in the unyielding pillow, turn on a soporific radio phone-in about ecology and finally drift into sleep.'

Jerome's monologue caused Venetia inwardly to marvel. Its matter was familiar, banal even, but its delivery so unerringly reproduced both Jerome's insecurity and his capacity for shifting narrative style that she wondered whether it was necessary for him to undergo similar traumas to achieve this level of authenticity. The literary self-awareness, the *précieux* interludes, the uncomfortable use of popular idiom, how ill this fitted with the neo-brutalism of his appearance, how savagely it conflicted with the rules of literary decorum! A Cervantine *mésalliance* if ever there was one. But, despite its formal looseness, it reflected her own perception of Jerome more faithfully than any so-called reliable authorial voice could have done. Her gilded fillet and snood quivered with sisterly concern.

13

Song of Innocence 1

'Nous n'habiterons pas toujours ces terres jaunes, notre délice . . .' – St-John Perse, *Anabase*

Jerome felt a swelling in the gum of the upper right side of his jaw. After a brief but fruitless consultation with Bonaventure, he decided the ache was too important to dismiss as a mere *problème du jour* and took appropriate action. Lining up a row of medicaments on the bathroom ledge, he began methodically to down them, rub them in, sluice them, bite on them till they fizzed: sodium perborate, clove oil, antiseptic and soluble aspirin. Jerome really knew his pharmaceuticals. His basic collection was so heavy that when he flew it had to go as hand-luggage to avoid a swingeing excess. Anyway, you never knew what the pressurized atmosphere inside the plane might lay on for you next, from dry elbows to hair-static; once he'd come down with a carbuncle the steward had had to lance, a duty made tolerable by Jerome's martyred smile, ever so St Sebastian the sky-waitress had told her friends. At the end of the row of remedies was a solitary Dalmane, an emergency sleeper only to be used after the inefficacy of the others had been incontrovertibly established. He eyed it covetously, thinking of the oblivion which would allow him to link up his earlier healthy, acheless state with some future similar Nirvana in a woozy rite of passage. Pethidine would have helped that pain. Or willing the beta-endorphins to flood his brain. But his weakness of spirit stopped him even from this act of supreme weakness; and he sat on the lavatory till the quadruple assault on the hapless abscess should begin.

Some moments later, he stood up with a jolt, looked in the mirror and asked: 'Are you Peter the Great or are you not? Would you let your boyars see you laid low by a boil? Was this the spirit that launched a thousand dockyards?' David was quite frightened when he came in for a piss and found Jerome flashing his eyes at his own reflection and, to conceal and eliminate the tedious pain, drawing a false Muscovite curlicue on the end of his moustache with Venetia's kohl.

'What doing?'

'*Do* use the auxiliaries, you sound like an Apache. This is what you do when your nasty old body lets you down. You can't just let it ride, unless you want people to think that maybe you're a born-again Christian. Or giving a bad impression of Job and the boils. Did I ever tell you about them?'

'Shan't,' said David, with childish logic.

'I'm sorry, darling, it's not fair talking to you like this. I so love us being equals. It reminds me of the time when Shelley snatched a baby from its mother's arms on Magdalen Bridge and started questioning it about its Platonic pre-existence. I think metempsychosis is a lovely idea, don't you?'

David's intelligence, Venetia used to say, was like Natalie Wood's in *Driftwood* when she learned the rudiments of the theory of contagious disease in ninety seconds flat.

Either Jerome's remarks were too obscure or David was reluctant to pursue them. The child wandered away in silence.

How lovely his innocence was! How his face shone with the blind blessedness of a child! Jerome felt almost dirty, corrupting his mind with the souring revelation of knowledge. Why break that open membrane of his mind, deflower his innocence, send him remorselessly towards disillusion and the false honesty of the sceptic?

128

14

Flying Fearlessly

Mealy-mouthed they were not. Their conversations were conceived with the clashing but studied position-taking of a pitched battle. So sophisticated a knowledge *toti mundi* underlay their tortuous opinions, so many qualifications, ambiguities and defences, that it had become impossible for sentiment or direct candour to bubble up and pierce through the opaque aqueous surface tension. Their exchanges slid this way and that with only the taut membrane of their shared other-worldliness to keep it from falling apart into nonsense. Each, too, was so conscious of the stylistic devices of the other – discerning here a zeugma, there a chiasmus, here an imagination-stretching catachresis – that it was a cause for wonder that two such self-conscious people dared speak to each other at all. Those forces which potentially silenced them, stemming the flood-tides of their restless liquid reservoirs of minds, were always outweighed, however, by the mutual love, almost self-identification, that *precipitated* speech. Often, by the end of their conversations, it would have been possible to tell them apart only by the masculine and feminine timbre of their voices. Their use of language made them interchangeable and with interlocking words reinforced their love.

Venetia once heard herself saying: 'Oh God, I wish we could sometimes just have a natter about something ordinary, don't you?' Jerome didn't even bother to answer. Even before the sentence ended, she knew it was rubbish. They had so little need for banal exchanges that to engage in them would have been highly artificial, no more than yet another exercise in transferred identities. More important, the bridging together of their two selves was so tight that they knew each other's practical needs well before they were articulated. Consequently they didn't attempt to. There was, it was true, much to be admired in the way other people addressed one another with short bursts of information or opinion and lightened their bareness with *double entendre* and witty jumps. But this was a function of language beyond their own aspirations; succinctness, economy, clarity all had more value for them as words than as concepts.

They were in their natural habitat, the aisle and window-seat of an aeroplane, as they returned to the West Coast after a holiday in New Orleans with a grand old man of letters who had sucked them dry of ideas in his now desperate search for inspiration. At such times they half-realized that several novels must simultaneously be being written on the subject of their lives. It was an eerie feeling, worse in some ways than the most vigilant police surveillance. They had delivered themselves, with freedom and honesty, into hands which were now at liberty to alter them arbitrarily, recast their experience, shuffle the jigsaw of their lives in an infinite number of deceiving permutations. They alone knew the truth. Or so they arrogantly believed.

'You be Sancho Panza. I'll be Don Quixote,' she said. 'It's time I delivered a measured disquisition on a theoretical subject. Wouldn't it be more fun if we did it through a kind of literary prism? Only you don't need to watch out for intermittent lucidity in what *I* say. I'm sane to begin with; and anyway, I think the Romantics were right to think that Don Quixote was right all along.'

She abandoned whatever she was doing – too insignificant to escape oblivion – and, turning towards Jerome, stroked his army fatigues.

'*Das ist der Anfang eures Frühlingszeit,*' she began.

'Make up your mind, darling, you can't be DQ *and* Sarastro.'

'You remember what you said about hating yourself. *I* believe, on the contrary, that hating yourself is the best solution, that guilt is one of the most fruitful human emotions.'

'So what was Tallulah Bankhead on about when she growled out that stuff about "Conscience not being like a liver; you can get along without one"?'

'Stick to the Sancho idiom, my dear. I remember at school reading a whole book which sought to demolish Catholicism by insisting on the psychological devastation it wrought. Instilling, recognizing and formalizing guilt. The sacrament of confession, the remission of sins, casuistry, the fearful reduction of self-redemption to the indispensable acknowledgement of our repeated transgressions. For us moderns that's like the death of the human spirit, and somehow irreconcilable with the concept of a benevolent and omnipotent Deity. If God had intended us to feel this painful responsibility for our own natural shortcomings, He was somehow deficient in the characteristics which by definition we ascribe to Him – and that's a logical *non sequitur*. I suppose I prefer those wild late Greek accretions on the notion of God's creation; the hierarchical levels emanating outwards and downwards from the Ultimate Fount, in which man's position is clearly less than angelic and more than animal. Fishes and plants definitely at a lower level. At least it allows us to understand the urge to sin that singles us out as humans, and it dispels the incomprehensible "man in God's image" idea. We fall and we rise morally like barometers, and our experience of sin makes the concept of virtue more assimilable. I've always found the Original Sin allegory to be a kind of over-simplification. And I've never understood the point of Lucifer, except in the crudest Manichaean terms. But if good and evil are coexistent and equal, how come we don't all reach a mutual agreement to act well and subjugate the bad in us, to recognize the collective benefits of virtue, a kind of visionary Christian *phalanstère*? Because *God* makes too many of us, distributes his gifts in the most outrageously capitalistic system and forces us into a version of self-interest which suppresses our instinct to do good. Evil's no longer the mere negation of good, it's the logical conclusion of materialistic deductions.'

'Hi, I'm Mandy,' said a bright voice at Venetia's elbow. 'Are you totally comfortable? What can I do to make your flight just *perfect*? A Manhattan maybe, or a screwdriver?'

'That's very sweet of you.' Venetia smiled at her. 'We're just fine.'

'OK,' answered the stewardess with a slightly Chinesey intonation to give it lightness. 'Have a nice flight!'

'Let's take your case,' Venetia went on doggedly. 'By now you've managed to persuade yourself that surrendering to your sexual nature is good and authentic. You believe you've made sense of it by allowing it full rein, by magnifying it, deliberately putting yourself in homosexual environments and, in the process, subscribing to a very ordinary notion of normality (i.e. what everyone else seems to be doing). It's like someone very dim going on stage dressed as a Druid and carrying mistletoe and a sickle just because the rest of the chorus are doing it. But it's behaviour that only makes sense in a specific context. And you're transferring that eccentric, localized view of normality into a moral dimension where it's meaningless and wholly idiosyncratic.'

Jerome lay back and stared at the aircraft's ceiling in silence. From time to time he lolled his head sideways and looked at Venetia.

'I know how hard it is not to believe that what one does is somehow natural, preordained – by one's past behaviour or God or both – and therefore perhaps it's morally neutral. But you wouldn't be doing what you're doing unless you had an *esprit malin* egging you on, daring you to defy convention and prove to the world and yourself how *dirty* you can be, how flagrantly opposite your conduct is to the established norm. Whether or not the responsibility for it lies finally with you. You're dismissing the world, defiantly and childishly, as some kind of unreflective lumpenproletariat. Which if it only possessed your delicate sensibility – impossible, of course – would end up applauding, even subscribing to your own views about sex, love and mutual irresponsibility. And yet you also know that the product of that change would be a bleak and ravaged world. Not only would you have lost that delicious *frisson* of apartness, but you wouldn't even have the alternative image of cosy and virtuous domestic morality to calm your errant imagination.'

'Psycho-Catholic mumbo-jumbo. Thou talkest in clouds,' thought Jerome, while recognizing its probable truth. He

132

looked out at the clouds in which she was indeed talking. His own self-appraisal often followed the same pattern as hers. So what was the appropriate Sancho Panza retort? It takes all sorts? We all have our problems? Remember the Alamo? It would be unfair to Venetia to articulate something so intellectually down-market, even in jest. She'd expended a lot of energy on this chat. And she liked to be taken seriously.

'My main awareness is of the general superiority of homosexuality,' he drawled. 'It pre-empts much of the need for spiritual exchange, it releases a tiresome humour like a medieval bloodletter, it allows one to give in regularly and briefly to an obviously biological urge and it clarifies my relationship with women. I can compartmentalize the benefits and stimuli I get from other men; and I don't need to force those boundaries to overrun each other, except on those uncomfortable occasions when I myself momentarily confuse them. Sometimes I can actually see homosexuality as a metaphor for a future libertarian world-picture in which all these advantages would be universal. Imagine – even from your own special point of view. Our friendship and mutual love writ large, the paradigm for a world released from the conventional sexual thrall and its vile institutionalized corollaries. No domination or submission except in the most innocent kind of play.'

'Oh yeah, and what about women? What little interstices will they live in? What a nightmare. All you preternaturally young young men modelling your self-regard. By the way, how old *are* you?'

Jerome had never told her. He smiled in self-deprecation.

'Are you two fabulous English people enjoying your flight?' Mandy's farm-girl figure loomed beside them. 'I sure hope so, that's the only thing I care about, right?'

'Everything's just great.' Venetia smiled. 'Don't you worry about a thing.' Then she picked up the thread unerringly and went on, 'But seriously, the world would have to be *taught* all that. Against its will, like an artificial experiment in eugenics.'

'It's nothing unusual for the world to be taught things and finally to accept them. Only their effects have tended

to be a bit ephemeral. The ethics of colonialism, the discovery of an anthropocentric world in the Renaissance,
the destruction of the idea of an idealized Great Chain of
Being through Newtonian physics. All of these were learnt.
There's nothing unrealizable in the notion of a universal
intellectual revolution. But you're right. I don't really want
it to happen. It would threaten my sense of separateness
and taint it with human mediocrity. Let's think about it,
though. What would happen if homosexuality became the
norm? Clearly there would have to be breeders, otherwise
where would we men get our boy friends? But that would
merely act as a practical force. Whereas the celebration of
love between men would sanctify a new society. I wouldn't
want to go back to all those high-minded rhapsodic apologies
for faggots in Plato. Yacking on about ideals and souls cut
in half when all they want is to get laid. Perhaps it could
bring about a reversion to the pre-Industrial Revolution idea
of the stem family. Replacing our boring little present-day
nuclear ones. Nu-*clear*,' he spat out dismissively, 'more
like nuclear fission if you look at the divorce rate. We
could have a community of loving friendships, untrammelled with the competitive obsessions and embittered
constraints of the straight family. An extended kind of
family in which sexual contact didn't imply ownership
but just became an expression of solidarity and released
libido.'

'What about the argument that the ramifying stem family
couldn't tolerate nonconformism? It was OK that everyone cared for each other, but it was impossible for anyone to challenge the tribal standards and engage in illicit
experiments.'

'That's just it. Modern homosexuality has an extraordinarily high tolerance level and tends to regard sexual aberrations
as merely accidental (while taking very strong stands on
moral and social corruption). A strong cohesiveness which
of course *can* become – and historically *did* become – a threat
to centralized authoritarian control. None of that neurotic
Strindbergian claustrophobia, family members trapped by
their own defensive fetters. And full allowance made for
the males' tendency towards nomadic gregariousness, their

rejection of domestic routine, their concern for children and the provision of role-models. All in a climate of complete sexual freedom.'

'More like a brazen Utopia. There just wouldn't be enough Venetias to go round. You're the victim of two illusions: your own and the claims of the homosexual conspiracy. You *can't* be serious.'

They drifted off temporarily into a comforting silence, satisfied that they'd done justice to their own and each other's arguments. But that, too, could never be true, as they were both intellectually idle and too concerned with exposition.

This kind of unprofitable exchange was in effect a kind of spiritual communion. Such conversations took on the stilted sound of declaimed *da capo* arias in an *opera seria* and what was most significant in their discourse was what they did not say. Questions of actual importance were passed over and ignored in favour of playful, formalistic argument leading nowhere. How was Venetia able to love Jerome with a passion that utterly excluded sexual desire and jealousy? What bound Jerome so tightly to Venetia that he was able to resist the romantic blandishments, the adventurous life of a homosexual so constantly held out to him? How could they resist together if one of them threatened to fall or desert? How fragile was the whole edifice? None of this got answered, let alone asked.

The conversation revived and drifted with a falling and rising rhythm according to their energy-levels and the commitment they felt to its fluid matter. It lasted throughout the rest of the flight, with breaks for Mandy's ministrations. It still sputtered on as they readjusted to their return home, where the first event of note was the arrival of the cleaning-team from the Logistical Purity Clinic: two sour plain-faced men and a girl, all EST graduates, dedicated to the furtherance of cleanliness through the spiritual regeneration of your apartment. Venetia, eager to chatter about the underlying meaning of their lives (and to stop fretting about the New Sexual Dawn), met only with surly robotic rebuffs. *She* was clearly beyond redemption. Their minds had apparently been evacuated by all freedom and self-determination; exercises in self-abasement had worked their magic and shrunk the dimensions of their inconveniently unstructured former lives. Seizing vacuums and plungers with severe purpose they cleaned for God.

15

The Call of the Tame:
Venetia with a Straight Man

Venetia's sublimated libido was temporarily on vacation. She had accumulated a backlog of frustration so intense that it demanded some form of release. Given that she would never jeopardize her love for Jerome by trying to seduce him, she was forced to compete with him on the open market. Furthermore, she hated to inflict on innocent David the consequences of her sexual tension. He would stare at her and redouble the strength of his all-powerful weakness whenever she threatened to do so. His glottal cries took on a peculiar plangency that reminded her of her pro-maternal duties and invoked the spectre of Adelaida. She could never superimpose her own cruelty on to the existing scar-tissue left by his mother's abandonment of him. At times like these she became so conscious of her responsibility towards the child that she felt, almost as an obligation, the need to jettison her frustration. But how? And with whom? Had she not virtually disqualified herself in the sexual competition by her unqualified surrender to Jerome? The narrowing of her sexual horizons was not so much natural shrinkage, more a disappearing point.

Jerome, on an assignment in San Anselmo, photographing some Indonesian driftwood for a mail-order catalogue, had taken David along with him. Venetia asked Nicholas, her employer at the gallery, to take her to a party. At least that would give her a framework in which to operate, the familiar exchange of subliminal taunts and invitations. So what if you don't like me? I'm gonna fucking well make you talk to me. I know you're gay, but does that mean I don't exist? Am I reduced to just an invisible piece of Berkeleyan sense-data? You're prettier than me, but I can get you. Who're you trying to fool with all that opera stuff? I know you're straight.

Nick said he'd take her to the opening of the huge syndicated 'Art of New Guinea' exhibition. The idea nearly floored Venetia and aborted her plan, so strong was her abhorrence of the ethnographic. But she recovered her nerve, primly reminding herself of what Picasso had said about the blindness of those critics who'd considered Melanesian art to be a mere construction of dim anthropological beliefs. She would force herself to see them as something expressive, magical even. Fetishes. That was it. Anyway, she was going for the men not the masks. Nick gave her some bitter advice about how to behave. 'None of that well-brought-up British shit. No hanging back. Forget it. Just come across as sexually available. Some kind of female Lothario who's wandered in from a singles bar. Hot for American guys. And none of those headgames with converting faggots. It never works. If they want conversions, they'll talk to interior decorators.'

His advice on her appearance was even less realistic. In the face of all the evidence, he visualized her as a kind of New Wave dyed doll, an industrial wraith. Adelaida perhaps, Venetia definitely a no-no. She thought Nick's judgement fallible, anyway – you had only to look at the terrible slag he lived with. So she agreed with herself on an ensemble that would somehow give her the air of an ethereal wisp; something like Mia Farrow dressed as a *coryphée*. Maybe she didn't really want to get laid after all.

As Venetia strove for the look, her ample breasts swelled rebelliously and she struggled to press them down. Her Venusian hips seemed triplet-bearing under her despairing gaze. Reducing, vanishing, firming, how sadistic it all sounded. All she could do was give in, live for the present, think fat, somehow use her voluptuous opulence as a sexual asset. The *Latinos* liked that sort of thing, after all. *And* they were easier to deal with than those scrubbed Wasps, all locker-rooms, clean jaw lines and jockstraps, but with none of the compensating homosexuality. At least with a *Latino* you knew where you stood. You could project on to him some kind of operatic persona, a Manrico to your Leonora, an Edgardo to your frail Lucia. *And* they made most of the running themselves. She so liked to lose her characteristic noisiness and give in to the drilling eye-beams and facial seductions, the ego-washing balm of their ancestral voices.

So the outcome of her quandary bore a marked resemblance to what she normally wore: enveloping folds with strategic pleats, *effectiste* slashes, effects without causes, as Wagner complained of Meyerbeer, and trails of material. Dark and visceral rather than airy and astral. An earth-mother, not a Squeaky Fromme. She would have liked to have been able to lift David from his cot and hug him to her breast, crooning lovingly and laying her head gently against his puckered face. Without him she was nothing.

Outside the museum, the flailing mass of *le tout* San Francisco embraced and squeezed, seeing and being seen in its eternal parish *Totentanz*. Characteristically, it had assembled to render homage less to a faddish artistic cult than to itself. It was make or break in the mutual exchange of appraising stares. Learnt and natural self-confidence sussed out the intruder and the weak-spirited. Venetia felt like St Perpetua thrown to the lions; only most of these were more kittenish than ferocious, man-eating only in their sexual orientation. Nick contrived to use her presence as a badge of cosmopolitanism and made her feel that, to reinforce his anglophilia, she should perhaps be wearing the helmet and trident of Britannia rather than her present panelled marquee. He introduced her to purring Ganymedes and hectoring, bearded Ajaxes, aged prima donnas and creased Clinique-débâcles; and he watched her diffident progress. While *he* needed no credentials other than his professional standing, Venetia was forced to summon up her latent reserves of party-trash to penetrate the iron barrier of insularity. Since *everyone* had come, the multi-bricked wall of opposition was immense. How did one deal with it? Couldn't she find some all-purpose Jericho-trumpet formula to bring about its total collapse? How easy it was for, say,

President Kennedy with his, 'Ich bin ein Berliner.' That was all very well if you were a charismatic philanderer in charge of the world; but what if you were a stray, trust-funded Anglo with mental overdrive and glandular dysfunction?

Inside, the crush had broken all records, and tempers were beginning to fray. Even with her inbuilt English upper-middle-class radar, Venetia found it difficult not to press up against unknown backs and gem-strewn torsos. It didn't, at all events, seem to matter that much, the Americans seemed to accept all this physical contact as a necessary, even desirable, aspect of the occasion. Even when expensive viragos collided, it was much more an excuse for good-humoured mutual recriminations than for bitten-back *froideur*. Venetia became freer with her elbows, loosened up her shoulders as for a clash with a wing three-quarter and began to feel more American. This was the city of the '49ers, after all, the gay home of rough-and-tumble. (She remembered the night of their cataclysmic victory, the hysteria in celebration of the city's vindicated sexuality; those Michigan taunts of 'Beat those Gays from the Bay Today' had been triumphantly flung back in their rash teeth.)

A switch of Asian hair hung disconsolately away from the head of a shrill Jewish princess. A discarded Cuban heel had left some complex-ridden *Chicano* temporarily unbalanced. No one stood a chance of getting anywhere near the *margaritas*. A drink, honey? This is the fucking Sahara desert.

Venetia messed around with her flat heels amid a cache of rhinestones, bending down to pick one up for David. While her sisters were kicking around in newspapers and soft-drink cans in ravaged London, she was wading gravidly through semi-precious stones. Like some grape-treader in a designer-vat by Des Esseintes.

So far nobody had been straight. Had she really come to live in a city where heterosexuals wore badges saying, 'Hi! I'm straight'? Even the air was sterile, all fecundity sucked up like chlorophyll by the eucalyptuses in Golden Gate Park. Season of mists and mellow fruitlessness. No atmosphere could have been less charged with philoprogenitive promise. *Homo sapiens* milling in the serious foreplay that preceded the stereotyped throes of unprocreative lust. In a few hours' time, all the urbane and not-so-urbane men would be lunging at each other's orifices. In stygian caves, at Land's End, through drilled wall-holes, on chained slings, in bubbling jacuzzis and under sybaritic lawn canopies. Girls would be tucking themselves up with D.H. Lawrence and travel-brochures, dreaming of the princes who would only ever come in drag.

'Hey, I like your décolleté, kind of 1930s Balmain. All the other women look like nothing beside you, I mean they're the *worst*. How *dare* they insult Art like this, can't they see what messes they are?' Camper and ever camper it trickled along, meeting only with Venetia's dreamily half-interested eyebrows. She didn't want to culture-club *him*. She wondered why it was that women sounded like freakish *monstres sacrés* as soon as they emulated this drivel. No wonder women never understood the point of Rosalind Russell in *Auntie Mame*; the whole deception was that she was really a gay Everyman, smiling bravely through the tragedies, endlessly redecorating her apartment for a morale lift, emanating the staunchest love through the holes in her histrionics, life-enhancing through the straight-shaming obloquy. In a woman it sounded like a genetic mutation, in a man it sounded like normality.

'Venetia, my dear, how perfectly adorable you look. Just looking at you makes me feel more European.'

In the space between those two sentences, Venetia had resigned herself to the knowledge it *was* futile to hope to ignore this approach. The wheedling, cajoling insincerity was too professional for her to slink away and hide, or escape like a shy amateur. This was going to be a severe test for the cosmopolitan chic, which, while remaining dormant in her, had so rare an airing in the way she chose, at present, to run her life that it was impossible to predict its efficiency.

'Hello, Sibylla.' She said this before turning. It was all the more jarring, then, that the resigned breeziness of her greeting should be so suddenly transformed into authentic admiration when she actually saw the artful vision. Aslant the unforgiving spotlights, Sibylla had contrived to angle the shadows so that they fell immaculately into alignment with the layered silhouette cast by her own darknesses: the gossamer veil, the black osprey feather that swept upwards more imperiously even than the tilted nostrils, the continental shelf of her bosom, the low swing of her arms as they came elegantly to rest in front of her in a position that suggested the beginning of the permanence of statuary. The vogue in SF for Sibylla was of a kind to justify her queenly demeanour.

'You look *sensational*,' Venetia continued, recovering from the falter in her address. They bumped cheeks without surrendering a zillionth of hauteur. 'That neckline, it's so exactly like Ingres's Mme Moitessier. God, I wish I could look so good, and you've even managed for your necklace to plunge in *precisely* the same way, so tantalizingly fragile. You really should be an art director, nobody knows like you how to re-create an image.'

'But then, my dear, you'll always have the advantage over me with the sheer *originality* of your appearance,' Sibylla countered with a flash of polished enamel. 'I must say that even when Javier and I were doing our Grand Tour, we were amazed by the *daring* of you Europeans, the sheer *audacity*, and yet I don't think we ever met anyone quite so original as you.'

Not even in the travelling freak show in Trieste, Venetia's mind continued on Sibylla's behalf, not even in the Hieronymus Bosches in the Prado. She beamed at Sibylla, though the effect was confined to the lower part of her face. She made a highly strung gesture involving her right hand and her uncoiling chignon, a point-loser if ever there was one.

'I'm so glad to have bumped into you, Venetia. We see one another so rarely and, even then, there's never any time to talk. I mean really talk.' A nuance of threat had become rather marked in the other woman's voice. 'One's always so busy, so *distraite*, you know how it is. And I've been meaning to try and get you on your own. I've got something rather awkward to discuss with you, something I think you should know. Why don't we find somewhere less crowded? *Si nous faisions un petit tour de l'exposition?*'

There were a lot of qualifying endings to that lightly lifting conditional clause that Venetia could think of. She recovered some ground, however, and a little credibility by acting on Sibylla's invitation and taking her arm to guide her away from the mêlée. Sibylla acquiesced, confident in knowing that her burnished pale-oyster gown floated and gently fractured the surrounding light as they gracefully outmanoeuvred the persistent crowd that re-formed immediately after their passing. There was a lot of heavy sugar around her neck. Older than Venetia, more secure, less prone to intelligent self-questioning, more practised – because more ambitious – in the glacial flash of the *beau monde*, she allowed herself to be sashayed away in a movement which, given the elegant co-ordination of the two women, suggested an unhurried measure in an antique cotillion. They circled around the backs of the throng, eliciting furtive, almost involuntary glances of admiration from those women, and even more from those men, who felt they might have something to learn from this fluid pairing, this walking in beauty, so unlike their own insecurity and nervousness.

Sibylla was a woman of enormous influence and superficiality. Jerome, from a position of undeclared hostility, called her The Point (defined by Euclid as having position but no substance). She had married a department store. To ignore her was an act of supreme defiance. Her expensive elegance, too, was legendary as well as being the subject of ridicule from more modern women. It was true that when she swept in to pick up some groceries, she tended to look as if she was about to elope.

'She's seriously pretentious,' he'd complained. 'The kind of woman who, if a cruel and malign fate forced her to live in a 1930s pebbledash semi, would stick on a pedimented Grecian porch and then not see the joke.'

And still there were weaknesses in her on which one could play: the vulnerabilities of one whose position came from new, American money, a lot of it, and yet who believed herself to be a sprig, no a branch, of ancient European culture. She found the novels of Henry James impossible to understand, not because of any difficult words or tortuous syntax, but because the central conflict between American morality and energy and European sophistication and guilt seemed so absolutely meaningless. She was herself a living proof that they could coexist.

'How is Jerome? Hasn't he come tonight?'

'No, he's away, but he's really not too keen on this kind of thing,' Venetia answered.

'What a pity, I should love to have seen him. Did you both enjoy that party at the Loos' the other evening?' she asked.

'Enormously,' Venetia replied. Why was Sibylla holding back on what she really wanted to say? Ingrained *politesse*, presumably, or softening up.

'I find Filipinos so hospitable. One can see it in the way they've produced such *perfect* domestics, so neat and clean and incredible with children. I do have to admit, though, I do find them the teensiest bit dull, just a little bit lacking in the originality department. I thought Jerome looked bored rigid when he was talking to Benita – you know, kind of glazed over yet trying to smile all at once?'

Here, perhaps, was a clue at last. It was hard to tell, through the anodyne padding, where Sibylla was leading.

'*Puisqu'on a abordé ce thème-là,*' Sibylla continued. 'Is he *happy* in San Francisco? He's so brilliant, so *exceptional* I find it incredibly hard to fathom what he must be *really* thinking deep down inside, behind those perfect manners.'

'He loves it here. Both of us do. It feels like we've finally found a place where our lives can flower unimpeded.'

Sibylla turned from her to look with apparent attention at a warlike shield painted in the colours of dried blood. It might have transferred its meaning to her address as she came to the substantial meat of what she had to say.

'I've thought long and hard about whether I should discuss this with you, Venetia. I know that your life seems even and satisfying at present, and I wouldn't want to do anything to upset that, I just hate to destroy beautiful things.' Venetia's gaze strayed to the scarlet nails Sibylla displayed so beautifully, half-concealed by her gestures like velvet-sheathed feline claws. 'But I really feel that I have to say this for both your sakes. I'm only trying to help.'

She looked back at Venetia for a moment, before continuing. 'I've lived in San Francisco for many years now, too many, I really don't care to remember!' Her hand went up to her neck, less to feel the tangible evidence of deteriorated skin than to emphasize her humorous self-deprecation. 'It's an extraordinary city, quite extraordinary, the most marvellous mixture of a pioneer frontier Wild West town and a neat little European spa and of course it's got this fantastic *tolerance*, you can behave in just about any way you like. I sometimes wonder what those old '49ers would make of the city now; they were pretty wild, sure, but some of the things you see today, I think they'd be reaching for their Bibles or their six-shooters or whatever it was they carried in the line of handguns.'

Venetia guessed that Sibylla's bag concealed just such a weapon, nicely chased and enamelled, with a pearl butt maybe, but lethal none the less.

'Really, just about anything goes, and I guess we should be proud of our record on minorities. Sometimes it's pretty terrible to hear what other Americans say about us. You'd think we really deserved our reputation as Babylon by the Bay; but in the end, whatever anyone says, I'd rather be a San Franciscan, it's OK by me.'

She paused, and drew Venetia aside beyond earshot of a pair of art-lovers they both half-knew.

'The thing is this – I really don't know how to say this – if you want to get on in San Francisco, if you want to be a success (and don't kid me you don't), there are just a *modicum* of rules you have to obey, just the smallest guidelines, more a question of etiquette than morality really.'

'What are you trying to say, Sibylla?'

'I've nothing but admiration for the way you've presented yourself in California. Everybody adores you, you're so amazing, so charming, so *refreshing*. But I have to say this, it's *Jerome*. He's all those things, too, of course he is, and so *dreamy* to look at, everybody quite fell in love with him from the moment he first appeared. And as you know, I personally am utterly stricken with him, I could almost be jealous of you, only I think you're equally fascinating, my dear. I just wonder, though, whether he isn't going a little far, maybe taking gay liberation just to the limit, partying a little too hard. Both of us' – she blazed her eyes to check Venetia's intervention – 'both of us, you and I, absolutely accept Jerome's sexual orientation, let's get that straight. He's absolutely entitled to express his sexuality in whatever way he chooses. But there are consequences, you know, implications . . .'

She infused each word with a weight of meaning too forceful to be ignored.

'I must tell you a story, then I guess you'll see what I mean. Someone – I won't tell you who it was, there's no point, but she's a very dear friend of all of us – anyway, she was driving along 10th Street, I think it was, on her way to get her car fixed. It was some time on a Sunday afternoon, no one much around – you know, kind of deserted like the city gets. But she gets snarled up at an intersection and while she's waiting for the traffic to move off she looks down a side-street and there's this huge pick-up truck parked, you know, in one of those really dirty streets with no houses, just dreadful old paintstores and stuff. There's the regular quota of gays circling around, not doing much, just filling in the time, they didn't seem particularly interested in one another. No action. I mean nothing *visible*. And there, right in the middle, there's Jerome, she got quite a shock, and, my dear, he was in such a state, lying in the back of the truck, in a condition, well, words fail me to describe it. He looked frankly, as if he'd just been had by the entire passing-out grade at West Point.'

Ah, here were her true colours, Venetia realized, as the crimson rushed into her own face.

'He was wearing the most bizarre clothes, all ripped and torn and covered in what looked like oil, and his pants were just, well, *hanging* off him. Apparently you could see most of what was on offer. He looked like he'd been there all night and the rest of the day. God knows if he was doing drugs. Sa – . . ., our friend, was just too shocked to stop and ask. But, Venetia, it was such a terrible sight, really the *worst*, so *tacky*, we thought we just *had* to tell you, it's our duty. Because if he's going to let everything go to hang like this, and not care, not even *care* about who sees him doing what, then things are going to get really difficult for you. You do see how I'm telling you for the best, we terribly want to help you.'

Venetia had listened with mounting exasperation. She dreaded the unfolding of the story, because its dénouement could shock her either as a revelation or as a moral parable, but more because she longed for Sibylla to repress it, to realize how hurtful it was and how this pretence of solicitous concern was absolutely, utterly bogus. Her use of words alone showed that, even if it had not been transparently evident in her steely face. The gibe about West Point, the sick fashion-details, all pointed to a prurient thrill, a triumphant sense of a power to destroy Venetia and her fragile happiness. It was the most shallow manoeuvring in the seedier reaches of social competition, intended as a slander. Venetia was reminded of an idea in the Buddha – what was it? Something about the slanderer being like one who flings dust at another when the wind is contrary; the dust does but return on him who threw it! She determined to produce a counterblast to sting the kohled eyes of her enemy and leave them smarting, streaming with remorse. Through her rage, a rage fuelled and stoked by words as they rushed and roared through her mind, she was vaguely aware of bystanders beginning to strain to overhear the impending altercation.

'I'm not in a position,' she began, 'to speculate on what your motives may or may not have been in telling this shabby little story. I don't know what you hope to gain by it, although I'm pretty sure it's not my social welfare. If it's intended as a genuine piece of advice, then forgive me, I'm afraid I can't accept it as such. I'm well enough disposed towards you to believe you may have the best of intentions. But I cannot allow what you've said to pass without defending Jerome.'

Her voice began to rise slightly after the strained politeness of her preamble.

'As you yourself admit, Jerome is absolutely entitled to express his sexuality in whatever way he chooses. There are no secrets between us. I have never been excluded from his sexual life, I understand and accept it. What's more I have nothing but admiration for the way he's accepted what to him is an unassailably normal sexual orientation and lives it to the full.'

'I don't think we're arguing about that,' Sibylla said.

'I don't really know *what* we're arguing about,' Venetia replied hotly, wondering what direction her diatribe should take. 'Look' – she opted for an honest directness – 'this is 1982. Jerome is living in San Francisco, the most sexually liberated city in the world. He's hot-blooded and has the natural appetites of a man in his prime. He is extraordinarily attractive and besieged with sexual invitations. Surely he has every right to behave in the way he does. It's the current fashion for gay men to be open and promiscuous, it would be odd and perverse if he chose any other. Can you imagine him deliberately turning his face from all this honesty and truthfulness and deciding to jump back in the closet or hang around public lavatories like some furtive old queen? All that's happening is that he's conforming to the new model, and it's a terrific model, because what it symbolizes is the end of years, decades, centuries of deceit, lying, hypocrisy, personalities stunted by repression. If I was a guy, I'd be right out there storming the barricades, proving just how sexual I could be. The kind of sex you describe in your tight-lipped, evasive way is actually a huge political statement, a cry of grateful freedom. I'd be horrified if Jerome just let it pass him by without seizing it, embracing it whole-heartedly.' Her voice was rising in a crescendo of passion, though she had sacrificed none of her fluency. 'And if you and your friends don't like it, then I only have contempt for you. What it reveals is your inability to come to terms with the truth as it is and the rights of all men. Your liberalism is just a feeble façade, skin-deep, you're just skulking behind it in a world of self-deception. I'd rather you were a self-confessed redneck, at least then you wouldn't dress up your intolerance as some kind of phony Californian bleeding-heart concern. Really, I can't let you get away with it.'

'I'm sorry you feel this way,' Sibylla said quietly, her voice more caustic than silver nitrate. She took a tissue from her handbag and snapped the clasp shut with unmistakable finality. 'It's a pity you're not able to accept advice with the graciousness it deserves. Goodbye, my dear.'

As she spun on her heel, the small crowd of onlookers erupted into applause. Taken aback by this spontaneous acclaim, Venetia beamed shyly at the men who went on

clapping and smiling, turning to one another for confirmation of the courage and drama of her performance. 'Good
for you,' one of them said in an exaggerated English accent,
and then, reverting to the native idiom: 'Right on and
tell her, lady.' A flush of pleasure and embarrassment
suffused her face, and she found the rapture of her reception
disproportionate to the importance or expertise of her
speech. But that, she realized, was an integral part of
camp: the seizure of the second-rate, its deification and
theatricalization, the instinct to change ordinariness into
art. She walked past her admirers, acknowledging their
attentions as best she could. Her head bent this way and
that as she looked at them from under her eyelids and
the fall of her bandeaux. It was only afterwards that she
regretted her lack of panache and, going over the scene
again in her mind, changed it so that it became a regal
progress, all gracious and slow wavings from the elbow
and the fixed smile with which the House of Windsor
disarmed.

She was now again on her own, fending for herself in the
mêlée. Her triumph gradually insinuated itself in her mind
so that she was content to dwell on it mentally, savouring its
pleasures, without going through the necessary motions to
cement her success by sharing it with others. What she had
not realized was that her conquest had signally confirmed
her unusual resolution to seduce a man. If she could ward
off Sibylla so robustly, she could certainly deploy that
same strength to secure a lover. But she was still happy
simply to review what had passed amid the press of the
unknown crowd.

She found herself being introduced to a dark-blond Viking
who stood incongruously silent in the screeching aviary. His
largeness seemed to make him impervious to the thrashing
Homintern; the darting glances from the swimming, deep-
set, moustachioed eyes bounced off him like blunted arrows.
He presided over the sensual Babel with all the impassivity
of U Thant at a session of tempestuous delegates. Venetia
realized that his supremacy was founded not so much on
his warrior grace as on his inviolable heterosexuality . . .
His entire presence was alien to the faded widows and the

breathy female socialites, inured as they now were to the staying-away power of straight men. *Conlige, virgo, rosas.* It's now or never. Had Priscilla said that to Elvis? Could one *be* that outspoken?

She deployed her specialized armoury of sexual attractions, moving her orbital eyes languidly as she drew him aside from the Odyssean gang of suitors. It was clear, her intuition told her, that he complied largely through the chance she offered him to escape their siege. Still, it was a start, and she could build on her advantage.

'You look kind of uncomfortable with all these guys. Like everything else in this city, it's more like a Halloween party for Judy Garland than anything else. Did you come to see the art?'

'I guess so. I've been reading Margaret Mead and Ruth Benedict, and I just wanted to see these things. I feel kind of serious saying that, but I really am interested in this stuff. All those weird ideas about cargo cults and sexual initiation, it gives you a sense of proportion. Men in California, especially gay men, think they have all the answers. But all they really know is how to sublimate their celibacy – flower arranging and bitching each other up.'

Venetia felt much the same. They talked about the statues and shields, warlike objects that suggested his own aura, as she assessed his cloudy intelligence. It was clear that if Jerome felt floored by the gay idiolect, Tom would have been totally at sea in it. His manner was ponderous after the frothy leaven of the rest. But, 'Is *he* beautiful!' she exclaimed to herself as he launched his leaden way through the thickets of conversation. He spoke of his slender reading habits, his partial surrender to the anti-intellectual prejudices of his class, his half-hearted defence of Reaganomics. Supply-side sado-monetarism and the radiant promise of Silicon Valley; nothing revealed even the most tentative side-stepping of the Great American Dream. She embarked on what she still regarded as her expatriate responsibility: an exposition of the English sickness, a despairing elegy for the intellectual beauty of London, a self-exoneration for her rattish abandonment of the sinking ship. She composed her sentences with a kind of jerky awkwardness, fearful of seeming over-literary.

His gaze grew more intense, his ice-slide eyes more caressing as he listened to her nervous delivery. Every word she uttered made her more foreign to his nurtured Americanness; but his appreciation contained no Jamesian apprehension, no anxiety about the hereditary duplicity of the European. Her counterfeit energy gradually drained away as she absorbed the unclenching sensuality of his response.

'What I love about you English is the way you can say really *terrible* things in exactly the same tone of voice you use for ordinary things. Do they teach you how to do that in high school?'

Venetia thought sardonically about the terrorized nuns, browbeaten by nubile girls and thankful if they could instil the mere rudiments of the catechism. But perhaps the confessional *had* taught her how to present malicious evil as the tiniest of venial sins, to dissimulate and make secret mental reservations, to explore the sophisticated reaches of amphibology and casuistry. But surely he didn't mean *that*?

They had moved almost imperceptibly out of the social carnage and found themselves in a draughty lobby filled with mediocre plaster casts of classical statuary. 'Circulate, circulate,' Nick hissed in her ear as they entered; but now her object was nearly accomplished. She told Tom about her life in San Francisco and so angled her opinions about the liberating effect it had had on her as to leave him in no doubt about her sexual availability. Soon their dialogue became almost quiescent as they approached the certain conviction that they would imminently be making love. She wanted him to remain taciturn, to strangle at birth his predictable ideas and concentrate on his dominant expertise, the filling of his pliant victim with sensual anticipation. Internally she was writhing like Laocoön, a Second Empire actress making the transition from enticement to surrender. Most of the skill was actually his, but she had contributed the intimation of the ductile core within her brittle husk.

During their moment of recognition they were able to still the nervous compulsion of their talk. Tom tailed off into generalized admiration for the femininity of English women while Venetia concentrated on presenting her body in its least matronly vector. Many Californians had accused her of divorcing herself from her body, of seeing it as an external encumbrance rather than a harmonious complement to her spirit. Holism and self-esteem. But even at a precipitous moment such as this, she believed herself to be inhabiting a body at war with her soul, a kind of aggressive neo-Petrarchan dualism in which her spirit struggled to free itself from its mortal prison. Some improvement, it was true, had been wrought by her exposure to northern California; it was at least possible for her now to itemize her bodily assets, to make a graded comparative list in which her eyes outshone the heavy volume of her pelvis and her vivacious mouth and chin undid the damage inflicted by her embonpoint.

'Let's leave all this behind,' Tom said with a valedictory movement of his head which brooked no refusal.

Venetia half-heard the distant odious vernissagespeak and dimly saw flexed and preened bodies presenting their high asses to the New Guinean fetishes in contemptuous dismissal. The mass philistinism, overlaid with the need to use the exhibits as social adjuncts like inert conversation-pieces, gave her a sense of purposefulness and clandestine adventure. The fragile foundations on which she was building her relationship with Tom at least had the solidity conferred by honesty and had needed few of the contrived props of fantasy so much in evidence in the other gallery. She could not, however, be sure of his reactions. There was always the inescapable alienness of the American, the understanding that there could be little falling back on shared assumptions and interchangeable humour. It was still extraordinary for her that, despite her bedouin rootlessness, she could never entirely cast herself into the prevailing national mould and remove the fetters of her background. She was responsive, volatile, suggestible and curious; yet a kind of insecurity, at once associated with and separated from her physical movements, prevented her from absorbing and aping foreign mannerisms beyond mere parody. Jerome believed this to be inextricably connected with her strong femininity and her sexual self-denial. She had substituted for the firmness of a sexual persona a reliance on a hybrid farrago of values to understand who she was. So with Tom there could be no mutual signs of identity. Both of them had taken refuge in archetypal stances, drawing apart as they displayed the constituent parts of their personalities. Yet the very effort of this exchange had allowed them to build up a sense of shared isolation, he through his sexuality, she by her cultural exile.

They left excitedly for Tom's house, since Venetia felt anxious not to disrupt the institutional regularity of her temporary home. Their breathy conversation was wayward and cursory, and seemed increasingly like a kind of nutritional carbohydrate to counterbalance the energizing spinal tremor, the onward rush of lust. Their movements and gestures were oddly controlled, as if their excitement fed off layers of self-restraint. She reacted badly to his apartment and temporarily felt her commitment sliding as she absorbed its details: bookcases filled only with technical journals and college programmes, the dingiest kind of South London net curtains, an immense Betamax, dioramic photographs of pre-earthquake San Francisco, a gloomy montage of wood and cotton thread in a design that reminded her of the Thames estuary flood-warnings. Nothing to alleviate his singleness. She remembered how earlier, at the gallery, she'd spoken with an elegant, fluting Chinese who'd told her about Feng-Shui:

'The art of living in harmony with your surroundings. Channelling the energy, the *ch'i*, so that it flows between the arrangement of the room, the furniture and your own energy-field. So important, my dear, so few people understand it, that's why they become so neurotic and jumpy – damaged by the jagged lines. The disorder, mirrors that cast an irregular image, so many things . . .'

Tom's room broke all the rules (though she couldn't yet speak for his energy-field). It implied a great deal of pressure on him to live outside its confines. In a sense, though – and in an effort to reaffirm her resolution – it allowed her to see him as a creature of transience in whom she had no need to invest any futures. The intellectual and cultural Red Sea dividing them would need no Mosaic superego to cross it, since her project stopped short of so arduous a span.

'I'm glad we met,' he said in a new *sotto voce*. 'You have

a strange kind of mystery. Will we get to understand each other?'

The implied long-term optimism of the question was so starkly at odds with her reverie that she felt like a fraudulent intruder. She was, after all, self-consciously behaving like a marauding homosexual.

'I like you a lot,' she compromised. 'At the beginning it was just the relief of talking to somebody straight who seemed to be aware of exactly what he was doing at an exhibition like that. But I find you sexually very attractive.' She looked away apprehensively before beaming on him a brave glare of sensual ardour. 'Most Americans make me really nervous. I just can't catch up on all that prehistory of quarterback camaraderie and the hideous competitiveness of it all. But you seem more gentle, more tender. In that army of gays, you were like a boyish Viking warrior straying from his longship.'

'Let's get blasted.' His voice had changed register again as he tried to deflect her from mannered Anglicisms. He wanted now to be like a primate, uttering only the minimum noises necessary to arouse her re-emergent libido. His large hand was caressing her shoulder and drawing her closer to his craggy Nordic head.

The joint released her strangled naturalness and she was able to relax, feeling only the imprint of the rough sofa on her back and the strong tensing of his muscular body. Recurringly she imagined herself to have assumed a different identity, to have divested herself of all the messy superstructure laid on her mind by the carbolic Assumptionists, by the magisterial Tannoys of the Sorbonne corridors, by the incestuous *flaneurs* of the Courtauld, by her life as part of Jerome's circus. It was as if Tom had pentecostally broken through to her virgin core, stripping away, through the mutual impossibility of retaining it, all the redundant bondage of the past. Release, white candour, tactile strength. Could there really be such sulphurous lust within so kaleidoscopic and factitious a sensibility?

Their love-making (as she described it later to Jerome) was interesting for the fact that it was primarily she who coaxed Tom out of his Waspish reticence. She felt particularly triumphant at having run down the length of his undulating back with her moist tongue. He buried his head between her breasts and felt both dominated and protective. They half-slept languorously like gays, side by side like spoons in a drawer until his dark voice rearoused her from her somnolence. Her thrusting and bucking body, sedated and stimulated in turns by the grass, reacted like the body of any sluttish Hollywood starlet eager for a bit-part. The morning was sour but handleable, and they recognized the flawed rapport which had cemented their loneliness. No, it wasn't the same for girls. Nor was it the first time she had reached this conclusion (and inwardly railed at Jerome for its injustice), a conclusion paradoxically so inconclusive that it was certain she would again and again put it to the test. But she felt nothing for Tom. His presence was entirely mechanical. She longed for Jerome.

When she came to ask Jerome for his expert views on how to extricate oneself from ephemeral sex, he was too caught up in his own absurd jealousy to answer her.

16

Jerome: Kensal Green

'Jacques était paresseux, comme tous les vrais artistes.'

Jerome lay in bed, looking at the ceiling through half-closed eyes. He was trying to understand something, trying to co-ordinate a rabid dream in which Chilean militiamen mutated into Berlin transvestites and moronic brigadiers spoke with babbling glossolalia until their teeth crumbled. As he slid inexorably into consciousness and the heavy furnishing of his room replaced the outsize contours of the looming Estadio Nacional and the Votivkirche, the seaside funicular in the Taventziener Strasse, his unrested brain turned to his habitual Jungian search for the symbolic orders that the dream might have contained. Instructions for his future conduct and self-knowledge? None of the *dramatis personae* bore any resemblance to himself, or, for that matter, to any potential, as yet unrealized, persona he might be harbouring. The distance was immense. He felt closer to being a fundamentalist rabbi or a spaniel-breeder than to any of these ready-made suggestions. Perhaps there was *something*: the epicene Germans and the South American militarism – the twin polarities of *machismo* – might really conceal a secret hankering, his contempt might in fact be a longing. They did, after all, afford an unassailable code of values in which everyone knew the rules (and that was something he liked). You couldn't be a field-marshal and wear a dress; and then, again, you probably wouldn't want to run the War Office if you cherished a silicon implant. No one could challenge their assumptions without undermining their whole *modus vivendi*. He, on the other hand, was, as he knew, in a quagmire. His own personality had a relentless fluidity which was permanently open to question. The morass of battling moral and aesthetic values, the absence of exemplary goals, the whole porous susceptibility left him as wearily confused as a scattered backgammon board. Why was there no Alamein to test his decisiveness and reveal a paragonic man of action? Why no *Diez de mayo* in which he could discover reserves of leadership and resolution?

Much of his morning sickness was taken up with these dispiriting questions. Characteristically, it was not until the mid-afternoon that he could abandon his melancholy self-critique and resume life within its given parameters. The days were thus divided between aspiration and compromise, self-regard and oblivion.

He decided to walk to the cemetery at Kensal Green after tidying up the flat and finishing the rough draft of a magazine article. His obsessive untidiness was the one single factor which made Jerome worry about whether he really *was* homosexual. Surely he ought to be scrubbing and prinking. Ransacking the household departments for new scouring-powders. Tying up old letters with pink bows. Colour-coding the ornaments. Putting the jockstraps – especially the one last night's trick had left behind – through the second spring-flowers-fresh conditioning rinse cycle. Starching and name-taping the sports sox. First, though, he turned his attention to the *magnum opus* which lived at the back of his head, the script of a Catholic Hollywood epic, *Fisher of Men* or *Curiosities of the Curia*. So far he had only got so far as a tentative cast-list; it would star Hedy Lamarr au Diable, Stefanie 'Earthly' Powers, Rosary Cluny, Rock of Ages Hudson, 'Efficient' Grace Kelly, 'Pope' Joan Crawford, Peter 'Vatican' Sellers, Romy Schneider/Romish Neider, Jean-Paul II Belmondo, Divine, and, in the cameo role of Monsignor Merovido . . .

It had been an energetic and constructive day which had caught him unawares after its sad start. Previously the week had seemed to establish a pattern of monotonous idleness and repeated dizzy nauseous spells as he slumped the four-foot drop out of his brass bed and dragged himself through beads of spilt cat-litter towards the putrescent contents of his Utility fridge. 'Self-respect comes from self-discipline,' he thought, as if he'd seen a platitude embroidered on a Victorian sampler. But somehow he could never subscribe to the sentimental instructions that others had laboriously invented. They could never be allowed to impinge on his cultivated otherness. So he let the garbage fester until the slime seeped out in rivulets on to the kitchen floor. Dust had heaped up into uneven *cordilleras* and blown about in competition with the fur-balls of the cat. But that afternoon he had at last been able to clean up, acting on his suppressed knowledge of the simple equation between neglect and nausea, sloth and fungus. *Trompe l'oeil* painted mould in fashionable closets was one thing, liquid garlic humus another.

The day was bright, and his sense of conquered sluttishness made him walk fast and with even strides. He could have been walking to audition as a housewife. He strode purposefully, like a YMCA recruit, through the dirty streets that he could now see through a filter of moral purgation. He could disregard – hardly even register – the detritus around him. The banked and gutted electricity-meters, the disembowelled vinyl car-cushions, the plaster-spattered antediluvian light-fittings. A cyclone of swirling fanzines. He walked his superior way, thinking how, had he a more theatrical self-image, he might have sung out: 'I'm the man who broke the bank at Monte Carlo,' fortissimo, like the azure-eyed gold and white panther Peter O'Toole in *Lawrence of Arabia*. Certainly his demeanour reflected the same self-assured panache and the sense of elated solitude amid the desert places. He passed the brown blocks of Ladbroke Grove, the dusty plane-trees and hydrangeas, the recessional tyre workshops and glaziers – lest we forget – crossed an invisible canal as the walls narrowed towards the traffic-lights. Past the builders' partition scrawled over with: 'Rude Gay Aircrew Skills' – now *that* was eclecticism for you. Great black rubbish bags swelled and spilled their contents, torn apart like Jezebel by dogs. His scarlet-flash Puma baseball boot sank noiselessly into a dog-turd. Christ, the only issue that would get him to stand for a political cause would be a pooper-scooper ordinance! Hot, black drivers exchanged ritual insults between egos as bruised as the tyres on their cars. Traces of liquefied rubber still clung to the road surface. Lead fumes shimmered prettily in the motionless air.

It was a relief to reach the leafy Grecian portals of the cemetery. He stood back to look at the classical motifs. Then, walking down the avenue of trees, he felt a sense of widening possibilities, his freedom to choose any sarcophagus-strewn path now unimpeded. He slowed his pace gradually, absorbing the shady prospects of Victorian granite pyramids and modern mica headstones hung with photographs of dead Cypriot expatriates. There seemed to be no order, no chronological arrangement, certainly no aesthetic divisions. The noseless Winged Victories of Samothrace flew heavy-footed over recumbent bogus-medieval Goths. The carved impedimenta of an Edwardian admiral lay heaped beside an infant's premature resting-place, only a forearm long. Jerome had visited the cemetery before, vainly trying to locate the grave of an Italian opera-singer, but finding, as today, only the nameless levelling of death.

As he walked through a whitethorn thicket, away now from the path, his attention was arrested by a strange and incongruous object. It seemed to be a swollen bladder made out of some vegetal substance, and was hung around the base of a fluted vase. The grave was of recent design and covered with pieces of some greenish marble-substitute. A silver hairbrush lay in a glass case nailed to the stone surround. The marble gave off an oddly unreal reflection from the tree-shaded sun. Bending down to read the inscription, he made out: 'Dedicated to the memory of Lorenzo Urquijo Maura, beloved son of Spain, disciple of Christ, indefatigable crusader for the Army of Truth. Died, October 13th, 1978, aged 33. And of his adored sister Adelaida, cruelly murdered by the enemies of salvation . . .' Jerome rubbed away a small patch of lichen which obscured the remaining words: '. . . *Que en paz descansen. La paz que les fue negada en durante su vida mortal.*'

His mind wandered momentarily in recall of *his* Adelaida,

the silent glowering virago, the sullen rebel. How strange that he should be about to see her in Madrid – albeit *à contrecoeur* – and that her beautiful Beethovenian name should be commemorated here on the grave of some Catholic martyr! He leant forward again and pressed the belly of the dark bladder that hung so sinisterly over the mortal remains. It was heavy and seemed to be filled with some viscous liquid. But he could find no opening through which a liquid might have been poured into it. Curiously it seemed to be a seamless pouch divided into two swollen sections by the black cord that held it to the vase. He tried squeezing the contents from section to section, but the binding was too tight to allow any movement. He sat back in the long couch-grass, looking at the bladder and trying to concentrate: on what it might be, what meaning it might have in this isolated segment of transplanted Spain. At first he dwelt on the idea of witchcraft. Dimly he remembered something from a classical author – Diogenes Laertius, was it, or Aulus Gellius? – about Aristotle habitually wearing a leather purse filled with heated oil against his stomach, no one ever knew why. There were many cases of desecration and sabbats in London cemeteries, but on the whole they turned out to be no more than the pathetic clamourings of hoydenish suburban landladies. Perhaps he had seen something like this in a dark *acuarela* by Goya: some part of the demonic baggage of a tormented hell-hag in the throes of death? Or some medieval curse filled with fermented bodily fluids, ready to gush with stricken menstrual flow at the prick of a bodkin?

At that moment Jerome heard the sound of branches being pushed aside and the heavy tread of an approaching person. He hastily drew apart, his mind split between his repulsive speculations and the presentiment of danger. Pressing himself behind a tangled bush, he watched the arrival of a curious figure dressed from head to foot in a kind of iridescent dark-green material. The woman – for it was probably female – seemed swathed in bands of sea-weed, fringed with teased-out fronds of drifting algae. A kind of aged Undine, a sea-water-nymph displaced out of her element, become lumpish and earthen. For a moment he was reminded of something Venetia had once said; how she liked to daydream and oneirically to compare herself with the pantheon of the ancient Adriatic, seeing herself as an etiolated aquatic creature surfacing to seize the Doge's ring. (Jerome, exasperated by her silliness, and in an attempt to quash her pretensions, later sent her a postcard he'd found in Berlin of a pig executing a perfect Olympic dive.) But Venetia's spirit, aquatic or otherwise, was firmly elsewhere, in mud-sodden Marin County. And this apparition gave out a feeling of never having been seen before, of intruding irreversibly into the confines of his life and laying the foundations for a new direction it might now take.

He watched, caught up in the sprawling briars, as she sank to the ground in an attitude half-way between prayer and exhortation. Her body became pyramid-shaped and remained motionless a few seconds, like some mystic architectural excrescence sculpted in airy green tissue on to the surface of the grave. Jerome could see no visible sign of a living form encased in the hieratic pyramid. It had no identifying features, no alleviating bumps or hollows, nothing to extenuate its solid regularity. Her stillness was somehow more threatening even than if she'd been a restless Fury flapping her wings as she battened frantically on to some hubristic victim. It seemed as inconceivable that she could be transformed back into a human being as that a pillar of salt should be made to revert to the shape of Lot's wife.

A thin humming sound issued from the top of the figure. As it swelled in intensity, a sudden movement thrust her arms into the air to remove the emerald swaddling-ribbons from her head. They fell away with miraculous speed. Why had Jerome assumed that they were some kind of intricate many-layered mummifying binding? A magnificent head was revealed, an erect, authoritative and leonine head with a profile of extraordinary vigour. She seemed to be trying to articulate words, or song-sounds, but the firm line of her mouth betrayed no enunciatory movement. As she continued emitting the inhuman noise, she broke the immobility of her body again and bent down towards the talismanic bladder, staying close in front of it for a few moments, then leaning back to resume her original position. Jerome craned his neck to see what had happened, if any part of the inexplicable tableau had been altered. In effect, a small glass circle now lay beside the bladder. A magnifying-glass, a telescopic lens, a rectal smear? Its shape was slightly irregular and it seemed to have a jagged edge protruding from its perimeter. Was it a burning prism, the end of a kaleidoscope, perhaps? Despite its circularity, it might well have been the Aleph, the final enlightenment, one of the points of space which contain all other points. Maybe a closer inspection would reveal the infinity of creation, all the miraculously coincident atoms of matter, perhaps even the tattered labyrinth of London which Borges had glimpsed in the dark cellar of the Calle Garay?

She turned abruptly towards him as if she'd been conscious of his presence all along. The crooning wheeze ceased suddenly and she scrutinized his anxious features. Nothing he could do could alter the untenability of his position, his feeling of a child caught in some unspeakable misdemeanour. He smiled weakly in an attempt to normalize the situation. But her iron failure to reciprocate left his mouth hanging in a stupid contraction. She spoke in a southern European accent:

'See here, it has five deep grooves in the surface. It's a broken bottom of milk-bottle. I like to think of it refracting the cosmic rays of providence on to their hallowed corpses. Can something so humble, made of mere sand, achieve something so divine?'

Jerome's reserves of social adaptability were being sorely stretched. This was trial by ordeal, being stuck into the pages of a novel and told to fight your way out as best you may. He'd rather have been strapped to a ducking-stool or locked in a cubicle with a urolagniac. Or lowered on to Catherine the Great with a pulley.

'I believe that the ancient Egyptians used shards of crystal to venerate their dead,' he lied.

The woman appeared not to hear this feeble sally. She bowed again to untie the bladder. Brandishing it operatically, she rose and walked towards Jerome. He started back and automatically seized a thorny trunk to prepare for some mysterious onslaught. *O magnum mysterium!* As she offered the sinister object like a votive donor, he summoned up some drama-school poise and gravely, majestically even, received the presentation. He figured that even a manual operator like Joseph must have mustered some imperious dignity to accept the bizarre and largely useless gifts of the Magi. The woman floated away and left him clasping the dismal object.

17

Venetia: Story about Miletos

'Dearest Jerome,

'I'd survived a supremely uncomfortable ride perched on top of some wool-bales on a lorry from Çeşme. In those days I hadn't yet developed my present Edwardian attitude to my skin, and I'd decided to lie and sunbathe on top of the soft texture, cushioned against the appalling bumps in the road surface. I did some isometric exercises for my thighs. Soon I realized that the driver, as he was roaring along crashing his overworked gears, was trying to set up some kind of periscopic arrangement with his wing-mirrors so he could watch me reclining there – an Ionian Mme Récamier – in unconscious abandon. Or at least that's what it looked like. Naturally I suppose I'd have been upset if a Turkish lorry-driver had ignored a sumptuous European voluptuary lolling and stretching so frustratingly close to his field of vision. He dropped me in a small village and offered to buy me some food before he went on to Muğla. I was aware, of course, that to accept would deepen my compromise; but I was also more than a little defiant, slightly triumphant after my solitary travels in Turkey, proud of my ability to radiate a sexual negativity while maintaining a friendly approachability (a distinction which in retrospect I don't think the Turks really appreciated). He bought me something called *tavük gogüsü* – lovely all those umlauts, don't you think? – a sort of gooey milk pudding made with chicken. If you can imagine, a sort of savoury sago. So I tried very hard to battle through it smiling bravely and spooning it down with artificial relish. He was stocky and muscular, dark and swarthy, with the kind of luxuriant moustache that drives you guys crazy; and a regular stubble which seemed oddly porous and filled with copious sweat. OK. Calm down. I watched him intently, trying to establish what sexual magnetism his kind of physique and fierce expression could exercise over you lot. I'm afraid, though, that women will always find that kind of animal obviousness, with its promise of insensitive abuse, extremely resistible. Combined, of course, with their well-known sexual ambiguity. So unlike the equivalent macho phenomenon in Western societies.

'I felt fraudulent, as if I was conducting some clinical experiment on a helpless laboratory rat with electrodes hanging out of his head. I just sat there appraising him, sizing him up – come on, don't be crude. He was so vulnerable, so boyish through his cruel Ottoman façade. Like a grave Benedictine novice hidden inside a steely Seljuk warrior. I was so interested in this ambiguousness that I could only stab limply at an olive and peck at the dry salted red mullet; and this too I felt must be a disappointment to someone from his world, used to simple appetites and pleasures. After establishing our tacit understanding that he stood no chance, that he'd never get to ravish me, he was courteous, even quite interesting. I had, as usual, been so patronizing that it seemed inconceivable that he could actually *know* anything. I believed him to be pure instinct, a simple construct of sensual appetites without any information or intellectual calibre. But he knew about the early predominance of the Ionian cities. He even knew about pre-Socratic philosophy. He said something like, "Here we invented the ideas that led to the atom-bomb and that substance came from water and returns to water." A better summary than you'd get out of a lot of Western students banging on about theoretical physics and rarefaction and cosmological mensuration. I liked him very much and felt guilty that I could only reject him sexually with such finality. Perhaps one overestimates the importance of that kind of rejection to people who are more *primitivo* than oneself. Maybe they find it just as easy to come to terms with as we do. Or rather as *I* do. It's so difficult, how can one *know*?

'He left me drinking *raqi* and watching the ants processing along a festering sluice. He'd pestered the bartender into giving me presents of baklava and pistachios, feeling it to be his duty to involve everyone in his own hospitality. Then he walked away towards his truck and I began to wish I could somehow make amends – alter my background and sexuality at will, demolish all the barricades I'd set up around myself and respond to him in the uncomplicated way he'd responded to me. But I'll never be able to be that sort of chameleon. And all I could think of was how he'd constituted yet another sexual stereotype for *you*; another Action Man permutation – oil-stained overalls, a sweaty tee-shirt, the infidel sweat oozing in the curly velvet hair under his armpits. I could almost sense your lascivious response, your desire to surrender to those atavistic embraces, your ability to project on to yourself the characteristics of a sexual model.

'Anyway, enough of the sleazorama. You're so *predictable*. It's only a literary construct, after all. What was happening – to the innocent viewer, at least – was that a slightly incongruous pair were having lunch together in a hot landscape. Venetia and Mehmet, who would never meet again. After he'd gone I felt lethargic and heavy. I hardly even listened to the barman's directions about how to get to the ruins. The heat was just crushing down on my head, my brain felt like scrambled eggs – melting, perhaps. You remember that bit in *Don Quixote* when he thinks his brains have melted because he's put on Mambrino's helmet full of curds? I could easily have reached the same extreme. The Turk was just reciting a formula, a litany, a vapid incantation. It had a meaning and could be acted upon; there was a direct transference between what he was saying and what I should do. But I was so overcome by my own deepening torpor that I could only think of him as oddly superfluous, not part of the *pattern* of that day, a kind of excrescence on my private awareness of things.

'I set off down the rocky slope, almost blinded by the white afternoon reflected light and having to focus on the dark-green cypresses that lay ahead. But even this didn't work. My vision was somehow trapped by the dazzling stones in my path. It was half the difficulty of negotiating the meandering path, half a compulsion deliberately to torment my own eyesight, to absorb the luminous glare without flinching. Perhaps I was trying to prove something to myself – that I was physically part of this alien place, that with all my overcrowded mental furniture I could still be an integral part of this aged and flinty solidity. The stones were all irregular and unyielding, so much so that at each step I felt my ankles being painfully twisted and wrenched from side to side. The plainness of the spectacle was entirely without relief. Occasionally I saw a lizard or a train of ants, vestigial movements on the static ground. Everything seemed ossified. Especially since the whole region was still inhabited by the dead reminders of Miletos's past as a bustling commercial port and intellectual centre, all silted up now in this foetid alluvial plain. It used to be so important in the Greek world. Do you know that when they put on a play in Athens called *The Fall of Miletos* after it'd been sacked by the Persians, the whole audience burst into tears and the dramatist was fined 1,000 drachmas for upsetting everyone so much? I felt what I always feel at classical sites: the danger of succumbing to an over-rich historical imagination, the error of those boring old dragons at Versailles, the misconception that describing the effects of auto-suggestion or bogus ESP can be remotely interesting. It's about as interesting as telling one's own dreams to anyone except a lover.

'But as I approached the site itself, I was overwhelmed by the sensation of having stumbled and shambled my arduous way towards something very special. It just wasn't like everything else, it didn't fit into the scheme of things. If I'd been a continuity girl, I'd probably have rushed around rearranging everything. The persistent whiteness had made me more than a little dizzy and I found it strangely difficult to transfer my vision to something less harsh. As I've said, there was something compulsive in that head-flattening blankness. All I'd distinguished so far had been the violent accidental outlines of millenarian rock, the ring of rather Scottish mountains. Gradually, though, I was encircled by the pastoral Arcadia, the smaller scale of the ancient city, like a sixteenth-century poet happening upon an artistocratic masque. Trees and bushes, little pools full of frogs, even a water-snake thrashing about hideously in a sort of antique cistern. Masses of water everywhere, with stepping-stones and strange recumbent shapes like turtles lurking under the surface. Odd really, when you remember that this city used to be a port till it was "silted up" and now it's five miles inland, and the big hill you can see – Lade, it's called – used to be an island! One of the things about Miletos is that unlike, say, Ephesus, it hasn't been tarted up and transformed into a kind of antiseptic film-set. Even Elizabeth Taylor's barge in *Cleopatra* looks more authentic than some of the reassembled and polished Lego at Ephesus. Miletos just lies there and broils *sans trêve*, abandoned and remote.

'There hardly seems to be any reason why such an immense metropolis should have inhabited such a desolate and unaccommodating space. There was an inscription – something like, "The senate and people of Miletos, the first city settled in Ionia and the mother of several other great cities in Egypt and the East and other parts of the world." How *could* it have been? All I saw was a smashed-up lion couchant, some piers of an aqueduct, scattered plinths, the outline of solid and substantial buildings which probably had had drainage and all sorts of mod cons. Everything was covered over with rubbish and thickets and the residue of the Ottoman village – with its vile mosquitoes – that had been plonked unceremoniously down in this fabled spot. Ozymandian slabs and pedestals, isolated hieratic columns planted at unfathomable street-junctions which now just looked like levelled right-angles. I saw lots of signs that it had been built on a grid-iron pattern, like an American city; in fact Hippodamus, who developed the idea of grids and planned the Piraeus, came from Miletos. There was a hideous Roman baths, dedicated to some old baggage called Faustina, all lumpy and solid beside the airy Greek stuff; but it was fun to make out the *frigidarium* and the *sudatorium* and to see that it had had *lecture-rooms*, for Chrissake; must have been like an English public school. The amphitheatre *was* exciting, with its huge marble front; but I was even more moved by the stench inside its vaults and the *vomitoria* and lots of bats flitting around like lost extras from Transylvania. And always the perspective of the receding sea, the cleft mountains extending farther and farther into the Aegean. I was so hot that I wanted to bathe my swollen feet in a pond; only the glimpse of that water-snake had made me wary – the last thing I needed was a slimy reptile wrapping itself around my marble calves. Yes, I can just hear you saying, "You'd have made a hopeless Minoan priestess, they had to *handle* snakes."

'Don't be idiotic. I wasn't even trying to reconstruct the past. I wish I had been; I envy people with a *real* sense of historical transference. But I was still firmly in the pedestrian present. And I *mean* pedestrian. My feet were running with sweat and my thighs felt distinctly overstrained. Just as if I'd been some tired housewife in a Luton shopping-precinct, I took off my shoes, recognizing what a hopelessly impractical choice they'd been. Suddenly I burst out laughing, remembering an episode in London when I'd been watching a seriously tacky strip-show in Macclesfield Street. A midget girl who looked like she'd come in on the bus from Ealing was standing clutching the side-curtain, wobbling slightly to a cracked record, wearing a garish lurex garage mechanic's overall and the most outrageous pair of corrective sandals. How could she have dreamed of maintaining the illusion of sexuality while wearing those shoes? Perhaps it was in fact peculiarly apt: they were a cryptic item of clothing to arouse mysterious erotic feelings in those tawdry men. Perhaps I was the only one who didn't get the point. Anyway, at Miletos it seemed very funny. And I enjoyed the fact that so simple a stimulus had triggered an extraordinary association of ideas which was unique to me. *Nobody* in the world could have united Miletos and Macclesfield Street. Ever. And with such rich visual detail. And then I remembered a bit in Ezra Pound:

> 'Conservatrix of Milésien'
> Habits of mind and feeling,
> Possibly. But in Ealing
> With the most banky-clerkly of Englishmen?

'It was *absolutely* exact, but, Christ, there *did* seem to be some kind of prophecy about it. So many points fitted. Maybe I was living out some imaginary coincidence, some incredible continuum which would soon drop one in the middle of another poem, helpless, gripped by someone else's dream. I wasn't too crazy about the "Conservatrix" bit, let me tell you, but let's not push the prophecy angle too hard.

'I'd bought my own shoes at the Fine Show salon at I. Magnin in San Francisco – you remember, it's like a 1950s hotel lobby – and I'd talked at great length to the assistant about the conflicting claims of fashion and personal idiosyncrasy – one of those inevitable *colloques* we get into in San Francisco. He made me feel like a *creative* dresser, someone whose unerring instinct anticipated the crowd, a new Queen of Chic who'd forced Cher to look to her Los Angeles laurels. How could he know that one day those shoes, so perfect for clattering along between North Beach restaurants, would torment my swollen feet with their pinching elegance? And remind me of a louche fascination with the London underworld, the Maltese flick-knives and overheated libidos underneath copies of the *Standard*?

'I sat in a heap on a pile of rubble which, for all I knew, might once have been the centre of the *agora*. I'd seen so many comparable sites – Pergamon, Sardis, Smyrna, Didyma, Priene – that I didn't feel the need to locate and identify everything from my *Baedeker*. The whole landscape had a feeling that was far more important than its constituent parts: an amorphous, numinous force. I'd read something about magic sects – S – E – C – T – S, darling – in the city, Gnostics with miracle-working amulets and something about an inscription which repeated the name "Miletos" seven times, talismans and things, the seven Greek vowels of "Jehovah", I can't really remember. That numerology you sometimes go on about. But there was something definitely eerie about the whole atmosphere. You could almost believe that all those mythological stories had taken place here, mortal women had given birth to monstrous, portent-laden abortions or mated with swans or showers of gold. It was so impossible to relate these decayed but resplendent ruins to the everyday activities and pressures of Milesian city life –

I thought of it somehow as a bit like London in the '60s – that I just gave up the mental effort, depeopling my mind and simply concentrating on the immediate accessibility of everything. The fluting of a single column became incredibly vivid. I looked for hours at fallen capitals, bits of friezes and veined marble. The fact that there was no one else there made it an infinitely private experience, as if I was spiritually set apart, reacquainting myself with the real canons of aesthetic form, uncluttered by all our flirtations with the baroque and all the travesties of true proportion. So much of our modern faddishness unthinkingly rejects the mathematical virtues – equilibrium, symmetrical volumes, the Golden Section, things like that – that it was extraordinary to rediscover suddenly their unchallengeability. Their obvious virtuosity. As if expressionism had never existed!'

(Jerome, as he read this part of Venetia's letter, groaned inwardly, but perhaps, even through his scepticism, he sensed that she was going to reveal something: the mystery of the Marabar Caves and Lord Jim's shrouded act of cowardice simultaneously discovered, the true history of Mrs Rochester, a *coup de théâtre* to make Venetia's wayward behaviour less opaque, more easily understood in some kind of continuum. But what? A sudden awareness of time? *Durée* and foreshortening? A momentary insight into a Coleridgean sublime? A snake-bite?)

'We should always remind ourselves of classical form. Our particular psychoses, romantic variants on solipsism and social alienation, are deformed and misshapen creatures, Fuseli monsters fed by Grand Guignol and the grotesque. If we could only see ourselves as sectionalized Leonardo anatomies, magnificent in our regular, volumetric proportions, equidistant one from another, equal in value and formal characteristics. Our age so concentrates on disequilibrium, asymmetry, on voluntary *dérèglement des sens* – all to achieve some elusive notional ideal of exceptionability, uniqueness, idiosyncrasy, unpredictability, the special insight. So what was so visionary about Baudelaire and his cronies? Most of what they saw was borrowed from Poe anyway. I'd rather read a treatise by Boileau any day.'

(Jerome felt his own artistic preferences – for Blake, John

171

Clare, Huysmans, Genet, Böcklin – to be under attack; and he fell to speculating about why Venetia should have embarked on this epistolary diatribe which, it was instantly clear, tended to falsify her own real views. Was the effort of recall so strong that she had actually recovered a lost identity? She seemed to be adopting extraordinarily contrasuggestible opinions.)

'What I most abhor is the modern absence of rules. Only classical antiquity – and its derivatives – understood the importance of formalized canons, the need for a purposive ideal, the enshrining of perfection in models like Zeuxis and Apelles who, for all their physical evanescence, remained as usable abstractions. I feel that it's much easier to understand art if we retain these points of reference, even if they do sometimes bring about questionable practices like plagiarism. The problem with modern aesthetics is that it's so subjective, a chaotic morass of idiosyncratic theory and practice, each artist his own critic, every man in his humour. We can't have any *a priori* criteria. Each time we're confronted by a new artist or movement, we're forced either to accept or to evolve for ourselves a whole new body of critical ideas to assess and understand them.

'At all events, those old Milesian relics seemed so canonical, so irrefutable, that I began to lament the complete fragmentation of experience which today's civilization prizes so highly. I realize that it's absurdly regressive and unrealistic to think like this; now that all those Goths and autodidacts have hurled down the temples of academicism, you have to be either crazy or very brave to try and re-erect them. But sitting in that archaeological decay, I felt depressed by my own isolation. And by the fact that that isolation was just a single unit in the whole modernist conspiracy, the conferring of autonomous categories on everything, whether they're morally evaluative or aesthetic or whatever. I thought initially that I should be getting all morose about the transience of mortality and human ambition – like that odious Lope de Vega fretting over his literary effusions at the ruins of Saguntum – but I knew that to feel that would be as artificial and second-hand as Lope's own elucubrations. This other feeling was so dominant, so ineluctable, that I was almost physically overwhelmed by my notions of order and formal rigour – even though all the buildings and statuary were in such disarray.

'I allowed these speculations to drift on in an uncontrolled stream, just like the river Meander near by. They have no resolution, the polarities are as fixed as Dionysian and Apollonian, Florestan against Eusebius, Sarastro against the Queen of the Night. It's rare for me, though, to feel on the side of the angels – *non Angli sed angeli* – because the ordered hierarchy of classical form finds no expression in my own life.

'Eventually my lethargy became less focused and I progressed – or rather regressed – into one of your cyclothymic torpors. I suppose the heat was very intense, and the contours of the buildings became like an evanescent mirage without any defining colours or framework. I became like an empty vessel, or an outcrop of the rocks, with little consciousness of what or where I was. I've always wondered what happened to Christ at the Transfiguration, what anyone there would actually have *seen*. I too was immobilized, lifted out of my normal self, become something other than my usual persona. Imagine my shock, then, when I realized that this intensely private experience was being invaded by another human being.

'I'd momentarily looked back towards the mountains, hardly even seeing their different dimensions and shadows. But my attention was suddenly seized by the image of a person on a donkey, carrying a parasol. It was all too Tiepolo for words. Something like Aunt Dot or Father Chantry-Pigg in the *Towers of Trebizond*. It would have made a fantastic murderous image in a Pasolini epic, the visitation of Retribution on a decayed capitalist Caesarea. If you'd seen it as ominous, that is, which I certainly did in my very special frame of mind. As the person approached, I became convinced that he was sent for a specific mission – a Vietnam seek and destroy – even if it was only aimed at dissipating my self-absorption.

'It was a woman, a large and erect woman, perched with the utmost delicacy of balance. Her movements, the donkey's faltering steps and the bobbing parasol were all in unison. The heat seemed to reduce the image to slow-motion and eliminated any spasmodic jerkiness it might have had. Like a stately imperial progress in a Tiepolo fresco; a look that Mae West might have aspired to with her oiled Schwarzenegger bearers. Or Hester Stanhope languidly perambulating towards a distant caravanserai. All the surrounding scenery had lost its force, as if some avant-garde film director had changed the relationship between foregound and inessential details – fuzzed out the hills. I watched transfixed, no other feeling or thought engaging my attention. Part of me wanted to cry out, to arrest the movement of the film and insert myself into it. But it was as if I had no motor reflexes, and I knew that the sound would die on my lips. She passed close beside me, although it seemed that she never registered my incongruous presence. Then, as she processed in front of me, she slowly turned her head and bowed, revealing a fluttering *mantilla* on her head. Nothing more, just a majestic inclination of the upper body. Like a Habsburg duenna condescending to an inconvenient emissary. I could have been a burnt-out church, a superannuated hoarding or a pile of shit for all the interest she showed. And then she passed onwards, no more than a fleeting spectre.

'What was extraordinary was the fact that her appearance managed to expel any effect of memory of my previous aesthetic crisis. It's only now, writing to you, that I've remembered it properly. Because at the time it just fizzled out. An odd effect, as if a riveting pageant in a Heidelberg street had so distracted a German idealist that he'd resolved to abandon for ever the single-minded search for the meaning of *Kunstgeschichte*. I suppose, in a sense, it fits into the pattern of both our lives – our willingness to allow our intelligence to be submerged, annihilated even, by erratic phenomena that we perceive at the most superficial level. Colours never seen before, physical perfection or deformity in a man or woman, ephemeral sounds that mean more to us than the whole history of Western music. We'll never be intellectuals. What do you think, darling?'

18

Jerome in Rig: Macho Picture

'They perceived that corporeal friends are spiritual enemies
They saw the Sexual Religion in its embryon Uncircumcision.'

Venetia fluttered around, a noisy and volatile servant,
helping him with the preparations for his sexual foray.
She had become accustomed to all the precise logistics
necessary to produce in him that temporary security which
was, in turn, necessary for definitive conquest. No Kutuzov
she, no victories despite herself, no lethargic dalliance with
Romanian paramours in the face of battle. All her energy
– and indeed her love for Jerome – was dedicated to the
elaborate and sanctifed ritual of bedecking: the leather
dalmatic, the denim alb of the ordained conqueror. Don
we now our gay apparel. Often Jerome had talked to
her about the unfathomable closeness of their lives, its
transcendence of sexual stereotypes and its evolution from
tentative amusement to Loctite ESP. One of the oddest
aspects, he felt, was that their love had intensified his
masculinity. Earlier, listening to the rapturous programme
music of the homosexual Saint-Saëns's *Rouet d'Omphale*,
he'd compared his affinity with Venetia to the curious
effect that Omphale had had on Hercules. Omphale, a
powerful Lydian queen, had received the super-hero as her
slave, fresh from his machismo-baring exploits (which had,
however, contained that disturbing ingredient of intelligent
resourcefulness which sadly detracted from the horny image
of dumb brutishness). Strangely, he had succumbed to an

exaggerated and theatrical effeminacy, happily spinning with Omphale's beauteous handmaidens and exchanging his exiguous lion's pelt for the gilded distaff and brocades of a Heliogabalan eunuch.

> His lion spoils the laughing Fair demands,
> And gives the distaff to his awkward hands.

By contrast, Venetia's enveloping femininity had strengthened Jerome's masculinity – at least within the unreal parameters set for it by the current version of homosexuality. But only cissies liked girls. She, while secretly wishing that he would soften his exterior and make the impossible leap back into apparent boyish vulnerability, had gradually come to terms with his present self-image: a surface identity which now seemed fixed and admitted of no clear future change. It had something to do with the labour-saving certainty of her role, her amused acceptance of the knowledge needed to prepare the strict inventory of his appearance. She ironed without creating creases, kept the amyl nitrite neatly displayed in the icebox (in order of expiry date), knew how to fold leather without causing cracks, felt instinctively the rightness of the white against the blue bandanna and moderated his tendency to overdo the ironmongery. He, in turn, had overcome his early misgivings about this aspect of their joint lives. Earlier, whenever he felt the schizoid uprush which forced him on to the streets, the repeated sin like a dog returning to its own vomit or a tongue relentlessly probing the site of a tooth-extraction, he'd felt also the need to incorporate that preparatory phase into the limits of his privacy, cutting at that stage the loose tentacles which connected him to the heterosexual world. Now, however, Venetia had thrust herself even into this sanctum and he positively encouraged her voluble and deft participation. She was able to imagine herself backstage at La Scala knowledgeably discussing Bellini and laying out the slashed doublet and capacious codpiece of an operatic megatenor; while he enjoyed the sensation of complicity – something like reform-school desperados planning an anti-authoritarian rebellion, a breakout from some serried Dickensian dormitory.

She gratuitously pressed his abdominal wall of muscle and then withdrew her hands, knowing that he knew that she knew that she could never achieve such smooth surface-tension. He never used his physical superiority as ammunition against her; but it was important to her morale to avoid recognition of it. Along with everybody else who saw him, he adored the features of his peerless body. Only his smooth knees gave him cause for concern, since he had read in a Catholic novel that bald knees denoted cowardice.

It was like the exaggerated sessions Eugene Onegin squandered in preparing himself each night:

> Three hours at least he spent, before
> He issued from the closet door [how prophetic!]
> Resembling Venus, when she passes
> To join the masquers and assume,
> (That giddy goddess) male costume.

'My intuition tells me you won't be able to carry off the full leather tonight. You seem a little insecure. Let's get you into something which stays within the confines of masculinity and yet allows your intelligent sensitivity to shine through.'

'Oh, Christ!'

'I suppose there's a danger that that'll fix you up with someone too young; but I *so* like you in the role of the protective *slightly* older man' (important, that 'slightly', as she knew from experience). 'You know how those twenty-two-year-olds like to be told things, with their big eyes widening in amazement at the sheer breadth of your life. You remember that cute little French soldier from Charleville, Mezières? You can lift them out of their dim little lives, carry them off on a white stallion, sweep them off their sneakers with exotic tales of the *demi-monde*. Your velvet larynx is better even than a meal-ticket.'

'That's just it, Venetia, that's exactly the role I least like to play. Of course it works, but it makes you so conscious that no one else is acting or talking in the same way. Our formalized narrative, fully formed sentences, adverbs everywhere, subordinate clauses. I *long* to chatter on freely in their fractured *lingua franca*, their lightning associations of ideas and their phenomenal timing, all the electrifying drivel. It's all a problem of language acquisition; and the more expert you are as a linguistician, the less able you are to project yourself into another linguistic register. Imagine overhearing what I've just said in the Ramrod. Oh my God!'

He desultorily fingered some wayward hairs in his moustache. If only, if only. His adventurous life was peculiarly liable to this reaction. If only I could be Franco Nero for a day, if only I could wear a harness with aplomb, if only I looked like that, if only I could reverse time, if only I could *clean up my act*, if only . . .

'What a dilemma.' She was kneeling, rolling neat joints *à l'anglaise*. 'What about taking Louis back to Europe with us and setting up an immersion course in street talk for over-educated gays? He'd be a fabulous instructor, only I don't think anyone would concentrate on what he was saying. Do you think his kind of charisma survives thirty?'

'I should care. At least I never possessed it, so I don't have to mourn its passing.' The beginnings of a pout formed on his prodigal mouth and edged into the seriously disagreeable as her large breasts surfaced in front of him.

'Here, take this.'

Theirs was a strange courtship. She consolidated her position by servilely bedecking his body in preparation for the perpetual tournament in which he proved his manhood. He retreated from involvement with his vanquished paladins to lie in her Provençal embrace, a paradigm for a neo-*chevalieresque* society. But one in which they both knew there were too many cracks and interstices.

'I *love* the feel and smell of clean 501s,' she murmured, her polymorphosexual fingers buttoning his crotch from behind. He really did have the cutest ass. Not that she lusted after it in him, but she sure wanted it for herself. She helped him on with his laced workboots, biting back her disapproval but mollified by the softness of his airy white socks. She herself liked a wide variety of textures – moiré, shagreen, shantung, matelassé, lute-string, georgette, crêpe. How unlike the nineteenth-century composer Vaucorbeil, who held velvet in such horror that he suffered paroxysms of anxiety when invited somewhere for the first time, terrified that the dining-chairs might be upholstered in the hateful material. Venetia's passion was for the extravagance of natural fibres rendered unnatural – a striving for the liquefaction of her clothes – but she acknowledged that she must always compromise with Jerome's prescribed range.

Jerome bit back his preference for dirty 501s. He was eating a heavily mayonnaised tuna and alfalfa sandwich, holding it hugely with both hands in his adopted American style. In between mouthfuls he put the sandwich down and picked up the slender joint to feed his head. 'I love you very much, Venetia,' he found himself saying, conscious that everything they were doing implied the contrary. 'You're very special. It's so incredibly lucky you're not a man. If you were, all your qualities of intuition, sympathy, intelligence and honesty would make me run a mile. While, in you, I love them.'

Cruel hypocrisy unlike the lovely delusions of Beulah! But he could no longer prolong his address while his appearance gradually grew in conflict with it. Dejanira cloaking Hercules in the poisoned tunic of Nessus, cladding him in alienation, miscalculating so poignantly her role as saviour of their marriage, effectively sending him deeper into the predatory vortex of psychosis. Out there were just too many Ioles, any one of whom could destroy their love with a flounce of their fatigues.

'*Pecca fortiter*,' she murmured as she kissed him goodbye, casting down her gaze. Her hand fell limply from his shoulder.

Walking down 11th Street, he played the eternal game. Pass, dismiss, pass, dismiss, pass, be dismissed. Stop, register, fix with acid stare. Lose patience. Back three steps, recover morale. Self-assert, self-project, self-efface, self-destruct. He walked past a clinched couple, leather Siamese twins stinking of urine. Glistening totem-poles butt-buttressed Ringold Street, overworked musculatures strained for release from their emotional constriction. The *de rigueur* architectural decay, manufacturing rubble, desolated car-lots and smitten Hopperesque diners. The nearness of the docks a constant reminder of insecurity and transience. Spleen and garages.

Then the spike. He found himself in the middle of a seventeenth-century allegory, a market-place of moral errors in which he and, he suspected, many others acted dumb, took more care to conceal their wisdom than their folly.

There was little to relieve the darkness. Only the brief flare of lighters or the low spark of a cleated engineer's boot as it impatiently stomped and struck the kerb.

Creosote, whose source you could probably locate in the bonded crevices of the telegraph poles, fanned into air already maritime with tow and sea-pitch, the exhalations of hawsers, the strong black oil that seeped over cranes and winches. But these intimations of the sea were blocked off by the immediate landlocked squares of masonry like mere spaces bonded by brick and cement with their air of desertion and inhumanity. Long time-lapses defined the uneventful rhythm of the area: the silences between the tinkling bells of a mission priest carrying forth the viaticum; the funereal, fog-muffled booming as ships warned of approach; the friction of workman's denim as the waiting, vigilant wall-leaners changed position, their expectant asses tiring of muscular tension; a drunk lurching out of a café, roaring imprecations, damning America, his wife and America's wife, sick from the grease and fat that sat immiscibly among the stomach fluids screaming out for the dubious pacification of alcohol. And the light gleamed lazily with a viscous slowness on the few reflective liquids and surfaces among the dark masses: on hubcaps and spilt battery-acid, the rainbow slick from leaking oil-tanks.

Then there was the mortifying Babel, the cryptic Villon-cant that so eluded him; the distancing safety-curtains which could always keep him on the European side of the proscenium. How could all those words come out of all those American heads? Shouldn't they just be brash and dumb? It needed clear-sighted, straight-talking Sam periodically to remind him of the sense of identity gay Americans found in self-parody, the artificial pretence of carnival, the exchanges of descriptive flights of language, sit-com transcripts and stichomythia, communication that transcended the sex-first, understanding-later barrier. He thought of Borges's reminder that all language is an alphabet of symbols whose use presupposes a past shared by all the other interlocutors. No wonder it wasn't making sense.

Two guys stood stiffly beside each other, occasionally fondling an ass or a shoulder, their eyes glazing over with boredom. Probably two new lovers; next day they would have had bad sex and never see each other again.

A huge studded black gauntlet appeared on his own shoulder and began to stroke his scapular. Turning round, he confronted the dark colossus face belonging to the fist. Good tight skin, a friendly cruel glare, but there was a slight whiff of antiseptic to cancel out the aphrodisiac leather and *completely* disqualify the suitor. Jerome smiled shyly, almost apologetically, as if it was somehow his fault, and walked away.

His meeting with Syreeta, Most Feared Bitch of Upper Market, had emphatically shown how minimal were his chances in the loud-mouthed colossal-steamroller drive-everything-before-you stakes. Phew! Had he *crumpled*! Anyway, a lot of gays went overboard for shyness, especially in an Englishman. What was it that Seattle Corpus Christi stevedore had said? They just *loved* to discover the abandoned sexuality and chaotic values which underlay the surface of proper British rectitude. Rectitude schmectitude, he didn't even have that. Oh dear, Charlus and Jupien would never have gone through this, at least their torture was physical, not linguistic. His thoughts wandered to the eighteenth-century Duke of Queensberry, just leaning his worm-eaten body against a balcony in Piccadilly and summoning stray whores with contemptuously thrown sixpences. What an enviable *reductio ad absurdum* of the elaborate courtship ritual he was at present engaged in!

The grass helped, of course, in spite of those rumbling National Institutes of Health warnings about its interference with oral communication. Oral what? But he would first exploit his looks in this temple of looksism; his attitude meticulously composed for maximum Pearl Harbor impact.

Two men beside him stood unsmiling and avoiding

one another's gaze as they twiddled with each other's nipples, network roulette, like sedate housewives looking for Hilversum on a radio dial. How and when *was* it that tits had been rehabilitated from their heterosexual ghetto to become erogenous zone *numero uno*? No one even mentioned them before 1978. The pair broke off momentarily for a slug of beer and some bantering dialogue, then reverted to the serious pectoral-play, progressing into gradual crotch-massage, albeit sensitively bypassing their beer guts en route. Their sexual gestures were rigidly codified, divorced from recognition of each other's diverse personality. All they had was a kind of frowning, concerned fraternalism, like fundamentalists waltzing at a Salt Lake City *thé dansant*. But these ones were pretty nice, Jerome thought, '*Pulchra sunt ubera quae pendula supereminent et tument.*'

Mysterious Americana, pre-Columbian codices beyond all comprehension. Perhaps here was the elusive source of all human language, the decipherment of Linear B, the code laid bare, the fount of knowledge among these winking Hypocrites. Then little Samuel, shyly catching and avoiding Jerome's glance, there and not there, pick up and turn down ad lib, who cares? *I do, but I'm fucked if I'm gonna show it.* Jerome toyed with his options and, in a supreme Lytton Strachey gesture, interposed his body between Sam's and an aspiring soldier-consort. *Where was the innocence, where the submerged truth? Man in the Resurrection changes his Sexual Garments at will/Every Harlot was once a Virgin, every Criminal an Infant Love.*

'Jerome, you don't seem to understand, it's terrible, it's all gonna end in the destruction of the world, that crazy cowboy in the White House, he's gonna engineer the end of everything, there's no point in us even being alive now, how can we be *doing* this to ourselves?'

The chiliastic terror was probably just a metaphor for sexual misery. Or so, at least, Jerome explained it to himself, so circumscribed was his own life in its routine, so shielded from political concern in its sexual straitjacket. Half of him wanted to comfort the boy while the other half backed away in fear from these self-revelatory arcana. Sam's eyes had the steady brown limpidity of a new-born calf's, and no aspect of his countenance betrayed the searing exploitation to which he had repeatedly and masochistically exposed himself.

'I saw this movie on TV. It started with a real ordinary class in school then the teacher disappeared and a woman came in in a kind of military uniform. She just took over the class and it was incredible, you could *see* her twisting the minds of those kids and they were just like you and me – well me, maybe. She made them talk about their allegiance to the flag and question all their beliefs, it was like brain-washing but real subtle. You see, there'd been an invasion of America and she was a Russian agent trained to do this kind of thing to the new generation.'

'Undermining their morale?' asked Jerome, encouragingly.

'Yeah, that's right. But she did it so efficiently, it even made me think about the time I swore allegiance. I knew the words backwards, but I never even thought about what they meant. It was like saying Hail Marys. And this movie made me see how it was all false, that nobody could really have any beliefs any more. Maybe the whole movie was beamed in from Moscow and there were weird kinds of thought-control in the rays. Nothing seems certain any longer, I'm just so confused by everything.'

Sam had been a prostitute since he was fourteen and had serviced the city and naval dockyards of San Diego. The first time Jerome met him, Sam had come over and said: 'Hi, I'm Sam, I'd like to know you.' And pointing to a beautiful girl sitting at the bar, he added, 'I'd like you to meet my sister too. She used to be my brother.' Jerome tried to single out the remaining male features of Sam's sister while Sam, describing the queues of grimy stokers, smelling of pitch and sweat, who had clamoured for his mercenary favours, sighed and said, 'One can get real tired of sailors.' Jerome said he would have to think about that one. Sam, impressed, suggested a three-way.

Jerome thought of Sam's ancestors serenely sowing and reaping on a Sicilian hillside, untroubled by these perplexing Transamericana. He was overcome with compassion, but felt so constrained by the barriers between them that he was unable to articulate anything. Moreover, he was obliged to maintain some kind of sexual persona (and would have gone to the moon to find out what it was). He just seized the boy protectively and hoped he'd intuitively sense the depth of his co-feeling.

'Sometimes I just go to bed and lay there, I can't go out. It's so weird being in this bar with you, I can't explain, but I was thinking to myself: "This is Hell" – I have this very real picture of the Devil, a strong, strong image. Technicolor. But then you being there made me feel it was all right. I can't understand why we keep coming back. I suppose it's a kind of security, even though it's dangerous, destructive, terrible. All dark, like a womb. What do you think Hell and the Devil are like?'

'I think maybe the Devil's a bit like Nancy Reagan or some fat old queen, all bitter and raddled and loving it when we get all fucked up and don't know what we're doing. I guess all the pictures we have of him are just like convenient symbols to help us make sense of an abstract idea.'

'Yeah, I can't take all that Garden of Eden stuff. But sometimes I think that Paradise was gay. You know, before Eve got there. God created man in his own image, right, so he'd have to be perfect? Then along came woman, the snake, all those nasty things.' Sam gulped excitedly at a Budweiser, then stared moodily at the pool-table, a James Dean *sans le savoir*.

The dialogue had distressed Jerome. He longed for the boy to get it right, to cancel out these dark and random mouthings and replace them with exact, imaginative words: '*sed tandem dic verbo, et sanabitur anima mea*'.

With Sam, Jerome felt overwhelmed by the inefficacy of all the standardized sexual overtures. Not only was the boy's projection of his fears too insistent to allow for a posture of disinterested neutrality, but Jerome believed himself so secure in the disproportion between Sam's preparedness to lay himself down the line and his own toying affection that he felt compelled to introduce himself into the other's malaise. He could not profane Sam's *horror vacui*.

In some ways he felt better, perhaps partly through *Schadenfreude*. But two things were foremost in his mind: a genuine rush of fellow-feeling (transcending his confusion

184

at Sam's train of thought) and a delight in the prospect of impelling security towards him by force of sexual domination. Sadism as compassion, strength through weakness. He was, as so often, quite close to loving. If Sam had slashed his wrists, he would have adored him. Come live with me and be my love. Hey nonny, nonny no! Or rather, get the fuck out, this is getting heavy.

'What right did my parents have to bring me into this goddam awful world? I didn't ask to be born. They must have been really fucked up to want someone to live in this pit. I reckon they really got off on the idea of tormenting me, putting me in the firing-line. I guess they'd only really be happy if I was a corpse in some foxhole in Vietnam. At least that way they wouldn't have to face the truth about me.'

'Surely all parents only want their children to be happy?' said Jerome without conviction, nervous about the resurgent paranoia and aware he'd done little to stifle it. Yet he felt that he could manipulate the boy's despair to his own advantage. This barrage was just a little bit too like a psychotherapy session, and he'd long since abandoned his role as sympathetic counsellor to the inadequate. That – a long phase of his early adulthood – had led to too much living by proxy, too easy a deflection of his critical gaze from his own neuroses (though it had been a role in which he had, by all accounts, really excelled). But in a determined effort to exorcize his passivity, to accelerate his delayed entry into adulthood, he had contrived to become brusque and impatient and allow his eyes and attentions to become cold and wander from any supplicant, to become an abrasive carborundum from which the weak shrank apprehensively. Now, confronted by this *enfant maudit*, he had allowed Sam's insidious helplessness to penetrate to his old malleable soft-centre, and was finding the long-dormant responsiveness upsetting. It meant that his adoptive personae were no longer watertight, that they could not be diluted and reconstituted at will – and that that will was not his own.

'I really like you, Jerome. In fact I love you. But, Jesus, we both know that you're using me. You're as weak as I am, only you keep it all hidden behind your tight British face. You're just a big baby, you never learnt anything. And you're totally insecure, that's why you cling to that fish of yours. You use your freedom so's to carry on being like a teenager, just hanging out. What a fucking fraud.'

All of which had such crystalline truthfulness that Jerome felt grimly chastened. Could his whole performance be reduced to this skeletal Stanislaus Ryan subplot?

'Sometimes it frightens me, Sam, just to see how much you understand; how you never get confused by any of the bullshit. You make me see things that I'd only dimly understood. My mind's like a muddy pond beside yours.'

'That makes me feel good. You're an innerleckchul and I can make you think.'

Jerome was conscious that they shouldn't be talking like this. He was losing points both to Sam and to the big-league battleships cruising near by. He resolved to move Sam away from the combat zone and lay siege to his solitude.

'It's kind of strange, our relationship. But that doesn't mean I want to mess you up.'

Soon they went home. Sam's room contained a small bed with rumpled, greyish sheets, a set of weightlifting equipment, a shoal of pornography and several photographs of naked men carrying outsize accessories like chain-saws and pneumatic drills. In the corner stood a vase of dying lilies. Jerome fistfucked Sam until he lost consciousness and Jerome got scared.

19

Adelaida

One of Adelaida's earliest memories was of a visit to the Murillos in the Capuchin church of her native Cádiz. Perhaps her unchildlike revulsion against their Italianate sentimentality, perhaps the influence of the rampantly phallic topography of the city – which she was later to experience again in San Francisco, both cities being built like ulcerations on a *glans penis* – sowed the seeds of her later anti-natural personality. She had walked though the motions of a Spanish childhood and adolescence like a spectre at Walpurgisnacht. Always clever, she dismissed her own achievements as immaterial while retaining a clear sense of her intellectual and moral superiority. She had had a relationship with a well-born *rejoneador* – he wore a poignant pigtail in his patent-leather hair – until her fiery androgyny undermined his self-esteem and toppled him from his elegant seat. She had stood rigidly, expelling sparks of blazing fury at the overdressed pilgrims transfixed before the oxen bowing at the shrine of Our Lady in the marshlands of El Rocío. A spiritual chasm had opened between her and the superstitious outrages of those naïve compatriots as they surged forward through the iron railings to wrest the Virgin from her sanctuary and shoulder her high through their own mêlée in a movement suggestive more of desecration than of celebration. A Mother Superior had wrestled with her beneath an impassive Zurbarán of quinces and pomegranates as Adelaida cried out to Heaven for vengeance.

At this early stage of her life, she was inclined to understand her nonconformism merely as a *casus extremus* of the normal kicking against the pricks. She read only the plays of Calderón and applauded the saints and the criminals, the rapists and the mass-murderesses, the anchorites and the persecutors, for their ardent cleaving to moral extremism. But she could never understand the force of the perennial Eucharist which could placate their tormented souls and reconcile them to Christ. Her father, a courteous and pacific admiral, once discovered her examining her breasts for the miraculous imprint of the Cross; she sat weeping, yet full of paradoxical restraint, sure of her exclusion from the redemptive power of grace. His confused, blustering reassurances made her throw up as she twisted and squirmed in his awkward naval embrace, staining his uniform with dark vomit. Later that day, she had left Cádiz and travelled to Seville.

The hot plain with its limitless vineyards and huge water-ducts and flumes had seemed as featureless as her blanked-out mind. The bus drove through the shimmering humidity past cardboard cut-out bulls and biblical olive trees towards the foetid city. She was conscious only of the importance of movement and unconstricted space. Nothing happened to her. But as they approached the outskirts of Seville, an elderly woman next to her took out some holy pictures and, shuffling them like a tarot pack, passed them surreptitiously into Adelaida's unwilling hands. The woman murmured appreciatively at the anguished contortions of the Crucifixion.

'See here the blood that pours from His wounds. And here the pricking of the Crown of Thorns. His forehead bathed in the sweat of fear, the eyes that sweep towards Heaven. And these His limbs writhing as He gradually suffocates, His head falls into the hollow of his neck. Can't you feel the agony as He shifts His weight from limb to limb, the nails ripping through His hands, blood gushing and mingling with the dirt and sweat, all the organs inside crushed together, falling into a mangled heap like offal on a butcher's slab? So much pain, such despair, abandoned, killed, tormented by the cruel deicides.'

But the old woman met with no reaction from the iron-masked refugee.

Adelaida went to a poor quarter of the city near the Macarena. As she passed the church, she recalled how the image of Our Lady inside had been created Captain-General of the Nationalist forces during the Civil War. Mechanically she laid out her exiguous belongings in a bare and airless room. It contained nothing but a bed, a table, a print of St Justin and St Rufina and a single coat-hanger as emphatically apparent as a single tooth in a dental desert. This had the curious design of Spanish hangers, a long-stemmed handle fixed under the usual arc. Adelaida lay down, her mind destitute of sensation and memory.

The sight, however, of the coat-hanger began to disturb her complacency. It seemed as inexorably *there* as the claustrophobic streets of Cádiz now were not. As she focused her beautiful eyes on its contours, it began to advance and retreat like the Holy Grail before the postulants of Montserrat. She became accustomed to its erratic waxing and waning; and its shape became less well-defined, seeming progressively to mould itself into the iconographic symbols of Christianity. The Greek *tau* became the blood-stained limbs of Christ Himself, became the ithyphallic fetish, became the serpentine figure of the Saviour. Her religious despair had made her the victim of bombardment by all those sacramental props alienating her from God and from herself. Finally her own innate violence imprinted itself on to the image and it hung static and hard-edged in the unmistakable form of a bloodied pick-axe. Her passive reverie turned into a murderous Via Crucis, each Station of the Cross marked by a suspended weapon of lead. A swelling diapason from the *Seven Last Words on the Cross* filled her drained head and then, as suddenly, was silenced. The axe was all axes, she Judith the slayer of Holofernes, Jael driving a nail through Sisera's temple, Charlotte Corday bloodying the bath-water of Marat, a Red hit-girl laughingly shooting the Bishop of Jaen in a swamp outside Madrid. Her destiny could no longer be in doubt.

This extraordinary event could not but scar her deviant

mind. It might have created an indiscriminate murderess had not her later political alignment concentrated her death-dealing compulsion into something which at least made sense to the modern world. Her enforced solitude in Madrid allowed her to generate a strangely revisionist attitude towards her adolescent certainties. All those aspects of Francoist totalitarianism which had seemed to her least tenable, most constraining, now opened out like immense glittering boulevards of enlightenment. Extrapolating from her poor father's liberal tolerance of her venomous rebellion (her father a sad pelican pecking his own breast to succour an asp with his blood), she came to see in his withdrawal of authority the cause of her floundering in the seas of bad faith. Where he should have been navigating he cast her adrift. The raft she now clung to had the shape of an axe; and she allowed her gratitude for its rescue to direct her into the outer limits of political terror. Unable to resolve her religious crisis, she determined with the full force of her devastating candour that God had abandoned her.

'I became like an animal,' she said in a rare moment of self-revelation to Lorenzo. 'It was as if I had no possibility but to kill. I have no compassion because I cannot understand the feelings of all humanity from which God has set me apart. He made me as I am as certainly as if He had been the Devil.'

That was as much as she could say. The power of sustained speech had slipped out of her mind. Furthermore, she had an almost superstitious fear of giving Lorenzo power over her. The more she uncovered, the more he would understand and so be able to out-manoeuvre her. The peculiar thing was that her runic articulation found no corresponding compensation in her brain. It, too, had been vacated. Suppression of speech had entailed suppression of thought. Only a fanatical certainty was still in residence.

When she visited London, she used this taciturnity to foil the many assaults on her virginity. She had, in effect, already lost it deliberately, in Vicenza, in a slavish attempt to accelerate her womanhood. The compliant victim had been unknown to her until the night of sexual consummation. She had bled and bitten back the first tears she could remember since childhood. Afterwards, London allowed her to obliterate the bitter experience in the dark embrace of its anonymity. There she had no history, no cultural past, and her life was entirely linear. She learnt about detonating mechanisms and timing devices, contraception and the psychoses of Mother Ireland, weapon assembly and the limits of democracy, the lives of shopgirls and the errors of anarcho-syndicalism. As her thought-processes became reactivated, she saw that her mind had a unique capacity for sifting out in advance any material which would not serve its purpose. (It was this ability which caused her to graduate, two years later, from Stanford *summa cum laude* in computer sciences.) Single-minded and technically brilliant, she'd emanated a lethal expertise in the rank, bald-plushed niches of Kilburn bars. While absorbing the details of flawed conspiracies and textbook ideas on infiltration, she remained silent and aloof, able simultaneously to radiate dependability as an ideologue and a kind of pseudomonoglot apartness.

She had scarcely been able to visit San Francisco during her course at Stanford. Inured as she was to evidence that she could only discount, she found it intolerable that this metropolis should so dedicate itself to a loose-limbed libertarianism. So she remained at Palo Alto until the swelling in her womb became a kicking and a prompting of her conscience. The arrangement with Venetia for the child's future occurred to her with such devastating clarity that she surprised even herself at the lack of thought she devoted to it.

Her release from David left her unscarred, her only concern being with the unsound political confusion of his adoptive mother. She acted subsequently as if her womb was extinct and all her secondary sexual characteristics neutered. She felt no lasciviousness. Her libido had been exorcized. It was calamitous, therefore, that her consorting with fascist compatriots brought her into the orbit of Lorenzo Urquijo's physical perfection. In a whitewashed room deep inside an Ávila *finca*, they had met and talked without humour about many things, while outside the Falangist cohorts abandoned themselves to a rustic bullfight with all the innocence of Goya's *peleles*. The gleaming sclerotics of Lorenzo's violet-irised eyes had outdazzled even the blinding walls, and she had the sensation of sloughing all her bitter sorrow in his angelic presence. He seemed to her like a Giordano archangel injected with testosterone, a creature as distanced from her perception of feminine manhood as it was possible to be. So ingrained were her habits of self-repression that she was surprisingly able to sustain their fervent conversation. But she was all the time conscious of a resurgent wildfire that threatened to transform her glacial exterior. Later she allowed Lorenzo to visit her in her conventual basement in Atocha where he seduced her with inhuman violence. She was unable to release his scissoring thighs from her own molten limbs. Their orgasm was like the rictus of death. And still she tried to divorce her mission from her sexuality.

20

Song of Innocence 2

His body slumped low in a sofa, Jerome was reading aloud to David, who sat beside him attentively, as upright and formal in posture as Jerome was slovenly. The child drank in the magic words which meant nothing to him.

'Once upon a time there was a king and queen who had an only daughter. Her beauty, her sweet temper, and her wit, which were incomparable, caused them to name her Gracieuse. She was the sole joy of her mother, who sent her every day a beautiful new dress, either of gold brocade, or of velvet, or of satin. She was always magnificently attired, without being in the least proud, or vain of her fine clothes. She passed the morning in the company of learned persons, who taught her all sorts of sciences, and in the afternoon she worked beside the queen. At luncheon time they served up to her basins full of sugar-plums, and more than twenty pots of preserves; so that she was universally considered the happiest princess in the world!

'There was in this same court an exceedingly rich old maid, called the Duchess Grognon, who was horrible in every respect. Her hair was as red as fire, her face of an alarming size, covered with pimples; she had but one blear eye left, and her mouth was so large you would have said she could eat everybody up, only, as she had not teeth, people were not afraid of it; she had a hump before and behind, and limped with both legs. Such monsters envy all handsome persons, and consequently she hated Gracieuse mortally, and retired from court to avoid hearing her praises. She took up her abode in a neighbouring *château* that belonged to her, and when anyone who paid her a visit spoke of the perfections of the princess, she would scream out in a rage, "It is false! It is false! She is not charming! I have more beauty in my little finger than she has in her whole body!"'

Jerome invested his reading with arch climaxes so as to stress the story's truthfulness and the resemblance it bore to the vicissitudes and over-simplifications of life as he himself conceived it: the division of the world into immiscible groups, the huge distortion of assets and defects, the impotent petulance voiced by the bad and the weak in the absence of more constructive remedies (a little like his own when he was periodically subject to a spiritual equivalent of Grognon's turpitude). What a story, he was thinking, what moral finesse, what élan!

He was interrupted by David's familiar squeak. 'Jerome bear, big,' he said. 'Hump.' That seemed to have been the only word he'd picked up on. He said it again, tailing off into a long, breathy, super-plosive 'p' at the end. While his mouth remained open, rounded with the energy expended on the consonant, he leant upwards to stare into Jerome's face. His childish flabbiness seemed now tautened as if he were expecting something to happen, some leap of the story out of the bland confines of its pages, some re-enactment of its irreality in front of them.

In the face of this distraction, undercut by David's turning from docility into interrogation, Jerome wavered between a firm resolution to continue the reading and an instinctual sympathy with the physicality of the child's reaction. Perhaps it was right to break off the narrative and expect it to go on in some different way, independent of the dry volume in which it was trapped, closer somehow to the shape of the room and its empty spaces where princesses and monstrosities might caper and metamorphose at will. He himself sensed that there was something wrong about the cramming of so much rich animation into a small buckram thing which gave off no emanation, no clue to the myriad ramifications it held within. And yet the story would have no meaning outside itself; all the formalism of the narrative depended on squeezing it into its conventions. He *knew* what Gracieuse and Grognon were, *who* they were, in a way he would never know who he and Venetia were.

'Bang goes the book,' he said as he shut it with some violence. 'I expect Grognon does something really horrid to Gracieuse. Cuts off her tits, maybe.'

David was busy now anyway, and couldn't care less. He'd got up off the sofa and was squatting down, building a kind of ziggurat of toy American cars. A huge Oldsmobile formed the base to a pyramid triangle of lesser Mustangs and Fords crowned with a Dinky Morris Minor Jerome had brought from home. He then carefully placed a stray geodesic dome over the whole confection so that it looked like an exhibit of immense importance, an emblem, perhaps, of the crisis at General Motors or an indictment of the gas-guzzler. His ability to switch centuries was really mercurial.

21

Work

Venetia leant disconsolately over the parapet at the summit of Broadway, encompassing the titanic view of the downtown area with her bleak, vitreous gaze. On rising she had blearily slalomed through piles of discarded clothes towards the theatrical mirror whose pitiless bulbs she knew could never extenuate the increasingly unpalatable truth. It was one of those days when she looked at her reflection and saw only a shapeless object like a burst mattress. She was getting old. Each day the cutaneous elasticity sagged only to be replaced by an outpressing, semolina-like bulk. This time, this grey morning, her perennial concern with fugitive time and the ravages of her once translucent skin was overlaid with a deeper, more visceral malaise. She became almost tearful, until she remembered the dire graffiti: 'Fat Girls Blubber a lot.' She felt, *ça allait sans dire*, like a gargantuan coelacanth; but she was also overwhelmed by one of those hollow depressions which, after reading *War and Peace*, she had come to recognize as symptoms of the Vera Rostova syndrome. An awareness that during certain limited (she hoped) periods everything she said or did, while being perfectly acceptable in itself – unupsetting, bland even – would make those around her curiously uncomfortable, disturbing either their pools of complacency or their peaks of elation. Not embarrassing or rude; just disquietingly redundant, like a plastic pineapple ice-bucket. And the corollary always loomed achingly monolithic. She would never to be able to exorcize this sporadic dimness, never glitter and coruscate, never have recourse to the dazzling Princess Helene Kuragina alternative – the presentation of self as a supremely physical creature, a presence reduced to an emblematic pair of marmorial shoulders. Shoulders which could subjugate the most hardboiled adversary. No salon would ever be orchestrated by Venetia's lumpy contours; no Nevsky Prospekt would defrost at her scorching advance; no meteoric diplomat would lose sleep over her millenarian calves.

The familiar solution swam irresistibly into her cross mind. Surely she could compromise with marriage to a desiccated intellectual and resign herself to a matrimonial life of ashen Ciceronian asides? A stability punctuated only by the pedantry of some latter-day Casaubon? Would it really be such a sacrifice? Like the colossal buildings clustered around the Transamerica Pyramid, their apices lost in the enveloping Pacific fog, she could perhaps afford to lose a portion of herself, sublimate her higher but misdirected aspirations to the safe nebula of disappointment and alleviate her distress in ordinariness?

'Jane, Jane, tall as a crane, the morning light creaks down again.' The line, which lived always at the back of her head without ever becoming intelligible, swam to the front, the line from Edith Sitwell, the Plantagenet Byzantine Czarina of Moscow Road.

A Chinese family straggled irritatingly up the steep slope from Taylor Street, noisily parading their ethnic malabsorption and jettisoning firecrackers in their wake. The windows around all shone darkly with monotonous encumbrances of yuccas and succulents: that inescapability of design which no one in San Francisco seemed to know how to change or better. There was a dryish flailing of viridian leaves as though before a cyclone. On the distant Bay Bridge an automobile accident attracted a noiseless flock of sirens and lights. The cracks in the parapet were like a corpse's hair. Gradually the lowering fog turned to a drizzly veil which formed barely perceptible droplets on her violet plastic mac and the emerald perspex sunglasses she'd put on in a vain attempt to alter her mood and sequester the spectre of Vera Rostova.

Few of her efforts to assume a more satisfying persona through changing her clothes bore any fruit. They just left her with a raging civil war between her inner and outer selves. If only she were a gay man, permanently equipped with all-weather, all-mood, all-lover contingencies; the battleship-grey pixie-hood artfully thrust out from under the sage-green parachute jacket in case of rain or the momentary need to pass unrecognized. The leather that was either practical or a sadistic signal, the running-shoes that got you away. This jealousy was deeper than it sometimes seemed. She could never fully accept her informed admiration for homosexuals, based as it was on something far more complex than the reiterated – and enraging – accusation she heard of penis-envy. It had something to do with Jerome's easy oscillation between inner self-pity (of colossal proportions, but so easily sexually-surgically removed) and an overbearing knowledge of and confidence in his variegated assumed roles. Each exterior he adopted was as circumscribed as the outfits of Barbie Doll. Tinker, tailor, soldier, sailor, lumberjack, cowboy, policeman, clone. The fact that his contradictory personality could inhabit so many diverse uniforms never interfered with his standard-ized performances within them – or so it appeared to her in her sourest moments. No such simple paradigm came to *her* rescue. All she seemed capable of was floundering in a welter of infinite choices; like an ex-nun aghast and whimpering on her first foray to the bedecked hangers of a department store. Several motives underlay her own decision that morning. But she was nevertheless at war with her clothes, a sad and resentful dark beast prowling inside a glittering crystal donjon. She was haunted by the fear that one day a furious Japanese assailant, his face contorted with resentment, might attack her in the street and rip the clothes from her back, screaming, 'You're not the kind of woman I designed these clothes for.'

In the gallery she could not allow herself to think too hard. Neurotic self-absorption got in the way of commerce. The emphasis was on surrender to the caprices and foibles of others, on the contrivance of false interest and the boosting of variously erratic aesthetic judgements. She was made to feel like a seventeenth-century Quietist, like Miguel de

Molinos deliberately 'drowning himself in nothingness' so as to be a blank sheet on which others might write their irritating characters. The evening before, her attempt to leave early and evacuate her cumbrous brain had been foiled by the arrival – the entry of the Queen of Sheba – of an eighty-five-year-old socialite wearing silver lurex greaves in honour of the forthcoming exhibition of Hellenistica at the De Young Museum. She had thrust out her shins until her withered frame almost overbalanced, and invented a brazen discourse on Macedonian ceramics, a *tour de force* of vacuity. Christ, Venetia wondered, *is* this city full of freakish females? Maybe all the gays – what was the proportion, 30 per cent – were creating a new race of madwomen who had to resort to the most outrageous eccentricity just to grab attention. First Sibylla and the scare of Venetia's ostracism, now this. Venetia had smiled throughout like a Rossetti damozel, Lizzie Siddal listening to an over-the-top Mrs Siddons, half-appalled at the woman's presumption, half-flattered that she should have gone to so much trouble to impress a mere gallery assistant with intermittent bulimia.

'You look *exhausted*,' said Nicholas. 'Been hanging out with that nasty Brit again, I suppose. God, those guys make me sick with their phony-assed vowels, all teddy-bears and Mummy and baroque mausoleums.' Nicholas's immediate perception of England had been imbued with a strong precipitate of *Brideshead Revisited*, which he'd watched half-comprehendingly with his dank Baptist girl friend. He's not even gay, Venetia thought angrily, how dare he mimic their drivel, the sacred prerogatives, and stray into that magic territory? His presumption offended her sense of propriety, her desire to compartmentalize humanity so that her own exceptional capacity for cross-cultural feeling might be thrown into relief. She would have liked to zap him with curare, insert barbed suppositories into his unexplored rectum. He didn't even *look* right. But then, oh God, nor did she, nor *could* she!

How sad that her repertoire should be so limited! She tried again and again to look different. It was in this characteristic alone that she ran the risk of ratting on her self-imposed financial restraints, casting penury out

199

and, like Marie Antoinette, earning the nickname of 'Mme Deficit' and ordering 172 dresses a year. Everything she wore seemed like a hybrid. Her most delicious experiment in personality transformation through clothes had been in London once, when she wore the shirt Charlton Heston had worn as Michelangelo in *The Agony and the Ecstasy* and which she'd stolen from the studio wardrobe at Cinecittà. She'd felt an empathetic *alter ego*, a *doppelgänger* suffuse her body, flat on her back on a scaffolding, the stirrings of inner sonnets and egg-tempera. Yet how she resented the attempts of others to discard their given selves! That very day she had been outraged in Poland Street – *Poland* Street, for God's sake, in the year of Solidarnosc! – by the sight of a procession of nightclubbing slags in crinolines, bustles, eyepatches and sashes, taffeta ribbons and pompadoured hair, like tiered *campanili* missing naught but the storks, their dreary Ealing voices chafing against their dimly understood nostalgia. She had wanted to hector them in the dry and precise orotund periods of a Sotheby's 'Works of Art' course lecturer, to correct and discipline the silly creatures. But she had passed by, allowing resentment to fester in her already atrabilious memory. How unfair she was! Had she seen the same sight transported to the groves of Sumatra or Cochin, she'd have thrilled to its strangeness, eagerly tried to identify their anthropological signs, wallowed in exoticism.

'Jerome's coming by this evening to take us out for a drink,' she said to Nicholas.

'Do we have to? You know I don't like him. How is it that you and Jerome relate together, anyway?'

'I don't think you can really understand. I think he needs the security. Inside him there just might be a straight man struggling to get out. Of course I should hate that if it ever happened. It would be so disappointing to be loved by a mere heterosexual, some dumb breeder. I couldn't handle the ordinariness of it. With Jerome there's such a fantastic sense of complicity. In some ways it's the only way we can perpetuate our defiance of convention. And explore a new version of living together. Apart in the things that don't matter, together in the things that do.'

'Isn't that a little perverse? You're swimming upstream,

honey. I just see a rather childish experimentalism. And I can see God knows how many problems ahead. He leaves you for a lover, what then? You meet a straight guy – preferably with a vaguely gay sensibility – who can give you your own babies and love you normally? One of his lovers decides to blow you away, you know how vindictive those queens can be? Etcetera, etcetera. How can you handle all those dangers?'

'First of all, I *like* the dangers. It'd all be dead without them. And my control of life has always been a little fragile.' Her jaw slammed forward as if to underline the security of her own values. But she fidgeted with her hair and might have been retracting a false impression. 'Sometimes I think about all those possibilities. But all that happens is that I'm left marvelling at the way our love can withstand them. It's like a city being besieged by a vast invading army. Even to the point where Jerome, at least, is acutely vulnerable to the dangerous beauty of the hostile forces. But just so long as I allow him to skirmish, to play at conquering and surrendering to the enema – enemy – I *know* that he can only love me. I want him to be free, he wants me to be dependent. And anyway, his freedom is illusory, just sexual releases and the belief that he's understanding other people. He doesn't understand them, of course, it's like a recurring course in mystification. Sex and bafflement each time. No wonder he needs my strength and love.'

'But why do you limit yourself like this?'

'Are we expected to know why? Isn't it enough to know *what* we can like? We both have a lot to lose, sure. I guess we've both invested a lot in this thing, and it's bound to be a little precarious. If *I* left, Jerome would be thrown over to sink or swim in the gay pond he hates so much. If he left, I'd be left with an unfillable gap and no father for my child. Self-interest keeps us together as well as love.'

'Aren't you sacrificing rather a lot?'

'Only the things that I'd never appreciate if I had them. You're projecting on to me your own prejudices. Let me tell you one thing. The one aspect of it all that worries me is that I am in fact conforming to the straight model. It's a marriage with pseudo-celibate ingredients. Like a copy – only if you looked at all the constituent parts you'd never recognize the original. In a sense I hate that, because I want it to be something Jerome and I have created from nothing. But I have to recognize in the end that it satisfies my love of order, my love of making patterns out of chaos, my brickbuilding mentality. Do you understand what I'm saying?'

'No way, José. I think you're on a collision course with Miss Destiny. I hope it works out, for your sake. Only don't expect the rest of the world to leap at the chance of copying you creeps. It's strictly for the loonies. There's ways and means of fixing up a marriage. Yours is so tortuous, it's like you needed to travel to the moon to pick up some dust before planning your rock-garden in Daly City.'

'Part of the deal is that straights like you should never understand. Just imagine how I'd feel if the world started to like it. If *Time* magazine ran a sympathetic feature on our marriage. "Feisty heiress bankrolls aristo Castro clone and adopts terror scion." I'd rather be condemned by a specially summoned Vatican Council. I love Jerome and David more than you'll love anybody. Hey, let's hit the peppermint schnapps.'

A sexy boy was delivering a sub-Ernstian *frottage*. He was rangy and open in his strenuous movements, secure in his hybrid role of art-acolyte and Badlands cowpoke. Venetia felt lustful and doomed. She longed to be trodden on by those heavily buckled boots, struck and then fanned by the cowboy hat, buried in the tumescent folds of leather. Jerome could have done it, fuck Jerome.

Surreptitiously swallowing a heavy-milligram Valium, she took delivery. Surrogate sex, the delivered *frottage*. But the moment of tension was brief, the recovery complete, like the acupuncturist's first prick. Could anybody ever understand her? She knew that equilibrium came from conquered stress and the acknowledgement and acceptance of anxiety; not from the easy Californian removal of the symptoms. Perhaps only Henry James would have understood her alien diagnosis.

All this mind-junk crumbled when a client came in.

'I'm looking for a diptych that I can cut in half for the two closet doors in my bedroom. Do you have anything Renaissance?'

His Dobermann pinched its nostrils as imperiously as its owner.

'Try the Uffizi,' she muttered. Then, 'That sounds ritzy,' she corrected out loud. 'What a thrilling idea. That'd be real co-ordination.'

'I'll handle this, sweetheart,' said Nicholas, scenting danger.

Venetia sat staring out of the window until the idiot client had left. A derelict black jittered down the street, internally dancing, a grin on his sadly mobile face. Braving the rain and his own hopelessness. Yet it was less distressing, Venetia thought slyly, than the private misery of most of the people you passed in the street whose tightened faces concealed injustice, divorce, rejection, disappointment, murder, penury, bleak, hard times.

'Now that is what I call *out to lunch*,' said Nicholas, conspiratorially looking over her shoulder.

'What the hell would you know about it? The bloody balanced voice of American liberalism, the Jewish prince from Pacific Heights? The nearest you'll ever get to madness is a TV documentary on Bellevue. Anyway, I thought the point about San Francisco was that you had to be crazy to survive.'

'The point about San Francisco, honey, is to sell pictures. So let's bite back our darling tears of compassion and finish the print inventory.'

That evening Venetia found that Jerome had already gone out on a sexual reconnaissance. She called a travel agent to inquire about flights to Rio de Janeiro. 'Oh, I see, the Carmen Miranda number is it, got our fruitbowl *chapeau* out, have we, flying down to Rio with Dorothy Lamour? It's not just coffee they've got an awful lot of in Brazil, sweetheart,' answered the camp *basso profundo*. She put down the telephone.

22

Song of Innocence 3

Jerome was reading, wrapped up in a wolfskin rug. He was gayed out, and racked with headaches and nausea. At intervals he broke off and stared obsessively at the composition of the wolfskin and its minute gradations of colour: for, if truth be told, a condition as yet unfulfilled in most aspects of his life, the book was inducing a state of glazed indifference. Wallow or deny, indulge or defy, what the fuck. It was a novel by a late-nineteenth-century writer whom he knew, from external sources, to have been something of a Catholic bigot. Parched desert saints raged around, outdoing one another in self-inflicted ordeals and trials of self-abnegation, sitting for hours without stirring from the contemplation of their own wormy excrement; crawling with lice, streaming with polluted lymph from torn blisters, flecked and pied with fistulas they'd ceased to notice in the fanatical glare of Christianity. All this was set in contrast to the lush overblown landscape of a cypress grove at Daphne near Antioch where decadent pagan Romans and Syrians languished beside the river Orontes, promenaded and did pleasurable things to each other amid the singing of linnets and nightingales, lulled by the scent of tamarisks, and lay on carpets of tuberose petals until the darkening foliage swallowed them up in delicious oblivion . . .

He received an affectionate and highly suggestive telephone call, producing the distinct feeling that he was being asked to make a choice, as if he'd reached the 'pick 'n' mix' counter at Woolworth's, and the salesgirl was *definitely* coaxing him towards the truffles. But he failed to recognize the voice and went back to his book.

The only interruption came when David insisted on a short walk in Lafayette Park. Jerome made him change into a sweatshirt with camouflage pants, and David insisted on carrying a silver attaché lunchbox he'd bought in the Part Mental Store, a look and ensemble later coincidentally popularized in its exact entirety in *Paris Texas*. Jerome was so disappointed by the park's familiar, anti-exotic garden – little more than a green parade-ground racetrack and lavatory for his four-legged *bêtes noires* – that he wanted to go straight home, much to David's annoyance.

As though to keep Jerome trapped, David went up to a child, smiling and gurgling at her, and touched her breast. The little girl's arm shot up in the air and she brandished her crimson ice-lolly, standing there like a replica of the Statue of Liberty, except that the torch was withheld, not granted.

She seemed to be trying out adulthood and a peculiarly vicious kind of capitalism. This became even more apparent when Jerome watched her forcing another child off her bicycle, screaming, 'It's mine, it's mine, you jerk!' fixing the other with a glare of amazing ferocity, then prising his hands away, spitting crimson sputum in his face and finally lashing out with her ballet-pumps. David was transfixed by the scene. Jerome, on the other hand, became more and more disengaged from the human psycho-drama and stared at the stupidity of a dog that held a stick in its mouth as it walked along. Jesus, what a giveaway, you'd never catch a cat doing anything so crass!

It was all too much. He dragged David home in a rage. Later, stricken with remorse at having rained on David's parade, he tore himself away from his book and announced they would play a game much loved by both of them. Jerome would say aloud and write down a narrative incorporating long names for animals. Each time David recognized one, he let out a shriek, and Jerome paused to draw an exquisite picture of the animal. Jerome's name for the game was 'Polysyllable Beasts', a name that had satisfactorily resolved itself for David into 'Polly Sybil Beast', so conjuring up a hugely enjoyable image of a smug and self-righteous elder sister in pigtails while, for Jerome, his enemy Sibylla loomed as the Aunt Sally. If he had expressed an honest opinion, David would have told Jerome that the picture of this little girl was far more interesting than the game itself and that it was this which made him throw himself into it each time with such gusto.

That evening the story went: 'I had a dreadful skin disease so I went to see a Paki dermatologist' – Jerome paused helpfully, but David looked blank – 'and gave him a catalogue of my symptoms' ('Cat!' shrieked David) 'only to be told that I was really well and the burden of responsibility' (again a helpful, but ignored pause) 'rested with me to cure myself. So I went to a bar just near the hospital' (exaggerated upper-class English accent – 'Horse!' the boy cried) 'where I met a lady who was busy fishing' ('Fish') 'for compliments, but I thought she looked a real dog' ('Dog!' David said without excitement, it was so *obvious*!)

After this game had outlived its interest, Jerome sank back and believed his paternal duties to be discharged. He lay on a sofa, muffled again in the wolfskin rug and watching with pleasure as David wandered around seeking more solitary amusement.

But the respite was brief. The child came up to Jerome again and asked him to close his eyes for a big surprise. Wearily Jerome acquiesced. Just another familiar game, he thought. The one where he tickles my ear with a feather or pummels me in the stomach. 'Open your mouth,' the boy ordered. Again he did as instructed. What would it be, a chocolate bean or a piece of days-old madeira laid upon his tongue?

The texture was fleshy and firm. He opened his eyes with a start to find David standing in front of him with his tiny childish cock pressed into Jerome's mouth. The child giggled and pulled away, enormously gratified by the huge dilation of Jerome's eyes, the appalled shock his whole face registered.

Christ, had he seen something? Had he surreptitiously accompanied Jerome on a nocturnal adventure and stored up the memory of some sexual encounter? Or did some curious instinct allow him to calculate the devastating effect of his action without really understanding what it meant? Or maybe some infantile psychological trauma was at work, some interpretable demand for help or reassurance? Whatever the cause, David stood doubled up with laughter, as innocent as May morning, till the tears rolled down his cheeks.

23

Amsterdam:
Professor van Amerongen

Professor Claes van Amerongen fondled the incunabula as if they'd been undropped Sicilian testicles. Their burnished surface and underlying asperity were a poor surrogate for the over-photographed fauns of Taormina. Concentrate, Professor, *focus* on the real *content* of those books. After all, they're only designed secondarily as physical objects, even these dull Milanese homilies with their crude xylographs. The book is what is *in* the book, not the book itself. Still, the library's exhalation of morocco could indeed paralyse the intellect and stimulate the baser senses. A blindfolded Jerome might have been transported to the leather pavements of Berlin and New York or the enveloping stench of *lederwasser* in West Hollywood and the Swish Alps: fantasies now substantially denied to van Amerongen – if, indeed, he'd ever inhabited them, except in a previous incarnation. His world was now circumscribed by the limits of senility alone. He allowed only the awesome image of Rita Hayworth's Alzheimer's dementia to cloud and interrupt the respectable median tenor of life. *Beatus ille*; but only up to a point. He missed the heady closeted days of his early life, albeit envying the present-day freedom conceded to the out homosexual. He was sensible and almost resigned. The brackish waters of the Prinzengracht outside accorded ill with the clarity of his analytic mind in which he had almost subjugated the anti-logical and disquieting agitations of the sacred fury. It was a process reflected more accurately in his pristine head, his polished, buffed skin, a bodily casing as regular as a new software print-out. A severity which, centuries before, might have emulated the ascetic exhibitionism of a fraudulent Capuchin. But this was in effect a self-imposed order, an altogether synthetic set of measures aimed at suppressing the latent memories of rebellion and anti-conformism.

Alicia his secretary. Wurlitzer his Weimaraner. Ignatius his conclave. Perrier his sustenance. Cornucopia his mind. Finite his hopes of salvation.

'A cable has arrived from Madrid,' said, presumably, Alicia. The voice was tailored enough. An aura of the 1950s, of Barbara Stanwyck and *style utilité*, the Festival of Britain and the corridors of a foundering Hollywood still clinging to a dying correctness.

'Thank you, my dear. How are you?'

She was due for a colostomy. What she said was, 'I have to have a skin-graft next week. May I be released from my duties?'

She was as disposable as a toxic-shock tampon. But he maintained the pretence of her usefulness; and enjoyed making her feel subservient, that hint of lesbianic games.

'It'll be a little inconvenient. But necessity before routine, epidermis before duty.'

Age before beauty, she thought, sex before marriage, yeah, yeah. Boopety-boop. Her petulant pout was something to see.

'I shall miss you,' he lied.

This habit of exchanging lies was now ritualized and inescapable. By night Alicia – the hint was there in her voice – dressed in hooped scarlet to exaggerate her embonpoint and ran around yelling in a lesbian idiolect. She loved to kick off her sling-backs and dance up a storm in her Fair Isle legwarmers, bad-mouthing pretty girls, a New Wave governess, Radclyffe Hall in zips, the Swell of Loneliness. When Jerome first met her she'd contrived to transmit to him, across the forbidding aura emanated by Professor van Amerongen, masonic signals that he reciprocated with a glance of astonished admiration at her incredibly successful duplicity. But her eyes had an infinitely Verlainean sadness.

The cable said: 'Blas' party on (San Lorenzo + 2). Ideological support requested.' Claes recognized Asdrúbal's mannered fear, the coded request, the caution instilled by Spain's decades of intimidation of the humanitarian liberal. A smile of annoyance struggled across his normally pursed lips at the thought of having to attend yet another political party rally on behalf of his ancient friend. The pique coincided with his sudden awareness of an unpreventable break-out on the nape of his neck, an eruption destined to mess up the regular contours of his cosseted physique. He wondered if he could lay his hands on some 'halcyon cream', the antiseptic ointment made from birds' nests that Ovid mentioned in the *Medicamina faciei femineae*. His sebaceous glands had always been overactive and he was prone to stress-related styes and dandruff, kept at bay only with scrupulous hygiene. There were, too, compensations for the persistence of these oozy secretions. His face, unlike the faces of more balanced secreters, had gone straight from acne to a sleek, heavy-pored ruggedness so elastic that the incipience of lines and scoring never seemed to flourish.

How like Asdrúbal to puncture his unaccidental life! To reactivate the inconvenient stirrings of a dormant, almost senescent, conscience! Stern Daughter of the Voice of God! O Duty! He stroked the surface of the blemish, irritably defying the rules of cosmetic propriety, half-hoping that, like the eventual demise of the spot, Asdrúbal's importunity was coming to a head and would burst, leaving him free of the lymph of guilt. He hated Madrid and everything it stood for. Its hot neo-Stalinist tenements made the rectilinear boulevards of Sofia look picturesque. He hated speaking in bad Spanish, the need, with his limited resources, to concentrate on *how* to say, not *what* to say, the difference between *langue* and *parole*, the Saussurian banana-split on which he always slipped. The exposure to ridicule was so inappropriate to so articulate a man! You had to speak in a peremptory tone and a Gatling machine-gun delivery which you would never dare to use in Dutch (though the phonemes, he had to confess, were more melodious than those of his own language). He'd never mastered the tenses and felt he must always be getting them wrong and sound like Ernest Ansermet bellowing at a cellist: 'Don't spoke! If you didn't like, you went!' On his last visit he had misappropriated some juvenile speech-habits – who was it, now, that he'd been consorting with – and outraged a *macho* boy. Mistakenly assuming *cojonuda* – great-balled – to be synonymous with 'terrific' in all its contexts, he'd applied it to the boy's mother, a Whistlerian matriarch of irreproachable womanliness.

Most of all Claes van Amerongen despised the liberal establishment, the dingy gravy-train that plied between the Café Roma and the Universidad Autónoma and came limply to rest on the conscience-stricken buffers of the political salons in the Calle Alfonso XII. Often in the past he had risen early to walk through the dawn streets of Madrid down to Lavapiés, where he'd mingled with the prawn-packers in the huge depot where the shelled husks cracked under his feet like the low-flying cockroaches of Guayaquil under the wheels of gun-toting Buicks. The presence of the horny-handed toilers had reassured him and dispelled the memory of the vapid posturings of the *salonnières*. The fishy texture of the air had connected with the calming Hanseatic herring of his home waters. But this had, of course, been evasive action. His deep-seated burgher puritanism always demanded some more positive resolution, some kind of adherence to a set of strenuous beliefs; and demanded, too, the illusion of social usefulness, of a contribution to the common weal; a means of sublimating his fastidiousness, a counterbalance to the mandarinism of bibliophily which so often left him fainting with its own inefficacy.

He had read that morning of a right-wing terrorist outrage in San Francisco. The news strengthened his so far weak resolve to conquer his initial reluctance to fall in with Asdrúbal's plan. He was peculiarly susceptible to a kind of short-lived revulsion after hearing of such incidents; and tended to speculate morosely about their global implications in long, self-addressed Conradian sentences. Now the spot on his neck throbbed dully, promising physical pain equal to the trauma of leaving Amsterdam. At least, though, its insistent presence filled his mind and diverted him from the impending Jesuitical self-examination on political ends and means, on Weathermen and the Red Brigade, on the immersion of the self in disinterested causes. He promptly decided to go. A strict Thomistic analysis of his motives might have revealed some wobbly *intentiones secundae*. A clearer intelligence than his would have called it the need to get off his ass. A rose by any other name.

In search of guidance and confirmation, he sank to his knees on a prie-dieu and wound a rosary around his hands. He knelt before his un-Dutch Maker. Yet the familiarity of his gesture was somehow subtly altered. The Glorious Mysteries seemed more technicolor than usual, more Grünewald than Titian, suffused with a luminous day-glo. *'Benedictus fructus ventris tui, Jesus.'* The well-rehearsed utterance seemed newly forged and revelatory; it refused to fall from his lips with the leaden monotony of a slogan. The ivory beads felt rockish, petrified, and appeared to give off irregular electric pulses as though on a malfunctioning oscillograph. Bouncing almost, autonomous, impelled by a force outside him; increasingly, with growing strength, they leaped and quavered as if in response to some manic alien console. Along the beads the electric message came. A tremor was passing through them, a cableless cable, a semiconductor trying to conduct his conduct. No longer was he in Amsterdam, but in Madrid. A shrouded room, seemingly decked out for the exequies of some rickety infanta; a crow crone in black serge and a Byronic young man with a cold, hell-dredging gaze in transfixed adoration before a polychrome madonna, its grooved patina as reflective as the high contours of the man's Tartaric cheekbones.

Professor van Amerongen strained to receive the elusive image as it receded and advanced like an indecisive army. Then he was able to focus on the double Pompeo Leoni sculpted group, its immobility now as marmoreal as a Carrara hillside. He gradually *saw* the telekinetic imprint: a pair of votive donors winging their mystic way without intermediaries from Spain to Amsterdam, the ancient refuge for Spanish heterodoxy. Its precision and clarity astonished him, accustomed as he was to his own unvisual perception, his muddied appreciation of concrete things, obsessed as he knew himself to be with the *Ding an sich*. While its contours ate into his vision with the tenacity of etching-acid, he became aware of an odd incongruity. Some element of the whole was wrong; like a Sloane Ranger on Christopher Street, or a 'Dykes on Bikes' badge pinned on an angora breast, a Marlboro in St Peter's, a Caroline divine in St Tropez or a divine Caroline in a leather bar. The apparent imperturbability of the picture was being undermined by a paradox that struggled to assert itself against the iconic stillness. It emanated, Professor van Amerongen noticed, from the young man, with the sinister insistence of a worm wriggling through the eye-socket of a skull. *José Antonio Primo de Rivera presente* . . . *Fuerza nueva* . . . *16 de julio* . . . *el hombre ha muerto pero su espíritu vive* . . . JONS . . . arrows and a yoke . . . pulsating now in the young man's forehead like the bezoar-stone in a death-dealing basilisk. He was radiating political darts, expelling them as inexorably as Bernini's St Teresa received the ecstatic shafts of divine union. Even as the old lady perceived the bloodied stigmata of the moribund Christ, His twisted musculature dimming her perception of her own withered body, Lorenzo's sacrilegious train of thought gathered momentum and intensity. It solidified in fragmented pictures like an Edwardian jigsaw puzzle. El Caudillo . . . the heroic *estado mayor* at Burgos . . . *Muerta la libertad* . . . the epic cavalry charge against Abd el-Krim . . . the humiliation of Hitler in the railway-carriage at Hendaye . . . the national reconstruction . . . the women auxiliaries at the Castillo de la Mota . . . the Organic Law of State . . . Falange . . . Falange . . . *vivan las cadenas* . . . eugenics and oligarchy . . . *catequismo* and benediction, angels with épées, the celestial battalions . . . *Gerra y Santiago matamoros* . . .

Wurlitzer moved his neck affectionately against the professor's tensed calves. Drawing level with his master's head, he froze to re-enact the attitude of the Madrid frieze so that Claes's starched religiosity mirrored Guillermina's and held its posture as the signals' climax abated and their clarity became fainter. Gradually, by degrees, the professor reinhabited his own body, repossessing his own mental furniture temporarily distrained by the aggressive

Spanish bailiffs. The various parts of his body resumed their interdependent lives, and he extended a newly prehensile arm to encircle the dog's huge neck. All the continuity of the dog. 'My own, my inalienable *animal, mon semblable!'* Claes murmured. 'Only you can keep away the demons.' Reassurance, soft and almost edible, rippled along the dog's back and swam in his lugubrious eyes. The two grizzled warriors clasped one another's spirits.

Alicia's bulk loomed intrusively on the threshold, interrupting Claes's gentle transition from the disturbing tremors to the familiarity of his love for Wurlitzer and recalling him to the prosaic features of his library, his microcosmic prison. But what could *he* know about prison, even analogically? Had he been in the Algeciras slammer?

'I'll fly to Paris and take the Puerta del Sol to Madrid. Please make the arrangements for me. My trip will coincide with your hospitalization. By the way, who actually donates the skin? Do people lie down under an anaesthetic having their legs flayed? Rather Auschwitz, don't you think? I hope you don't get a donor with an irregular sebum secretion.'

Alicia's gorge rose, nauseated even through her own lie. It was even worse than the reality she had to face. At heart she had already been preparing herself for the alteration of her scarlet ensembles to accommodate the vile colostomy. Now the professor's concentration-camp sensibility made her feel as if she had both operations to face. An inner *and* an outer scraping.

'Will you walk Wurlitzer for me while I'm away?' Her heart leapt at the prospect of so invert-enhancing a duty. 'Just remember not to let him jump into the canals. Sometimes he thinks he's a seagull.'

Alicia's responsibility lasted only a week. Wurlitzer contracted nephritis and died of a surfeit of lampposts.

24

Jerome Pitches Camp

'And perpetual children are tedious' – Thom Gunn

Two inclines formed the Castro valley and there was a traffic intersection where they met. Although the slopes were gentle in their gradient, there were so many men scurrying around that it looked almost as if they were helplessly struggling against gravity and being pulled down until they settled like spillikins in a heap at the traffic-lights.

Their movements were, in fact, astonishingly aimless. Under a cloudless sky – except for the thin ruler-shaped fog-bank which hung above Sutro Heights – they seemed to be careering towards nothing in a world in which there were apparently neither women nor children. This odd lack of purpose struck Jerome as rather sinister, and to fit in with the sense of life being conducted as a kind of child's game that he'd already observed in other aspects of San Francisco. Everything was very public, much stress was put on the impression of fullness and self-sufficiency; but the effect was of an animated toytown, insulated from reality and as mechanical and meaningless as clockwork.

Jerome swung his camera-lens first towards the top of the street, the portal which announced its frontier with the real world beyond. An art deco theatre, proudly re-Odeonized and consecrated to the gay movie pantheon it repeatedly disinterred – Joan, Bette, Marilyn, Lauren, Judy – who smiled out from their glass frames, the only women on the male reservation. (This was, after all, the city where, some years later, armed raiders were to hold up a store and demand the handing over of the authentic red slipper Judy Garland had worn as Dorothy in *The Wizard of Oz*.) Inside there was a Wurlitzer which came up out of the ground and sank back, after the film, with a raucous and sentimental rendition of 'San Francisco, Open Your Golden Gate'. Jerome saw all this, his eyes endowed with the X-ray vision of previous memory, and the gilded Churrigueresque latticed miradors that hung like voluminous royal boxes over the organ.

In the doorway of the dry-cleaner's next door a nun stood examining a huge, polythene-wrapped bundle of clothes she had just collected – a change of habit, no doubt. Her wimple and coif framed a face sugar-iced in pink foundation, eyelashes so weighed down with double-lash mascara that they were blacker even than her walrus moustache – which had, it was true, been frosted, glazed, basted with a pale glitter-gelée that to some extent counteracted its immense bulk. A Sister of Perpetual Indulgence, Sister Motorsexual Homocycle perhaps, or Sister Vicious Power Hungry Bitch, whose appearance seemed intuitively to coalesce all the elements of Jerome's and Venetia's lives. Gone-wrong Catholics, up-front camp. While Jerome was adjusting the shutter, the nun walked away, past the gay bread-shop towards the first of the many gay bars that lurked behind their mock-Oklahoma swing-doors. She disappeared inside with an unnunlike swish. One sister for seven thousand brothers. This was the oddest part: the clear passion for creating a microcosm of the world in which everything referred to homosexuality. A world fluttering with the pink pound, the lavender dollar of faggot capitalism. Perhaps it was this that Dante foresaw when he herded the queens and the usurers into the same circle in Purgatory.

Panning down the street, Jerome saw a gay hairdresser (fair enough), a gay travel-agency, a gay pharmacy, a gay solarium, a gay gym, a gay bank. Perhaps there was a gay greengrocer where you could pay gay money for gay potatoes, the kind you don't have to peel, you just put them together and they scratch each other's eyes out. But the shiny playground concealed a deeper unease. Not only was there a new argument, a more rigorous self-questioning by the leaders of the Homintern about the feasibility of this womanless world, but there were signs, too, of the encroaching doubts prompted by mysterious pandemic diseases. It was one thing when they started opening night-clubs called Interferon and Flagyl (to replace The Mincing Machine and Nightstick), a bicycle-shop called Tetracyclin and a flower-shop called Intestinal Flora. The way allusions to diagnosis and medicine were beginning to multiply. Yet only a few isolated serious voices predicted the end of the Old Hedonism. The New Celibacy was as yet unheard of and would still have sounded like a far-flung rock-sect. No signs of traumatization had appeared, there were few cracks in the surface of the shiny pink gay machine. Jerome himself felt only the mildest unease.

The buildings were so undistinguished that he found his attention wandering towards the elaborate criss-cross of the telegraph wires and a group of workmen digging a hole at the intersection. Even they looked gay with their for-once real working clothes and the bantering laughter with which they turned their labours into a party. The red flags that hung from their wagon like the warnings on a cow-catchered locomotive were as sexually charged and inviting as the red handkerchiefs worn in a back pocket to lure the twitching forearm.

There was no escaping the fact that Jerome was more interested in the human ecology than its surroundings, which should, professionally, have engaged his attention. The casual, self-assured men were electrifyingly watchable as they bustled around in their paradoxes. While they were all antiseptically squeaky-clean in their dress and hygiene – apart, that was, from some calculated oil-stains on their jeans and the few overlooked scuffs and trails on their shoes from nameless liquids – there was something supremely dirty about them. The blatancy with which they displayed their sexual attributes. Their self-abandonment to the supremacy of sex. Smiles of self-satisfaction and mysterious triumphs. The lazy grace of their bodies, which seemed encased in something, an outer carapace or layer of iridescence. A grace generated in most by bravery and self-consciousness, controlled in others by fabulous extroversion.

Jerome studied, photographed, absorbed, dismissed, mocked and envied. The *désinvolture* of their shambling, moseying, thigh-pronouncing walk lured and enticed, more shameless than the writhings of Liane de Pougy and Cléo de Mérode in lewd tandem. An aura surrounded each man, somewhere between self-advertisement and boyish reserve, and allowed the less beautiful sometimes, often, to outdo the merely beautiful in pulling-power. If you could enter a room with that quality alone, Jerome knew, you could be as plain as a pikestaff yet galvanize the whole auditorium and seize on whichever willing trophy you chose. (Jerome had ended up with some real dogs that way.)

And then there was the childlike feel. The apparently unaffected spontaneity with which they touched, like babies helping each other over a difficult patch in the sandpit. The sense of brotherhood, originating not just in the inheritance of persecution but in their collective desire for the commitment of friendship, the love of equals, which could replace the love they often sacrificed in sexual gratification. Not sinister, like Freemasons, but open-hearted and generous. Their companionableness seemed to bypass the creaking artifice through which their straight counterparts established such male bonding, team spirit, religion and the violence of sport and drunkenness and ox-like allegiances. If you were a half-way successful queen, you ended up with a chain of sisterhood that stretched all over the world. You could arrive in, say, Gothenburg and be pretty sure that somewhere in your bulging address-book you'd find the number of some local you'd had in, say, Portland, Oregon. It was something like the camaraderie of war.

The slope of Castro Street was like the escape chute from an aeroplane that precipitated you down into the safe womb of childhood. As they went about their daily business, Jerome could sense that they were all acting, playing, consciously like children. They invested each new experience – the making of a date, the purchase of a magazine – with a veneer of wide-eyed receptivity (which often, sadly, masked a hugely blasé detachment).

They ate ice-creams with aggressive gusto. Their gaze

focused rapidly on any brightly coloured objects – especially each other. Everything was a toy, as in Pope:

> With varying vanities, from every part
> They shift the moving toyshop of their heart.

It was probable, Jerome speculated, that the mass of them were compensating for the scars of their actual childhoods, the cicatrice of children transformed into the cockatrice of lust. Perhaps they'd had no real childhood. Now that they were grown-up, adulthood could be, should be, turned into a game. Fassbinder had done it, exaggerating his baby-ish temperament and tantrums, running his film-crew and actors as if they were an obstreperous squad of lead sol-diers who could be maltreated, battered, cajoled, coupled and uncoupled, abused, reconciled, *quod libet*. Egotism and narcissism seemed triumphant, a prototype for the straight yuppies, the self-regard of San Francisco itself writ large.

They were promiscuous in their mutual praise – and in a few other things, too – egging each other on to ever dizzier heights of false security, children being brought on, forced on to an infinitely receding maturity.

'Hey, I like your tee-shirt!' (Doesn't she realize what a crêpey turkey neck she's got?) 'That's a great haircut!' (Got past the stage of covering up the recessions, have we?) 'I just loved the party at your apartment last week!' (Isn't it about time you learned that sophisticated queens need a little more entertainment than a sprinkling of sex-aids [sex-what?] and a bunch of out-of-towners screaming about how they're ripped to the tits like they were Bette Midler gotten stuck in the groove?)

They seemed to have careered on, relinquishing responsi-bility as they went. But it wasn't all faults and fecklessness, that contagious fecklessness, deadlier than leprosy, which blighted Jerome as well. Some of it was for real, and could be compared with the instructions in a Renaissance cour-tesy manual. Hadn't Castiglione and all the others wanted us to indulge in elaborate compliments, manouevres and ego-boosts to oil the machinery of social – *social* – intercourse? It sure did make a lot of things easier. Especially when you were dealing with the acute, bruisable sensitivities of gays.

Jerome, anyway, wasn't that uptight about sincerity and was as susceptible as the next man to blandishments. His day could be made or unmade as easily as a bed with a duvet. How often his spirits had soared, as when they liked his voice or fingered his real-European Lacoste with the honeyed purring coming out of their fingers! And as when that truck-driver from Ulan had smiled and said, *'Du bist der einzige der mir gefallen hat!'* Or plummeted, as when someone said, 'Yeah, you're real nice, but *I'm* a little *busy* tonight.'

Perhaps all sub-cultures evolved these reciprocal signals to raise a collective morale threatened by external condemnation or condescension? He would have to think about that one.

Was all this childlike behaviour new? Did it have something to do with liberation and closets permanently vacated? A dim memory came to him of Proust going on about the peculiar decrepitude, senescence, yes that was it, of bachelors, something about their 'morrows being void of promise'. Looking around, however, he found exactly the opposite. Nobody looked older than they actually were, most looked (and behaved) years younger. What had happened? What had changed?

They *were* good-looking (or, if not, they had been). Job-lot Apollos. If, that was, you accepted the strict *convention* of their appearance as boy-men, just as you had to accept the convention in pastoral poetry, or *opera seria* or Japanese Noh plays. Jerome thought that many of them were probably gay because they'd been repeatedly impressed with the idea of their own beauty.

'The trouble with good-looking men,' Venetia had once sighed, 'is that they're too interested in other good-looking men.'

Jerome was beginning to feel a little uncomfortable with his camera. He had been subjected to hostile glances which suggested that the Castroites resented the presence of this apparently rubbernecking photographer-voyeur. There wasn't much to record anyway. The interest lay in the *meaning* of the place, and that was better understood by speculation and experience than by oh-so predictable snapshots. Even while he'd been fiddling with lenses and light-meters, in fact, Jerome had been reflecting on the symbolism of these men and their habitat, deliberately forcing himself to dwell less on their physical shell than on the implications of their behaviour. Where was love? Sex seemed to have been pried away from the solid rock of European romanticism. It had its own autonomous life, its own rhythms, easily apprehended like the clanking sounds of the body-building equipment. It had been corralled. While in the act of sex or its preliminaries, he stopped short of this profundity and took in only the outer, sensory features, he knew that in doing so he was restricting his vision and falling error to the intellectual blindness condemned by the Puritan Ranters: 'Filthy blinde Sodomites called Angels men, they seeing no further than the formes of men.' He thought that was what they meant, anyway.

He felt in need of a rest, but could not face the pressure of the bar, where the mutual assessment and point-scoring made your head spin. He walked a little farther along Market Street, away now from the Main Gay Drag, turning his back on the most spectacular experiment in convention-rocking he'd ever seen. A queue of frou-frou fantasticks outside the San Marcos shed an odour of sterility over him as he strode by purposefully, surprising himself with his own masculinity, pleased to have these willowy, squirming pansies against whom to measure his red-blooded hunkiness, humpiness.

221

25

San Francisco: The Café Flores

The café was a light and airy confection, green with spider-plants and hangovers. Its glass sides let in too much light for the homosexual sensibility.

Jerome didn't feel too good. Something was fermenting in his gut and his herpes were coming on like harpies. He'd been to the clinic the day before and the doctor had taken one look at them, cried out: 'Wow, they're a classic!' and rushed off for his Polaroid. His venerealogical history was now so extensive that it had been transferred on to microfiche. He'd sure rustled up some pathogenes in his time.

He could feel the girl's burgeoning compulsion to talk to him. Her pretence at eating conflicted with her nervy drags on a joint which she held in a metal hair-clip she'd pulled out from behind her bulbous fake moon-rock earrings. Gloria Swanson, he remembered, *Sunset Boulevard*, flashing semiotic danger-signals, the predatory female, *das ewige Weib* poised to suck me into her faded life and mercilessly spit me out. His total exclusion zone had been effectively breached; and it was now impossible to create a diversionary tactic on the other side of the table, where a couple sat playing a hermetic game of backgammon. The girl played with impatient petulance, jerking a cigarette percussively in and out of her horrid mouth, her slumped bovine body belied by the darting movements of her head and hands. Cyclamen talons swooped overfast on to the innocent dice, the counters clicking like the speech of arrhythmic Hottentots. Opposite, three despondent Belgian cowboys sat coming to terms

222

with their dim sexual prospects in the incestuous city. Overwhelmed by the sadness of the suicidal Brazilian music and craving the security of their rented tethers at the Maastricht rodeo. 'Ce patron, comme ça, il est bien . . . il m'a touché les fesses . . . fascisme sexuel . . . pas dans le coin, là-bas . . .'

'Would you like to come to the private screening of my movie?' Her question was peremptory and didn't seem to allow for the idea of a refusal. 'We were up filming last night from twelve till seven in the morning. I was doing MDA, I mean I just *had* to, those creeps were so boring always asking for more takes. Grody to the Max, I was really coming unglued. *Totally*. Yench! I had this fantastic number at the beginning. This young guy Tom is out front singing "Mony Mony" and I'm at the back dressed up like a cute little bunny and messing around like the Harlettes.' Here she imitated her performance in miniature. 'At the studio on Natoma Street, 8-millimetre, I mean a *real* movie. We're showing it as a double bill with *Sink the Senate*, you know, the disaster movie with Lesbe Sensuus as Senator Hayakawa? It started off with my having just like this one number, but they liked my rabbit so much I had to come on again for the finale.'

There was no need for Jerome to intervene, so sure was her narrative conviction. 'Did I tell you about the time when we were driving on the freeway to Los Angeles? I was doing seventy-eight miles an hour and we were stopped by this cop who said he'd been following me for twenty miles to see if I was weaving around but I wasn't and he was kinda nice so he warned me about the speed and gave me a calendar from a travel-lodge. I just thought, what if I'd been doing ninety, what would I get, what speed do you have to go to get a TV?'

Jerome fidgeted with his parachute jacket and snapped off some hanging threads. He sipped his camomile tea. 'They're kind of unpredictable, the American police,' he said. 'I never know what to expect from them.' His own experiences with the SFPD had been rather specialized.

'Are you *Australian*?'

'No. I'm from London. But I don't really live there. I spend a lot of time travelling. I like it here a lot.'

223

'Because of the guys? You look like you've come here to fuck around. It's always the same, you guys from Europe just come over and fuck all our men.'

'Getting our own back on the GIs who ravished our mothers, maybe. Anyway, American men don't seem to mind too much. And you girls seem to make a lot of allowances. My room-mate says she couldn't live with a straight man, all that *machismo* in the kitchen would drive her crazy.' He looked down and caught sight of her boots sprawled pigeon-toed under the table. They were so grossly clumsy that Jerome could not decide whether they were antiquatedly fashionable or merely orthopaedic.

'Yeah, but what about all those tantrums, the hysteria, the cracked poppers in the icebox, the shit stuck to the shower nozzle?'

'¿Nosotros trabajabamos en una pastelería, aquella amiga colombiana y yo, te acuerdas? Mira, nos trataban tan mal, eran francésas de aquellos tan antipáticos que siempre te dan un montón de trabajo y luego no te pagan. De todas formas, mañana nos vamos para Madrid. '¡Oye, sabes una cosa, que ha bajado tanto el peso argentino que ahora te cobran un millón para una cervecita!'

This was more interesting, he felt. If only the gibbering slag would allow him to listen. The other girl was describing how the nurses and doctors in Lirne had just gone on strike after turning down an 85 per cent pay-offer, then an attempted political coup, in English now, to a hopelessly ill-informed American; he made her feel infinitely intelligent, but infinitely old. She switched back to Castilian to talk about laundry with her Argentine lover.

'And there's my mother still believing that gay men wear dresses. She came here once and refused to believe that all these super-macho guys were gay. Who're you trying to fool?'

The Argentine's father had expelled him from their military tenement in Bahia Blanca. In the end it was for the best, 'armando follones ... y yo te lo juro ... you, bueno, la gente así ... me tuve que marchar ... desgraciado ... es cuestión de super-vivencia ...' He kept pointing at the girl as if she'd been taken in adultery. Her face, too, was intent, in mock-seriousness, emoting and empathizing like crazy, and she touched his body to hang on to their fragile relationship. A Spanish magazine beside her blew open and the pictures of grinning socialites were blitzed with Californian psychobabble. She was cleverer than all the others; but her need for popular acclaim forced her *à rebours* into the lives of the stupid. Jerome could sense the fast wheels of her mind frenetically reduplicating their activity in order to control their own complexity and sustain the unintimidating façade, the bathetic mouthings.

'You can imagine how I felt, like I was *hysterical*, I was just tearing the hair out of my head,' said the nasal slag, clutching her rats' tails as if in proof. '*And* I wasted my Mandrax. *Nauseous.* And me a valley girl. He's that sleazy type, I can't imagine how he's my boy friend, I'm just totally repulsed by him, you just can't mellow him up, you understand, you're a Taurus too.'

Jerome had lost the struggle to co-ordinate the two simultaneous floods. What *was* it he was supposed to be learning by exposure to this exercise in dichotic listening? Was it going to improve his conversation? He felt floored by it. He was hesitant, subtle and self-doubting; to that extent he was guilty of un-American activities. It certainly didn't make this shouting, assertive world any more intelligible. He was relieved to see Aaron, his hairdresser and temporary guru, sidling his Cincinnati way into the café. 'Hi, God, he makes me feel so fat!' said Aaron. 'Remember how we all wanted to look like Elizabeth Taylor? Well . . . now we all do! Hey, I bought a new car, the cutest little rattlesnake you ever saw. The most fantastic colour, kind of desert sand. My shade,' he said, pointing to his head, forgetting he'd been bald for several years.

'Let's hope you drive it as well as you drove that baby ambulance,' said Jerome with unconcealed British sarcasm.

'How're you doing? Has God showered on you all the loveliness you so richly deserve?'

'Not really,' Jerome answered, 'unless you count getting herpes on my ass.'

'That's too bad,' said Aaron sympathetically. 'So you've been traumatized. When *will* you learn to synchronize your

moods and avoid all that tensed-up pressure?' He turned
Jerome away from him and began to massage his neck and
shoulders. 'Just try and treat it like I did when I had hepatitis.
You can't imagine how depressed I was, all I could do was
eat peaches and chocolate-chip cookies. What you have to
do is be *grateful* for what your body is doing. Expelling all
those nasty toxins stored up by bad colonic movements. So
you have to imagine yourself exactly at the affected point
of your anatomy – travelling down through your veins, like
driving a kind of microscopic ambulance. *Then* you'll be able
to empathize with your body's action and the herpes will
seem like a logical expression of your body's natural will. So
that they can live out their natural life and then disappear
back into your system. Just let me concentrate on helping
your herpes, you'll see how fast they disappear.'

Jerome thought he would be as well-advised to follow
Pliny's advice about transmitting diseases into someone
else's body: if you were stung by a scorpion, you whispered
into an ass's ear: 'A scorpion has stung me.' And the ass
soaked up the pain, took the rap. So much for the march of
scientific advance.

Aaron was choreographing a ballet provisionally called
Quaalude à l'après-midi d'un faune in which a Very Beautiful
Drugged Boy would perform a dream-dance on his points,
and then, clinging to a more informal mode, would stumble
aleatorically around an empty stage. The movements were
to be a loose variation on Aaron's regular cardiovascular
callisthenics. He had a boy in mind for the part (though
that was not the only part he had him in mind for);
but at present he was busy, too preoccupied with the
manufacture of articulated cloisonné flea-collars for cats
(his idea had caused an epidemic of feline head-droop for
miles around). Aaron's neck throbbed as he described the
boy's animal grace.

'You remember Nijinsky in the *Spectre de la Rose*? He has
the same *diaphanous* quality, like a very delicate asparagus
leaf. Sometimes I feel he just defies gravity, like Jayne
Mansfield's tits. Nothing can hold him down. God knows
I've tried.'

'I always felt Nijinsky was probably hugely overrated; and

that he needed Diaghilev like he needed a hole in the head. Some overweight Russian impresario who was really only interested in surrendering to the entire Monaco militia. Just don't let yourself get sucked into *that* role, sweet Aaron.'

Aaron was over-susceptible, a character Hemingway would have screwed up into a ball and chucked into the waste-paper basket. Like a *manso* fighting-bull, a Ferdinand too in touch with his own body and psyche. Adelaida would have crushed him like an ageing meringue. Or Gabriella Krocher-Tiedemann exacting her vicious revenge on the innocent in distant Entebbe, Kalashnikov-butting their pliant heads.

Jerome looked across at the cartoon the poison slag had been drawing on a grubby pad streaked with lipstick. It was a grotesque picture of an aghast mother, staring wild-eyed at the infant-sized but perfectly formed leather queen, equipped with goggles, gauntlets and harness, to which she had just given birth.

'This is the most beautiful man in northern California. Right here.'

'Then why's he smoking a cigarette, for fuck's sake?'

A cadaverous young man swept past their table, his dancer's body clad in leg-warmers and surmounted by a raddled, embittered face. He collided gracefully with a pair of unimprovable gays who brushed themselves down and went straight to Jerome's head. They walked with their arms thrust out in simian fashion and exaggeratedly co-ordinated with their leg-movements, their rolling *al fresco* gait reinforced by the heavy pressure on both feet and the slight curvature of their legs emphasized by the full ass of their 501s.

'I think it's stupid of you to help somebody still your own spirit.' The reptilian, lentil-fed girl spat the accusation at her anaemic brother.

'We found this *perfect* Jesuit church on the beach right outside of Goa. Manfred walked in and just like *screamed* with excitement. It was all derelict with like little bits of gilt and plaster angels everywhere. I just lay down on the altar steps, my head was just *swimming* with all the acid, and now all this baroque glitter, and Manfred found a whole chest in the *sacristy*, do you say? And it was full of these fantastic vestments all purple and gold with bits of filigree

227

silver thread like some kind of wardrobe for the Broadway production of *Hadrian VII*. We laid them out on the beach and slept on them, right under the stars, the palm trees leaned over and fanned us, the sand was like the most *giving* kind of mattress, all we could hear was the splashing of the surf, the great Indian Ocean. Then this *divine* Indian boy came and joined us, it was so hot when he started talking dirty in Urdu and he screamed like a pig when he came, it was just unreal . . .'

(When they goe in the Streets [of Goa] the Portuguese hidalgoes step very softly and slowly forwards, with a great pride and vaine-glorious majestie, with a Slave that carrieth a great Hat or vayle over their heads, to keepe the Sunne and Raine from them. Also when it raineth they commonly have a Boy that beareth a Cloake of Scarlet or of some other Cloth after them, to cast over them: and if it bee before Noone, he carrieth a Cushion for his Master to kneele on when he heareth Masse, and their Rapier is most commonly carried after them by a Boy, that it may not trouble them as they walke, nor hinder their Gravities.)

'The problem with Marcus is that he really gets off on those South-of-Market sleazoids. What a waste of a beautiful guy. Just fucking around with his thumb up his butt. He should be fighting in El Salvador or something.'

Hands moved meretriciously but without elegance. Mock outrage, ill-synchronized head-bobbing and chin-thrusting, drug-reddened third-eyes under chiselled bangs. The performance arts, chameleons coming on as camellias.

'He's a Southern belle, can't you just *smell* the mint-julep?'

A heaving lesbian broke into howls of derision as the speakers poured forth, 'Man! Woman! Desire!' and clutched on to her triumfeminate of acolytes. She had won one of them in a slave auction and had put her into a shapeless shift with a logo that read 'Fit to be tied'.

'Shit,' said Aaron. 'Aren't they *tacky*? I'll bet she's had a strapadicktome. You can tell they're dykes, just look at their fingernails. You know in New York now you can buy 14-carat screw-on gold words you fit on the end of your fingernails saying things like "Virgin" and "AVAILABLE". I just don't see them going down big in the world of fisting.'

Jerome tried to overarm his way through the surging waves of chatter, but had already lost interest in his own view on ballet (although he'd intended to dazzle Aaron with a pyrotechnic display of erudition as spectacular as any entrechat). He was overcome with a numbing stupor; then was instantly reactivated by the seductive odoriferous leather newly beside him. What *was* it that was so inescapable about leather, that second skin so much more exciting than the real thing? He was transported to the girl in *Wozzeck*, slavering at the sight of the soldiers, and panting to Marie. It was hardly a person, more an artefact rendered extraterrestrial by the mirrored aviator glasses and the blank elimination of susceptibility. Black, silver-metalled lenses like the lacquer blinkers of a fly. The untidy, unclassified nature of the place could scarcely accommodate so perfect a specimen, so unadulterated a paradigm. He seemed to threaten to drive out the chaos and the *flaneurs* like money-changers from the temple. Jerome would have liked to watch this diaspora, all the detritus scattered to the far corners of the earth, leaving them together, survivors of the cataclysm, new sons of Noah poised on the brink of a purged creation. He nervously swallowed some Perrier and spooned down some yoghurt.

'You realize you're negating the beneficial effects of those things by digesting them in a state of high tension,' said Aaron.

'Frankly, my dear, I don't give a damn.'

26

The Weird Sisters
of Hammersmith

Sharon and Doreen – insistently pronounced 'D'reen', with a gobbled 'o' – devoted much of their energy to weaning Jerome away from the blandishments of real women and converting him to their own weird sisterhood. When not engaged in this Sisyphean task, they primped and patted each other, murmuring suggestions and endearments, bursting with sarcastic disbelieving shrieks, mutually washing and stroking like tireless kittens until they looked so exactly alike that neither could possibly have any objection to any eccentricity or deviation in the other's appearance. The result was two perfect clones with fierce moustaches concealing eternally pouting lips, hair whose millimetrical precision would have aroused envy in a topiarist and apparently poreless skin which none the less soaked up moisturizer as thirstily as gossip.

Jerome, of course, looked the part as well, although a hint of serious masculinity clung to him, more in the shyness of his responses – especially to these two screamers – than in any real physiognomical ruggedness. This was irresistible to Sharon and Doreen, who dreamed both of being such a man and of being possessed by such a man. It was galling – yet *fabulous* – that he so obstinately withheld himself from their sewing-circle.

'Oh, puh-*leeze*! Can't you ditch the dreary old slag just for one night? What *is* this passion for fish? It doesn't do anything for your image,' said Doreen. 'We'd give you a good time if it's a woman you're looking for. Sharon's been practising her contractions, haven't you, dear?'

Sharon shimmied in his laddered 501s to prove the point. A leather strap peeped through a tear in his groin at the exact place where his femininity was most flagrantly contradicted. He leered at Jerome with such single-mindedness that, had it not been for an almost imperceptible cast in his left eye, the unflinching gaze could have featured in a pop textbook on sexual enticement.

'You're such a gorgeous man, Jerome,' he said. 'I just wish you weren't so brainy. Heaven knows what's going on in that masterful *brooding* head of yours. Tell you what, if I get to fuck with you I promise not to say anything at all, I'll just be the roughest trade you could possibly want, you'll never even know I've *got* a brain, like Frankenstein's creation half-way through the operation, just body, all *body*.'

His pupils dilated as his speech became more excitable, Jerome fiddled with an overlong curl behind his ear. He was in the middle of one of his periodic efforts to declone, and his hair was gelled in spikes like quills upon the fretful porcupine. It really was a hassle, though, and he appreciated the virtues of short hair: no parasites flourished, conditioner became redundant, you didn't have to think about ways of doing it and, above all, you ran no risk of getting your hair caught in a tree and dangling there helplessly like Absalom strung up for Ahithophel.

'Come on, you guys. You cannot be serious. It's cracked-record time. Do we have to wade through all this shit again? When I need sex from either of you, or both of you, I'll give you a call. Tell me what's been happening.'

'Well,' said Doreen with all the breathy emphasis of a preamble to a long session, '*wouldn't* you just like to know. Maybe if we didn't spend so much time changing nappies, we wouldn't have to ask. Sharon's getting into nappies by the way, now she's doing so much water sports. Isn't that right, treasure? I'm thinking of buying her a rubber dummy and groundsheet to go with the dildo.'

Jerome's temper was wearing thin, yet he hung on, first because Sharon and Doreen were world-beaters on the hard-core scene and secondly because he liked to feel the pulse of the new, perfectly formed science of clonology.

Sharon came back with an armful of drinks.

'Ooh, that Sharon,' Doreen said. 'She's got more bloody muscle on her than the meat counter at Sainsbury's. Practising already for Qantas, are we?' he went on. 'You're not allowed to spill a drop, otherwise they throw you down the emergency shute.'

Sharon had just been accepted for a job as an air-steward. Being a sky-waitress had a lot of advantages. You could display an all-year-round *bronzage*, kick your heels in expensive hotels in faggot Meccas (Sydney, New York, etc.), collect book matches from Spikes, Ramrods, Probes and Vices all over the world, and get to bend over a lot in Club Class. *And* there were those heavenly Lufthansa ball-bearing, ball-breaking stewardesses.

'A Malibu and Amaretto and lemonade for you, Doreen, a Daiquiri for me and a big butch pint of lager for you, sweetheart,' said Sharon, distributing the drinks with a certain masculine purposefulness but even more of the finesse of a Filipino butterfly houseboy. 'That means you and I get blasted to kingdom come, Doreen, and Jerome just spends all night in the john. How about recycling the beer a bit? I just love to taste it the second time round. You know those parties they have in that warehouse in Amsterdam where the whole place is deserted and you think nobody's come until you realize they're all in the toilets kneeling under some Dutch guy like cocker spaniels with their tongues hanging out? You should *see* those toilets, fabulous ceramic tiles and all Victorian brass fittings like something out of *Interiors*. Seems a shame to waste it like that, I'd like to *live* there.'

'Ooh, *he's* nice,' Doreen swivelled and broke in. 'Hiya, dreamboat,' he added. Ten faces looked around, ablaze with hope. 'Not you, shitpricks,' Doreen spat, '*him.*'

The subject of attention turned, a neat flush of scarlet rising to the level where it precisely bisected his neat faun-like ears, their tips left ivory, their lobes roseate. It looked to Jerome as if he was one those queens who only looked around to deliver a withering blank-out and pass on like the Bad Samaritan;

in fact he was so struck by the hungry trio that he seemed to forget the unpromisingly camp overture and allowed the blush to settle and drain as he stood his ground and took in all three in brave turn, his eyes sweeping from one to another like high-intensity searchlights under the solid flaps of his lashes. His mouth had somehow filled with gravel.

'Hi, this is Jerome and John, and I'm Jo,' growled Doreen. The shift in gender was instantaneous, the camp inflection of piccolo obbligato bottoming out and replaced by a double bass cadenza. He wanted to continue, 'and you must be Josephine', but for the moment at least, until they knew each other better, he knew Marlboro Country tonality had to be sustained. 'Have a drink.'

'Thanks. What do you have to drink to get a fuck round here? How about a Coke? I'm on sulphate and anything else makes my throat burn up.'

No problem about integrating *her* into their sisterhood, they all thought at once. He joined their group as naturally as a docking liner. Why hadn't they met him before?

'My name's Frank, by the way. I was watching you guys earlier and trying to work out who does what to who.'

Doreen was ogling Frank's body determinedly so as to prevent this conversation from getting too general. Two strange queens moved a little nearer, but Jerome, observing their Arthur Scargill pleached thatches, realized it was less with the object of eavesdropping as of steering clear of the overhead fan. Sharon found himself looking at the clusters of lustrous hair that peeped out around the rim of Doreen's vest (which clung tightly to his torso, making his shoulder-blades, lats and breasts appear even more substantial) as his friend turned his gorilla-back on him.

Sharon's ambition was one day to wake up metamorphosed into Olivia de Havilland, wearing a sensational crinoline, in mid-descent of a marble staircase, at the foot of which would be her beaten rival, whom she would magnanimously raise up in an act of forgiveness witnessed by 10,000 extras.

'She's off,' he complained to Jerome. 'Give her an inch and she'll take nine. Just you wait, her voice'll break soon, like a boy soprano's only in reverse. She'll never keep it up. Come to think of it, that's always been her problem. Wait till you hear this. I was with this guy the other day. He was kind of Robert Redford, well, maybe just a bit. He had funny lumps on his cheek, anyway, and his back was a bloody lunar landscape. But he came on all handsome and irresistible and took *for ever* to cruise me, the naff queen. I get her home and she says she feels uncomfortable because she's too sober, so I make joint after joint and give her these dirty great swimming pools of vodka. Gradually she unbends and loosens up, and then she goes all butch and starts talking in an American accent and leans back and says things like, "Yeah baby, suck my dick," and I say, "Come off it, sweetie, you're not in America now just 'cos you once had a fortnight's AwayGay in New York," though I'm thinking actually she does look a bit like she's got jet-lag. *Anyway*, when it comes down to it, she's so stoned that she doesn't even get hard and just stumbles around knocking into the furniture, shouting at tables and chairs like it was their fault and they'd got up and hit her. Pathetic, you should've seen the state of her. If that's an attractive man, then I'm the Princess of Wales's stepmother. In the end I put her to bed with a Valium and Otto, that's my dog – poor thing, he's got no balls – got in beside her. It was good in a way, 'cos in the morning she had one of those foul hangovers when the only thing you feel like is sex. It sure made up for the night before, quite restored my faith in the macho male. He did things with my bootlaces you just wouldn't *believe* . . .'

Jerome was drinking too fast in order to conceal his inability to take part in this conversation. His assets, anyway, he knew to consist primarily in his looks and his mysterious quietness, the latter a real winner with these logorrhoeic canaries, these yapping caponized story-tellers whose fluency would have conferred privileged shamanistic status on them in a more primitive culture. He wondered what it was that made Sharon tick, if such a manic piece of exploding clockwork could be said to do anything so banal. On reflection he felt that Sharon's life had probably been permanently embittered and his energy galvanized by the fact that, when it came to it, his upper lip lacked the necessary spaciousness to grow a moustache as bushy and glossy as Doreen's.

234

'I don't know what they see in D'reen,' Sharon pouted. 'She's just a shop-girl under all that slap. She can't fool me. Somebody must've told her she looked like Harrison Ford a *long* time ago, but *me* – *well* . . .' he sucked in his cheeks. 'Can you bear so much beauty in one person?'

It was getting to be a strain to listen now, and Jerome craned forward so as not to miss the *mots justes* in Sharon's distilled wit and wisdom. The music suddenly seemed mind-numbing, a repetitive high-energy riff topped by a raunchy black girl who did little more than bawl out the names of gay resorts – 'Key West! San Francisco! Berlin! New York!' Huddersfield, Russian River didn't get a mention – too unrhythmic, or maybe a bit esoteric. At all events, Jerome was getting a mega-headache. He began to wish he was back home, stirring rusk and Brussels-sprout purée. The weary hissing conversations idly flapped along, trapped like sand-flounders in their own monotony.

Burble, burble, burble. Doris Day . . . jockstrap . . . Nuit d'Amour Marigolds . . . colon outrageous . . . Mildred Pierce . . . ball restraint, the *green* one! . . . customs officer at Tenerife airport . . . locked up with a German shepherd . . . *prima donna assoluta* . . . Armani, Alfredo . . . swollen lymph glands . . . right up the pipette . . . Bobby Womack and Rock Hudson, yes! . . .

'Oh God, you're so *amusing* these days. Ever since you picked up with that spooky blond runt from Chicago. Jesus, I really hoped she'd be the dumb kind but all that happens is she teaches you how to talk too much. God, your mouth is so big you can't help wondering where it's been. You know, like chest-expanders, only for mouths. I've heard of tunnel-vision, but tunnel-*mouth*, uh-uh!'

'You're a fine one to talk, you could always get a job as a sword-swallower.'

'Then I got cruised by this heavenly Danish guy . . .'

'So that's what's called bringing home the bacon! How did you know he was Danish, did he have it stamped on his bum?'

'No, I couldn't see among all the herpes scars and cigarette burns. But he did ask me to brand it on for him. I'll just have to go to Texas to get a branding iron, you know, the designer ones in Neiman-Marcus . . .'

The clones looked as eager and preoccupied as weasels, their moustaches, eyebrows and crewcuts quivering and bristling with alertness. Some unseen eventuality seemed constantly to await them. Their idea of paradise was to fly to New York for Hallowe'en or the Palais d'Extase (where the balcony groaned under the weight of infamous excesses). It didn't matter if they were dumped forty-eight hours later in the baggage check at JFK; the ecstasy of the sexual gyrations and the chemical stratosphere justified the foul aftermath.

Jerome's bladder began to prick. Casting self-consciousness to the four winds, he made his way to the lavatory. The contrast between the plain door and the exotic interior to which it led was reminiscent of the most fabulous Arabian fantasies. But the interior could not be so easily confined. As he opened the sesame door, it leapt out at Jerome as if it had been a coiled-up spring, waiting with expert timing for release. The walls shone with a greasy, semi-precious effluvia created by the yellowish lighting. On them black and white super-realist drawings of impossible, glowering, jut-jawed *Übermenschen* advertised leather bars in Liège, Karlsruhe, Bologna, Malmö and other cities of potent sexual mystique. A large knot of men stood waiting in a line which Jerome found classically English. But he could see immediately that they were not merely waiting; but rather absorbing some kind of anticipatory erotic aura. The *1812 Overture* was playing. (Would Tchaikovsky, tormented with homosexual guilt, have applauded this use of his music, and heard in the torrent of urine some angelic harmony?) The few men who were pissing used a low silver trough stretched at their feet. But their faces concentrated on the reflection of their whole frontal body in the dark bronzed mirror before them. Jerome joined them and, fixing his gaze exactly on their model, looked at the image of his penis and realized it was microscopically, subtly enlarged by some mysterious convexity. But the effect of this was dulled by the sudden extinction of the lights, a musical climax of cannons, bells and percussion and a hectic cross-hatching of stroboscopic light. Jerome watched his piss as it cascaded in the light like a tinkling shower of golden moidores.

A sanctuary within a sanctum, a spectacle as fantastic as the circus-parade outside the shrine of Urolagnia Immodesta and the Diversional Narcissus. No wonder these guys hung around like bemused acolytes. There was an ironic disproportion in the over-stagemanaged production number devoted to the most basic of human functions – one which for most people was an unmemorable, inconvenient interruption, but which here assumed, through the confused mystiques of shame, regression, humiliation, self-love and exhibitionism, the status of a cult tricked out with the paraphernalia of idolatry.

On his way back, Jerome looked down through a glass screen at the dance-floor. Droves of men with bared torsos lubricated with sweat performed a mirror dance, apparently a kind of ruleless self-expression not a million miles from Isadora Duncan, a celebration of the colossal power of physicality, yet in effect subject to a shared complicity, display reduced to muscular agreement. The whole panorama heaved and swayed, eerily silent through the sound-proofing, the entire rhythmic rationale of the movement replaced by the conversational stabs and flickers around him, this seeming as oddly stressed and irregularly frantic as German *Konkretmusik* from Darmstadt. In Jerome's direct line of vision stood a beautiful boy of about nineteen, almost motionless, gazing around him in beatific pleasure, bolstered in his tense and defiant sexuality by the reassuring horde. When he gradually moved, without feeling the *need* to move, just embarking on a loose-structured journey – his hair brightening and darkening, his eyes registering only an indistinct surging, a handkerchief soaked in ethyl chloride occasionally gripped between his teeth, Jerome sensed how the visible ecstatic oblivion cast off in him the mean pressure of the office or the bus-depot or the bland lying in bed in the absence of reasons to rise. But his temporary heroism was counteracted by the shorts he wore. They had a zip down the back – Irish shorts in the straight world, pragmatism in the gay.

Sharon and Doreen stood now beside a blown-up airbrush

picture of a pair of heavily chained engineer's boots stomping down to crush a helpless wrist and hand that tried simultaneously to clasp its oppressor. As they chattered and postured, the juxtaposition seemed as surreal as if a pair of fluffy tea-cosies had been set down beside an Exocet.

Could it be, was it *really*? They wouldn't *dare*. No, it *was*, a leather queen kneeling down, not to pleasure his lover but to adjust the inside leg of his chaps, slewing them carefully round to the front, much as a dowager would bend down to sew up a sudden gash in her niece's fragile organza.

'Ouch!' said Jerome as he banged his head on a pair of rubber waders that hung decoratively from the ceiling. He looked back up at the legwear reproachfully, but the waders swung with masterful unconcern.

'Fabulous!' said Sharon, using one of the eleven different inflections he'd perfected for that seminal passe-partout word. 'Get a load of those three queens on the sofa. Who do they think they are, the Three Graces? She's Grace Jones, she's Princess Grace of Monaco and she's . . . um . . . er . . .'

'Grace Quirrel,' suggested Doreen.

'Grace Abounding,' volunteered Jerome.

'Who's *she* when she's at home?'

Clones seemed to scurry about with a shy cast to their shoulders. 'You don't know what you're missing downstairs. There's this incredible leather aerial ballet, six guys hanging from the ceiling.' Downstairs the music was so loud that the clones conversed by screaming alternately into one another's ears, their eyes swivelling away as they did so. It became a kind of tennis-match, a stichomythia of shouted banalities batted back and forth and punctuated by pauses for bright laughter.

'You're a good colour.'

'Eye-beezer.'

'A-gain?'

'Well, we booked for Mykonos but the travel company folded.'

'The night before Joe and I landed in San Francisco . . .'

'You wire it up, plug it in and then it just takes over completely . . .'

'He went mad and shaved it all off. I couldn't stop him . . .'

'The tessitura's shrinking, nothing she can do about it, she just can't get it up there any more.'

'If he was really a lawyer like he said he was, then what the fuck were all those copies of *Plumbing Monthly* doing on the floor . . . ?'

'Eventually you just can't fight any more and you gradually die . . .'

'His best friend ought to tell him, but then he hasn't got *any* friends, let alone a best friend . . .'

'It had petals cut on the bias down the neckline and they all *rippled* when she walked. And these *incredible* opalescent paillettes with a snaky kind of rouleau hem . . .'

'We just wouldn't even *think* of going on holiday. This year it's either the double-glazing or the hostess trolley . . .'

There really *must* be more to life, Jerome fretted, than Mardi Gras, dirty jockstraps and persistent generalized lymphoid eropathy.

'What disease do Mayfair hostesses die from *not* having? Maids!'

'My parents are coming on Sunday and they're bringing a whole lot of bedding plants, so I was trying to decide what to do first, whether to weed out the buttercups and bindweed in the back patio – ooh, they're terrible this year, I've never seen weeds like them – or maybe I should paint the new shutters in the study, only I couldn't get the exact colour I needed till Thursday, so there I was in Safeways with my trolley just crammed with different kinds of . . .'

Jerome's eyes strayed upwards as a colossal screen lowered itself from the ceiling. When it was in position, a video was projected on to it of the scene when Joan Collins and Linda Evans, Alexis and Krystle, slug it out in the Carrington lily-pond. The queens went wild, whooping and yelling as the unladylike blows rained and the women's coiffeurs were reduced to Medusan aquatic plants.

Surely the world was right, Jerome thought. All of this was so deeply anti-natural that some kind of hormonal dysfunction was busily at work; and the gay world would pump its endocrinological mass around its pathic body until (after passing through gradable steps of effeminacy, womanhood and lesbianism in turn) they reverted, maybe, to being biological men. It was time to bring forward the *paradis artificiel*, to take off his tee-shirt, tuck it into a back pocket (so that it would swing appealingly, drawing attention to his cute ass) and hit the dance-floor and the amyl nitrite. Hell, that was better. A wall of mirror in front, the beginnings of a sweat trail fertilizing his back and trickling down over his coccyx and into the hollow between his buttocks, an army of men giving rein to their physicality, music like the drug of love. He wouldn't be on his own for long, and if he was he didn't care. He slid into electronic automatic pilot.

27

Jerome in Notting Hill

Closely guarded lives and nurtured paranoia seeped from the pendulous and indeterminate stucco of the sparrow-loud square. Trashed lives; fearful lives full of half-measures, always approaching some elusive climacteric, yet baulking at any kind of resolution. Adrift in a dense and transient landscape; solidarity only in this collective insecurity and sought obscurity. Like segmented fruit, lives here were mere adjuncts to one another and prey to the acid corrosion of intrusion. The etiolated grandeur of Ionic portals and abandoned balustrades, houses in reverse presenting their buttressed rears to the alien gutter. Like the houses of San Francisco, their fire-escapes clamped to their *fronts*. Horizons and space were blocked by these cloud-bearing fortresses. Enclosing so much moral diversity and nonconformism. No orthodoxies left. Post-war virtues spurned and maintained only in a kind of indulgent nostalgia smiling at the eclipse of moral certainty; a faint smirk of recognition of the kitsch-movie value of discretion, honesty, reserve, dignity, silence. Under attack now from the new Titans, the dispossessed in possession, the buildings beleaguered by their unforeseen denizens, Mycenean lion-gates sheltering the un-Greek.

A white child scraped the tyres of a car with a sliver of Plexi-glas. A black one rolled marbles into the mouth of a dead cat. Two young women apprehensively eased their fleshless asses into the acidic grass, screeching nocturnally at their crazed offspring. The half-hearted wail of a police siren was already dispirited by the larcenous flood. Three

241

self-confident Jamaicans, with aureoles of dread, like so many Apollos burned the pavement with their *folie de grandeur*. Shrinking adults, cowed into heaps of plastic and clingfilm, surprised disappointment and limited expectations, newly aware of the weird apocalypse-calypso. Argentine exiles were in conclave, incommunicado plotters in *bombachos*, doomed proxy *montoneras* locked in futile assemblies. The fluttering headdresses of polychrome Ukrainians were livid against the matt eau-de-nil of partition walls. Weeping secretaries, downwardly mobile as Icarus, were spreadeagled by their own pointlessness. Opportunities and self-esteem escaped through rotting architraves, slid perceptibly like slime through the roach-cracks. Berberis of dusty aniline, part now of the organic mouldering, feebly illuminated the dismal confines of an exploited tenement now benefiting the pitiless coffers which once were filled under a bed in Vilnius. Blotchy children, who ached with urban guile, set up their embryonic street hierarchy, power clinging to the tendrils of their hair. Threatened Tuinal-droppers from the upper and outer echelons intuitively sought out the up-market stallholders of the Portobello Road, pressing avocados with contrived bravado in order to shut out the bulking plantains, yams and ginger roots that swamped their vision. Mumbling bundles of synthetic fibre fiercely navigated barbed trolleys and sickening brats. Cheap Spanish cologne that smelt of lime cordial and creosote. Pitted, ravaged, elastoplasted lives.

Amid the dreary archipelago, Jerome clung to the sinking flotsam of his own neuroses. Self-pity was easier if you could relate it to social concerns – and that could best be maintained at close quarters. While his own problems seemed diminutive and self-indulgent beside the tangible squalor, he also felt that they had a right to survive there, that they were not being force-fed in some sequestered area of privilege. Of course he was wrong (repeated the imaginary supercilious narrator he believed was writing his life for him). But he chose to ignore the cavilling doubts and caressed his own version. He bought American magazines and high-pulp fruit-juice, bicycled through the crowd in a cloud of soul-fusion, and harangued launderette attendants when he felt eloquent. He telephoned for hours, except when his unrealistic sense of domestic economy made him keep silent for days on end. When problems loomed, he turned away and, like the *Tolypeutes matacus* armadillo, rolled himself up into a ball. Believing that cellular tissue would regenerate more efficiently without the *Sturm und Drang* of his waking life, he slept continuously in a drugless accidie. He knew, though the knowledge was persistently inefficacious, about the terrible dangers of accidie. He had even read, in a diatribe by Cassian of Marseilles, of this affliction of a troubled mind, that it engendered boredom with one's cell, contempt for one's brethren, how it prevents some from making progress and leads us to make exaggerated claims for the advantage of being somewhere else, some spiritual distance. 'One's mind is in an irrational confusion, like the earth befogged in a mist'; but for Jerome the fog was too permanent for him really to understand the way out.

At other times he panicked and forced himself into a fever of activity, overcome with the Duchess of Malfi's fear 'if too immoderate sleep be truly said/To be an inward mist unto the soul'. And failing to get up in the morning, lolling in bed like a slag meant always, as Effi Briest had seen, the collapse of all discipline.

He was too lazy at the moment even to feed the cat, however much it cried before passing through the hunger-barrier and resorting to resentfully biting off the leaves of a probably poisonous gardenia.

He missed Venetia, it was true; primarily out of pique that she might probably be enjoying a more uncomplicated life than his own. He wished sometimes that she could have her lustrous head forced down against a pustular Arab crotch, that she could be made to love the Estonians, that she should wait permanently in line for festering Polish meat; maybe then she would understand the promiscuous peaks and troughs of his own odd life, its temporary sacrifices in the cause of redemptive pleasure; its frequent plunges into actual *boue sans nostalgie*.

When Venetia called him from Marin, he found it hard to respond to her opulent self-satisfaction. His head ached from the excesses of the night before. And as he sprang listlessly to

243

answer the telephone, the cat dived for his ankles and left him sprawling beside the instrument, which, happily, was right beside him on the floor behind the sofa. This was no random impulse on the cat's part; it was a play in a calculated strategy originating in the theory – empirically enough tested – that the maximum annoyance ended in a placatory feed-up.

'David and I went out with the Red Cross to help the mud-slide victims at Santa Cruz. You wouldn't *believe* their despair, women just standing in the debris crying. Do you remember those pictures of the 1906 earthquake when everyone gathered excitedly to watch the spreading inferno below? Well, this time there was no sense of elation, no spectacle, just ghastly all-consuming despair. The stench was indescribable, the furniture all reduced to pulp, an oozing quagmire of spilling freezers and cesspools, everything brown and· streaky. Quite a sight. David loved it and kept clutching huge handfuls of slime and throwing them at the housewives. So I strapped him into a papoose and he liked that too. Do you think he'll grow up to be a bondage queen? I couldn't bear it, it makes people so dreary, they don't have any friends.'

My God, thought Jerome, should anyone be allowed responsibility for children? Even when she embarked on some charitable enterprise, Venetia could never fully sacrifice her frivolous detachment, her contrasuggestible ethics, her invasion of his own private world and its Eleusinian mysteries. Her adenoidal, *surexcitable* voice sounded like the climax of a Barbra Streisand finale, especially now that it had adopted so many American mannerisms. It had a hectoring, stentorian quality, even when she was seeking affection. It had made people nervous in European hotel lobbies, fastidious queens had poutingly drawn away from its orbit, London punks had lowered menacingly at the unstoppable decibels. Still, one had to make allowances for someone who had made so strange and unqualified a sacrifice of her innate sexuality and offered it up on the altar of Uranus.

'How are you getting along?' she asked.

'Well, England's fine. I miss you, but every time I see a fat blonde, I think of you.'

'You pig! Done anything interesting?'

'Not much. Hanging around with queens most of the time. Real men they call themselves. Last night we saw some avant-garde movies with Sebastian and Red at the Noir. Boys being crucified, roses turning into bandages, all to the accompaniment of anvils and a chorus of ravens, the usual kind of thing. Oh yes. There *was* a fantastic sequence when those two guys dress up as Spanish inquisitors and sit with their backs to us, arm in arm, watching a back-projection of flowers, rather Isaac Oliver, and the music sounded like you're wearing armour and someone's bashing your helmet very hard with an iron rod. At the end of the session a South American girl got up and screamed abuse at the director.'

'So unlike the home life of our own dear Queen,' Venetia said. 'And how's work?'

'I keep getting bombarded with requests to do commercial publicity and I'm just determined to hold out. If you do that, it turns you into a completely different kind of photographer. But I've done some pictures of children. The idea's to emphasize their likeness to their grandparents and I was really very pleased with that. The temptation was to draw moustaches on them and powder their hair, even dress them up in Fair Isles and collarless shirts, but I resisted. One of them was quite uncanny. She naturally angled her profile so as to make her features like her 'twenties grandmother's, the same eye-focus, the same slight shadow beside the retroussé nose, everything. I'd have loved to use David, but I'd have had to flog across to Madrid to get a picture of his grandfather from the naval archive.'

'Darling, that's just exactly what I want to talk to you about. Once I asked Adelaida what her father was like, and she didn't understand the question, and all she said was, "Physical contact," and rolled her eyes.

'I'm calling because Adelaida is in some sort of mess. The last thing I want is to confront David with his mother at his present vulnerable age. It'd be bad enough if she was reasonably balanced; but it seems like she's verging on a major collapse. She sounded completely dehumanized, robotic, with that horrid flat voice – the Castilian plain, I call it – dropped a few registers, a kind of technological voice, cybernetic tessitura. One wonders how she ever got on in California; she's right at the opposite end of the spectrum from all the consciousness-raising and intuition-expansion. How can I ever have related to her? I'm beginning to think she's demonic, like some kind of battening Barbey d'Aurevilly succubus. Maybe she achieves her nasty ends by operating a sort of compulsive energy-field. Suckers like me don't stand a chance. Especially if we have an inbuilt passion for radical chic.'

'I'm the last person to ask, Venetia; you know what I feel about Adelaida. It's hard for me to judge because I've never remotely understood her. I have to admit to a certain perverse interest in female violence. I've never been able to explain to myself the capacity for gratuitous sadism you can find in deviant women like Adelaida. As a matter of fact I had a dream about that the other day' (or was it night? – immaterial in Jerome's twenty-four-hour hypnic cycle). 'It was about the concentration camp at Ravensbrück. It went on and on, and then it got confused with Theresienstadt. I felt like a snake transfixed by a mongoose. The only way I could control my fascination and revulsion – even through the dream-sequence – was to follow a wild associative series through the name Teresa. And speculate about what the various Teresas would have made of a female concentration camp – Ávila, Lisieux, Maria Theresa, Espronceda's girl friend Teresa Mancha, Byron's Contessa Guiccioli. Perhaps Teresa of Ávila's prayer of inner quiet would have shielded her from Ilse Koch. Anyway' – he drew a breath and forced himself away from the vagaries of his train of thought, itself already filtered from its random oneiric source – 'what are you going to do about her?'

'I shall *have* to go to Madrid. Much as I fear and dislike her, she needs some kind of support. Although it's the last thing she'd confess to.'

Venetia's voice had assumed Adelaida's bitterness, squeezed out of her sinus, in order to state these horrid facts. Jerome looked for refuge and solace at the engravings in the libretto of the soporific Bellini opera he'd been listening to – garlanded fatsos and attitudinizing barbers with iron lungs. He could sense an ominous importunity in Venetia's voice.

'Please come,' she said, confirming his intuition. 'It would be so much easier if you were there. You could keep David out of Adelaida's clutches and act as some kind of solid bastion for me. When I eventually free myself from her gravitational pull.'

'Jesus, you really know how to foul up my hard-won serenity.'

'Come on, you know how much you appreciate *any* opportunity to show off your altruism. The egomaniac with a mission. *Del vieni, non tardar.* We can stay at Raúl's apartment on Claudio Coello, he's in Huelva. And you can spend all day at the Turkish Baths in the Plaza de España. Just so long as you're around to pick up the pieces after my sessions with Dolours Price. God, I hate her, why am I *doing* this?'

Just think about it sweetie. No one else needs your help. Urban terrorism is a lot more interesting than infant care. And you're getting addled in Marin with your army of analysts, neo-Reichian technicians, Gestalt therapists, rebirthers, orthobionomists, astral trainers, kinesiological irrigators, lymphatic drainers, interactional regenerationists, those marshmallow balletomanes masquerading as hard men who are good to find. Time for a bit of second-remove commitment. Just how many times *can* one somatize? What exactly *did* you learn from a Thematic Apperception Test?

His most recent *coup de théâtre* had been to find Venetia sharing her creativity with nature on the model of the Chinese in their public parks; she was singing her heart out to a tree in Golden Gate Park. He could imagine her planning her outfit for the meeting with Adelaida, despairingly fingering Israeli parachutist uniforms and glancing down at her recalcitrant cellulite. (No, that holster really would *not* reduce.) But she was politically so apathetic, he thought, how could she ever even associate herself with Adelaida's manic *pronunciamientos*? Shit, why couldn't Adelaida have been half-way OK, a teenage tennis star, a pianistic *Wunderkind, anything,* just a more productive kind of extremist? He suspected that her energies would have been more reasonably deployed had she been brought up in America and succumbed to a cheerfully listless patriotism. It was bloody Spain that had nurtured her inhumanity; the bitter

247

patrimony of Francoist materialism and its institutionalized conformism.

These reflections supervened after Jerome, needless to say, acquiesced to Venetia's grossly unfair proposal. At first he toyed with ratting on her and sending a Proustian telegram: *'Impossible venir, mensonge suit.'* His real anger was reserved for Adelaida. His relationship with her was, in any case, one of such reciprocal loathing that it was easier to offload on to her the full weight of his mere impatience with Venetia. He had agreed to meet Venetia next week at Raúl's high-tech apartment: a minimalist living-space austerely provided with aerodrome-runway lights, steel hospital cabinets, enamel kidney-basins that served as crockery, towering industrial shelving and exposed galvanized drainage-conduits. The prospect of its abortion-clinic chic further deepened the nascent despair in Jerome's swirling mind.

A girl outside in the street stood bowing and ducking at a baby, elaborately kissing her hand in a mock-baroque curtsey. Oh, the pain of needing to be liked! The extremes to which it drove one! The waste of physical and spiritual energy, all those enforced concessions which interfered with the conduct of one's own life! Jerome knew that he was caught between selfishness and the stratagems necessary for proving his unselfishness. And here was this sacrificial measure, the anguish of Madrid beckoning when apparently all he really had to do was kiss a baby and have done with it! His relationship with Venetia, indispensable, reassuring and life-giving as it was, seemed sometimes like a voracious maw which swallowed up all his depleted reserves of generosity of spirit. His realization of this – and more especially his articulation of it – was always accompanied by the bleak acknowledgement that *no* other facet of his life could be thought of as self-sacrificial. He liked to conceive of his love for her as an expression of innocence; and would sing to himself in a kind of Elizabethan beguine:

> 'Love seeketh not itself to please,
> Nor for itself hath any care,
> But for another gives its ease

And builds a Heaven in Hell's despair.'
So sung a little Clod of Clay,
Trodden with the cattle's feet.

Unable, or unwilling to express his love for her sexually, he associated it with a childlike contract in which he could annihilate his own vanity. Venetia had a sacramental power, conferring grace on his blitzed soul. Were she to disappear, he would have no other stake on which to bind the withering tendrils of his altruism. At least she provided for him scenarios – there seemed to be no other word – in which he could act out the given rules of humane behaviour and project the semblance of charity. Even his exposure to Adelaida had been engineered by Venetia, not through any awareness on her part of a potential beneficial effect, but rather as a result of her naïve belief in what she called her 'theory of coalescing personalities': the farther apart two characters initially stood, the more dramatic and satisfying their fusion would be. Generally these artificial collisions ended up like those of contrary magnets, doomed to a last-minute rotation. In fact Jerome's reaction to Adelaida had been more complex and had forced him to dissimulate like crazy. Adelaida's view of Jerome was immaterial, as she saw no advantage in knowing him; the resemblances with Lorenzo were too damning; and she sought only to axe him. For her, his leadership potential was negligible. Indeed, he would be a positive threat in any position of office. She could never imagine him co-operating with the political cells she had dragooned in Kilburn in between flailing choke-holds with Irishmen on activism furlough. So perhaps Madrid was holding out a redemptive prospect; and he thought of David with a pang of real love.

He walked across to a card-index balanced precariously on the broken leaf of a Victorian mahogany table, but stopped half-way to put on another swooping, long-breathed act of *Beatrice di Tenda*. The first action, with its threat of overdue work, was unthinkable without the mollifying panacea of the second. His work – meticulous and expert as it was – would always be jeopardized by this unwillingness to treat it as a self-contained activity. Its very private nature made him want to integrate it into the whole pantomime of life. The idea made him feel like a modern British playwright showing people not just acting but *doing* things on stage, sweating in a locker-room, eating, ironing, throwing up, pacifying lunatics, stoning babies. This was one of the things that really separated him from Venetia. Her work was effortlessly dilettante, cushioned by other people's resources, never an imposed constraint. His, on the other hand, was the only recourse he had to demonstrate his illusory independence from her. It made him feel wasted by *force majeure*. This arose not from mere *Schlamperei*, rather from the difficulties of his cyclic rhythms, the dizzying alternations between high-energy equilibrium and inert pessimism, a life veering like a drink-driver truck between the fast and slow lanes. Today he felt as if he'd come finally to rest on the hard shoulder.

He took a shower under the specially imported high-jet American cascade. His cat now lay on the floor beside him, energy dissipated, languorous through a miasma of malevolent halitosis. 'So who's my fierce little leopard? Just you be good, or nasty Lady Docker'll come along and turn you into a coat. What *are* we going to do, Lanfranc? Do we really have to go to Madrid?' It was, he hoped, a *num* construction, expecting the answer no. Surely those idiotic Latin constructions demonstrated the futility of human discourse! You knew the answer before you even asked the question! But there wasn't really even a question. His duty was clear. He would have to go through the customary upheaval, packing the heavy-duty cosmetics, the travelling library, the emergency lenses, and saddle poor, patient, cat-struck Seraphia with Lanfranc. Lanfranc, Anne Frank, why not just ditch Venetia and have a few steamy nights in Amsterdam? He couldn't be bothered to answer his own question or rehearse all the arguments he'd already so laboriously pursued. If the second shampoo lather produced the promised high gloss, he'd go. In this adventitious way, the decision was taken which launched Jerome's political career.

28

Ciudad Rodrigo:
Venetia and David

Venetia got fed up as soon as şhe arrived in Madrid. It was
hot and windless. Her throat breathed in gulps of dry air
that seemed to come from a malfunctioning, underground
radiator. And the sense of asphyxiation was compounded
by the exhaust fumes of the traffic, as extrovert as its drivers
and so relentlessly swarming that she wanted to scatter
tin-tacks in its path. She was swept by a city sadness, a
sense of powerlessness and oppression, which she knew
would linger until Jerome's galvanizing arrival.

Temporarily encamped in Raúl's apartment, her luggage unpacked, averting her eyes from its uncosy post-
modernism, she squatted on the floor and pored over a
map of Spain. David crawled up her back, scaling and
falling, clutching at her hair as he repeatedly lost hold
and rushed back for another assault on her North Face.
Her eyes flickered from Catalonia to Andalusia, Levante to
Galicia, and gradually came to rest on the remote borders
of the kingdoms of León and Portugal. The name of Ciudad
Rodrigo imprinted itself, its semi-bold type more forceful
than the familiar capitals of the capitals, its *echt*-Castilian
sound redolent of El Cid (wrongly as it turned out) and
the Gothic kings, a feeling of solidity and historicity. It
looked also as if it was in the right sort of geographical
place. If she grew hopelessly bored, she could escape to
near-by Salamanca and cruise some easy-prey academics. She

checked the gazetteers and read out the town's assets to David: two kilometres of circumvallation, Romanesque cathedral, Peninsular War sieges, typical squares and palaces, that sounds fine, doesn't it, darling? Help me pack. They went.

The palaces were as beautiful as she'd hoped, although the people who presumably lived in them were somewhat less than palatial. They looked mulish and slack-jawed and bore the signs of struggle in their faces. There was an air of unsatisfied longings, of sexual and moral tension. As she promenaded nervously with David, she was met by glances of hostile curiosity from the women and began to feel that she had – not for the first time – miscalculated her appearance. She remembered Lady Holland's dire warning, from nearly two centuries before, of the 'extreme derision and scorn with which a woman is treated who does not conform to the Spanish mode of dressing'.

She pulled David to a table in the Plaza Mayor and sat down for a calming chestnut shake. It frothed tantalizingly, and David spooned some off the top but spat it out after one taste.

'Yuck, don't they have proper sodas here?'

'Darling, don't be a bore. You drink your Coke and I'll drink my *horchata*.'

She toyed with a newspaper while he surveyed the passing scene.

'Hey, look at her, it's the Wicked Witch of the West,' David stage-whispered.

Venetia looked up, and all her fears for her own feminine credibility evaporated at the sight of this *ne plus ultra* of the grotesque. No sinister matron could even in the long school nights have aspired to such a coiffure, so processed that it looked like a lifeless wig. Her thick sunglasses had dark-green ophthalmic lenses which rested on a hawk-like nose more disfiguring even than the thin, beaky proboscis of the Duchess Marie-Louise of Parma. Her earlobes were distended by gold weights to a degree undreamed of by the most fervent African self-remodeller. Her mouth rat-trapped open and shut as she walked. Inexplicably hailed by a group of women, she sailed across and joined their huddle of self-assertive exchanges. Each responded to the others' cavorting and melodramatic gestures – mostly of outrage – as if invisible rods between them joined together facial muscle with facial muscle, arm with arm, admonitory fore-finger with admonitory forefinger. Perfect pleats swished around their varicose veins and their bulbous feet were thrust, desquamating and verrucaed, into tiny court shoes. All their conference revealed the sureness of their moral convictions; and a tight bank of self-regard hemmed them in from Venetia's alien stare.

It was only after a while, during which she passed from registering their peculiarities to overhearing their conver-sation, that she discovered how rudimentary their concerns actually were. 'Underwear's so expensive in Salamanca, it costs you a testicle'; 'Encarnación's granddaughter's gone to London on an excursion. I think we know what *that* means.' One of the fatter ladies opened her handbag and, after taking out a foil-wrapped suppository, hoicked up her skirt, rolled over on to one buttock and inserted the wax torpedo. 'What a beautiful sky,' her neighbour exclaimed.

'The trouble is that we Spaniards live with our heads in the sky.'

'And the sky's so boring it just goes up and up, like the price of everything.'

'Until the Americans blow it apart.'

Occasionally a profile hovered tentatively towards her, a flickering eye lizarded through its paint with only the mildest curiosity. It was inescapable that they had little need of her.

David was becoming restless. His attention had wan-dered from the street-life to the samba rhythms he was improvising with a teaspoon and glass. Venetia glowered, snatched the spoon away and paid the bill. Whether out of vagueness or ingrained insecurity, she left a tip that would have bought the proprietor a spring lamb. They left the table noisily, in a glare of publicity now: rich space-invaders who mocked the respectable aspirations of the townspeople. Shielded from the sun, they walked idly through narrow streets, pressed in by honey-coloured palaces stuck with heraldic escutcheons and wrought-iron grilles, the pavements so precipitous that the girls sat on them with their knees drawn up high above the gutter as the boys showed off in front of them, bullfighting delivery-vans. Eventually, overtaken by hunger, they went into a bar which was little more than a deep cupboard sprinkled with sawdust. Such food as there was flagged faintly on dusty pottery dishes, and David stopped to watch a bluebottle burrowing angrily into a grey tortilla.

The old men had the dry faces of spiritual certainty tempered by kindness. The edges of their eyes had been deeply creased by their courageous humour and afternoons wincing at the sun's glare in the corn-fields. They clung to the symbols of a Spain untorn by democrats or nationalists: berets, dark flannel waistcoats, greasy bandannas spilling from pockets, balding corduroy trousers. Venetia liked them instinctively, comparing them with the gruesome women and then immediately feeling guilty over such sisterhood-disloyalty.

'Can you tell me where I can find something to eat?'

The eyes of the men who stood at the bar as they picked at brains in batter took on a spark of curiosity and they guided her eagerly into the street.

'Over there you'll find a *mesón* where you can eat lentils, bean-stew, artichokes, asparagus, steak, cutlets, chicken . . .'

'Pork, omelettes, trout, mussels,' interrupted another, his beret quivering with excitement.

'Liver, kidneys in sherry, partridge, sucking-pig,' said a third. All contributed to the description of the cornucopia that awaited her. She feared that when she got there she would find little more than strained soup and scarlet sausage of brick-dust, unidentifiable gristle and lard. The eulogy of the restaurant became so clamorous that David backed away and tripped into the gutter.

'Come on, darling, we'll see what we can find. I bet you'll love the asparagus.'

'I want a triple bacon burger with a side portion of French fries and a banana milkshake.' It was an old joke of which he never tired. Earlier a big-eyed child had shyly, solemnly held out a plate of garlic potato crisps and David had gracelessly and with great theatricality pretended to throw up.

'We'll see, darling, we'll see.'

The restaurant was called, oddly, El Sanatorio. This seemed to refer more to its valetudinerian timetable than to its restorative powers. The meal lasted one and a half hours: twenty minutes of unhurried waiting, seven minutes of eating, eighteen more of waiting, twenty-two more of eating, fifteen of eating, thirteen of waiting. David timed it exactly on his Mickey Mouse watch. 'May you benefit!' said a chorus of friendly strangers, referring to their meal. Towards the end, David poked desultorily at his quiver-jelly with a two-pronged fork. Venetia, meanwhile, was rabbit-fascinated by a naïf painting on the wall opposite which advertised a sports club called La Liebre ('The Hare'). The picture showed a start-eyed hare being used as a football by a team of muscular heroes.

'Under the circumstances,' David said, as if it were a complete sentence.

'I know what you mean. You see, Spanish people don't really mind. They've been like that for years. They love their lives and they don't want anything to change. The ones who do, go away to London or Paris or New York. One day you'll grow to understand and love them and see there's more to them than just silly old people who tweak your cheek and shout a lot all the time.'

The overhead fan screeched and stopped and a quantity of fly-carcases dropped on to the table. David started to arrange them in the positions of a football field until Venetia imperiously swept them into a napkin and deposited them in the bowl of a plastic hydrangea.

'Urgh, sometimes you really are the pits! How *can* you be so squalid?'

'What an enchanting child!' offered a new voice. A large jolly man had abandoned the bar to come and speak to them. 'Are you German?'

'No, we're Irish,' Venetia lied, dodging the possibility of a confrontation over Gibraltar, or the Falklands. '*Southern* Ireland, not where the fighting is.'

The man seemed satisfied with the answer which was, for him, *muy católico*, very *comme il faut*. It seemed to require no elaboration.

'Do you like bullfights?'

'Not much,' she replied. 'I can't speak for my boy.' She turned to David and translated the question for him. He rolled his eyes and hit the roof.

'No, I don't think either of us like them much,' she continued.

'I'm sorry. Here in Ciudad Rodrigo we have the bull-mania. All around you will find fields full of the bravest fighting-bulls in Spain. In Ledesma, in Vitigudino, in Sancti Spiritus and Tamames. All the best *matadores* come here, El Litri, Paguiri, Vázquez . . .'

Although Venetia enjoyed a good list, her lunch had made her disagreeable.

'I think the whole thing is disgusting. Imagine how much pain the poor animal suffers.' She surprised herself with the vehemence of her denunciation.

The man looked blank, as if she had resorted to English.

'What justification can there be for inflicting such agony? It's inhuman, the animal is nobler than anyone involved. How can you tolerate such a thing?' She couldn't stop.

'One has to eat,' he answered laconically.

It took her some time to understand the connection between the question and the answer. She had never before thought of bullfighting as a livelihood. Life, she reminded herself, was a struggle for these people.

'When do we go see the uranium mine?' asked David.

The hotel receptionist had a lot to answer for. He had told David about the near-by mine in sign language, miming explosions and glass rods going in and out of silos. Venetia had censored the last part and refused to translate for them.

David as yet seemed to have very little notion of the country of his origin. Spain made him slightly cantankerous and impatient and, above all, demanding. On their arrival in Madrid, he had insisted on viewing the pandas in the zoo, where they sat appealingly in water-barrels stripping bamboo branches at high speed. David stared, as entranced, if less voluble, than the Spanish children around him, and pronounced his verdict: 'Black eyes. They look like they've been mugged.' How on earth was Venetia to reverse this relentless urbanization of the child, this disenchanted sophistication, *urbs in rure*, that threatened to carry him farther even than herself or Jerome into a wilderness of their own making?

'We don't,' she said *ex cathedra*. 'Show this nice man your watch and tell him how it works.'

David held up his wrist to the bull-enthusiast and launched first into a welter of microelectronics and then, seeing he was not being understood by the fat pig and ascribing this incomprehension to stupidity rather than a simple language barrier, told a complicated biography of Mickey Mouse with all the voices.

'Darling, do be quiet.' David looked justifiably hurt by the cancellation of orders. 'We'll go to the Plaza Mayor and you can have a Fanta, then it'll be time for a siesta.'

In the early evening, Venetia went out alone to buy some anti-vertigo pills. The chemist reassured her and told her to keep out of the heat of the sun. On her way home she pressed herself conscientiously against the high walls.

Right on cue, bitch on heat, alligator on tit, stoned on *tinto*, a grotesquely Madridified youth swaggered up to her in the street of Giants and stopped as she shyly, sullenly, furiously walked on. He looked pretty much the town shit.

'Cutie, you're *hot*,' he snarled in his bit-part voice. 'If they put you in the Atlantic Ocean, it'd boil over.'

Six out of ten for conceit (literary), she thought, ten out of ten for conceit (behavioural).

They rose early from their rest, too early to prepare themselves for the evening *paseo*. It was bound to be a disappointing event, anyway – a constant surge and flux back and forth, then mandatory inspection and feigned consideration of pen-knives, saucepans and ancient flesh-coloured brassieres in shop-windows. Venetia took a deep breath and tried another tack.

'I think it would be really nice to go for a walk in the evening sunshine. We could walk all the way round the walls and then I'll buy you that plastic statuette of General Franco with all the medals; it's lovely, I do agree, to die for.'

God, she hated that obligatory bribery; but without it the concept of co-operation might as well be left entirely to the EEC secretariat.

'Yeah, OK, Neeshie, it's a deal.'

257

He was really eager, and she hustled him out in the rumpled clothes he'd slept in before he could change his mind.

As they sprang with an Anglo-American step up the sloping approach to the ramparts, a sudden flight of martins darted out of the myriad holes in the cathedral façade. They both looked up, startled, and Venetia sadly recorded the smashed entablature and eroded finials.

'Look, David. All those holes are there because the Duke of Wellington, who was a very brave and well-known English general, fired a lot of big guns at the town so he could get rid of the French soldiers inside and give it back to the Spanish.'

It was growing too complicated; easier to stop there. Anyway, the probable truth that the building had suffered years of neglect would have been simpler but duller.

'What guns? Where?' asked David, his eyes shining.

'Well, sweetie, it was a long time ago, but they were over there on those two flat hills.'

They had emerged on to the ramparts and looked out to the northern horizon. The ramparts were broad and spacious enough for a promenade; above them a brick-seamed fortification plunged outwards at intervals into a round stone look-out post. The walls alternated in strength between plant-strewn rubble masonry and cyclopean stone. Below them squatted minuscule arc-lights, eternally dark, for, as a lady had recounted to Venetia, their bulbs were inaugurally kicked in by *gamberros* on the day of their installation. Farther out, there were more concentric earthworks, some of them in a star-shaped Vaubanesque formation that would only have been appreciable from the air.

David was impressed. Conscious of the slight he was casting on her efforts to amuse him, he slipped his hand into hers and squeezed it, and she, in turn, was moved by this sign of kindness. He had, since arriving in Spain, bitten back his obvious distaste for many things criticizable; his mind was, she imagined, enmeshed with largely hostile views of squat, smelly people who were idiotically overdressed – especially his contemporaries – mysterious sewer-like exhalations, bumpy roads with no respect for the suspension perfected by Americans, unhygienic trash that came up to your ankles in street cafés, dogs that looked like anatomy lessons, a cult of spoiled brats who resented his California brawn and cool. He only mentioned these in passing when he was actually under threat. In a way, Venetia would have preferred a more candid wail of protest so she could explain and justify things and present the case for the defence. She'd enjoyed it when he'd kicked a three-year-old small-town flirt who tried to seduce him with sunflower seeds.

Now their sense of shared adventure was unconditional. Not only was Venetia fulfilling a cultural duty, a passion for history and a maternal concern, but David was launched on a cerebral militaristic enterprise that rivalled the siege of Cádiz itself. He was also trying to forget his awful diarrhoea, the kind that made you scared to cough (let alone fart). Detaching his hand from Venetia's, he zigzagged with frank inquisitiveness from vantage-point to vantage-point, as fleet as the lizards among the liquorice plants. He bent to grub around in the earth and straw – had you raised the temperature of the sun to that of a kiln, the ground would have baked itself into bricks – and examine ant-trails, frantic crawlings for no apparent purpose. He stroked the leaves of a fig-tree that struggled up through a machicolation and examined his fingers for sap. He sniffed the deposit. Finding a ripe fig, he squashed it in his hand and opened his palm to scrutinize the crimson and ivory pulp. He was all tactility.

Venetia meanwhile tried to force her attention away from the interiors of the houses which sank like doomed liners below her, level within the protective circumvallation. A cage of canaries and macaws doubly trapped in a glassed balcony; a gesticulating housewife, a row of drying fish, a crumbling palace for sale, a zinc bucket full of bubbling pig's blood – all absorbed her attention at the expense of the romantic fortification and the outline of the sierra. Gradually the surrounding land fell away. The rash of modern suburban housing ceased; and she caught sight of the Agueda river far below, half-hidden by a grove of intensely green alders and poplars and so sluggish that it reflected less light than David's silvered astronaut jacket. She leaned over the parapet to make a camera shutter of her hands and block out the avid lion's-pelt colours of the fields which besieged this oasis as obstinately as the unforgiving artillery of Wellington. It looked as if the gasping sterility had indeed encroached on the trees. She could make out dead branches and cracking leaves; and the church beside the disused flour-mill was roofless, displaying its burst and hardened intestines.

David looked down at the sweet-corn plantations.

'How do the farmers stop the people from stealing the corn?' he asked.

'I don't think they have to. Even here there aren't many people who are so desperately poor that they have to steal. They're all ultra-honest. Although in Seville I'm told there are gangs of boys on motor-bikes who ride around and snatch women's handbags, and even chop their fingers off with knives to get their rings.'

'Wow!' said David and was lost in thought.

Venetia's anger rose as she spotted a pistachio-green plunge-roofed Swiss chalet built just beneath the ramparts.

'Look at *this*, darling. Have you ever seen anything so awful?'

'*Yes*, it's horrid. I guess it'd make a good ski-jump.'

But his attention had already strayed, drowsy in the heat, to a donkey which pressed up defensively against the side of the wall below. If David were to lower himself in an exact perpendicular plumb-line, he could land on the donkey's back in full armour and ride in triumph to Persepolis. As it was, he would have to content himself with roaring down the middle of the rampart in a chariot drawn by four horses from Scythia.

David began to rattle the door of one of the sentry-boxes, locked, presumably, to keep down the birth-rate.

'David, it's locked. You can't go in.'

'Why not? Does someone live there?'

The diminutive size of the Spaniards – diminutive, that was, to a child accustomed to Californian giants – had obviously impressed him deeply.

'Don't be silly, darling. It's to stop people like you from getting in and messing it up.'

It suddenly became rather sinister and she was glad it was locked. She felt claustrophobic without even having penetrated its interior. What a punishment that would be, incarceration in this diminutive gaol, big enough for just two enemies with bowed spines!

'I expect they used to use it for punishing people in the old days. You know, a man and a woman who'd behaved badly together. Rather like in Constantinople – say it, darling.' (He did, obligingly and correctly, to humour her again.) 'If one of the Sultan's wives was naughty, the palace guards called janizaries – say that too' (he did, this time with less precision and worse grace) 'used to put her in a sack with a whole lot of cats who'd been starved for days and throw her in the sea. Which do you think would be worse, being torn to pieces while you were drowning or baking slowly to death in this smelly little sentry-box?'

She really must control this morbidity. His imagination was growing on a diet of horror-comic captions and it was most often she who embedded the sinister seedlings in David's mind. The festering cruelty and violence in his brain was beginning to contrast with the innocent playfulness of his sturdy body.

He had lost interest in the sentry-box and walked masterfully up to a group of children to take over their game of cramming pebbles into a glass jar. The ones he found were more original than theirs, multi-faceted, striated with coloured veins of orange and green, shaped like animals or fish; and their admiration for his superiority knew no bounds. He pacified their squabbles with the quiet force of his personality. Under an olive-tree, they sat in a circle, their eyes big with wonder at the foreign godling, and Venetia blinked at the flash of light as the sun fell into Portugal.

She turned around to face the children. The sunset had not succeeded in blindfolding her own memory and imagination. She was trying to reconstruct the predetermined image she'd formed before ever seeing the town. It was generically similar to the view she saw. Some details had been a little inaccurate; the cathedral was a little more peripheral to the whole, the modern concrete more concentrated than scattered, the tracery of crosses that interspersed the network of TV aerials less pervasive. But in all the essentials she had been right. She could have laid a sheet of tracing-paper bearing the imprint of her version over the plan of the town and there would have been no blurring of outlines, no angry cross-hatching.

Prophetic visions were something which she had bundled into the same dead category as her old theology of guilt. Yet this geometric sharpness of the picture spoke of an inner capacity, one of which she had never before been conscious, the power to foretell. She felt a little closer to Maimonides, the twelfth-century Jewish philosopher of Córdoba, who had struggled to reconcile Judaism with Aristotle, and had till now remained for Venetia a paragraph in a dimly remembered cultural history. His *Guide for the Perplexed* – what an extraordinarily accessible title for his lofty speculations! – told of the language of prophecy. Whereas reason makes the real, empirical world intelligible, its ideal transcendent form is seen only through the prophetic vision. She couldn't quite remember the details. It seemed that her recollection of the past was more flawed than her perception of the future.

It was irritating not to be able to pursue the idea, and not for the first time in her life she regretted she was not in a library. Frustrated by her imperfect memory (compounded at the time of reading about Maimonides by her own inattention), she tried to jolt herself back into immediacy, to *look* at things, register their form, see the interconnecting volumes, resume the painterly eye.

It was no good. The locomotive had really come off the rails. She had irretrievably strayed into the literary mode, those very lines of indirection and fustian pedantry which afflicted poor Jerome. With a final effort she stared intently at the double cube, one set on top of the other, of the keep of the castle of Henry II, strong and secure despite the precipice which fell below it. Somehow, though, it was too self-contained to engage her. Too finished, too efficient. The walls held more appeal with their ramshackle progress through crackling burnt grasses and mounds of broken pantiles. She realized that she and David had now walked almost a complete circuit and she looked backwards to where the ramparts curved inwards, embracing the solid houses within their circling arms. She felt it coming on her, the *de rigueur* literary analogy, the foundation of a metaphor, as relentless as David's diarrhoea. It was inescapable that the walk along the ramparts should be seen as an allegory of her chosen fortune: a delicate circumference of successive tentative trials, a self-exclusion from the compacted core, a skirting and looking outwards for the unknown, an earth-bound rooting in the solid foundation of history that stopped her from making the definitive break into the new. It was an overwhelming vision. Yet it did little to help her on to the revelation of self-knowledge. Something *real* had to happen for that to occur.

She lay quietly with the cool cotton pillow uncreased beneath her cheek – astringent as a lemon sorbet – staring at the beloved child beside her. He was wonderfully serene, his golden apricot-bloomed face like the mask of a Cretan sun-god, his sweeping eyelashes now softly fluttering, con-cealing his innocent eyes. Even at night he smelled of the noon-day. In many ways he was more hers than if he had been her blood-child. His rescue from dereliction, his fierce and expressive loyalty, his passion for Jerome, the tough independence that alternated with wild affection more suited to a paramour, all of these welded their hearts together. She hated being possessive, owning, controlling. Her own life made her cling to the notion of character unfolding from within, the flower of innocence inside. But she was forced to admit her deliciously proprietory rights over the sleeping orphan.

What, then, could Adelaida want from her? Or from him? Adelaida had been so characteristically leaden on the telephone that her motives remained locked in the secret coffers of her mind. How was Venetia to present David to his unnatural natural mother? Her belief in universal honesty was beginning to be eroded by the apparent need for ambivalence, amphibology, half-truths, all those techniques in which the dour nuns had so usefully instructed her.

The din outside cut short her sentimental effusions. The corporation dust-cart was revving its engine and crushing discarded urine-bottles; a hornets' nest of low-c.c. mopeds buzzed petulantly out of the bloody discotheque. It was two o'clock in the morning. Venetia allowed herself a certain justifiable pique and glanced anxiously at David. He turned heavily away, but the racket had apparently only scratched the surface of his deep sleep. She stayed staring at the window until her eyes drooped with a torpid blankness. Moments later, there was a faint rasping sound like the squeak of chalk on a blackboard. She opened one eye and saw an exophthalmic cat staring at her through the window. In its jaws it held a twitching fieldmouse; two dark circlets of blood streamed down over the hapless rodent from the cat's canines.

'Yes, dear, *well done*,' Venetia whispered wearily. '*What* a clever cat!'

It darted away, only to reappear thirty seconds later, more insistent this time and even more self-congratulatory. It had a monumental outline conferred by its instinctual victory.

'What on earth do you want me to do about it?' she asked. 'Applaud? Spit-roast it for you? Do piss off.'

To cancel out the bile and the prickly heat she felt (despite the night breeze that blew the gauzy curtain inwards, almost veiling her face like a recumbent bride), she composed a letter to Jerome. She'd begun the process of composition earlier when she bought paper, an envelope and a stamp. It had been extraordinary to watch the tobacconist gravely wrap the single stamp in a dead football pool slip with the brow-furrowed concentration Jerome used for his envelopes of cocaine.

Next morning, in the deserted bar, she and David decided to make a list of things wrong with Spain. With courteous fairness Venetia wrote a conciliatory introduction:

We are very fond of Spain. It is very agreeable and mostly very beautiful. These negative criticisms are not, therefore, intended in a spirit of hostility or, more important, of condescension. The following things, however, might benefit from change:

1. Belief in the magical, sacramental efficacy of shopping (V.).
2. Excessive value placed on physical beauty (V. and D.). This has terrible effects, especially on ugly women. [Here V. Pencilled in the margin: 'Results in grotesque

efforts to improve on the random gifts of nature. Leads to financial precariousness as in (1).']

3. Temptation to chatter for the sake of it (D.). Quietness = rudeness = *antipatico* (V.).

4. Underestimating the beauty of their old buildings (except in a spirit of blind cultural patriotism); and, like Athenians, prizing only the new (V.). [They built garages next to palaces, transport cafés next to convents, used armorial mouldings as shoe-shine stands, sold intact Romanesque cloisters to the USA, disposed of God knew how many art objects by evading export licences, tethered goats in church narthexes, sold off seventeenth-century organ-pipes to the no-questions plumber (actually it would be rather nice to have one pouring hot water into one's bath).]

5. Too much living in public (V.).

6. Too much smoking (D.).

7. Staring (V. and D.).

8. Getting too much olive-oil on their hands and constantly flicking it off while they speak (or that's what it looks like, anyway) (D.).

9. Not reading enough (V.). [She had never quite appreciated that only the really unhappy read as much as she demanded; and that even they were often too unhappy to read.]

10. Mistaking florid kitsch for elegance.

11. Seeing the outside world mainly with the limited curiosity of prurience.

As a symbolic postscript Venetia added a text that she had seen displayed in the window of a shop selling wallets in Arevalo: *'Plasticamos en el acto'* ('We make things plastic on the spot.')

'I think we should send the list straight away to the Ministerio Cultura de Whatever,' she suggested. 'They can issue edicts for the reform of customs.' The writing of the list made her a little sad. It reminded her of Jerome, with his passion for writing things down.

And yet, in the end, these people were more profoundly human than she could ever be. She sensed it and despaired.

Later she relented and felt she had betrayed the country which had given her so much delight and so miraculous a son. She made a list of opposing virtues to set beside the criticisms; and the list grew to be so long that it began to bore her with its sickly bulk, like an inexhaustible bag of boiled sweets.

29

Madrid: Jerome's Arrival

Before Jerome's arrival, Venetia diplomatically seized the opportunity to modify the disturbing severity of Raúl's Le Corbusier *plan libre* apartment. It was pointless to inflict on him an interior which could only intensify and add fuel to his pique. Just what is it, she wondered, that makes today's homes so different, so appealing? Pressing and turning a set of dials in a Bakelite field-radio fascia, she found a station broadcasting the strangled suburban anger of a falsetto punk. Happy in the *Verfremdungseffekt* it had on her, she delved into her sheikh-sized luggage and started to distribute lengths of soft-textured material over the uncompromising Finnish angles of triangular chairs and self-assembly shelving units. She cast and flung like a eurhythmic *danseuse*, imposing chaos on order, singing as best she could a wiry, strung-out song. Whirling like a Konya dervish, she obliterated the contours of a 1950s Zaragoza hospital instrument-cabinet, the dazzling forceps reduced to a velvet bulge. She festooned a slatted aluminium mezzanine platform with variegated Manila shawls like a ballooning washing-line. Nothing remained of the aerodrome runway lights, the casualty stretcher that served as a sideboard, the peninsular eating-unit made from grenade-boxes. All the angularity became membrane and diaphragm, the high-tech utilitarianism a lush, billowing D'Annunzian *morbidezza*. It looked as if a homosexual parachute-brigade had landed.

Jerome was late and bad-tempered. He had circled in a stack over the bald, parched hills and the harrowed fields of burnt sienna outside Barajas, watching the spirals of heat rise from the flattened summits and thinking morbidly of the 8,000 political prisoners shot there in the winter of 1936. A brusque customs official had dared to detain him, and his indignation had led him to counter with a fluent diatribe on the dispensability of public functionaries, so plunging himself further into unnecessary trouble. Each time he carried drugs through an international frontier, he effectively maximized his chances of detection by such strategies. It was not so much a matter of deliberate policy as a manifestation of his resolve to act wildly. Precipice-living. The cocaine was solidifying in his top pocket, the marijuana crushed in a prickly bundle against his crotch. Everything emerged intact from the interrogation except for his battered sense of self-importance. He could never understand the humiliation he felt when sucked into the aggressive embrace of paid officials. The frisson of outrage and the pouting retaliation must have had a sexual origin.

David cried out when Jerome arrived and dropped his encyclopaedia as he rushed towards him. It was as if he had undergone a radical metamorphosis: from the absorbed, inward child buried in other people's knowledge and counterbalancing Venetia's wild outwardness to a piping *amorino* flying down like a Bavarian squirrel to land in the arms of a Paschal redeemer.

The lovers' embrace was serpentine and histrionic, an animated Pontormo. They hugged until their arms ached. Jerome saw immediately how far her concern for his stability had taken her. It was evident even in the writhing clasp she used to express the complexity of their feelings. She and the room were somehow floating and rounded, with a rare kind of superimposed curvature. She had out-textiled Christo in a harmonious half-hour. Furthermore, her delight at seeing him was unforced. Each time she saw him after a prolonged absence she felt their relationship reverting to an innocent set of simple dance-steps. She imagined that the choreography needed no relearning, that their natural motor-energy would coalesce in a joyous *pas de deux* that sprang fully formed from their intuitive bodies. Jerome, on the other hand, was more realistic and never lost sight of the awkward framework of their love, acknowledging that more often than not cygnets became ducks and remained all too earthbound. This disparity in their perception meant that Jerome often tried harder than she to sustain the fragile bonds; while Venetia sometimes blindly believed in their marvellous strength. Since it was Jerome's self-indulgent actions that so often threatened to break them, she had tried to overcome this imbalance by pretending that his fragmented life was somehow necessary to her own life's continuity. He, while recognizing the probable effects of everything he did, had all the characteristics of an auto-destruct. He exaggerated and stressed his intangibility, he made sure that she thought of him as doomed, finally persuading himself that she could only ever be interested in a literary construct of fatalism: a present-day combination of Chatterton and Rimbaud, a kamikaze poet whose lines were written in spilled semen.

'I've brought drugs, pirated opera tapes, trace-mineral capsules, papaya enzyme, zinc, Polaroids of Lanfranc, a birchwood Romanian abacus, a short-wave wireless and myself, in that order of importance – an entire Spain-survival kit. The *total* life-support system.'

'Darling, you think of everything. You should be working for some dizzy marchioness. Kiss David before he starts screaming. He's adopted this peculiar high-pitched wail since we came to Spain. Cultural acclimatization, I suppose. Jerome, I've been sick, some kind of trauma of the digestive tract. Where's that papaya? Have *I* missed *you*! My tormented creature of the night.'

'What's this? Are you *smashed*? At times like this I really start to despair. What do you *mean*, "tormented creature of the night"? You make me feel so predatory. Like one of those owls in the Vaucluse that hover around preying on small rodents – mice and voles. Maybe there's a real analogy there. Those little rodents are my one-night stands. While the owl is *really* only interested in cats. It swoops down on them and has a more or less vicious battle, then carries them off to eat somewhere else. Food to go. And that's *you*.'

Venetia ignored the possibly real implications of this cruel parable and clasped the back of his neck, pressing her lips ardently against his forehead. She remained in this embrace for some time. All she needed was his physical beauty. Her partial capture of his defences was enough.

'What's for lunch?' asked Jerome. He smiled a real bobby-dazzler.

'I thought eggs. How'd you like them? Benedictine?'

'No, I don't feel like eggs. Too much albumen. Hey, do you remember those loony bits in Swift when he invents wild derivatives? The one about eggs and Alexander the Great? I'll read it to you.'

He took out the book he'd been reading on the plane.

'"Alexander the Great was very fond of eggs roasted in hot ashes. As soon as his cooks heard he was come home to dinner or supper, they called aloud to their under-officers, 'All eggs under the grate'; which, repeated every day at noon and evening, made strangers think it was that prince's real name, and therefore gave him no other; and posterity has been ever since under the same delusion." How about that?'

'Why don't you try and think in straight lines for once in your life? This is a rescue-mission, not a literary soirée. I'll make something authentic. Cuban eggs, you know, fried eggs on rice.'

As Jerome walked towards the shower, shedding clothes as he went, she stood watching his receding form, the fleshly fire revealing itself gradually from its elegant shell. All she could do was *be* there, a silent spectator at the perfect *baldacchino* of his shrine, forced to repress her passion for fear of rearousing his hostility. She stood like Niobe, then moved frumpishly towards the kitchen, at each step adopting the frowsty weeds of the Spanish *ama de casa*, needing for authenticity only the tangible impedimenta of bleach and garlic, tomato purée and lye, oil-cloth and spatula. Amid Raúl's metallic domesticity, she shed her lust.

'I called Adelaida this morning,' she said as they ate her uneatable *gazpacho*.

'What the heck is *this* – okra gumbo?' he asked, as his spirits plummeted.

'She seems to have got herself a new kind of paranoia. She went on a lot – so far as she's capable of going on a lot – about sexual terror-tactics. She's wondering whether the controlled imposition of sexual stereotypes can bring about the elimination of political dissidence. Or something.'

'Could we save Adelaida for later?' Jerome fingered his scented crew-cut as if Adelaida – or even Venetia – might suddenly mutate into Delilah. 'For *this* I left England! Let's take David out to a bar. I'd like to go to that sidewalk café. He'd *love* all those transvestites. You remember the way they cruise around hitting businessmen in the crotch with their fans.'

Spain had changed a lot since their first visit; on their way to the bar a porno barber had tried to requisition them just downwind from the very *guardias civiles* who in Franco's era would have bludgeoned, electrocuted and garrotted him.

Later they sat surrounded by shrieked assignations while Jerome recited the story of his visit to Kensal Green. The beginning of his account was marred by a crazed black who wandered among the tables, beating obsessively on a polystyrene container painted as a wireless set and holding its silent loudspeaker to his cocked ear. Really off the wall, very un-Madrid.

'I'm going to do a core-dump on you. This is a long one,' he said as he embarked on the narrative. At its conclusion, Venetia refused to say anything until he passed her a joint under the table.

'I don't know what on earth it means. How *can* I know?' Being more systematic and reflective than her often impulsive *innamorato*, she began a careful and schematic analysis of his story, a Virgoan trying to fathom the imaginative vagaries of a Cancerian. She thought at first that he might again be deliberately trying to exclude her from his wild cerebral landscapes by thrusting this impenetrable mystery at her in the full knowledge that it could never make sense to her literal and methodical mind. Another warfare tactic from her adored Adolphe, his cruel yet weak stratagems designed to keep her behind her own lines. She had hoped that in Madrid they might be able to cast aside some of the complexities of their love, sloughing off its cumbrous excess weight and absorbing some of the impassioned simplicity with which she imagined, from her desultory reading of Zorrilla and Bécquer, the very soil of Spain to be impregnated. But Jerome

271

had nevertheless contrived, since his arrival, to re-erect the familiar barricades around himself; first by alluding to the unequal, predatory aspect of their relationship and then plunging her into this anachronistic carnival of pastiche homosexuality.

God, these queens were tiresome! While she could understand and relate to the factitious exaggeration of masculinity in London and California, she felt that this Spanish parade of strident androgyny overstepped the absurd. It might just work on the boards of some tatty pier-theatre in the north of England. Here, its technicolor immediacy made her feel redundant, a victim, she suspected, of some shock plan of Jerome's. These feelings so overwhelmed her during the course of his narrative that parts of it had eluded her, and she needed all her resources to recall and piece together its Woolfian elements.

Spanish queens seemed to stand around looking eager for some unseen object, squeezing their clutch-bags, straps looped around their wrist, against their glandular breasts so tightly that they might be mistaken for soldiers on the offensive. Their bouffant hair was wispier than that of their straight contemporaries through constant teasing, and their shirts – Hawaiian, silk, pleated cheesecloth and long-collared moire – were on an ambiguous cusp of the gender gap.

David was now pushing his way through a forest of lurexed legs. Whenever his delicate balance threatened to collapse, he clamped his hands on to pummiced ankles and shaved calves, eliciting murmurs and cries from the entangled transvestites. He was picked up and passed from embrace to embrace, his happy head nestling against plucked chests and swathes of chiffon and tulle. A gallery of glossy mouths opened and shut ecstatically in a Babel of maternal endearments long silenced by their seclusion in their ambisexual ghetto. Jerome rescued his foster-child from a bulky flamenco dancer and sat him firmly on his own masculine knee.

'If David's role-models have got to be gay, at least let's get him used to the rough male kiss of denim. The last thing we need is a *zarzuela* chorus-boy on our hands. So what do we think about the mysterious events in the cemetery?'

'What was *in* it? Did you open the horrid thing up?'

'I took it home and put it in front of Lanfranc. He sniffed around suspiciously. Perhaps he hoped it'd be catnip. But he didn't like it. In fact he bolted. I guess it was unfair of me to use him as a guinea-pig.'

'But what was *in* it?'

'I held it over the basin and slit the top open. Maybe I should have just left it and watched to see if it'd move or something. But I reckoned that if a *cat* could be so incurious, it was up to me to face the grisly contents.'

Venetia was getting impatient at these tantalizing details.

'When I emptied a little of the fluid, it came out as a slightly oily and cloudy liquid . . .'

David screamed, and the exposition came to an abrupt end as Venetia rushed to his defence.

30

Lorenzo the *Septembriste*

Had he been able to confess to a grounding in bourgeois literature, Lorenzo Urquijo Maura might have claimed spiritual descent from Alfred de Musset's mercurial tyrant-slayer, Lorenzaccio. The same single-minded, purposive self-view, the same antipathy to the abuse of power. As it was, he had definitively excised every link with the European liberal tradition, just as he sought metaphorically to convert the Pyrenees into an armed canal zone. At an early stage in his meticulous preparations for his *oposiciones* he had developed a belief in the fragmentation of the European corporate state and the need to implement the 1898 commentators' recommendation of Spain's special identity and separate destiny – its territorial imperatives as a peninsular block and the exploitation of its peculiar historic expertise in autonomous evolution, autarky and resistance to alien pressures. It was his passionate conviction that modern Spain had been contaminated by inappropriate criteria about the stabilizing effects of constitutional monarchy and laissez-faire economics, civil rights and NATO alignment. The last two issues had caused him some heartsearching when he found himself addressing a rally at El Escorial on the reduction of US armaments on Spanish soil. Part of him had seized on the opportunity to alter public opinion on an incontrovertible political issue while another part had felt the compulsion to silence his dissent in the interest of the body politic. But his flamboyant public persona – so at odds with his electrifying private taciturnity – had triumphed over his strictures on freedom of speech. It was probably as a result of this event that he had failed to secure a post in public administration. He, at least, remained convinced that an old-guard caucus had determined that his ideology was unsound and, more important, that he was likely to rock the fragile boat of coalition. Nor was his sex life on his side.

His crazed aunt – the only mentor he would tolerate – accused him of seeking his own destruction.

'My darling nephew, whom I love as ardently as I love the risen Christ, we must make a review of your convictions. Our country is riven apart between the traditional allegiances and the need to be seen to form part of the twentieth century. This is the only constant. When that misguided anachronism Admiral Carrero Blanco was blown six storeys high in this bourgeois enclave of Salamanca, it became no longer possible to ignore this fundamental tension. Success in public office cannot be achieved without the most delicate funambulism.'

Her 1890s delivery always reassured Lorenzo of the permanence of the Castilian ark. Although Guillermina had the intellectual curiosity to absorb current ideological changes – more through a kind of magic osmosis than any conscientious scrutiny of the press – her historicist perspective was always apparent even in her linguistic mannerisms.

Her parchment mask, serene in its myopia, remained sphinx-like as he tried to justify his miscalculation.

'Everything I've done has arisen from solid conviction. Nothing has been abandoned to chance. Even my sexuality has been deliberately chosen. You can only see it as the manifestation of decadence in a rebellious scion of your illustrious family. But it, my political ambitions and my self-love are all parts of an ineluctable plan. It isn't easy for me to ignore the dreadful demands of compromise. You'll see eventually, however, that I can transcend that need and replace it with our beloved virtues of obedience and sanctified ritual.'

Guillermina dreamed swimmingly that her nephew was a new Pizarro, rallying stony-hearted Dominicans to the sacred cause of forcible conversion to the True Faith. She had to know, on the other hand, that his purpose could never be so unsubtle. Subsequently she reflected that he must be embarking on some tortuous Machiavellianism founded on the central premise that his ends were best achieved through infiltration. His machinations were to be insidious, irresistible like the vapour from thuribles that made you godly perforce. The destruction of the multifarious enemy was to be achieved by crumbling its foundations like *migas* and erecting within its hollow shell a single crystalline castle of redemptive authority. All at the instigation of his unbearable strength.

She lit a Marlboro and sat back to watch the laser-beams.

'Frankly, darling, I have to say that I have always wanted you to be a Jesuit. Would it be too much to ask for you to divert your extraordinary manipulative powers *ad majorem Dei lariam?* You remember what Ignatius Loyola said about the overwhelming importance of recruiting beautiful men into the Society? So that the secular world could be more effectively breached and hard-edged duchesses could no longer complain that Christ's representatives on earth were so physically repellent? Your potential as a saviour of souls would be positively Pauline. And you might one day achieve the miracle of healing the split between the Vatican and the Society of Jesus and cover your magnificent head with St Peter's tiara.'

Lorenzo, meanwhile, had opened his shirt to take out a copy of Baltasar Gracián's *Oráculo manual* and was reminding himself of how the seventeenth-century moralists had recommended the use of intermediaries to accomplish one's gloryless ends, the withholding of power-conferring secrets, how a river is formidable only until a ford is discovered. His lovers, competitors, political rivals and family had expended much energy and ingenuity in the vain search for such a ford. But even his homosexuality was a source of strength. He had remained an obstinately Orinocan span and had fought off all such attacks with his piranha fleet of iron will. Adelaida, it was true, had nearly flung a cantilevered bridge across his broad stream, but he had demolished its piers with one deft explosion, cruelly confronting her with his Piers Gaveston, a sprawled blond giant from Malmö triumphantly smiling up from his pillow. No one stood a chance against his relentless promiscuity, his *amour propre* and his post-orgasmic ennui – a killer shark with all the emotional sensitivity of a pile-driver. Locks of his hair shaded his intent forehead as Guillermina got up to dance a stately, floor-clearing fandango.

'*Au contraire*,' said a substantial dancer later in a mid-Channel accent, 'you're very charming. Only my lover over there is more jealous than the most slighted of Spanish husbands' (this in Bay of Biscay Castilian). 'He's been known to trample live bullfighters underfoot.'

She – Venetia – had pointed to Jerome, who was thrusting David into the coat-check. His manner was so commanding that his rival was left open-mouthed, his protestations of honourable intent unspoken. Venetia hugged Jerome to pre-empt any further assault by the dago greaseball. Then she withdrew to wobble delicately in front of Jerome's sexual bump and grind. He was becoming reconciled to Madrid and the taut grace of his chassé expressed the ease of his acclimatization.

'Shit, I left the poppers in David's dungarees,' he panicked. What an obstacle to his kinetic oblivion. Turning purposefully from the expressionless Venetia, he faced the archaic figure of Guillermina, an alabaster *Commendatore* miraculously come to life in her solitary dance of self-celebration.

'My God! Kensal Green!'

31

Claes and Asdrúbal

Asdrúbal waited in the atrium of the Ateneo. He had panted across from the Calle de Alcalá, wheezing emphysematically in an effort of exertion that no one but Claes could have elicited from so fat a cat, so sleek a Greek, so shrewd a dude, so fly a guy. His supererogatory work in the upper echelons of the Ministry of Education and Science seemed like a sinecure to that small part of the world which knew or cared about its existence. To Asdrúbal, however, it was a crucial cog in the machinery of government, an indispensable flywheel which allowed him to act with corresponding self-importance. But his slender involvement in the programming of educational policy was more a base on which he could erect a smiling Aranjuez garden of overwhelming bonhomie. Nobody could detect the gargantuan effort he had poured into its construction, and only the most hard-bitten puritans found it pointless. At this moment he was trembling with philanthropy, his stocky frame ablaze with extroversion. This meeting with Claes van Amerongen would reinforce the inequality of their friendship to his own advantage; power was all the more delicious if it seemed to originate in a fraternal concern. This curious benevolent despotism had been easy to wield ever since Asdrúbal, during a casual tour of inspection of the Biblioteca Nacional, had first met Claes. The scholarly Dutchman had been discovered in a private research cubicle surreptitiously brandishing a pair of nail-scissors and cutting out the illuminations from a medieval manuscript psalter. A neat pile of gilded lettering and pictorial effigies of saints lay beside the plundered text. Asdrúbal, faint with admiration at the high-handed action, had hoped it might be some extraordinary and motiveless *acte gratuit*, a crime of non-passion, a testing perhaps of the perpetrator's nerve. Heaven knew what it proved. They had talked urbanely about its implications, and Asdrúbal had graciously digested Claes's many-branched explanation. The motive was simple kleptomania, but its exposition would have convinced a magistrate's bench of severe Lycurguses that some astonishing act of disinterestedness had taken place.

The two men embraced with the fervour of ex-conspirators. Claes, beholden to Asdrúbal for extricating him from a painful legal exposure, pecked the Spaniard's cheek, a continuing symbol of obligation. Asdrúbal, a man not handicapped by humility, magnificently dispensed regal boons. In an effort to equalize their relationship, Claes insisted on stressing how much his visit had involved an intolerable systemic upheaval.

'It's marvellous to see you, my dear Asdrúbal. Almost marvellous enough to make me forget my hatred of travel and disrupted routine. Spain has no place in my heart. Its only virtue lies in having nurtured a paragon such as yourself.'

'There we differ, my old friend. I *am* Spain and Spain *is* me. You cannot appreciate my qualities without worshipping the *madre patria*.'

This megalomania temporarily astounded even the world-weary professor, who regarded nationality as a mere accident, Amsterdam simply as a congenial womb for an uncomplaining and modest foetus such as himself. As they walked out through the venerable entrance past cringing domestics, he began to understand Asdrúbal's arrogance, ceaselessly consolidated as it was by a tradition of deference continents away from his own Northern egalitarianism. The ceremonious rite was re-enacted in the lobby of the Palace Hotel, and Asdrúbal fluffed out his silver linen and flannel feathers as much in a courtship ritual for Claes as in response to the fawning of the doorman. They drank whisky and gorged on corpulent olives. Everything seemed fat and sleek, even their creamy exchange of belle-lettristic endearments.

The shift into significant discourse was like an astringent dessert.

'The King leaves for Peru tomorrow. Some essential exercise, the cementing of Hispanicity some hundred and fifty years *ex post facto*. Ridiculous. God knows what those coca-chewing half-alives will make of our exemplary monarch. Perhaps they'll feel nostalgia for their own poor trusting Atahualpa; they should be so lucky. Lima *la horrible*. How *can* they have dismantled our beautiful vice-royalty. Americans, shit.'

Claes had never got used to the vertiginous changes in register which characterized even the most educated speech in Madrid. He himself sweated blood before dropping the obligatory excremental expletives into his own sentences.

'But Juan Carlos is achieving so much more than anyone would ever have dreamed from his pretty average military record. It's hard to assess him from our Dutch point of view. We're still stuck with the Duke of Alba and the Spanish Fury. But I'm inclined to admire him for not riding a bicycle. And you can't imagine Queen Sofía embroiled in a Lockheed scandal. I like their modesty, it seems so completely unaffected. Anyway, so what? Are you going with him?'

A well-aimed suggestion, implying a closeness to the ears of the Zarzuela palace which Asdrúbal, to his constant pique, didn't really possess. Their reciprocal feelings sustained many such illusions, as if their combined great age could stomach no lapses of sympathy. They were like two Gray Panthers bolstering one another's vulnerability before storming the Civic Center in wheelchairs.

'Unfortunately our delegation will be very small,' Asdrúbal lied. 'No, the point is this. After all these ridiculous attempted *coups*, we Spaniards are nervous about losing, even temporarily, the stabilizing presence of the figurehead of monarchy. The army is so restive, so resentful of the proliferation of political parties. The King's involvement with it is considered to be a *sine qua non* of our beleaguered democracy.'

'That is the one great fear which sympathetic Europeans share with the Spanish liberals. But are you seriously concerned about another military *pronunciamiento*? Surely the last one discredited political factionalism in the army to everyone's satisfaction? Especially when combined with the memory of the King's wonder-working defusing of the 1982 one?'

'Exactly, *majo*. And if he's away speechifying about the Peruvian economic miracle, what then?'

'I do see.' Claes moved to avoid Asdrúbal's exaggerated glance of interrogation. The elegant folds of his Milanese suit fell spectacularly back into shape. 'But is there any particular evidence to suggest an imminent crisis?'

'Next week there will be a rally in the Plaza de España, organized by the right wing. You can have no notion of how powerful their support is – both subliminal and overt. Now that various parties are spawning their own embryos, and old party faithfuls are seceding all over the place, there's a serious danger of popular sympathy rallying colossally to the right. There are many elements in the army not yet reconciled to democracy, and the extremists, who are so well organized, hope to exploit and provoke those hotheads into taking things into their own hands. I've decided upon a course of action which might affect the outcome of the demonstration. But first we must go and feast on sucking-pig and *natillas*. You Northerners always look so anaemic and undernourished. A little Mediterranean starch will improve your arteries. How *are* things in your wicked damp Sodom-on-the-canals?'

Claes distinctly enjoyed this bantering display of concern, used as he was to the acid condescension of Alicia. He was becoming reconciled to Madrid.

32

Carmelite Trip

Obeying the promptings of his insistent groin – there was
a kind of nice stomach ache which recurred, a mingling
of acidulous gastric juices, a contracting of organs, the
abdomen falling away to leave a void, more pleasure than
pain, that he knew to be the anticipation of desire – Jerome
left to get laid. By thinking about it, you could make the
feeling attack your vertebrae and then sit, like a herpes
virus, at the base of your spine. (Bending your buttocks
was helpful too; it made you know you were horny.) The
dancing of the neurons up the spinal column was as if the
spermatozoa had escaped from the vas deferens and swelled
promiscuously through the uncharted body. Perhaps this
was the writhing that Aquinas contemned as the appetite
act? Or the disturbance of the estimative faculty situated in
the dorsal part of the median ventricle of the encephalus,
the terrible *complexis venerea*, the neuro-secretory cells con-
gregating in the hypothalamus, releasing factors pumping
gonad-stimulating hormones from the pituitary gland.

He couldn't summon up the strength to justify his leaving
to Venetia. The sentences would have to be too baroque, the
excuses so intricate; he would have to work in countervailing
salves to set against his egocentricity. So he just said: 'I'm off
to the baths. Have a nice day.'

'OK, Mr Sensitive; a man's gotta do what a man's gotta
do.' She turned away. 'I've met some hardboiled eggs in my
life, but you – you're twenty minutes.'

Despite her borrowed wit, his disappearance put Venetia

in a really bad temper. For once she could not accept his freedom and wanted to feel that he belonged to her. It had something to do with her disorientation in Madrid; but also something even more visceral, a bilious resentment that in the end she knew to be at odds with her calculated precondition for their affair, the concession of total licence. She felt like an abandoned heroine in the last act of an Italian opera, and wandered grumpily around the flat murmuring in a sour contralto *Sprechgesang, 'Dov'e quel viso adorato? Deserta in terra. Sola, perduta, abbandonata* and especially *Crudel!'* The apartment seemed as alien to her as the colonial wasteland of Louisiana had to Manon Lescaut. She found that even David was a bore, as if some cocotte had been encumbered with a thuggish lovechild too reminiscent of its brutally absent father.

'David, come here and sit down. *Be* my, be my baby,' she said with all the breathy emphasis of the Ronettes. She fussed around with his bib and braces, tied an experimental balaclava round his head and then cast it aside and kissed him fervently on the nape of his neck.

'Wanna shit,' he said.

'You can't shit here 'cos your arsehole's in the White House.'

He wobbled away nevertheless.

She sat down and wondered what to do. It had to be something pretty large-scale if it was to match the enormity of Jerome's infraction.

There was nothing in the apartment to suggest a course of action. No books to inspire an expedition, no magazines to prompt a massive spending spree.

'What do you suggest, darling?' she asked David when he returned from his defiant absence. 'And what are we going to do with you? How about spending the day with big Angelines?'

Angelines was Raúl's divorced wife, a wizard with kids (which had been the main reason for her estrangement from her jealous, morose and perverse husband). Jerome didn't like her much. He was irritated by her domesticity and called her the J-cloth. She lived near-by in a house jammed with everything a child could want. The barley-sugar balusters and finials of her Alfonsine block were the clue to the sweet and amazing surfeit of toys it contained; the interior was like a propaganda-sheet for multiple parenthood, or an anti-abortion tract, so charming were the happy visions of romping babies, computing five-year-olds and squealing hair-pullers. David loved it there.

'Sí,' he said, reverting to his Spanish beginnings. His eyes shone with anticipation.

Venetia telephoned to arrange the visit, to the delight of both Angelines and David.

'Well, that leaves *me* free, and you're sure to have a wonderful time. Because Venetia is all grumpy and horrid today. You'd much rather be with all those lovely *niños formalitos*. They could teach Jerome a thing or two about good manners.'

Her sense of achievement at organizing David's day removed the cloak of ill-temper that had shrouded her morning. As her feeling of relief intensified she felt too that the self-indulgence stretching before her should itself be fed and pampered to prolong its effects. The fridge yielded up the Parma ham, poppy-seed bread, unsalted butter, olives, palm-hearts, *ensaladilla*, asparagus spears, *chorizo* and guava juice that she had bought and placed there the previous day (a mere shelfful, in her – biased – estimation). She laid the table as minimally as she could, anxious to avoid too much retina-searing from Raúl's surgical domestic objects. And then, when the mid-morning banquet was laid out in a magnificent array, she extracted a small paper envelope from the lining of her basque and placed it ceremoniously but secretively at the far end of the table. It was the oddest-shaped pudding she had ever seen, odder than any Floating Island or upside-down cake.

David sat beside her and toyed with her discarded *chorizo*-skin, dangling it with gusto into his pear yoghurt and sucking the dripping end. Eventually she stopped him – Jesus, what a gross-out – not so much from disgust at the hideous ensemble as out of anxiety that he should not spoil his appetite for Angelines's non-stop *fiesta infantil*, and in doing so alienate her maternal heart. As they ate, however, she talked to him in a low voice pricked with all the emphasis she gave to her words when speaking to a child – and indeed, even sometimes to adults.

'One of the best things in Spain is the way they treat their brats. Perhaps that's why Venetia and Jerome feel a bit *despistados* here. I know we treat you a little bit cavalierly; and When Did You Last See Your Father?' (Christ, Jerome's conversational tics were catching! And dangerously Freudian, shit, he'd never even *once* seen his father.) 'But I don't think it would really suit you, all that dressing up in sailor suits and pastel dungarees and getting chucked under the chin. I think a little rough toughness is more your style, such boyish chic, all tousled and confident, just like Jerome. Just you keep it up and you'll be a sensational guy.'

David smiled at the right moments and said things like 'Why?' and 'Yes', not as serious interjections, but to coax Venetia onwards in her sweet reassuring, custardy chatter. He adored being talked to, no matter what the content, tone or even the language of what was said.

After eating solidly, brain-numbingly through the food in front of her, Venetia's attention began to concentrate more and more on the secret envelope. She drained some juice and allowed what was presumably going to be a major internal fermentation – almost ptomaine-poisoning – to take place before stretching gingerly, slowly, towards the package.

Was everything ready? Had she left anything undone or unsaid, left any chinks in her self-confidence; or was it now safe to go ahead?

The intercom buzzed and Angelines presented herself on the threshold. And it *was* a presentation, an *apariencia*, girded all around with bandbox crispness, a sight of astonishing newness that one might have imagined was about to change one's perception of the world. She was dressed with extreme simplicity. No one pleat was less than parallel to any other in the tailored skirt, the bow on her silk blouse was tied with beautiful symmetry, although not quite so perfectly as to suggest it was ready-made. Her body was somewhere between slim and fat, at exactly that point where one doesn't ask any questions about improvement. The skin and teeth shone with health, the brow revealed the innocence of her needlessly contrite soul.

Venetia smiled at her, but felt awful. Did she *have* to be such a paragon? The only consolation for Venetia was that this disturbance had happened now, before she consumed the acid, and that she wouldn't therefore spend the whole day-trip hurling unspoken abuse and reproaches at herself for her slovenly trampishness and the unorthodoxy of her looks. Angelines could be the Archangel Gabriel to her bag lady, Marie Antoinette to her Esmeralda, Nancy Reagan to her Greenham Common wimmin.

Angelines, however, didn't seem to notice, either ascribing Venetia's unusual appearance to her English bohemianism (which she might anyway have possibly admired) or not wishing to dent her own perfection by registering surprise.

'You look so happy, so well.' And then, as little David came running up, squeaking excitedly: 'And look at the baby boy, what enchantment, he's divine!'

Venetia summoned her over to a Mies van der Rohe chair and gave her a glass of whisky, too flustered to remember the earliness of the hour. Angelines's polite refusal made her even more uncomfortable.

'Why are you in Madrid, my dear?'

'I've come to visit a friend of ours.' The last thing Venetia wanted to do was embark on an agonizing description of Adelaida and her part in Venetia's life. Angelines's useful-ness to her didn't include confidences about rule-breaking adoptions or political terrorism; better to leave David's ori-gin mysterious and rely on Angelines's no-questions-asked earth motherliness.

'You've come at an exciting moment. Everyone's terribly over-excited. It seems now as if we have almost a *season* for political activity. It's one of the prices we've had to pay for democracy. June is so over-filled with rallies and marches, the newspapers go crazy, even more parties get formed, it's a horrendous thing. I just lock myself up in the nursery – which is where most of the politicians belong.'

'I should have thought it would be terribly exciting after all that inertia during Franco's régime. Don't you feel liberated?'

'Of course we do. But sometimes it's impossible not to be nervous about the instability. At the moment, for example,

Madrid is *very* apprehensive about the big demonstration next week. It's sure to produce *incidents* and to polarize opinion even further. You can sense the tension in the streets, in the air even. Our democracy is so unstable, perhaps we shouldn't tolerate these immense expressions of public feeling. We Spaniards are so volatile, so *exaggerated* in our politics. Perhaps it's because we lack the parliamentary system and traditions of your country.'

Angelines smiled sweetly, as if she'd just conceded a point and was soliciting recognition of her generosity of spirit. But Venetia had heard it all before (and was to hear it again); it was far too early in the morning and anyway she wanted to get at the acid and fly away. She curtailed their discussion, politely but firmly; and then kissed her child goodbye, talking to him in Spanish to remind him of his birth and prepare him for the company of his compatriots.

Watching Angelines and David chattering excitedly as they entered the art nouveau cage of the lift (the one thing Raúl hadn't been able to streamline), her heart tightened. Perhaps David *preferred* ordinary people and only wanted security and routine. Perhaps his life was all a dreadful nightmare, a terrible B-movie in which she was always played by Gale Sondergaard, all her irresponsibility and bohemianism gone sour and destructive in a mixture of Miss Havisham, Scarlett O'Hara and Cruella de Vil. She was a wrecker of other people's lives; a destroyer, a Fury, a battening Harpy, one of those vile Greek female horrors that always seemed to come in threes; Atropos hard at work with her scissors cutting the thread of life, Clytemnestra raising the axe in the closet, Electra gloating over her revenge, Medea poised to kill her brother and scatter his limbs in the path of Aeetes; or some dreadful manipulatrix who twisted others to her own fell purpose, a monster of unspeakable selfish blindness, an exploiter, a tormenting crank, a frantic harridan, a deviant psychopath . . .

Christ, what a *mauvais quart d'heure*! This was no way to take a trip. A pretty inauspicious beginning for something which promised to make her even more introspective. She tried to remember a mantra for inner peace from her Nepalese days, but couldn't remember any and ended up saying Hail

Marys and holding her breath. The incantation was calming, it allowed her to finish off some slivers of *chorizo*, clear the table, flick her hair back and compose her mind all at once, and banish those cruel fantasies, recognizing them for the paranoid idiocies they were. Hadn't David even that morning turned his head to her on the pillow and smiled as if nothing else mattered in the world save her protection? He'd been full of love for her, radiant, pulsating. And she could at all events be secure in the knowledge that he regarded *her* life, Jerome's even, as normal, a kind of magico-realism, and would not be making odious comparisons with the tight regular battleship run by Admiral Angelines.

She went into the bathroom and fiddled around with her hair, straightened the carelessly flung-down brushes and tubes, checked her appearance in the mirror, once more compared her complexion with the most delicate Meissen and thought yes, OK, *fertig, alles in Ordnung*. It was a matter of seconds before she opened the envelope and took out one of the tiny dots of paper inside. Superman, was it, or red heart, she couldn't remember.

It clung a little to her palate before she was able to swallow it, like a sacrilegious wafer, she who could swallow great torpedoes of megavitamins.

Unlike most of the other times, she had no preplanned things to do, no special *regulation* of the day to accommodate the expected chemical clarity. Probably it was enough that she had released and unburdened herself from both Jerome and David; and that her day was an utter blank, a Roman spring or a condition-free sabbatical.

But the *externals did* have to be changed. Jerome, she knew, could trip anywhere, because his head was so much more important than his eyes. But for her the surroundings she found herself in really *would* not underscore the *extase*; their outlines bulked too large and square, like outrageously padded 1940s shoulders. She needed to avoid the day being vapid – not an unfamiliar feeling but one which took on particular urgency, now that the LSD had already begun to course through her bloodstream and produce the earliest, the cleanest rushes. Ideally the day should contain a sequence of agreeable visual and intellectual stimuli. It had to be some kind of sightseeing, she thought, given her desire to *understand* Spain, this city, its history, its – what was it? – *duende*, the quintessence (though, characteristically, she had nothing but contempt for Hemingway, Orson Welles and the other heavyweights who'd laid claim to the same obsession).

Summoned to the window by the siren of a passing ambulance, she stared out at the dull street without properly seeing the aluminium cafeteria, the glove shop, the black-bordered necrologies and the posters for lottery-draws pasted on to trees and kiosks. Dimly she remembered a visit to the Convent of the Royal Discalced Carmelites which had left her excited, transported outside the confines even of her multifarious life, bringing a sense of transference to another time and place, one which she could live in temporarily but wholly and from which she had, unlike the real nuns, a guaranteed escape-route. Yes, that was it; better even than a Hell's Angel funeral, a helicopter ride through the Grand Canyon, an early Buñuel. The stone ogres, dragons, elephants and sea-monsters looming out of the foliage in Duke Orsini's Sacro Bosco at Bomarzo, the caryatids by Primaticcio in the Salon de la Duchesse d'Étampes at Fontainebleau with their minuscule heads like the pin-heads of musclemen, the house shaped like a 1930s ocean-liner at Boulogne-sur-Mer, the crescents, obelisks and free-standing staircases that led nowhere but upwards in the observatory at Jaipur, the Tour de l'Apocalypse in Belgium, a hyper-rusticated tower crowned with huge effigies of an eagle, a winged lion, a man and an ox (symbols of the Evangelists) on the battlements, or even ... the cathedral in the salt mine at Wieliczka, a whole basilica of sculpted salt where the air glistened with crystals and was so intensely salinated that your brain seemed to undergo an abrasion-cleansing. Helsinki railway-station where colossal busts held illuminated globes ... even that time when the cardboard sets of *Traviata* at Orvieto collapsed into the audience, knocking the Queen of the Netherlands off her chair ... Shit, what trivia, how could she have got off on that? Camp was one thing, acid another. This realization made her feel curiously straight, probably owing to the fact that her normal consciousness had now permanently lapsed into theatricality. What if she devised *this* trip specifically to restore the past ordered perception of the truth?

But in that very *devising* there was a contradiction. Better to abandon herself to chance. At least the religious framework of the trip would likely make her regress to an earlier life, a time which seemed atrophied in history now, rather like Comte's idea of a *theological* phase of the development of civilization superseded by the belief in universal science. It would be interesting to see how she reacted to exposure to habits and wimples, scapularies and beads, the crucified God and the grieving madonna.

Half an hour later she got heavily out of a taxi, not entirely sure in her judgement of the drop, and stood in front of the convent. The square bustled with shouting, gesticulating crowds despite its evisceration for an underground car-park, and the journey had been a flashing, peopled stripe through the city. She orientated herself, blearily blocking out the modern junk and tottering slightly as she blinked at the great granite and brick façade. The semi-circular tympanum returned her gaze, only the serenity of its icy Toledan correctness mocked the inexactness of her sight. Gradually, however, as the motion of the taxi flowed out of her, she regained the fixity and clarity of her inner self, indeed, it was becoming a caricature of itself the more acidified it became. She was more conscious of this transition than of the buildings she saw; and she set to testing out the truth of the hypothesis by telling herself how each detail was increasing in definition and clarity. Her head was growing new sinews from brain to temple. The acid rushed and revealed to her the predominance of one feature over another, the importance and extraordinariness of the rubble, masonry and mortar, the incongruous and misleading labelling of the treasure-house within by this forbiddingly austere slab like a gigantic grave-stone.

She walked over to a wall behind her and leaned against it. It supported her back and gave her solidity during these early transitional re-markings. She pressed one foot back up against the wall and balanced on the other. It was very hot. In this position, persecuted by the sun, she wished she could metamorphose into a sciopod, the mythical creature which could run like hell on its single leg, then use that leg to provide a shelter from the sun, holding it up like a giant umbrella. Already she was hot and her brain racing. Acid was so hectic, so unrelenting, the important thing was to devise and canalize your thoughts into congenial and productive lines, not let greyness or discomfort or indeterminate fears press heavily through. At the moment it was enough to stay still and reassess the shape of the convent from this wider lens-angle.

What had inspired this melancholy, low-slung barrack? Now she continued to look at it but saw nothing as her mind filled with seeping historical data, literary trivia, religious believe-it-or-nots. The convent, she had read and remembered, had been founded by a princess of Castile, Juana, the daughter of Charles V, whose marriage to the King of Portugal ended on his death after eleven months. It was then a royal convent specially for princesses, yet dedicated to the most searingly poverty-stricken bare-foot order, Mount Carmel. This anomalous exclusivity hadn't seemed to disturb such foundresses. At La Helges near Burgos, too, the nuns had to prove their lineage and the abbess was a princess-Palatine, second only to the Queen, a 'lady of the gallows and the axe' with power of life and death over whole fiefs of cowering villeins. Had she sailed over the fields, her coif billowing, bearing down on hapless defaulters and striking them down with an executioner's blade and a murmured *Requiescat in pace*? The image of her grew bulkier and taller in the landscape of Venetia's mind, her face emerged from the folds of her cowl and took on the lineaments of Reverend Mother, no Adelaida, under the points of a diamond coronet on which one fall of serge had become caught. Stop, she yelled at herself, this way leads to dementia and paranoia, this has to be dispassionate, objective, external, removed from *me*. By a trick of her own invention – though others, too, had invented the same trick – she barricaded off the threatening road, and it was as meaningless, as non-existent as an amputated limb. Her hands stopped trembling; though she had not known they were anything but still.

291

Kicking purposefully away from the wall, she smoothed down her clothes and set out towards the main door. The cars being swallowed up in the subterranean maw boded well for the time transference, as if some trash-chute had been set up there to siphon off the intrusive modern ogres. By the time she sat inside the entrance hall, erect and soignée on a wooden bench, she had already begun to regress. It was only the immediate practical issue of securing a private, unaccompanied visit which kept up a slender link with the present.

The attendants stood around slandering and blowing cigar smoke at a human-scale picture of a nun, whose forehead was lined either by innate fastidiousness or theological doubt or acute moral disappointment. She floated above the guides with the elevation of moral intangibility. Their earthbound banter and grumbling hardened Venetia's resolve to rid herself of their presence and slide imperceptibly into the rarefied metaphysical aura of the nun whose symbolically bare feet hovered, as in the Assumptions and Immaculate Conceptions, between Heaven and Earth. Spotting a departing party of tourists, she joined them and then slipped through the door under wraps. None of the guides seemed to notice her, not even an elderly woman who had stared at her balefully as she entered.

No drastic alteration took place to her in the lower gallery of the cloister. She walked slowly and deliberately, unconsciously imitating the weightless footfall of a nun. Gradually the gliding became so noiselessly conspicuous that she began to realize it was happening and to understand its purpose. A fly buzzed around a window-catch. The ambience was of detachment from the meaningless trials of being, the transience of mortality, the fragility of the crystal vessel of life, the silent dropping of the petals of the rose of human love, the re-creation of the angelic simplicities in these blank severe walls and the earth-coloured flagstones. A kindred sisterhood was welling up, its sublimity and frailty heard in the nuns' voices as they floated over a crackling loudspeaker from their enclosed choir. She paused to look out into the centre of the courtyard. But the sight of nature, however unadorned, was a distraction, and she walked on to shock herself with the sudden mournful statue of a nun holding up a monstrance more as if it contained a burst of lethal lasers than the life-giving Eucharist.

This mood of borrowed austerity had come as an astringent shower to the normally unjudicious Venetia. Just as she was beginning to absorb and appreciate it, she found herself drenched in a psychedelic shift more akin to the coloured primary immediacy of the acid decade. A chapel of the Holy Family, recessed into the wall with folding tapestry doors, beckoned her to inspect its charming interior. But its charms in turn were too understated, too conventionally pious to distract her for long from the vast, overwhelming riot of the staircase beside.

Not a centimetre had been left undecorated, even if only with marbleized red striations as a gap-filler between the paintings. It was as if the painter had tried, with uncontrollable vindictive megalomania, to obliterate all traces of the builder's modest craft, claiming walls for canvas, repudiating architecture, emasculating the balustrade, fig-leafing the naked white plaster, like some cracked Counter-Reformation prelate. Could he have been some precursor of the video age, projecting iconic emblems of his own era on the studio walls, serried fragments of the cult idols of Christianity's late clawback? There they stood, dark and luminous, the Christ on the Cross, the dolorous Virgin-Mother, the Evangelists and the God-loved Magdalen; the heavy winged angels and archangels, Raphael, Gabriel, Michael, Uriel, Sariel, Jeremial: the modest self-effacing roundels of St Francis and St Clare, the *noli me tangere* helplessly hemmed in with eagles, putti and the scrolls of soured prophetic texts. The armoury and panoply of the rampant Church which bludgeoned the congregations of Europe back from Luther, and lured the savages of China, Japan and Peru to their first forcible schism-splashed encounter with the God of Israel.

Venetia had to look away. She snapped open her handbag and, unscrewing a container with one expert hand, stuck a finger inside and brought it up to her mouth covered in a rich slick of boysenberry jelly. That was better. It'd been worth lugging it over from the D'Agostino's in New York. She licked the finger clean, slowly, with the concentration of a child; but not so clean as to avoid leaving a purplish stain on her skirt as the hand fell back down by her side. Fortunately she did not notice and so was spared the paranoia her untidiness might otherwise have inspired.

Fortified, and with the feeling of another sense placated, she resumed her scanning of the walls. Planting her feet squarely and firmly, as she believed every serious art-critic must do – when they weren't having their high foreheads axed in by rough trade – she allowed her gaze to soar upwards to the upper level. Here the lushness seemed like high summer, the cornucopian days of a confident, colour-impregnated court in which the Royal Family ranged themselves behind a balustrade, the profligate Philip IV (his head filled with the sexual disgust and insistent self-recriminations he would pour out into the ear of his mother confessor, Maria de Ágreda), his disagreeable wife, Mariana of Austria, who drove him to sexual excess, prettified and bedecked with her one-dimensional haircut, the Infantas Marie and Carlos, heir and idiot apparent, doomed vessel, as Charles II, of the dregs of kingship. They presided over the staircase as if on a tribunal, flaring their nostrils at the squalor of the ascending criminals; yet they were so garlanded and their proportions so distorted, even dwarfed (were they kneeling perhaps?) that the gravity of their impact was undermined. Venetia liked the look of the Infanta Marie whose face was bossy and kind.

As she moved upwards past the curious perspectives and the false stage-flat vaulting, a weight seemed to lift from her shoulders and the clarity of her alert reflexes reintensified. This new lightness of being bounced back off a bizarre picture of a surprised beribboned lamb, arriving, like Venetia herself, at the top of a staircase. Was it an elaborate hoax, a frivolous pretend-mirror to undercut the spectator's pretensions to be more than the merest creature? Or was it a religious allegory of the soul surprised? Alternative interpretations began to proliferate too rapidly in her mind; she moved away to pre-empt insoluble speculations.

The upper gallery seemed blessedly simple, a modest conventual austerity, until she realized that the wooden grilles set into the walls concealed further turbulent confections of baroque exuberance. Each door might swing open to reveal its *tesoro escondido*; and the shock of revelation would cause the gilded paraphernalia of centuries to pour out, spilling over the plain red flags of the gallery floor and defiling their purity, just as the frescoist had done on the innocent stair-well. Venetia paused, to press a wooden door back into its resting-place and stem the imminent flood-tide, repel the besieging barbarianism, finger the dyke – whatever metaphor she happened to be trapped in.

What on earth was she doing here? An acid-ridden spinster, spinning hysterically, alone in a cloister and bombarded with papistical glitter? Why wasn't she at home with her child, placidly watching TV and fussing around finding God among the pots and pans?

Only a lying novelist could have invented a convincing motivation. A child-doll slept calmly in a glass cabinet, as serene as the recumbent Christ, who lay oblivious of the golden hole in his side. Our Lady of Charity was standing on a globe with a crescent moon above a canoe manned by tiny rowing Indians from the newly discovered paradisal island of Cuba. Mother and child were ubiquitous and in their varied forms, suffering, grieving, resurrected, radiant, frilled and ruffled, stained with tears of pearl.

Venetia drifted through in a neutral stupor. She wondered how many brain-cells she'd irrevocably lost. She was unable to relate these things to the theological instruction she'd received and wondered why so much passion had been infused into their creation. She began to feel tired, drained of energy and commitment and felt a surge of affinity when she looked dreamily at the portrait of Charles II. His elongated fleshy face, the strange stiff collar that stood under his disproportionate jaw, all had the same artificial freakishness she ascribed to herself in moments of self-dramatization. She read in her guide-book about his feeble life and the appalling corruption found in his body at autopsy – 'not one drop of blood: his heart was of the size of a grain of pepper; his lungs rotten; his intestines putrefied and gangrenous; one single testicle as black as coal and his head full of water'. The putrescence of that body, rampant even during Charles's life, had cast Europe into the War of the Spanish Succession.

Her eyes strayed upwards from the page, seeking something else on which to settle, anything other than these fat, bloated medical words and their disgusting import. A small window gave on to a garden and, above it, a blue patch of sky – 'Le ciel est par-dessus le toit, si bleu, si calme', she murmured pacifically. But her mood was so sick now, so overfed with decomposition and horror, that she stared thankfully at the frazzled trees, motionless in the inert and stifling air and seeming to cry out for transplantation to some moister climate. Dust rising from the ground had left thick, streaky deposits as it settled on the gnarled, asymmetrical trunks. They seemed cowed by their condition; the leaves were parched and had irregular excisions where browned portions had dropped off in despair. It was, she thought, as if one of Góngora's poetic pastorals had mutated, the profusion of nature had been reversed and deformed by human error: instead of the oneness of creation miraculously about to coalesce, all nature had been subjected to a Dresden firestorm as it struggled for survival.

Finding no solace, then, in this dry garden, Venetia went into a room described as the cell of Snr Margarita de la Cruz. Maybe this would be a true and satisfying asceticism, an exemplar for her prodigal uncertainty. The nun's portrait was not reassuring. She stood grim and menacing, her eyes hyperthyroid and expressionless, the huge slack, fleshy lips and the prominent jaw revealing her Habsburg origin. The Most Serene Infanta of the German Empire and the Kingdoms of Bohemia, Moravia, etc., Señora Margarita de la Cruz, daughter, sister, cousin and aunt of Holy Catholic, Caesarian, Royal and Most Catholic Majesties of the Roman Empire, the Monarchy of Spain and the Kingdom of France, Bride of Jesus Christ, King of Kings and Lord of Lords. Smartass credentials, Venetia mused; not a lot of drawing-rooms barred to *her*. Imagine being the daughter of the Holy Roman Emperor, and Rudolph II at that, that fanatical recluse given to locking himself in his Prague fastness and experimenting with mechanical pumps, perspective lutes, machines of perpetual motion and the inventions of alchemical adepts. The Emperor's daughter must have turned with relief from this crabbed

Maurist dream to the consolations of conventional religion. Her father turning away from God to scrutinize the magic ciphers of the introchemical universe; she, the modest, plain daughter returning to the fold like a docile sheep. Although that face . . . fanaticism . . . unworldliness . . .

Venetia brought out her book again and read about Snr Margarita's life: she seemed to have had miraculous powers as a thaumaturge and had been given to relentless meditation on death and suffering, even commissioning paintings of the skulls of her dead relations inscribed with the subscript, 'Let your eyes rest on these moral relics, the greatness and veneration of nations reduced to dust and ashes.' There was a story that when she heard of a lapsed Christian who had signed a pact ceding his soul to the Devil, she had prayed passionately and, taking a knife, slashed her breast and been blighted by the blindness that suddenly afflicted her and which doctors tried to cure for twenty days with corrosive oils. Destiny struck a cruel blow against a woman who had delighted in dressing up statues of Christ and Our Lady with pretty regalia. She had ordered a copy of the *Madonna del Popolo* in Rome to be placed before her, hoping that when her eyes might be reopened they should alight first on the image of the Madonna and the Child Jesus whom she had married; but that, if they did not, they would patiently wait until Paradise conferred that blessing.

Her cell reflected this inward sanctity: all her inherited riches reduced to a wreath, a pair of coarse slippers and a moth-eaten prayer-book. It certainly seemed more final, more concrete a sentence than the sentimental destiny facing Audrey Hepburn in *A Nun's Story*. Had Venetia been born an archduchess of the HRE, she doubted whether she would have sacrificed the fat largesses of the Hofburg for these tawdry and sad impedimenta, the miniature skull which Snr Margarita clasped fiercely in her hand in the pathetic Rizzi portrait.

The convent seemed to have attracted royal novices from all over Europe. A large group portrait showed Snr M. de la Cruz with Snr Catalina Maria de Eire, daughter of the Princess of Modena, Ana Doroten de Anstric, bastard daughter of Rudolf II, Snr Mariona de la Cruz y Austria, daughter of the Cardinal-Infante don Fernando, victor of Nordlingen, and Snr Margarita de la Cruz y Austria, daughter of Don Juan José, bastard pretender to the throne of Spain. They all stood side by side (chronology ignored), facing to the left in shy identical poses as if for a group photograph. All seemed resigned, only dimly aware of the regal status they had abandoned, bound together by simplicity and routine.

As Venetia wandered through the other rooms, she compared these grim paragons with the portraits of their secular counterparts, the caparisoned princesses and starched scowling matrons who'd opted for the world and its dubious but tangible rewards. Had the religious vocation set sister against sister, mother against daughter? Had the nuns all ended up like their stern foundress, bleakly cuddling a terrified lapdog? Venetia thought it must have been incredibly difficult to undertake the transition from the life symbolized by these imperious viragos in their jewelled farthingales to the meek imitation of St Francis of Assisi. She herself would certainly have faltered along the way, railed at God for demanding such sacrifices, questioned herself pitilessly for preferring flesh poverty to impoverished flesh. Indeed, she had already done all this in Kathmandu, although the contrast between Buddhist and Austro-Habsburg colours alone, to say nothing of the different rituals, beliefs and traditions, made it impossible for her to draw more than the most perfunctory parallel. Religion would always remain for her a thing of remote fascination, a solution that withheld itself from her; and she could only make sense of it by persuading herself that it made sense to other people (an ambivalent argument for such a determined sceptic). There were only isolated parts to which she could relate. She liked, above all, the notion of universal love and she appreciated the infinite iconographic portrayals of this idea. Here she saw it in a towering, surreal St Christopher striding through the gauzy veil of water wearing breeches rolled like the *maillot* of an Edwardian bather and supporting the burdensome Christ child with such patience, such forbearance, such unquestioning, naïve love.

The child threatened once more to reopen the wounds of her guilt about David, and it swelled to fill her vision, acquiring a clarity and disproportion, surprising-seeming. Before it naturally assumed the lineaments of her own child, she juggled with her focus to readmit the immense saint, whose dire relevance to her own life was not so apparent. She went up to the picture and stroked one of the fish that teamed and jumped in the river. She was disappointed that her hand didn't come away stuck with cool scales. It wasn't real, any more than the selfless love of St Christopher was real. Her understanding was too shallow, so literal; all the truths eluded her, as slippery as the darting fish.

Footsteps approached. She heard the murmurs of marshalled tourists, their caught breath interspersing with the authoritarian delivery of a guide. She slipped gracefully away down a corridor-gallery lined with unexplained Polish princelings and took refuge in a neighbouring room. Sidling backwards through the door, she turned to check out her hiding-place. It would have served its purpose as camouflage only had she been a gilded casket with one or more of her bones, a femur or a tibia perhaps, exposed through a transparent panel in her skin. For this was the relic chamber, hung with crimson brocade, piled from floor to ceiling, up the blue-tiled tiered steps, with gilt cabinets and glass-fronted canisters displaying here a calcified metacarpal, there fragments of splintered thorax, the abused foot of a martyred missionary careless of his own bodily decay: square reliquaries segmented like sewing-boxes, each compartment studded with diamonds and amethysts and treasuring even more recondite anatomy; the body of St Victor, lieutenant of the Theban legion, encased in enamelled silver in a chest from the dowry of Queen Anne of Austria; St Margaret of Pisidia, the Siamese twins – Sts Cosmas and Damian, St Casilda wreathed in flowers, St Teresa of Ávila – whose relics had helplessly, impotently accompanied General Franco to his protracted death. The precious metals strove to be as precious as the dead calcium and human minerals they contained: market value set against illimitable spiritual benefit, the tension between the fecund bullion of the New World and the fervent hopes of salvation which characterized the Spain of its Golden Age. The gilt formed an accusatory visual pun to remind her of her guilt.

Venetia was so dazzled that she would have liked to sit down and reflect further on this monstrous concordance of money and faith. The acid was not strong enough to allow her just to sense its progress into her veins and arteries (like some extravagant catheter) till it poured into a heart that palpitated with the apprehension of a wing-trapped bird. She found herself driven to wonder at it, to reflect meditatively on it, even to distance herself from it by consigning it to a dead historical world only tenuously linked with her own.

But she was not able to carry out this idea. From high behind a massive pseudo-Etruscan sarcophagus came a quiet buzzing, a whistling as of delicate machinery. So still was the religious blaze of the room that a noise she would otherwise have dismissed as the irrelevant importunity of some insect began to swell and reverberate, broad and resonant like a baroque organ-voluntary, a *vox caelestis*. And then she saw it, a darting bat that rose from its gilded lair and flew its course towards her as irregular as a feinting, beleaguered, decoying ship. She looked upwards at it, her pulse heightened, a small pearly trail of sweat starting on her forehead. It swooped at her head, brushed lightly, electrostatically against her ear and veered away without, thankfully *without*, tangling in her hair. Maddened with fear, she lashed out with her arms, turning herself into a flailing windmill, a transformation – human into windmill – more extraordinary than Don Quixote's metamorphosis of windmill into giant. But the bat had escaped, screaming in a low whine, back to some arcane habitat that probably ran with torrents of vampirized blood now dried and encrusted like a ruby intaglio on the reliquaries.

Venetia sighed and wiped the back of her hand across her brow. The whole thing was getting a little too much; she liked her trips easy, *allegro ma non troppo*; it might've been better to stay in and lay on something a bit more domestic.

'This is the fabulous treasury of relics, all the presents brought by the royal princesses as their dowry.' The Spanish guide was only seconds away, shepherding his flock with honeyed inaccuracies. Escape seemed impossible. If only she could dart past like the bloody bat. Quick thinking led her to abandon all hope of escape, and she lurked behind the door, ready to join the group of tourists from the rear as they gasped at the golden hoard. As they burst in, chattering and jostling, she contrived to fall in nonchalantly and unobtrusively – though she was acidically conscious of how little she resembled them and merged into their number. Her head buried in her guide-book, she walked on insouciantly amid them as they continued and now reached the end of their tour. Past a bright and empty locutory, they arrived back at their point of departure, harbouring this exotic girl like a dowdy *cordon sanitaire*.

The over-rich diet of sensations and aesthetic suet left her longing for something astringent, and she thought analogically with nostalgia of the citrus sorbet she'd wolfed down so gratefully between courses in the heat of an Atlanta summer. It became necessary to invent a similar counterbalance to the lush kaleidoscope of the convent.

'Take me to the Café Roma,' she barked at the taxi-driver, with the imperious aplomb of Lady Diana Cooper instructing an astonished bus-driver to convey her to Berkeley Square. Her mind was not running so much on what she could eat or drink at the Roma, as on the certainty that she would there listen to hard-nosed intellectuals, journalists cynically parading their disbeliefs.

Inside the café, she sat gratefully in a corner, slightly too far from the telephone to hear the rapid story being delivered down the instrument to an impatient editor. There was a sense of brisk interchange, a clash of stories and counter-stories, the ineluctable scoring of competitive points. Nobody hovered or dallied, for the purpose of the place was too deliberate. Venetia envied the women for their emancipated fluency, the practical unconcern with which they vied with their mercurial male colleagues.

'They found the body smashed beyond recognition on a rubbish-tip near the asylum. It seems the lynch-mob were mostly women, friends of the mother of the little girl he raped. When they examined the body they found . . .'

Venetia deliberately failed to hear the rest. The picture she was already piecing together from the unsentimental account weighed too heavily on her. Her eyes flicked around the room, past the intrusive, obscuring flannel bulk of a bystander, taking in the loquacious, rather under-dressed (for Spaniards) crowd. Near Venetia a girl was relating a story with such ferocity that she seemed unconscious she was repeatedly hitting her coffee-cup with a spoon or that her companion was wilting under the pressure. Beyond their table she saw the back of an elegant, leonine head, marred only by the slight pitting of a rash, but so formal and dignified in its carriage that Venetia wished she was sitting in a more strategic place to view its front. She remained staring until the head moved slightly to one side as its owner turned the pages of a newspaper. In that momentary gesture, she glimpsed a fine Nordic profile, deep-set intelligent eyes and an unguarded downward tilt to the side of the mouth visible to her. She cried out in recognition: 'Claes! Claes von Amerongen!'

As he turned to face her full on, his eyebrows raised questioningly, she got up clumsily and stumbled towards him, oblivious of the effect she created now that her spontaneous delight alone mattered. He did not recognize her for a short instant, despite her characteristic, idiosyncratic gait, the flustered Englishness of her smiling rush towards him.

'I don't believe it,' he said at length. 'The madonna of the picture-library. Venetia, it cannot be you.'

'I'm so excited I can hardly *speak*,' she cried, with an upward squawk punctuating the last word. 'I've gone so red I feel like an Italian tomato. This is the most thrilling chance encounter, my dearest Claes, how *are* you, what on earth are you doing here?'

'I've come on a rather extraordinary mission. I don't expect you'd ever have thought I was capable of an act of disinterested friendship. But here I am to prove it. I'll tell you all about it. Sit down, let me buy you a drink.'

They celebrated their meeting with Rioja, and Venetia toyed excitedly with the wire lattice that decorated the bottle. The first stage of their conversation was entirely banal, the exchange of necessary information to establish present circumstances, a kind of workmanlike transaction. It was a slight effort for Venetia to dampen down the still active acid flurries and adjust to Claes's stolid presence. While he described to her his strange compromise with

Asdrúbal, she busied herself with composing her nervous features and concentrating on this new, compelling experience which so completely blotted out her awareness of the bar around them.

'So you see, I've suddenly been plunged into the world of high liberal politics. It's all very unfamiliar; I don't think I shall ever get used to cynics acting as idealists. In Holland everything has to be consistent and systematic,' he was saying, until he began to unbend and lose his formality.

33

In Our Age

'What I envy you, Claes, is your unambiguous position. I feel somehow that the generation Jerome and I belong to is confronted with too many options, too prodigal a choice. And that paradoxically the *idea* of greater freedom is illusory, since the choosing of one option removes the possibility of all the others. Their very multiplicity makes their loss all the more poignant. While your role is secure. You use bibliography and scholarship as a kind of fulcrum which balances the centre of your inner contradictions and ensures your stability. What could be more fixed than all those incontestable truths about watermarks, second impressions, folds and galleys, all that dreary apparatus? And the fact that it's so meaningless, so lethally boring to the rest of the world, must make for a sense of defiant élitism – which is anyway *hugely* compatible with your own natural diffidence.'

Here she allowed her residual hostility towards Professor van Amerongen to surface obliquely.

'Jerome and I, on the other hand, have no such easy prop. We're adrift in our own experiments; and I, at least, find it increasingly difficult to anchor myself to any one set purpose. Even bringing up David – an extraordinary chance to satisfy my frustrated maternal instinct – was something I only partially accepted. I felt I couldn't commit myself totally to a biological role which properly belonged to somebody else. Perhaps I should be more like David's mother. I don't think she ever *floundered* in her life. I just feel lost, unsuccessful, pointless. And I know that contact with 98 per cent of humanity will always be denied me. Irrevocably. Through my inability – or unwillingness – to understand most of what goes on outside me.'

She would have liked to cry, quietly and unspectacularly; but Claes's presence was too intimidating. His Dutch stoicism would have interpreted her tears too severely.

'So much of life consists of coming to terms with your own limitations,' he said. 'Just seeing exactly what your mediocrity *is*. Eventually you'll find that easier and more fortifying than this perpetual agonic struggle. There are just too many culs-de-sac, too many diversions and *trompe l'oeil* perspectives. No one can see them all all the time. You have to learn how to identify them, so as not to be fooled by their false promise. Once you've established your own limits, you'll be able to understand and develop your abilities and stop chasing all those elusive chimeras. Will you ever be a *prima ballerina assoluta*, an aviatrix, a temp in a typing-pool, a management consultant in St Louis? I think not, my dear.'

Venetia recognized the truth of this and idly rearranged her dress as if to regularize her position.

'One of the problems I share with Jerome – or rather *used* to share with him – is the conflict between being a man of action and a man of ideas,' Claes went on. 'All my adolescence was peopled with heroic agitators, khaki-clad explorers, anaconda-wrestling canoeists, *alpinistes* brandishing crampons, fascists in and out of uniform – individuals whose sense of destiny was in fact confined to solving practical dangers; filled with moral certainties, immutable axioms as unchallengeable as a British passport. No self-questioning. Yet my very awareness of those paragons carried within it the seeds of my own alienation. I was constantly *reading* about them, poring over encyclopaedias of mythology and my father's boyhood Emilio Salgaris. The more *pabulum* I inserted into my eager brain, the more elusive the prospect of emulating them became. Perhaps if my personality had been more Quixotic . . . Had I in effect been *madder*, I might have been able to charge ahead, casting aside my scrupulous doubts, my prim reservations, and offer myself up unconditionally to some preordained life-style, some conventional kind of safe machismo. Just imagine it, looking at me as you see me now – an arid, blinkered and fastidious

Dutchman. There I was contemplating the life maybe of a crusader roaring Norman orders from a scaling-ladder, or a U-boat commander, binoculars around my neck, effortlessly navigating my battered craft of hero-worshipping sailors into Kiel Harbour. The more concrete the images became, in my fantasy, the more I was forced to stand back from them, furious with my intelligence and sensitivity, realizing how wholly inadequate I should be as a protagonist. I was too clever, at least in the ordinary sense in which we understand the notion of a clever child. I was also, of course, already homosexual. Now, after all these desert years, I recognize that it was the heroes who were clever – resourceful and energetic, like Hercules, not dumb automata performing some kind of parade-ground drill. I've simply modified my standards about what constitutes cleverness.

'At that stage I was merely conscious of an incipient old-maidishness, of intellectually prejudging and dismissing qualities like leadership, courage, things I was gradually coming to associate with weak-minded, pederastic school-masters, while subliminally I was aching, burning to possess them. The concepts, I mean, not the schoolmasters. So I retreated further into an impenetrable crust of cynicism, of nihilism almost, refusing any value to ideas and experiences outside myself; while remaining aware of a dreadful void within my own personality. I could produce fluent explanations, clear rationalizations, well-argued dismissals – to myself, of course, since I naturally had no friends. But I could construct nothing, all my analytic power was negative. And in the process my feelings about masculinity, or humanity rather, became crushed and mangled, so that I was only able to understand them in homosexual terms – the familiar transference mechanism. I was aware – horribly aware – of the elusive quality of these infantile models. So I could only make them real by using the homosexual factitious simulacrum. And at the same time this allowed me to remain sceptically detached from them, to mock them as intellectually crass. A vicious vicious circle.

'Now I can only imagine myself as myself. It feels as if my heart wears gold-rimmed spectacles.'

Venetia wondered if she could ever really conceive of

harnessing her future to someone like Claes. She thought their marriage might be something akin to the situation in Howard Hawks's *Bringing up Baby*, in which an heiress relentlessly pursued a timid palaeontologist Cary Grant. But would she really be able to do the Katharine Hepburn number, leopards and all? It was far more likely that their liaison would crumble into the dry embers of Dorothea Brooke and Mr Casaubon, and she would dream of Jerome as a resplendent, irrecoverable Ladislaw.

34

Adelaida's Request

It was going to be heavy. Venetia had telephoned Adelaida in the morning to arrange a meeting. She assumed a voice of breezy complacency, asked a string of well-mannered clichéed questions, but felt her energy and commitment sap away with the strain of it all. Adelaida, for her part, had never understood the mechanisms of politeness, or even seen their point; so that her answers were brusque and uninformative, and there was certainly no reciprocation – as there might have been with a more placid friend – of the emollient questions.

Venetia suggested that Adelaida should visit her at home, knowing that Jerome would be busy and that David could be reparked with Angelines. She had still not yet realized fully that David was the crucial subject of their meeting.

Adelaida, anyway, was unwilling to venture into Venetia's territory – borrowed and temporary as it was – and presumably felt scruples too about receiving her in her own. She suggested a bar near where she lived in the Calle de Rodas; and Venetia, knowing better than to gainsay or argue with her, agreed to a meeting that evening.

Jerome was delighted not to accompany her, and in the elation of pain avoided offered to stay in with David. It was not, in fact, much of a sacrifice, as he was beginning to find his taste for adventure under strain. His Spanish was being stretched to the limit, and his appreciation of argot-ridden torrents of admiration for his Nordic physique was flagging. It was far better, he was beginning to feel, to remain within one's own ethnic group where the competition was fiercer and the pressure therefore less fraying. There you could give in gracefully. Here his rarity coefficient was too high, and he sensed an element of bludgeoning in the attentions to which he was unwillingly being subjected. Nothing should, after all, be that easy, especially if you kept for your pleasures the vestiges of a Puritan work-ethic.

Venetia suffered her usual crisis of indecision about her appearance. Her friendship with Adelaida in San Francisco had been based so much on intellectual discussion that she had never quite fathomed what kind of physical presentation conferred the easiest conquest of Adelaida's unyielding misanthropy. There had, indeed, been no solid foundation for their bemused, dream-like friendship.

'I found her fascinating,' she would insist, protesting too much and hitting on a mendacious adjective in the effort of self-justification to Jerome. 'And above all I was so terribly flattered that she should single me out for her friendship. She wasn't exactly Liberace twinkling away at *le monde en général*; and it was rather a triumph to get her to acknowledge me, let alone make friends with me, rely on me. Everyone else thought she was married to the computers at Stanford. I remember how all the straight guys got really frustrated. Just imagine, a beautiful Spanish girl, to all intents and purposes completely mute but in fact pulsating with fire and intelligence. What on earth was she doing blocking out men like they were some sort of new virus? And what was she doing at a straight university like Stanford? Berkeley, yes, but *Stanford*? God, it was peculiar.'

'I remember thinking much the same. The only thing I could do was let you carry on seeing her in the hope that her claims to attention might eventually become apparent. Or perhaps some of your humanity might impress itself on her. There was a time, once, do you remember, when you came home in tears after she'd accused you of *betraying* yourself, I think it was, by squandering your patrimony and adopting just the pallid liberalism that she thought was undermining Europe under the nuclear threat? You were so upset, you could scarcely explain it to me. I felt then – and I must say I feel now – that you were allowing your love of eccentricity and extremism to run away with you and take you to absurd lengths. Just as we were a bit like a re-run of Harold Nicolson and Vita Sackville-West in *our* relationship, you two were like Lillian Hellman and Julia. The curious, *avid* intellectual mesmerized by a woman of conviction, a snake and a mongoose, Rikki Tikki Tavi.'

The telephone rang and a husky Californian voice asked for Jerome. He raised his eyes to the ceiling as Venetia passed the instrument over, trying to exonerate himself for responsibility for these unsolicited queenly pests. They traced him everywhere. She was not taken in. It was one of those physical, social interruptions to their marriage to which she had never learned to reconcile herself. Her face set itself firmly in a prim cast, her February face, which forced Jerome to adopt a peremptory and dismissive tone that confirmed this boy friend's prejudice that the English were terminally stony-hearted. Hadn't he gone to all the hassle of tracking Jerome down in some foreign Puerto Rican joint, couldn't he at least say hi without sounding like he was sitting on the john?

Venetia left the room to get ready. Jerome's *taedium vitae* billowed around him in huge flaccid envelopes. He imitated its motion by snatching up David and engulfing him in his big embrace. He took the child's hand and placed it first, finger by finger, in the whorls of his ear and then pushed the finger-tips rapidly backwards and forwards in the inchoate curls towards the crown of Jerome's head. David's sensitive finger-pads registered the odd feeling, which made him smile in a dazed kind of way. Jerome thought he looked for all the world like a cat whose nostrils had been inspired with a gust of marijuana smoke. When he released the boy's fingers, they waved around in the air, clenching and unclenching, palpating the void as if they might again regain contact with the mysterious phrenological bumps.

'What's your name, you naughty little saucebox?' Jerome murmured. 'David, powerful king, King of Kings, rock-solid. Do you know the story of the bomb at the King David Hotel in Jerusalem?'

David did, but, loving explosions, longed for the retelling. Venetia was now ready to leave and came sailing up to them with an expression of placid content at the enchanting Greuze-like double portrait they formed. Jerome broke off the narrative and David looked up a little petulantly at the interruption and, instead of saying goodbye properly to Venetia, repeated the word he'd found most interesting in Jerome's story – 'IRGUN' – over and over.

'Yes, sweetie, Irgun,' she replied, and kissed them both goodbye. Jerome was not quite sure about her outfit, but chose to keep silent for fear of undermining her fragile morale. She was wearing a rather severe grey tailored skirt suit and, underneath, a daring bodice, narrowly avoiding an intimidating but contemptible elegance by the addition of a pair of high-wedged espadrilles and a Basque beret. Very ETA, that last detail, she'd reflected irresponsibly.

A short metro-ride took her to an area of Madrid she hardly knew. The district was called Lavapies, but it was not in any obvious way a place in which you would have wished to wash your feet. A biting wind blew all before it, newspapers wrapped themselves tenaciously around her ankles, her eyes smarted with dust and her hair stood out behind her in a Struwwelpeter shock. Decrepit, grimy old tenements lined the dark streets, which were all the gloomier for the rectangular spaces of intensely blue evening light which tried unsuccessfully to penetrate the architectural mass, that 'subtle air of Madrid which can kill a man and yet not extinguish a candle'. A theatre had been allowed to dilapidate at a crossing that lacked the necessary geometry properly to be called a square, but which seemed to be the focal point of the quarter. The modern decades had superimposed tawdry affixes on to the house-fronts at street-level: chrome, plastic and aluminium that bravely, anachronistically summoned attention, amalgam fillings in the rotting dentition. The hideous fascias flared out, the shop-windows spilled over with the rampant merchandise of lamps and drills, quadruped (of some species) sausages, cans of beans labelled with pictures of smiling Galicians (where in trashy California they'd have read 'they're the classiest 'cos they're the gassiest'), squids in ink, bottled caviar, tripe with the texture of padded graph-paper, machine-made haberdashery, celluloid notebook covers, multinational nostrums and specifics, solidified mounds of Russian salad cross-gartered with stiff anchovies.

Had it not been for these modern intrusions, Venetia would not have been surprised to have been jostled by slumming *señoritos* in nankeen breeches and twirling quizzing-glasses. Certainly the children – give or take a pair of sneakers or a World Cup tee-shirt – had the unspecificity of all urchins, outside time, so ubiquitous was their Murilloesque gap-toothed facial uniform. She hoped they were not organized in some criminal guild like the brats in Bogotá, who'd not long since relieved her of an emerald of the highest *jardín*. Only the violent swerving of a car around her wrenched her back into a correct time-sequence and continental shift.

Everything was moving, almost artificially so, like the restarting of a frozen film-shot which instantaneously propels into motion a fervour of busy extras. Venetia began to feel self-conscious, rooted as she was to the pavement in her dazed curiosity, becoming herself a curiosity for the sunflower-seed-spitting gangs of children. They circled around her now, slower, leoparding, their eyes, some slitted, some circular, as they relished her discomfiture.

'*¡Quítate!*' she snapped as one of them fingered the back of her thigh. She brushed him aside, Katharine Hepburn sweeping off the river-leeches in *The African Queen*. '*¡Asqueroso cerdo!*'

Even this limited command of invective established her as a force to be reckoned with. One of the children, whose face betrayed more experience than the others, shepherded them manfully away, puffing himself up in the glorious role of her protector, Castilian and strong in his blaze of honour. Never again would he degrade himself with the sunflower-husk of childhood.

Placing herself gratefully under the tutelage of this dashing boy, Venetia asked him to accompany her to the place of rendezvous. They set off briskly, almost running with relief. Soon they were standing in front of a blinding neon cafeteria where Venetia said goodbye and gave him a pack of Camels. His smile of gratitude was the best part of the expedition so far.

The café could not have been worse. It might just have

passed muster as the surgery of a peculiarly sadistic dentist. Once the glare of polished metal had subsided, the serious blinding began from the Agent Orange wallpaper. Venetia tottered over the threshold with the resolution of Samson in the temple of the Philistines and, remembering her classes in perspective drawing, focused on a distant table which might serve as a vanishing-point and obliterate the rasping light-bouncing sidelines. Her visual integrity secured, she walked on and gradually allowed herself to be seduced by the high-spirited smells of coffee, aniseed, fried sardines and black Canaries tobacco, that clutter and lumber which the Spanish seemed cheerfully to shuttle around with them from antique bodegas with sawdust and aromatic casks to these simulacra of small-town America and back again.

Focusing ascetically through a snowstorm on the television mounted on the wall, she dimly caught sight of Sir John Gielgud dressed as the Pope. Instead of the sly, casuistical murmuring his mouth and face portrayed, he was shouting in militaristic Spanish. Sickened by the travesty, Venetia looked down to find the proprietor's eyes as wide at the sight of her as if she were an intergalactic time-traveller while his wife leaned back against the wall to stare with all the subtlety of a rude cat.

By the time she reached the table, early for her date and in need of stimulants, she felt able to make this surrender unconditional. In a way her eclectic mind relished vulgarity as readily as the most rarefied and etiolated of subtleties. It was, too, some sort of revenge in kind for Jerome's sexual self-debasement. Some unsolicited junk-food arrived with her wine: rubber-rings of squid and wasted olive. This, as well, delighted her, and she wolfed them down, watched by an aged drunk who made sympathetic gobbling sounds through his lecherous smile as each mouthful bounced down her throat.

The food was so calming that she ordered more, this time specifying fat slivers of tortilla, a dish of piquant mussels, asparagus as gross as bluebells, even a slab of hake, which she folded clumsily into the maize bread. She could not stop gorging, and she let herself be overtaken by a heady indulgence. The eating was so interesting and satisfying that she barely noticed how much wine she was drinking – although the waiter, who'd sussed her accented Spanish, smiled slyly at the thought of this foreign, Amazonian, *bonne viveuse* with the cantaloupe breasts. He had never before seen so well-filled a bodice. She knew that her skin was of such whiteness that, when she drank, the wine could be seen passing down her throat.

She moved her metal chair to one side so as to change the embarrassing sightline from the cauliflower warts that sprouted and clustered on the side of the drunk's sweating nose. As she did so, the chair leg scraped and rasped; and her relief was tempered with a sudden new shock as her foot struck an object under the table among the sugar-wrappings. It was spongy in texture. Overcome by curiosity, she bent down and saw a rounded piece of flesh-coloured plastic. It seemed so displaced there, so flaccid and mournful, that she picked it up and examined its smooth surface. With an appalled shriek of recognition she read a label on the underside: PRÓTESIS MAMARIA HERMANDI GONZÁLEZ. How on earth could it have got there? Shed by a woman rendered so careless by cancer that she hadn't noticed? Discarded by a perfectionist salesman sorting through his merchandise? Clawed off and dashed to the ground by a vindictive lover? The trains of speculation were infinite, yet all probably as novelettish and false as the object itself.

By the time Adelaida stood in front of her at last, Venetia was decidedly drunk. More important, the acid had not yet left her bloodstream and was starting to reactivate. The prosthesis had seen to that. It was with a dopy, glassy stare that she switched her attention back to her table-companion – whose gestures had become increasingly obscene as her gluttony grew more unabashed – and then to the formidable terrorist erect before her.

It would have been wrong to expect Adelaida to speak first, to make the running or puncture the embarrassment. Venetia launched herself upwards and embraced her, almost convinced that the pressure of her hug conferred the warmth and closeness she needed. Adelaida patted Venetia's shoulder-blades. Had you been fairly neurotic, this could have seemed perfunctory; but Venetia was so determinedly relaxed that she believed the gesture could have been a concessionary overture, the early clauses of a truce.

'I thought we should never see each other again,' she cried. 'It's as if you were just the memory of a story I read somewhere in a book. I'm so excited I don't know what to say.'

Adelaida's threatened *froideur* was melting. Perhaps with her mechanical, cybernetic sense of the justness and equivalence of things, she was gradually matching the helpless susceptibility of Venetia, her child's other mother.

'My friend, I hope I still have a place in your thoughts,' she said. 'What you have done for me can't just be forgotten. I'm not so inhuman that I do not think about you and David. I can't forget what I have done and how you rescued my son. It was right; and even had it not been right, my stubborn nature insists that it was right. I suppose it isn't difficult for you to speak of him to me?'

She drank from the glass Venetia offered and watched her cautiously over the brim.

'He's my whole life now,' said Venetia. 'I love him with a depth of love I'd never thought to find within myself.' That sentence didn't come out quite right; there'd been a moment when she'd wished to say 'of which I didn't think myself capable', but the alcohol snapped the sentence at the 'of which' and she replaced it with the slurred alternative. 'I know he's yours,' she continued. 'Your blood, your genes, your creation. But in every way now he's become my own. We're inseparable, everything I do is done with his happiness in mind.'

The television channel had changed now to a quiz programme. It included many forfeits for the intellectual casualties who failed to give the right answer. As Venetia watched with blank attention, a young man was being blindfolded with an apparatus made from red nylon hearts. He was then urged to put black stockings on to his girl friend's legs as she writhed and squirmed to guide him. When he triumphantly snapped a garter on to her thigh, there was a burst of applause and an electronic fanfare on the organ; and the happy couple were showered with red-heart confetti by a compère dressed in tartan breeches and a straw hat.

Adelaida seemed to be struggling with a piece of information that she could simultaneously neither reveal nor withhold. Her whole manner betrayed unease, a welling disquiet, and she composed her features with some difficulty to respond to Venetia's maternal urgency. Her fingers stroked the chrome surface of a napkin-dispenser; and one could see that, had she given full rein to her feelings, she would have pulled the napkins out and scrunched them up in nervous abandon.

'I know that it might seem as if my motherhood's a bit unorthodox,' Venetia said, 'and perhaps that David's childhood is a little *mouvementée*. But he's supremely happy with me and Jerome; he shares our sense of adventure and towers above his friends who seem like the dullest kind of pedestrians when he speeds by. He's an extraordinary boy, full of talents and surprises, rattling on about everything he sees. And tied to us by love, wanting desperately to share in everything.'

She kept insisting on that notion of love, a little too assertively, maybe, to conceal successfully her apprehension about Adelaida's purpose. She absorbed every one of Adelaida's facial reactions as she spoke; and was glad that she seemed in a state of *general* nervousness, so that no one special, particular movement appeared to be individually provoked by anything Venetia said. This was particularly reassuring after her cursory mention of Jerome's role in David's life.

There was a pause as they both drank in silence. Their eyes did not meet as each concentrated on her inner thoughts. Venetia found the wine sweet to her taste, as if it corroborated her emotional appeal and spread within her a balm of justification.

'Will you let me see him? It's imperative that I do . . .'

Once Adelaida had said it, her entire face seemed to slacken and lose the clenched tension around the brow, the strain around the eyes that looked like soreness. Had beseeching been within the canon of her physiognomical messages, it would probably have registered in her expression instead of the mere softening and slight vulnerability that did appear.

'I have a very special reason for asking this. I know,

Venetia, how can I not know, that I gave him up to you, that he loves you now as if you were his real mother. That makes me happy and takes away some of the guilt. That was the way I intended it. But I am facing something so terrible that I don't think I have the courage for it without seeing my child again.'

The lines reasserted themselves on her forehead. Turning away from Venetia, she watched the café proprietor watching her as he mechanically polished the counter with broad, circular movements of his hand.

Venetia leaned across the table and put her hand over Adelaida's. She squeezed it gently; but the eloquence of the gesture was undermined by an inquisitive element within it, a curiosity that made the handclasp not merely one of sympathy.

'I can't tell you about it now,' Adelaida continued. 'There is too much at stake. But the probability is that I will die soon. It'll be a death brought about by my own actions; but I cannot deviate from my purpose. The cause in which I shall die is higher than my own life. Sometimes, in my darker moods, it seems almost as if I am taking my own life. But it is this cause, this greater good which will justify me.

'So you see I must see my child. I shan't upset him or make impossible demands or insist that you return him to me. I must just embrace him. Now that I am on the edge of danger I can see only his face, his importance; some of my womanhood has re-emerged. Let me, Venetia; show me your humanity.'

Venetia leaned back, considering what Adelaida had said, the intentness of their close embrace now relaxed. Her head spun with thoughts incapable of resolution, such was their incoherence. It had been difficult enough just coming here, heavy with a sense of foreboding and mystery. Adelaida had not – though this was to be expected – smoothed the path of their conversation by any conventional preliminaries. There had been no inquiry about Jerome or David's health or Venetia's domestic fortunes. With characteristic directness, she had not tried to protect Venetia from the shock of her request. And Venetia was left now with a question which, however she weighed its implications, didn't seem to have an answer.

She remained silent for a while, eating lustily and then taking a handkerchief out of her bag. As she held it to her nostrils, she said softly, her voice muffled by the cotton: 'I cannot possibly answer you now. I have to think about the effect on David. He's too young to understand. Come and see me tomorrow at seven. Either he will be with me or he will not.'

The dark streets seemed to open away from her in a reversal of normal perspective, leaving her an infinity of space for her own reflections as she walked home. Although the crowds milled and chattered more even than they had on her arrival, the intensity of her thoughts was such that they might almost have been absent or silent.

How odd the course of her life had suddenly become. Was this what she and Jerome had meant by their original dedication, years ago, to the objective of a life unfettered by rules, ungoverned by the ordinary laws of probability? Did this accidental dilemma fulfil their joint will? And how could she justify to herself a life in which a day of such rank frivolity as yesterday immediately preceded one in which her child's stability was so severely threatened? It felt like the sour end of a party; and, once this image had occurred to her, she felt slightly better for its suggestion that her judgement was impaired, affected by the lees of the drug, and that she was confronting a problem which should be postponed until clarity re-established itself over the residual murkiness. In this realization guilt played little part. Somehow the train of thought which led to questioning her own responsibility for the boy was blocked off.

'She's always behaved with unbelievable restraint. Just think of how she might have interfered in David's life. All she needed to do was assert her legal rights.'

She kicked gently at the gravel path.

'I know,' Jerome answered gravely. His lack of love for Adelaida made him consider her rights and her request in a different light from Venetia. 'I'll always remember how we acknowledged the risk we were taking when we accepted

318

David. Do you remember, on the plane to Phoenix? It seemed a relatively small issue compared with the big portentous things we said about our own responsibility, our own capacity to look after him. But it was always there, that fear that she might change her mind. I never really believed that she entirely abdicated her rights.'

'But she did. That was the extraordinary thing. And she's kept her promise. God knows what torments of guilt she's been through.'

'You have to keep reminding yourself that the ordinary rules of human conduct don't apply to Adelaida. Her moral categories are so haywire. A Martian might recognize them, I certainly don't. I suppose if you remember how many tribes go in for infanticide, Adelaida's action seems positively selfless. But I think we just have to be grateful she didn't pull some terrible volte-face and try and reclaim him. Or let on to him what happened. Or kidnap him. It's amazing, really.'

They were walking beside the lake in the Buen Retiro park. Groups of children, their faces ranging from gravity to hysteria, swept past them in both directions. Under the abandon of their gestures there was something Edwardian in the children's demeanour, a combination of their elegant clothing and the formal landscaping which affected the way Jerome and Venetia perceived them. Except that their perceptions were uncharacteristically blunted, confined now almost in their entirety to the pressing issue they were trying to resolve.

35

Snake

It was Lorenzo's saint's day, an event he appropriately shared with the menacing bulk of the monastery of El Escorial. Each year he reflected on the miraculous coincidence between Philip II's *Weltpolitik* and his own; the unflagging authoritarian centralization, the efficient control of subjugated territories through a judicious delegation of power. In the morning he had visited his aunt. Her cloistered life in a darkened eyrie in Hermosilla resembled the contrived conventual apparatus of the termagant Queen Mother Mariana of Austria, even to the point of the shabby nun's habit which concealed her silk petticoats and scapulary. They had said the rosary together; but while Guillermina's mind ran in the familiar grooves of the prescribed mysteries, Lorenzo's leaped and jumped from notion to notion, a frenzied network of unfulfilled projects, a child's game of planned acquisition of political cells and concession of others, schemes for conciliating the intellectuals without alienating the workers, Marxist dialectic reduced to interior monologue. So strong was the momentum of his thought that soon he lost control of its thrust. Then all the icons of Falangism passed in procession through his fevered mind, a *chevauchée* of patent leather and grey tunics, eyes bandaged with sunglasses, recrudescences of gold and scarlet insignia, '*Cara al Sol, Uña, Grande, Libre*'. Not even his normal dismayed perception of the actual democratic farrago around him could surface to still the strident images. He could not compare, relate or quantify. The only feeling to overlay the sequence was an awareness that its force was not confined to him alone. Where else had it penetrated? His aunt's mind, he believed, was too deadened by prayer to receive even subliminal messages. No, the target was somehow distant and the recipient reluctant, insulated by his own prejudices and yet so bombarded by the ideological *Blitzkrieg* that his circumvallation was entirely ineffective. Lorenzo could not understand this.

That afternoon, once the unexplained emissary thought-Heinkels had returned to their hangars, Lorenzo was left idly maundering in the Prado. On this panegyric day of Hispanicity he could not bear even to pass through the Flemish galleries. He thought with distaste of Spain's disentanglement from Holland, of Rodrigo Posa's insidious cajoling of the imbecile Don Carlos, of the damned conspiracy to liberate the Low Countries fron Philip's beneficent autocracy – and of Verdi's celebration of these dire histories, another travesty by the misguided liberals of the Risorgimento. With relief he turned into galleries filled with late-seventeenth-century Spanish paintings, vast canvases of allegorical *vanitas vanitatem* and public ceremonial, *stupores mundi*, the supra-real obsessions to which the moribund Habsburg culture had dimly clung. Even his unshakeable faith in the efficacy of absolutism shuddered and wavered in front of these decrepit scions of dynastic miscegenation: Carreño de Miranda's transparently propagandist attempts to paper over the cracks with luminous paint, to heroicize his pathetic and mildewed subjects, the prognathous jaws rendered fraudulently spiritual, the sideways and pendulous coiffures an assertion of hieratic defiance.

As he stood transfixed, a small figure approached and quietly took up a petitioner's posture. Lorenzo was conscious first of the sweating recessions in his hair-line. He might have been a state functionary, an obstructive bureaucrat, a part-time torturer, a gay bank-teller. An acrobat or a lounge-lizard he was not. The classic Spanish relationship between torso and leg-length, the despair of eugenicists; the dumpy complacency of an evangelical missionary.

'Señor Urquijo, I have been sent from the Calle Espronceda.'

His sycophantic lips simpered and hissed like pink plumbing. 'A matter of great urgency. I have brought instructions regarding the demonstration on Friday.'

Interposing his stocky bulk between Lorenzo and the inquisitive near-by gallery attendant, he handed over a manila file. Lorenzo took it respectfully, a communicant receiving the sacrament. Such gestures had always reassured the Movement for the Promotion of Democracy, fixated as they were with ritualistic and masonic signals. So successfully had he feigned them that no one suspected the real political aims which underlay his activism. His social position, extreme moderation, playful insolence and above all his impenetrable beauty all sheltered him from suspicion. He had infiltrated as effectively as a venomous krait, had reached executive office and now stood at the very core of the movement, ready to arch his elegant back and strike.

36

The Calle Arenal

A small attic in the Calle Arenal lay festering at the top of a house overlooking the twin architectural monuments of the fatuous Isabelline régime: the remodelled Royal Palace, transformed into an uncontrolled mélange of neo-classical bourgeois *grand luxe* and Hispano-Scottish baronial, and the now moribund Opera House, the testing-ground first of Neapolitan divas and then of the aspiring beau monde. The greasy plasterwork of the attic had patches of mildew, like cotton-wool stuck on with engine oil. Rudimentary quadriplegic furniture cast baleful shadows into the pools of light from the mansards. A semi-totalled electric Sacred Heart might have bled vividly had it not short-circuited some time ago. One corner of the room was obliterated by a mound of indeterminate organic matter the colour of diseased mice. Damp lakes and pools stained the ceiling to the consistency of abused underwear. In these bedraggled confines sat the impassive Lorenzo, confidently manipulating the console of an electronic scanner; opposite him sprawled an Algerian catamite manoeuvring his poleaxed body into successive postures of inventive indecency, evidently sulking at the end of some violent dalliance. A woman leant against an empty bookcase, an expression of willed detachment on her half-deranged face. Somehow her appearance contrived to retain the tainted innocence of a Simeon Solomon drawing in spite of her spiky velvet hair and her scraped austerity. Her tough emptiness, sapphic-seraphic; the far end of the sexual spectrum from Said's voluptuous availability.

Lorenzo addressed her a pretty compliment, shitting in the milk of the whore-mother who had borne her: the classic Spanish formulaic metalanguage that predates the punk graffito. It seemed that her aptitude for computer programming, so arduously learnt at Stanford, had temporarily deserted Adelaida (for it was she) while she strained to ignore or countenance the vicious coupling of Lorenzo and Said. As she had wrestled with the intractable software, they had prepared for the imminent battle like Spartan warriors, cementing their solidarity in a maelstrom of thrusting and contracting, eased sphincters, engaged prostates and swooping, ululating Arabic gasps. Adelaida's adherence to an entirely idiosyncratic version of fascism was total; she conceived of a refulgent phalanx of bonded manhood eliminating the wayward urges of the weak and the misled; here travestied and made sterile. It found some echo in Lorenzo's visionary aureole, but that strange sense of communality was undermined by his addictive sexuality, so far removed in her mind from the ideals of political activism. In an earlier and less confused age she might have been a fervent Carmelite reforming refractory convents and suppressing free-thinkers; or an Amazonic crusader in beleaguered Krak des Chevaliers. Here her brief was less clear cut.

Said was doing crystal and felt threatened by the increasing hostility between Adelaida and Lorenzo. He suspected that she was under some kind of sexual thrall. Why else was she there? His upbringing in a Constantine bordello had not prepared him either for these electronic complexities (his idea of war being based on Tuareg legend) or for the showers of loose political rhetoric. He looked out of the window at the alien Austrian slate-turrets and the flocks of noisy sparrows; and the heated bucking of his semen-filled body began to subside.

'You remind me of Madame Zélie on the waterfront in Constantine. She too was cruel, she was silent and full of hate,' he said to Adelaida in Arabic. Even had she understood his language she would not have replied, so full of contempt was her stricken, preoccupied heart.

Lorenzo began speaking rapidly and forcefully through

a receiver attached to the tele-scanner: a choleric tirade of peremptory instructions, addressed to himself as one might mutter pieces of information to keep in mind all the aspects of an issue.

37

The Pain in Spain in the Ass

The statues of Visigothic kings stared impassively at the gathering *canaille* that swarmed beneath their plinths at a safely subordinate distance. Recceswinth and Wamba, Childeric and Roderic, Recared, Sisebut, Childasvinth. Their Dark Age solidity was beset all around by the flushed organic leviathan of the Madrid *populacho*. Like a stampede of bellowing rhinoceroses driven by a single momentum, the surge swelled over the formal parterres through chiselled privets, snapping and trampling the plants underfoot beneath the presiding melancholy of the eastern façade of the Royal Palace. Quicksilver coursing as if through a maze in some obscure Elizabethan alchemical experiment, as much in reckless abandon as with true purpose, it thrust itself headlong down the Calle de Bailén towards the Plaza de España. The new forces of barbarism assaulted the elegant nineteenth-century formalism like a human barrage as fearsome as the first Gothic horde that had ploughed up the Roman order of Hispania. Once the square had been a rubbish-tip, when Ferdinand VII impatiently abandoned his projects for its embellishment. Right beside the Royal Palace. What an allegory!

Asdrúbal, waiting near the statue of Don Quixote, saw only too clearly the approach of his political opponents. He gazed ruefully at their threatening ranks, his brow furrowed by the sight of such mechanical allegiance to the armies of reaction. Wasn't there something Quixotic in his own stance there, he wondered, as he raised his eyes ever upwards from the pushing, urgent throng to the incongruously bulky mass of the knight-at-arms? He too clung to an apparent anachronism;

his ideas of chivalric self-sacrifice mirrored the idealism of the Quixote whose sporadic lucidity so outshone the banality of pragmatism. Even in Asdrúbal's pulse-and-oil-fed appearance there was a trace at least of symbolic fleshlessness, a challenge to the stocky endomorphic neo-fascists, these Molochs who might have been fashioned by a malevolent enchanter. The patrician features and the nonchalant *sprezzatura* of his attitude would have sufficed to set him apart from this worldly rabble even in the absence of the ideological divide that irreparably separated them. God, what apartness, what chasms of alienation.

He held lightly on to the base of the statue, as if his life depended on it, or as if it might transmit some cold current of brotherhood. Balanced there, stabilized and secure, he retreated inwards and now hardly saw the mass of flailing arms and stumping legs, indignant faces lurching forward like the frieze on a Vietnamese billboard of people's heroes. This massed dynamism suggested wilful destruction and animalistic stress, *la bête humaine*, the memory of the riots of Aranjuez in 1808, a people drunk on demagoguery, the tearing down of citadels, the elevation of blunt idols.

Absorbed in his own reflections (either these or something like them), Asdrúbal began gradually to perceive the surrounding panorama at a height of more than six feet above the ground. He had created a strange two-tiered relief in which the lower half of jostling limbs were frozen in mid-motion while the static air and buildings of the upper half became animated and threaded with epiphanic light. Asdrúbal's perception of space had always been idiosyncratic, tending as it did to categorize and reassemble the compositional elements according to their relative importance in his selective brain. His detachment, urbanity and inner blamelessness now found expression in this horizontal duality. The bottom part – the creatures of realism and crude, hard-edged predictability – was flattened and compressed under the luminous upper sphere of unfilled space and possibility, a realm of vertical upwardness. It was a way of superimposing calm on the hectic dynamo beneath by staring almost sightlessly into the Empyrean, soaring towards a cloud-trailing world where the base clay of humanity remained undiscovered, unguessed at, a mere theoretical antonym of air. He related the picture to El Greco's painting of the burial of the Conde de Orgaz with its rigid stripe of differentiation between the heavenly and the terrestrial, a world riven by the immeasurability of human error, yet here reconciled by these rare exemplars of Catholic spirituality. Satisfying as this duality was, Asdrúbal knew that he too often touched a foot on the material ground. The imitation of Christ was way beyond Asdrúbal's capacity; there was dross in his body; he reminded himself of nothing so much as an engraved emblem which Claes had once shown him: a fat Dutch angel standing in oddly surreal Northern landscape, one hand raised to the sky and sprouting wings, the other weighed down earthwards by a rough stone; the aspiration heavenwards balanced by the dragging down of sin.

His feeling of insecurity and the moral push-me pull-you made his head ache with a kind of brittle occipital needle and he feared that his overheated brain might topple him grotesquely into the shallow square of pond-water in front of him. Voluntarily or *sin querer*, his whole body swivelled towards the reassuringly solid, ungainly obelisk behind Don Quixote and Sancho Panza. A flattening of the spiky effusions of his fear could be achieved by panning upwards from the base – at which a crude child's maquette of Cervantes seemed to be willing his own creation onwards (but was met by the stubborn rump of Sancho's ass) – upwards to the surmounting globe, smooth as a hip-joint on the clumsy femur of the shaft, stuck around with allegorical lady-continents, even the Red Indian Squaw of America, engrossed in their infinite reading.

Asdrúbal's mind, in its conscious state, was more blighted with orgasm than with Orgaz. But he could *see* clearly, he could *imagine* the symbols of goodness and fashion their images so that they blotted out the shadows. His life was correct and its lapses into error were only intermittent and could not undermine the even acceptability of his conduct. It was fortunate for him, he thought, that he was Spanish and therefore had at his disposal a pre-packaged moral schema so unlike the free, amorphous libertarianism into which Claes had been born. A very present help in trouble (though the

Anglican diction would have outraged him). Even when he had plotted the creeping alienation of his wife and their subsequent divorce, he had never seriously transgressed. The cruel action had been a kind of necessary moral salve to cure a sickness tantamount to a mistake which no God-created mortal could be expected to endure without incurring greater sinfulness. But this self-exoneration did not fail to prey on his mind in his later years, and he found it hard to take advantage of his release from marriage, despite the promptings of his strong libido. It was this that gave him his reputation for uprightness and unblemished probity, so concealed were the erratic stirrings of his lower nature. In a way, his life was a veil of correctness masquerading as goodness, and the public countenancing of this act had bolstered his security.

Idly glancing towards the Edificio de España, with no sense of purpose or direction, he found himself focusing more immediately on the surrounding sights that met his gaze. At the north-east end of the large square a rostrum had been erected and hung with banners and slogans, though its prominence was dwarfed by the modular skyscrapers behind. Their towering thrust was an effortless soaring beside the upward gasping of the thirsty plane-trees whose dusty, indented and cracked leaves were mocked by the ease of the airline logos that plastered the skyscrapers and climbed on top of one another, vying for pride of place nearest the sky of their usurped kingdom. The stepped ziggurat at one side (incorporating, mocking too perhaps, a tiny Madrileño granite façade into its own) needed only to narrow the span of its steps to suggest an infinite climb to the heavens, but, like Altdorfer's *Tower of Babel*, the enterprise exceeded the capacity of man.

In the north-west corner towards the liberating stretch of the brown meseta, Asdrúbal caught sight of a shining, burnished Mauresque cupola. Among so many reminders of Spain's determined modernism, it recalled the primitive African element in her history, the luxurious cruelty and barbarous elegance which pulled her back, like a pasha seizing a fair European concubine and dragging her into his oily hammam. It was this atavism, too, which drove the collectivity of Spaniards and caused their tinsel liberalism to crumple like a glittering mirage in which they had scarcely believed.

38

Madrid: One Way to Die

Jerome, Venetia and David had agreed together that they
would attend the political rally with Claes. In the general
mêlée on the platform, Jerome became separated from the
others. It was at this point that Lorenzo and Adelaida
launched rocket-propelled grenades against the rally. One
of them killed Jerome.

39

Formalidados

How to describe to herself how she felt? There were no metaphors for grief. It resisted even the words that sought impotently to allay it. Flaubert had written, on the death of his beloved mother, that 'it was as if part of his entrails had been torn out'. How that feeble image seemed to trivialize the sorrow! One could scarcely believe that he had felt anything at all, as though he had rushed perfunctorily to a medical encyclopaedia to find a parallel which only a compulsive writer could have thought adequate.

It was hard to see much at all now. Her reflection in the mirror had so little corporeality; a mere blur of blanched, drained skin drifted and flapped, refused to reconstruct itself.

Tired out by the failure of her jerky, willed gestures to persuade her of her own tangibility, met only by this mesmeric wind-blown flag, she tore herself away from the hard apparatus of light and form. When she wept, the problem seemed to go away because then she only inhabited a space bounded by the racking, effacing tears. The main thing, she felt, was to hang on to this certainty and to plunge inwards, freed from the disturbance caused by the outside phenomena which insisted she was dead.

She cried loudly, constantly, a mistral, surprising herself often by the guttural, dredging span of her weeping, tears that coursed not so much from her eyes alone as from the visceral recess of pain in which their stinging, watery journey began. The walls of the mortuary had gleamed sardonically at her, the streamlined, airbrushed antisepsis threw further into relief the messy disorder of her inner self, the tatters of her sorrow, as she sat, a trespasser on death, entranced by loss. Jerome's recomposed features, divested of the frenzy of their death-throes, mocked on as well, iconically, a flamboyant, vivid beauty like the beauty that had disappeared from her mirror.

It was only the irksome, pedestrian duties that followed in the wake of death which rescued Venetia from precipitating, like a wounded animal, her own death. The inspection of the body, the depositions and the forgone inquest, the telephone calls to the embassy where distant voices boomed and swooped, the tremulous form-filling and red-tape. Claes guided her through the maze and tried to divert her attention with his familiar, laughable pedantry, a clown from Soest.

'All this red-tape!' he sighed. 'So Spanish, so Southern European. I never think it rings true in Kafka. It reminds me. There's a wonderful Spanish novel written in the 1870s about bureaucracy. In the end, the hero, who's a charming, in-effectual old man rather like me, gets so bound up in red-tape that finally he cracks and shoots himself on a rubbish-dump. Such a tidy conclusion, almost like recycling, going back to the primeval tip we started from. By the way, did you know that the Spanish for red-tape – *balduque* – is taken from the name of a town in the Low Countries – Bois-le-Duc?'

Claes's clumsy sentences did much to comfort and distract her. Angelines rushed to shield David from the devastation until Venetia could bear it no longer and cradled and hugged him as if it was he that had died. She spared him none of her grief and poured her howling tears over him with the abandon of unrelenting misery. David's own mourning was more inward as he climbed back from shock into a kind of self-protecting coma. But the presence of Venetia, who clung and shook and turned this way and that, made him confront the desolate vacuum again, and thick silent tears bulged down his pale cheeks.

As soon as they could, they left Madrid.

When, in earlier and less raw or real moments of despair, Venetia had imagined her own death, it had been a matter of vast and spectacular *mises-en-scène*: hurling herself from the bridge down the 600-foot chasm of the Tajo at Ronda;

injecting herself intravenously with embalming-fluid from a drip-feed; crawling into a cage of lions, gambling on her affinity with cats until some catastrophic moment of violence; riding the underground on the Circle Line until the effort of remembering her place on the diagrammatic map sent her mad; dangling her legs in the wheels of an Amazonian paddle-steamer so that her body was progressively sliced and minced and fed to the caimans; walking out into a glittering Antillean sea, the gentle and acquiescent waves folding over her docile head; bursting into a committee of the Chilean junta to hurl abuse and grenades till her body fell forward, ventilated with a thousand bullet-holes; calmly raising a pistol to her temple at a reception at St James's; scattering lilies with a drowsy dust of venomous exhalations and lying down encased in velvet to breathe in the slow-acting poison; running out under a rocket at Cape Kennedy; concealing a cobra in her bedroom and acting normal; filling a car-wash with sulphuric acid-rain and riding through naked on a motor-bike; mixing senna with opium and poison in a suppository, to shit her way to perdition with diarrhoea dribbling down her leg in the vestibule of the Paris Opéra; weaving herself a garland of dove-feathers and impaling her breast on a missile in Red Square; breast-feeding a black mamba; coating a Clouet *éphèbe* with *Datura stramonium* and slavering over his toxic earlobe.

But she had read about Guadalupe Velex, all of whose immaculate planning had gone so hideously wrong and left her with her head thrust down a pool of vomit in a lavatory bowl. Most things went wrong; breathing was so tenacious, as her schoolgirl tantrums had shown.

Now, however, the sorrow of her plight made these imaginary deaths into the figments of her past self.

40

Oxford: One Way to Mourn

Her movements were as automatic as the too-soon gear-changes of the grey BMW. David lay stretched out beside her, uninterested in the regular expanses of hedge and field, culvert and beech-wood forest that glided past. Cows and sheep in alternation with modular housing-estates and villages. David never came to know the enclosed monotony of the Chilterns or the buttoned-up sense of *rus in urbe* which heralded Headington and Oxford. The lucerne and rape-seed, the fences of surburban *bricolage*, a country-side which could never be poeticized; just historicized maybe as a textbook lesson on strip-farming, enclosures and urban over-spill; exactly right for an eighteenth-century neo-classical tract on agrarian reform, full of empty metonymy. Venetia, although she saw these things, blanked them out as effectively as the prone child had done. The hardest part was adjusting to the *unseeability* of Jerome; especially on a journey, where in the past the sight of passing objects, lost pictures, had *meant* his presence, so mobile had been their joint and split-up life. She associated objects in motion with the prospect of reconciliation or with shared adventure, the excitement of whirling David around in the vortex of her passion for Jerome. This, though, was movement without momentum. It seemed to originate in a void; it led to no outcome; it petered out even before it began.

So the prettiness eluded her. The hanging lushness of the hillside park, the gilded Camelot weather-vanes fluttering from Gothic turrets beyond Edwardian villas, the processional bridge lined with translucent globes, the cut-out tracery of a chinoiserie parapet, the huge climax of the monumental curving street. Where before she would have believed herself within a magic cyclorama, now she just swung the wheel and believed only in death. The buildings had died along with the outer fringes of her eyesight and nerve-endings. She had never liked Oxford and its willed self-consciousness. More than anything, it had meant a flabby conspiracy, run by determinedly small-scale poseurs, at best allowing her friends to work out their false selves and learn to stop talking about things they knew about. She liked her posturing professional. Too many dons' wives had swamped her with their shabby fundamentalism, with their hatred for her private wealth and apparent lack of social concern. One pinning against the wall by an earnest geneticist had confirmed her exasperation for life. Dons had a permanent subscription to a conceit and arrogance that masqueraded as humility. It was all a horrendous sham which her life had not unfortunately been able to ignore.

'Lay your sleeping head, my love, human on my faithful thigh,' she said to David as she crashed the lights. She was oblivious to all but the cocoon of love within the car. Flocks of secretarial students jumped back on to the pavement, patting their ruffled cheap finery back into place as she roared past, mouthing, 'Home, girls, you scumbags.' *Cloaca de ignominia! Vil razón!* It was all so neat, so paradigmatic, as if some educational-cum-architectural sub-committee had sat down with a progressive PTA to design a machine for student living. A segregated area for the begrudged tourists clustered forlornly under a bogus-looking clock-tower, daydreaming of druggy shopping precincts in Stuttgart and Limoges. Over-serious undergraduates, pale and ablaze with reddened pus, jealously clutched cartons of milk and nibbled digestive biscuits to compensate for the communal dinner they'd been too timid to attend. Laid-off car-workers, the new aristocracy now that the whaler of state had gravidly rolled over, squinted blearily at the scrawny girls and vaguely tried to relate them to last night's blue-movie session. Above all there was the silence, the resentful and suspicious pursing of thin academic lips trained to marshal arguments, nay, to provoke and pick, scholastic dialectic as an applied science. It was a place where bitter articulacy was bred but found no expression in human intercourse. Just a quiet rumour of housewives, the squeaking of pram-wheels, the undermining disco-wail from shops for desperadoes. It could all have been taped and used without offence in a crematorium. Perfect for Venetia's plan, had her synapses been working.

David stretched and let out a beautiful world-weary sigh. So she didn't even have to make her own noises now. They had made their way to the Banbury Road, contravening a barrage of traffic regulations with every stab of the accelerator. Neither of them minded – David's head being as yet unclouded with the notion of external control, Venetia's being invested with the idea that she was inside an armoured tank with caterpillars that killed. Tiring of the trailing students who dimly filed along the tramlines of her vision, she turned into a side-road and stopped. David looked at her, his face radiant with trust and dependence. 'PMW,' he said with a big smile.

'Yes darling, *nice* PMW,' she answered conscientiously. God, these conversations were fun. She wouldn't swop them for dinner with Oscar Wilde. He tucked his little python into his shirt-pocket so that its head lolled out at the world.

'*Much* nicer than that silly Lacoste alligator,' she said, 'what a *fierce* snake. Do you think he'd squeeze all those *nasty* dons for Venetia.'

'Dons,' David echoed, and farted.

'Come on, darling, out you pop.'

In the street, they walked quietly and happily, clasping loving hands and trying to equalize their pace. Every now and then David gave a little hop and swung slightly from her guiding arm.

'Will you look at those bricks!' she said in a temporary confusion of her California and baby registers. 'Just like a public lavatory.'

The sun came out and David put out his arm like an aeroplane. 'DC 10, Venetia, no crash.'

Her heart tightened as she remembered Jerome grabbing David by an arm and a leg and laughingly swinging the child around and around in a circular flight-path. Help, my angel, my splintered beauty, help, all the things you are to me, never shall I . . . Her thoughts lost coherence as the pain rolled over them.

They walked into the park. Venetia strove to repress the welling despair, to keep it down as it threatened to surge through her head. It would numb every diversionary tactic she tried, grip at her throat and temples, linger at the corners of her eyes and make it hard to breathe, interrupting the regularity of her heart-beat. Maybe those grimly cynical analysts of late-nineteenth-century positivism were right after all; love, passion, misery could all be reduced to a set of symptoms, clammy palms and disrupted lymph-distribution. Hysteria a mere heightening of the blood-count? But she knew that nothing now had any importance, whether it was the truth of a theory or the history of the world. All that counted was her loss. The whole purpose of her being had been wrenched out like a Caesarian foetus.

The values of her ancient class bubbled back to the surface as she saw the need to maintain stability for the sake of David. What on earth went on in his mind? Could he make any sense of his fractured experience? Perhaps this present *lapsus*, all her inner turmoil, seemed to him just like the customary boredom of her separations from Jerome? How odd that in two people who adored one another there could be so different a perception of the same thing. She felt it to be her duty to keep him calm and, if indeed her speculation was right, to maintain the illusion that Jerome's absence had no importance. The result was a strange mixture in which the anguish of her words bore no relation to the relentlessly cheerful, babyspeak expression she lent them.

'It's you and me, sweetheart. No more light of our lives, our darling man. No one could have loved us with such passion. Oh God, let it not be true, let him be alive, put together his beautiful body, limb by limb.'

'Limmm . . .' repeated David, smiling upwards as she caressed his ear.

'Why did it all have to come crashing down? Think of all the meaningless, mediocre people who might have been killed. Help me to bear it, my only love, help me to understand, make the pain go away. Kiss Venetia better; be what he was to me, love me, darling. Pretend he's coming back. More ours than ever before, our flammula, animula, vagula, blandula . . .'

The tears in her eyes threatened to reveal the true content of what she was saying. At all events, she had reached the point where grief challenges the brain and cuts the cord between feeling and language. The constriction in her throat, the tightening bond around her heart, the imminent tears could not be ignored; the senseless game with the child was too elaborate a masquerade. She squeezed his hand with overwhelming pressure, and he looked at her, frowning.

All around them stretched a placid summer picture. Tennis-players practised their service, cricketers hurled their off-spinners down the nets, girls in pairs lay with pink backs, giving impatient and petulant shrugs as they revised the dullest of textbooks. Only an irascible old man broke the calm as he held a conversation with himself about the cricket. The trees towered and spread their foliage, the birds sang, the children raced and chattered, just as they were supposed to do in an urban pastoral. Venetia and David drifted through. An observer would have imputed more purpose to the child's walk than to the zombie amble of the graceful woman. But it was she who was pursuing a plan.

The sluggish river moved along its muddy course through willows and tangled tree-roots. Swarms of mosquitoes hovered and darted. All along the bank an uprush of cooler air mingled with the August haze.

'Look at the pretty ducks, darling. All the beautiful male ones and all the dowdy ladies. What horrid frumps! Doesn't that look fun, just swimming around and eating! Is David a duck?' She was surprised at her own ability to slide back into the familiar register.

'No,' he answered firmly, giving the word a Spanish intonation. 'Not duck, DC 10.'

He seemed hell-bent on self-destruction. Why a DC 10, of all aeroplanes? Did he want to be just another air fatality with metal-fatigue? Or was it all a strange premonition of her own longing for death?

Venetia stared at the water. *Her* element, the element of

the city of her name, of her astrological sign. Here too it was *slow* like the lagoon beyond the Zattere, turbid and unhealthy, dotted with leaves like superficial scars. David was quiet now, as intent as she on the leisurely flux of the brown water. It was a moment of infinite stillness. Their lives had reached the point of ultimate conjunction. Their hands were clasped so tight that it would have hurt had they kept any earthly sensation. Somehow she had dragged him into the blankness of her own head, the time when life died because it contained only death. They stood and watched, floored by their own immobility. Like two more trees on the river-bank.

Would she be too worried about the practicality of the thing? Like Celeste Lavenent in the Goncourts' journal, who only persisted in her attempt to drown herself because of her *amour propre*; and who was anxious, in her utterly conscious state as her head bumped against a cable, that a dog which had jumped into the water might get hold of her in a 'tender spot'. Discounting this, picturing the ending now, she imagined a vivid and painterly death. Perhaps she'd be able to see it even while it was happening. That way she could feel it was somehow creative, an affirmation of her *making* self which had gone under in the infertility of her life. Re-enacting the death of Ophelia, perhaps, garlanded with flowers, her hair and white dress streaming against the current as she glided through the fields of barley and rye, the image coming from Rimbaud rather than Shakespeare:

> *Sur l'onde calme et noire où dorment les étoiles*
> *La blanche Ophélie flotte comme un grand lys.*

A slipsliding kind of death, aimless despite its grim finale. And it would be the one time when she *asserted* something. The paradox would be that in the negative act of self-destruction she was making her first positive statement, no longer hedged around with qualifications and conditions like her messy life. It seemed, in her moments of premeditation, that she was looking at somebody else's death, a death for which she would have no moral responsibility of her own. If it referred to her at all it was only to demonstrate that

339

a particular life had come to an end. A dim life, a failed experiment; not like the life whose extinction had drained her own of meaning. That had been a savage death, full of sound and fury signifying everything. Hers would be fluid and soft, like her clothes and movements and the modulations of her voice. A motion of clouds or water, of flags or stalking cats.

Obscurely, obliquely, anxieties and demons from her Catholic past insinuated themselves into this private feeling, this confrontation with her own tested will. In part she felt them to be intrusive obstacles, distracting her from the semi-heroic enterprise.

And yet they kept on coming. When would be the time for repentance? Perhaps she could make an act of perfect contrition immediately after casting herself into the water, as she lay under the surface weeds divested of grief, like a sleek fish, listening to the deadened bells? But wouldn't that seem too calculated? Did it have the right 'goodness of disposition'?

By staring and standing, feeling her temples prick with a creaking cardboard vacuum inside, she was able to fight off the attack that threatened to overwhelm her with all the paraphernalia of Rome that she feared so combatively.

She wanted to say something to David, but it was easier just to stand there. They were almost dying there and then as the terror of everything abandoned their minds. But she said:

'This is what it's like, *tesoro*. Just a nice kind of nothingness. All easy and laid-back, California, no hurt. *Immer zusammen*.'

A little current of rebellion quivered through his body, an affirmation of life which jostled against the certainty of death. The tremor ran up his unformed spine and limbs and damaged her complacency. She was suddenly conscious of the grass and the small tufted hillocks at her feet. The mesmeric enchantment was falling apart. David's movements became more assertive, more persuasive, and the void of her brain was flooded once more. She felt the pressure of his fingers, the smell of damp earth and overblown flowers.

He moved apart from her and bent down to stare at the minnows in a pool carved out of the muddy bank. Watching them dart from side to side, he snatched his hand out of Venetia's and pointed excitedly at their silvery flitting. He was so firmly reabsorbed into the life of flashes, sparkles, colours and light that the dark cloud overhanging them had been burst asunder, detonated by his simple gesture. She was left stranded, gazing wide-eyed into the distance, faintly ridiculous now. She seemed like the statue of a goddess whose cult has fallen into desuetude, stripped of all superhuman powers and mystique.

For once in her life she changed her mood without an excess of self-consciousness. David's escape from her hold had left her on the brink of her carefully nurtured death-wish and now she would have to walk backwards with him into the penumbra of their half-life. She *had* to have his agreement, in whatever form he could express it. That quietness beside the river had seemed to convey acquiescence, readiness for death even, a willingness to be with her in whatever she did, right up to the chilling point of oblivion. But it had passed, or maybe it had never meant what she believed it to mean. He had dragged her back to life as surely as if he'd actually saved her from drowning. Now she would be faced again with all those residual Catholic scruples, the heinous unforgiveableness of two mortal sins, the burning of her unshriven soul. Why was there no simple way of just ceasing to exist? Something like a horse deciding to die and facing the wall until it dropped dead. Would that will to die be a mortal sin?

He was running now, his wobbly legs moving with surprising agility over the uneven ground. She would never recapture him. Each movement stretched to breaking point the umbilical cord with which she had hoped to draw him to his death.

The physical distance between them expressed the widening gulf between their immediate targets. He was a child again, chasing imaginary living things, his head a whirl of spasmodic impressions, butterflies and plants. She was a spent force, thwarted in what could have been either bravery or cowardice, encircled by a stockade of abstractions. A burnt-out Roman candle, she thought to herself, and smiled at the recall of the familiar Protestant jibe.

David ran back and pushed her with two outstretched hands. She instinctively steadied herself, thrusting her weight back towards him; and the suicide was securely aborted. She picked him up, swung him round to face the slender arc of the bridge and leant her pale face against his flushed cheek. The blood and warmth passed into her spectral figure.

'Baby rescues mother in drowning bid,' she whispered wryly. 'Not Virginia Woolf, just silly old Venetia. Can't she do anything right? Another fine mess. Can't even kill a baby. The My Lai wimp.'

She was OK again.

Part Two

1

News from Somewhere

His fingers gently palpated his neck, a fluttering meditative movement that seemed all the more purposeful since he was sitting slumped uselessly in front of a silently flickering television screen. This in itself was curious and unusual. Jerome had long since abandoned television, a decision reinforced by his recent obsession with the image of another, less sane television viewer sitting sedately beside a propped-up corpse freshly bathed and powdered while a severed head boiled and reduced on the kitchen stove to ease the removal of its putrefying flesh. It was all the more peculiar, then, that Jerome should have apparently overcome this fearful image and allowed himself to sit there, deadened by the meaningless cathode rays.

'What on earth are you doing? Have you got a stiff neck?' Venetia was more interested in the curious neck-exploration than anything else. 'Are you feeling all right?'

'I'm OK,' he answered in an ill-humoured tone. 'Fine, just these bloody swollen glands again. I know it sounds like nothing, but it really hurts. I'm sure it's this that's making me feel so lousy, just the way I was when I had glandular fever.'

Without knowing why, Venetia was beginning to feel increasingly concerned for Jerome's health. She had become so accustomed to his ebullient expansive temperament that these bouts of listless sweating and unexplained apathy seemed like either an affectation or someone else's illness, an imported or even a fabricated malaise. More and more he had stopped looking at her directly. His face was creased and tight with a new and constant anxiety. Their openness with each other was such, of course, that he had described to her these creeping symptoms, and had, in so doing, wanted her to understand and sense his illness, unspecific and generalized as it was. Once, when she had been in Rome for a week, she found on her return that he was visibly worse, hunched in a feverish, glass-eyed torpor; and it had seemed to her painter's eye that all the light had gone out of his face. Now this shading was more permanent; it seemed to be overwhelming him with the same relentless dulling force as the hepatitis which had so nearly destroyed his liver.

'Don't worry, darling, it's probably some mystery virus,' he reassured her, addressing his remark over his shoulder as he continued to stare at the screen. 'Soon it'll disappear spontaneously and I'll forget all about it.'

'You seem very confident. I expect people were just as cavalier about Spanish flu when it first hit them,' Venetia said. 'Until they started dropping like flies. I really think you ought to see the doctor. A complete medical and maybe a homoeopathic screening. Please, darling, it would make *me* happier. I can't bear to see you like this, they must be able to identify it and treat it.'

'Do stop nagging,' Jerome answered in a tone of voice flattened by impatience and the wish for solitude. 'It'll go away, these things always do. I'm so revoltingly healthy really.'

'All right, my love, I promise not to go on at you. I know I'm making it worse. But *please*, just for me, I'll fix the appointment.'

Jerome got up and walked across the room. Looking at his retreating back, Venetia could sense his clenched expression, the exasperation felt by the naturally strong when overcome by illness. It was just as well that she could not see his whitened knuckles, the drawn sullenness around his temples and the slight flushing of his cheeks and the sides of his nose. Less visible still were the spasms in his lower chest and the sensation, with which he was becoming increasingly familiar, of some odd malfunction in his body, some biochemical imbalance, a surge in his endocrinology perhaps, a bustling of malevolent cells or the pulsation of erratic lymphocytes. Had she intuited all of this, her apprehension would have redoubled to become a visceral fear. As it was, she felt helpless and inadequate, defeated above all by his refusal to bear his pain with his usual fraternal openness.

Later that week she found herself lying on the floor wrapped in the end-fringes of a Turkey rug staring into the eyes of David, who was, like her, trying not to laugh as he chewed on the battered, balding fur of a toy marmoset. It was the kind of thing she enjoyed most of all, a feeling of absolute oneness in the craziness of the world, a closeness of love unimpeded by pretence or secrecy. David took the moth-eaten leg out of his mouth and hit her repeatedly with the animal's flabby head, gurgling with delight as she pretended to feel pain in her unbruised breasts. Spurred on by her ideal reaction, he began to increase the force of his blows until they threatened to become less innocuous. But she went on smiling and wincing, yelling and laughing until the infinite intimacy of their game, closed off as it had seemed from the imperious world, was interrupted by the telephone.

'I've done what you asked,' Jerome said. His voice was pinched and several times quieter, breathier than usual; as if his mood was as effortful and strained as the concession he'd made to her solicitousness. 'I saw the doctor. He referred me back to Dr Durkheim. Christ, what a pain, he kept me there for hours doing blood-tests and scans, blood-gases, everything. I felt like a rat in a vivisectionist's lab. We'll get the results pretty soon. Anyway, he made all sorts of encouraging noises, and he's sure there's nothing to worry about.'

So why do you sound as if you're fading away, she wondered. Why the pallid vibration of disease? A voice slowed, fractured and intercepted by illness? She humoured him by reciprocating his breezy unconcern; but she was overwhelmed with apprehension, and knew he would be away for long stretches at a time, assuaging his uncertainty in the throes of lust. This was a comfort she could not offer, although she recognized that its efficacy was far greater than that of her maudlin sisterliness. Whenever problems arose that could not be solved between them, or when he suffered the emergence of some deep-hidden anxiety, he escaped from her coils and tried to find, in the otherworldliness of sexual satisfaction, a temporary stemming of their effect. Sex therapy, she called it, half-accurately and with some scepticism. Turning from the telephone, where she'd stood for some moments in a sour reverie, she went off to the kitchen – her London kitchen, the one she most loved – picking up David as she went. Soon, as she wiped her brow among the sizzling pans and scattered trails of herbs, the question of Jerome's health had receded and diminished.

It returned with redoubled force nine days later. Those days had been tense and strained. Even David seemed to have become rattier and more unreasonable. Venetia had tried out several strategies to defuse the atmosphere. She had borrowed an old Citroën and taken Jerome and David to look at her favourite sights: a secret valley of beech-trees and flintstone; some seventeenth-century pigsties built in the style of an Arabian fortress. David had cried, and Jerome had acted like a blasé tourist, humouring Venetia condescendingly for her caprice. A visit to friends in Gloucestershire had done little more to alleviate their gloom. Afterwards, Venetia's girl friend had taken her aside and said confidentially:

'I do worry about you, Venetia. Sometimes, I think I just don't understand you at all. I don't know what you're *up* to. Especially when Jerome's being so difficult. You can always tell with him when something's up, his politeness is just a little too brittle, he's over-enthusiastic about things you *know* he doesn't care about, you can feel a great *sadness* underlying it all. Tell me what's the matter! How I can make it better.'

But Venetia couldn't, she herself didn't know the answer. Although she resented being the stronger partner, the one who held things together when melancholia loomed, she shouldered the burden nevertheless and hoped that the mood would pass like a child's forgotten tantrum. Her face wore a fixed smile, she used more adjectives than was usual, a hectic flush often suffused her pallor. These external signals that betrayed her effort seemed, even so, to elude her own family, and she watched their continued apparent insensitivity with growing resentment.

The second telephone call was even more infused with suppressed anxiety than the first. Jerome asked her to do something, which alarmed her, perhaps unreasonably, for being the first time he'd made a request.

'Will you come and meet me here? I'm walking home through the park and I need to talk to you. Bring David if you like.'

'Of course, sweetheart. I'll be there in twenty minutes. Near the Broad Walk? We can have some sticky cakes at Maison Bouquillon.'

Always the evasive and skittish tactic, the refusal to confront things head-on, the diversion she thought might bypass the truth.

David seemed pleased at the prospect of a walk. He went upstairs and chose some new clothes, of his own accord in honour of the occasion. His *pièce de résistance*, a sign of the anticipatory joy he was investing, was his antique Mr Freedom satin jacket emblazoned with rock-star decals and the repeated legend 'Far Out'. David was already visibly resentful not to have been a child of the 'sixties. He shouted and bumped into things as he got ready. He threw tee-shirts on the floor, tearing them out of their drawer in a parody of a temperamental starlet. The noise he made was deafening, a combination of Sioux war-whoops and mindless chanting as he trailed socks and knickers anarchically along the landing and the stairs.

'Your capacity for mess rivals Jerome's,' Venetia scolded. Secretly she revelled in the child's security and self-confidence that allowed him these excesses. How easy it was to forgive the beautiful and charming! 'I'm sick to death of picking up your clothes. Either you've got to stop or Lucy's got to learn how to deal with you.'

Lucy, *maîtresse en titre* of David's baby kingdom, was a stolid Peruvian nanny who had shown no sign of clearing up after her charge. Faced with a bout of exuberance, she tended to clasp her hands to her cheeks and utter incomprehensibilities in Quechua. A mountain-sickness blew through her words. This particularly infuriated Venetia, since she knew that Lucy knew that she could cope with Spanish invective and it was therefore safer to resort to the language of the sierra.

'Dan, Dan the sanitary man,' David shouted, his newest English discovery, 'Went to bed in a lavatory pan.'

'That's enough, now stop it,' Venetia snapped, and he realized that her imminent loss of humour meant that to continue really was to tempt reprisals. Smiling disarmingly, he stuffed several pairs of knickers untidily back into the wrong drawer.

'Come here, sweetie, let's look at you! Yes, you look divine, quite the little Marc Bolan, you horrid little heartbreaker. Do you love me? Show how much you love me.'

He did a strange kind of smiling dance and then, in mock embarrassment, rushed towards her and buried his head in her crotch. His arms circled round her ass and his hands described spirals on her buttocks. Gradually he slipped down her legs until he was looking upwards at her with the cataracty gaze of a fawning spaniel. She bent down to pick him up and walked happily out of the room. She was singing gently, 'Il mio tesoro in tanto' from Don Giovanni, and the world was Elysium and Elysium was love and the blessed spirits and trumpets and paeans.

David saw him first, from miles away, from beside the old tree-bole stuck with fairy creatures. Venetia followed his pointing arm, and she too made out the distant figure sitting on a bench, looking out at the flecked waters of the Round Pond. His image was indistinct, blurred by the hot haze of a London August, swirled around with dust specks and particles of heat. He remained motionless as they approached, uninterested, it seemed, in the sudden movements of ducks or even the capsizing of a toy yacht, blown over by a gust of sirocco. Groups and pairs of idlers walked past him, obvious Italians and deep Scandinavians, Iranians whose clothes could have concealed bombs in the service of God; but his indifference was total. It was only when Venetia and David stood immediately in front of him that his rigid pose relaxed.

'Oh, there you are,' he said as if awakening from a dream. 'You look great, I don't know which of you's the more chic. David, my duck' – maybe he hadn't been quite so impervious to his surroundings if, as it seemed, he got his metaphorical endearments from them – 'do you mind terribly leaving Venetia and me alone for a while? There's something we've got to discuss. Here, I've bought you an aeroplane book, why don't you go and read it over there by the bandstand?'

David, as Jerome well knew, had not learned how to play alone unless he had some written words to inspire him. And now even Jerome's present looked set to fail, judging from the child's crestfallen face. Yet he took the book and frowned at its cover as he wandered off. 'Come and get me when you've finished,' he said.

'Of course, darling, we'll give you a shout,' said Venetia. 'Don't go too far.' Her voice, too, was a child's voice, thin and high and innocent. They watched him in silence as he walked away, already turning the pages of the book.

'How can one person bring such happiness?' Jerome asked, still staring after the child. 'Suffer little children . . .' He took Venetia's hand and pressed it between both his own.

'What is it?' she blurted out, too tense to restrain her question. 'What's happened, what's going on?'

There was a pause as he squeezed her hand harder and seemed to be preparing her for a disclosure of disaster.

'I really don't know how to say this. It's so terrible. I've been trying to think of ways of breaking it to you gently.'

'I'll say it for you, darling,' she said, forcefully. 'Is it AIDS? Have you got AIDS?'

The word had hovered unspoken in recent conversations, a lurking unthinkable terror. He felt a tremor cross his body.

'Yes and no. That's the only way I can describe it. First, let's get it straight, my chances of survival are quite high. Apparently there's a huge difference between what I've got and the full-blown thing. My symptoms are what's called persistent generalized lymphadernopathy, that's those bloody swollen lymph-glands. But on top of that the most recent test reveals whether or not you've been exposed to the AIDS virus – HTLV III. And I have.'

He began to cry; or rather he allowed silent tears to roll

down his cheeks. His body remained still, there were none of the spasms of weeping. Venetia slipped her hand out of his and, moving even closer beside him on the bench, put her arm around him.

'Whatever happens, darling, we'll always have each other. My dearest love, my love, my love.'

He laid his head on her shoulder and they remained still for a long while. Occasionally one of them increased the pressure of their hold on the other and they stroked one another gently, like cats from the same litter. Venetia cradled Jerome's head with one arm and, circling his neck with the other, fretfully smoothed the short hair behind his ears. Eventually emerging from this moment of the highest, least sustainable intensity, Jerome straightened up and seemed resolved on speech.

'We've been through so much together,' he murmured. 'No one could ever have thought this could happen to us.'

He looked at her intently, his eyes still filled with shining tears. And then, just as soon, he looked away, down to one side like a timid schoolboy uncountenanced by something too forbidden to confront.

'Tell me, Jerome, explain to me exactly what it means. I'm so hazy about it all, it's just a terrible word, what's going to happen?'

He took a deep breath and wiped the tears from the corners of his eyes. As he began to speak, the mucus in his nostrils started to thicken, and he blew his nose to clear it. The action seemed so ordinary, so matter-of-fact, that it must have strengthened his courage to continue.

'Well, as I said, I've been exposed to the virus, and that means I'm infected. What the test shows is the presence of the antibodies the body produces to fight off the virus. They don't really know how operative the virus is, and I could be perfectly all right for years and years. At the moment, and I have to stress, they really don't *know*, they reckon that about 10 per cent of patients with antibodies positive go on to get fulminant AIDS. You don't actually *have* AIDS, not clinically, until you get one of three opportunistic infections that show its operation.' The litany of technicalities seemed to do him good, to lift the horror from the plane of personal despair and somehow accommodate it to the reassuring pages of an encyclopaedia. 'One's a peculiar kind of pneumonia, then there's Kaposi's sarcoma, which is a ghastly kind of skin cancer, and then there's the worst one, the thing that really scares me, fungal meningitis, when you grow fungus and abscesses on the surface of your brain and get paralysis and weigh about five stone, and you develop – a kind of senile decay, dementia, Jesus, don't let me get that, I can cope with all the rest . . .'

He relapsed into silence as Venetia hugged him closer again; and he noticed that she too was crying in little gasps, her eyes cast down in despair.

'They'll come up with something,' she said. 'All you've got to do is hold on for a little while, I know you can, you're so strong, and nobody's got more will-power than you. Just you see, darling. I *know* it'll be all right. All *right*' – she patted his shoulder in frantic reassurance. 'Fine. Just don't worry, I'll help you, you know I will . . .'

He smiled weakly, more of a sop to her effort than a real access of strength. After some moments of silence, he turned back to her, calmer.

'Let's not talk about it any more now. I think we're both in a kind of state of shock and I don't think we can take much more. Maybe later, I'll tell you more about it. Just now I feel as if I've been through one of Tamino's ordeals in *The Magic Flute*.'

Whether he had been able to calculate its effect or not, the mention of the opera galvanized them both back into their usual strength; and dispelled the atmosphere of some extraordinary cataclysm destroying their whole selves. Almost simultaneously they turned their attention to David, who, unknown to them in their cocoon of misery, had been casting nervous glances back in their direction.

'I'll go and get him,' Jerome said, standing up. 'I hope he hasn't seen too much. Heaven knows how we're going to deal with him.'

Venetia watched Jerome as he walked away and registered the bracing of his shoulders, the straightening of his spine and the purposeful thrust of his hands into his pockets, all strategies to prepare himself for the role of strong father.

Two elegant red setters chased one another around him, and then raced away in glorious ignorance. Venetia's mind was so overwhelmed by Jerome's revelation that it didn't seem fully conscious or capable of absorbing its significance. She felt strangely tired, as if acceptance of Jerome's fate was the only possible, exhausted response, at least in her present state of stunned shock. She felt as if she had been awake for many hours, a blank vertiginous state that stopped her from thinking. The corners of her eyes were puckered against the sun.

Jerome picked David up, and Venetia could not decide whether or not she wanted them to play together. If they did, then she would be made so poignantly aware of the brevity of the life left to them together; if not, she would worry that Jerome's decline had already begun and that nothing would ever again be as it had been. As it was, Jerome and David seemed to be having a slight altercation, so that Venetia was released from her dilemma; and she realized, with gratitude, that the practicalities of life must continue, children must be instructed, arguments settled, family power-struggles resolved.

She had suspected all along that Jerome's illness had a sexual origin. AIDS had implanted itself some months earlier in San Francisco, where its spread was already starting to traumatize the gay community. She had talked about it with Jerome, never thinking of it as a serious personal danger, considering it only as an interesting new abstraction (rather as if she had been thinking, through an effort of historical reconstruction, about what the moral and philosophical repercussions of syphilis must have been for seventeenth-century Europeans). She had observed, though not with precision or real understanding, how sexual habits were gradually changing in California. Faces at parties had worn uncharacteristic frowns, and there was a new and compulsive subject of conversation whose seriousness was alien to this playground culture. She had wanted, as a liberal spirit, to share in the discussions; but felt excluded by virtue of her sex. Gradually the anxiety deepened and strengthened. Someone she had met died. A long-established pair of lovers broke up when the suspicious nature of one partner forced him to eliminate even the remotest chance of contagion. A familiar bar she'd vaguely associated with S. and M. suddenly closed (or so she'd assumed, wondering alternatively whether the steel bolts that secured it were not some new sexual furniture, some mysterious advertisement for what could be found inside). The San Francisco *Chronicle* had carried long explanatory articles and agonized over the question of infectivity and transmission. Friends had begun to talk about weight-*sustaining* diets, fearful of any evidence of weight-loss. But Jerome had seemed to maintain a great distance from these things; and now, in retrospect, she reckoned that his uncharacteristic detachment and silence should possibly have been interpreted as a danger signal. Had there been some premonition? Or had he, indeed, even already experienced the first unclear inconclusive symptoms? Had the mildest tremor of nausea led him to block out the possibility of infection and outlaw the very existence of illness?

As the two approached her, she found it hard to correlate Jerome's healthy, strong appearance with the inevitable fact that they would from now on be living a different life, bound and constrained by illness, every aspect of it seen through the deadening filter of a sick decline. It felt like a sentence of unimaginable cruelty, partly because it contrasted so grimly with the carefree simplicity of their life up till now, partly because she, like most people, she imagined (without wishing to belong to their number), was unable to see the illness with any clarity, divorce it from dark moral undercurrents.

She had gone far in her deliberations, far indeed for someone who felt that her capacity for thought had deserted her.

'These aeroplanes are boring, not like the real thing,' David was saying. It had always been impossible to hoodwink him. 'Let's go home.'

As they walked slowly back, the child ran off at tangents, like a dog covering many times the distance of its owner. He seemed to have sensed nothing of what had just passed. Jerome, entirely in control of himself, took advantage of David's intermittent absence to continue his explanation.

Venetia was amazed that he already seemed to be trying to adopt the protective role, the calming voice of the surrogate husband, casting her, not himself, in the role of victim.

'First of all, I want to say that there is absolutely no danger for you or David. AIDS can only be transmitted' – (his naming of AIDS seemed over-deliberate, a characteristic anti-bourgeois refusal to resort to euphemism) – 'by exchanging really intimate bodily fluids, a bit like hepatitis B. So we'd either need to mingle blood in some bizarre sacrificial way or have sex with each other, and somehow I don't think that's going to happen after all this time!' He smiled in self-deprecation. 'So you mustn't worry about that. And apparently the current theory is that saliva is OK, the virus can't live in it for long enough to make glasses and things dangerous. Anyway, you know how obsessively hygienic I am. I gave the doctors a real grilling about this, and you know I would never do anything to put you and David in danger. So all we can do now is wait and hope for the best.'

'What do they think *will* happen?'

'They just don't know. Apparently the research in America and France is racing ahead – there's some sort of professional rivalry – and they hope they'll produce a vaccine, maybe in five years' time. They've done really well *already*, to identify the genetic blueprint of the virus so fast. But then, again, a vaccine's not a cure, so God knows what the chances of that are. There's got to be a Nobel Prize in it for the scientist who gets there first.'

'So you're going to have to live indefinitely with this uncertainty, not knowing whether you're going to get the disease and die or just moulder along like at present?'

'I guess so. It's a pretty awful prospect. Worse, in some ways, than if they'd given me a terminal prognosis, at least that'd be definite. It's going to be *really* difficult, we'll both need a lot of courage. And the doctors have warned me that it's going to be made a lot worse when the press gets hold of AIDS. So far, if they think about it at all, they dismiss it as an American problem, and of no interest to anyone except a few dispensable homosexuals. But just imagine what it'll be like here when people really start to get it. The gutter press'll go crazy. It'll be like thalidomide and Stephen Ward and the

Black Death all rolled into one. You know what the English press is like when sexual scandal goes public.'

David, passing them on one of his diagonal trajectories, pulled Venetia away from what must have seemed like just another boring, earnest conversation between his endlessly over-articulate pseudo-parents. Grabbing her arm, he propelled her willy-nilly towards a group of children. They seemed to be examining some mystery at the foot of a tree-trunk and shouting with delight as they made a fresh discovery. The cotton dresses of the girls were becomingly muddied and streaked, unknown to their oblivious tomboyish wearers. David stopped a certain distance from them, shy to proceed further, yet entirely absorbed by the magic spectacle. Venetia, more blasé and certainly more preoccupied, made impatiently as if to return to Jerome's side.

'Stay, stay,' David whispered impatiently. 'What are they doing?'

'I really don't know, my sweet, and anyway, I've got important things to talk about with Jerome.'

Always before she had joined in David's fantasies and speculations; they were like secretive Venusian conspirators, sharing in outrageous mysteries more solid, for them, than the mundane deficiencies of reality. Her answer consequently seemed unnaturally harsh and dismissive to the disappointed child. He had hoped to initiate her into some unspeakable rite, investigate some outlandish ceremony, and she had rebuffed him cruelly with a drearily rational excuse.

When they emerged from Kensington Gardens into the Bayswater Road, Jerome deliberately guided them home through the bustle of Notting Hill Gate rather than the placid side-streets they normally used. He felt that the noise and activity would distract them, maybe justify their silence. Even so, despite the success of this plan, there was a sense of desolation in their dogged path, a kind of fragmentation as each one of them shrank into an individual train of preoccupied thought. It was a dispirited trio which finally disappeared, straggling, tired and silent, behind the heavy front door.

2

Living and Learning

'I think maybe we ought to get the practicalities of this bloody thing absolutely straight,' Jerome announced briskly. In delivering the sentence it seemed he was adopting Venetia's persona at its most uncompromising.

She was taken aback, used as she was to his evasive scheming, the soft, sophisticated but well-intentioned duplicity necessary to his many-pronged life.

'Hang on, darling, I'll make us some coffee.'

She wanted to gain time, to adjust to this new pragmatism. Once in the kitchen, she prolonged the business more than was absolutely necessary. She brushed the cat and, ruffling his fur in reverse, puffed squirts of anti-flea chemical into the pink skin-core, through the dead black husks of parasites that clung to the curly abdomen. She rearranged the jars of dried herbs as if they'd been face-down cards in a child's conjuring trick: oregano, dill, thyme, cumin, the basil Isabella had brought her from Tuscany. Under the Welsh dresser, she found the disconnected pieces of a wooden train, locomotive, tender, carriages and guard's van, which, after picking them up and wiping them clean, she reassembled and placed carefully on the table ready for David to uncouple again and hurl to the floor as from a tremorous viaduct. While the coffee percolated the telephone rang, and she surprised Joseph, not normally so favoured a recipient, with her voluble conversation. The stories she told him wound and unwound, their second-hand conversations reported with pedantic detail, the stalling tactics so obvious to herself yet so mystifying to others. By the time she poured the coffee, the filter was dull with dryness, no trace of residual moisture gleamed among the grounds. She put macaroons and some left-over madeira cake on the tray.

'I thought you must be arranging to elope with Joseph,' Jerome smiled. 'You're such a creature of impulse. Promise you'll stay with me, darling, don't leave me.'

It was no longer funny. The frivolity had been overtaken by the lowering cloud of unspoken fear that hung over and between them.

'The first thing is that I've been assigned a counsellor to help me deal with this. He seems pretty nice, a Canadian called Mark Carr. He told me that he'd left a perfectly OK job as an air-traffic controller in Vancouver to study psychology and then qualify as a doctor. Now he's so hooked on the problem of AIDS that he's thrown up his entire past and come to London to dedicate himself to helping the victims. It's like something out of a Dickens novel, all that selfless uprooting and sacrifice. And the world won't even recognize his work; they'll be so caught up in their own prejudice. Why on earth should these squalid people need help, and help, what's more, provided by the state? I'm sure I'll like him. He's so intellectual, but he seems to understand everything. I only hope I don't make things too difficult for him.'

'You'll have to cut down on the cultural allusions,' she suggested. 'I really mean it. If he's going to help you, you must try and keep things as simple and direct as possible. You know how confusing you can be.'

'Anyway,' Jerome continued, ignoring her presumptuous advice, 'there's nothing specific that I'm supposed to do. No diet, no medication, no special régime. Obviously it's sensible for me to live as healthily as possible, to minimalize the risk of secondary infections. They really don't know what'll happen next. Durkheim said I'd probably moulder along like this for a while, possibly for ever. It's odd, he seemed to be backtracking slightly because when he delivered the bombshell he went out of his way to point out the dangers and prepare me for the worst. His voice got really squeaky and excited when he was describing fungal meningitis, and he dwelt pretty heavily on the slides he showed me of Kaposi's sarcoma. But now he wants me to act as if this is as far as it'll go. I'll remain symptom-free and the virus will just lurk around, maybe spontaneously decompose, like the hepatitis B one. He told me a lot of fantastically complicated bio-chemistry, something about DNA and coating the molecule with proteins and retro-viruses and the double helix, Christ knows what it all meant.'

'Maybe you really ought to try and understand it,' she insisted. 'You know how impatient you are. You do tend to assume you've understood things just because you can reuse the words with apparent authority. And for my sake, too. So far I've no idea what the virus does.'

'Well, basically it causes the immune system to break down so that it can't resist infection. Not just colds and mumps and things, but those three very special opportunistic infections I told you about. When a virus enters a healthy body, it's detected by the macrophage cells which then alert the T-helper cells to produce the immunological response to attack the invading ones. With AIDS that can't happen. The HTLV III virus infects the T-helpers, they're no longer able to recognize and destroy foreign viruses: in fact, they work in reverse, producing more and more replicated virus. Meanwhile I've got to expect more night sweats, sudden temperatures, fluctuations in weight and a ghastly kind of lassitude, just feeling unwell in an unspecific kind of way. I can't stress this too much, but they really don't know what to expect. There just isn't enough clinical evidence to go on. I don't *think* they're trying to jolly me along; but it does seem that full-blown AIDS is still a fairly remote possibility. Essentially I've got the virus but not the disease. There may be a long incubation period, there may not. Of course, the body anyway lives in peace with a whole lot of infections all the time. This might be just another inoperative virus: apparently some people hardly know they've got it.'

'All the same, it sounds as if you're in for a pretty difficult time; they wouldn't have given you a shrink otherwise.' She paused. 'I'll do everything I can to help you and nurse you when you're sick, you know I will.' She couldn't quite reciprocate his breezy manner, and a tense seriousness crept into what she said.

'Yes, darling, I'm really going to need you. You've always

understood me so incredibly well, you'll have to be even more understanding from now on. They said that I'd probably get difficult and irascible, the periodic depressions will make me irritable and difficult to live with. I can't tell you how delighted they were to hear about our life together and the way you can always be here to help me. Apparently they get really worried about the solitary gays who've got no one to lean on. Especially what Mark Carr calls the street-gays, the ones whose lives revolve entirely around sex and cruising. God knows how they'll cope with it. Because, of course, sex is completely out of the question.'

'Completely? Aren't you allowed any kind of contact?'

'Well, they're trying to devise something called "safe sex". Roughly speaking that means no anal or oral sex, just a kind of messing around and mutual masturbation, a bit like the things naughty English schoolboys get up to in the dorm. You know, after Matron's tucked them up and says: "No talking after lights out" – as if *that* was all they had in mind. Apparently that reduces the risk of cross-infection. And in America it's already becoming the norm, it's what people automatically do, they don't even have to agree on it in advance. But I told Mark it was a bit unrealistic and that I, for one, would rather forgo sex altogether than compromise like that with half-measures, quarter-measures. Anyway, there's no one I can do it with without revealing why I have to, and that's too complicated. God, we've fought so hard for the right to sexual self-expression, and gone so far that I don't think I, for one, can settle for something like that.'

'Yes, I can see that,' Venetia said. 'I think I'd feel the same in your position. But I suppose we ought to expect a lot of tension if you're having no sex at all. You haven't exactly been a celibate monk up till now, and it's going to be a pretty drastic kind of adjustment.'

'I'll have to stick to it somehow. Not only am I a threat to other people, but apparently there's a danger of reactivating the virus if I sleep with someone with the same symptoms. I've got to try and keep it dormant, a bit like a benign cancer. Christ, it's going to be awful. What's going to happen when I just feel ill *all* the time, lying in bed not wanting to get up and snapping at you when you try and help? . . .'

His disciplined control, the restraint he'd decided to adopt for this bleak session, was beginning to dissipate under its own strain. Sensing it, Venetia snaked out a hand to reassure him.

'I'll understand, of course I will. You've been so wonderful already. I think you've been quite heroic.'

He stared down at his hands, the extension of his spindly soul, convinced that they could no longer be the means of contact with the world outside him. His psychological reclusion found its counterpart in this contraction of his physical area of manoeuvre. His body seemed intermittently there and not there, prone to accidents of light like a cast shadow; no longer a primed machine with hydraulic working parts and cartilaginous joints but a framework that slipped and decomposed. And under the surface of his healthy, olive skin, dark shapes were lurking and massing like a Turkish flotilla.

'The hardest thing,' he went on, 'is that I've wanted to protect you from it. Even when I had the strongest suspicions about what was wrong, I just felt that *maybe*, by some miracle, it might fizzle out to nothing and you would never need to know. But it was so idiotic to think like that, because now that you *do* know, I feel as if an enormous burden's been lifted from my shoulders. Of course, that means you two have got to shoulder it with me. There are going to be some really bad times.'

'What about work?' Venetia asked. 'Are you going to be able to carry on?'

'I don't really know,' he said. 'I think the sensible thing would be only to accept commissions if I know I'm going to feel up to it. We'll see.'

Work had, of course, occupied only a relatively low standing in his life's priorities. It was not as if its loss would bring a profound crisis.

'You must never worry about money, at all ever,' Venetia reassured him, with only the mildest embarrassment in her sincere generosity.

'Should we stay here or go back to California?'

'I asked the doctors about that. On the whole, it'd be more sensible to stay here. First of all, because I think I want to,

362

something to do with facing a crisis and returning to your earliest home, don't animals do that? But the important thing is that I can probably get the best attention – I won't say treatment, because there isn't any real treatment, just alleviation of symptoms – in England. I've already pushed and hassled to get to see the experts I have seen, and I guess I might as well stick with them. Anyway, I like them and trust them. And medically America doesn't seem any further advanced, on top of which there's all the problems of medical insurance. We'd probably end up paying a fortune on hospital fees. Apparently there are already really sick AIDS sufferers in New York who are just dragging themselves round the streets because they're too poor to pay for any kind of hospitalization, and Medicare isn't adequate to deal with it. On top of that, it sounds as if quite a few Americans are actually coming to Europe to seek treatment, they're so desperate about the impasse back home. The Institut Pasteur in Paris is fast becoming a kind of Lourdes. These rich Americans keep turning up and asking for anti-viral agents which haven't even been properly clinically tested. They're prepared to try anything even if it stops their blood clotting and they suffer all sorts of ghastly side-effects. The things they've come up with so far have all been more or less toxic. So I think, on balance, we might as well stay in London. It depends on what you want to do as much as anything. And, so long as I stay stable, in my present condition, just sero-positive, there's nothing to stop us spending time in San Francisco. I'd feel a bit insecure if you suggested going off to live in New Caledonia or somewhere. So long as we have access to the hospital here, that's all that really matters.'

'So is the idea that we just try and carry on as normal, as if nothing had happened?'

'Roughly. I don't want anything to change, and as long as I remain stable, nothing need change. Sometimes I panic and think I'm going to die and that we ought to go off and live in some fabulous place, maybe a houseboat in Kashmir, until the terrible moment. But I actually think that would be harmful, I think it could almost *make* me die, precipitate things. The conviction that I was moving off to die would in itself kill me off. I'm afraid we're going to have to make do with the semblance of normality, however awful we ourselves secretly know it to be. I'm sure this is right, I've thought about it an awful lot.'

'It certainly seems the best way to me. And all I want is that circumstances should be ideal for *you* to help you recover, and I'll do everything in my power to smooth your path; I'm pleased in a way that you want to stay in England. My bourgeois heart tells me it's best, the whole idea of climbing back into the womb with all the familiar things from the past. But one question I can't get out of my head, it recurs and recurs and I cannot decide what to think. What, if anything, do we tell our friends? Need anyone know?'

'I've wrestled with that one, too. In some ways, there's absolutely no point. With all these things you've got to ask yourself *why*, what purpose would be served by it, would things be better in the end if you did it? So why should we tell anyone else? I suppose I feel that I'd like to, first because I'm on the side of honesty and in a dimly liberal sort of way I like the truth to circulate. But also, and this is the dangerous part, I think I want sympathy from other people. Or is it pity? At least I want them to know what I'm going through – and you. And I think in the end that that's wrong, it'd be better to leave them in the dark and face this on our own.'

'But whatever we say or don't say, they're going to start guessing and speculating. You yourself admit that you're probably going to be ill with some regularity. Aren't they going to wonder what causes those recurrent bouts of sickness?'

'I suppose,' he said after a moment's thought, 'that that all depends on how much publicity AIDS gets in the newspapers. If they go over the top – as I suspect they will – then I guess people are going to start putting two and two together. What I foresee is a lot of rumours arising and then somehow solidifying into fact. I think probably we *shouldn't* tell anyone at this stage and maybe needlessly upset them and even *start* an uncontrollable spiral of rumours. And, of course, there's always the danger that some of them might take it badly, panic about infectivity, even make moral judgements; and there's the chance that it could get into the wrong hands, and I can think of lots of ways in which my position would just be unbearable. It's going to be enough of a battle fighting the disease itself without having to fight on other fronts with the world at large. The last thing I need is extra emotional pressure and stress from explaining myself, defending myself, correcting people, fencing off their bloody curiosity. But if, as you say, it becomes impossible to conceal it, then maybe if anyone we trust does ask directly, I think we should tell the truth.'

'And, after all, the truth is that you haven't got AIDS. You've got the virus but not the disease. I know some people might think that's a specious distinction, but, let's face it, it's the one the doctors make.'

'Sure, there's some security in that. Though I think you're right, no one's really going to accept that distinction.'

'Anyway, I don't really understand why we *need* to bring anyone else into it. Haven't we got each other and David?'

Venetia characteristically cared so little about the world outside her family that the alternatives they had considered seemed less than urgent. The strain imposed on her by sustaining this courageously rational conversation was beginning to become acute. All she really wanted to do was hang on to Jerome and cry.

'Of course we have, and that's the most important thing, it matters more than anything else. The whole bloody thing is meaningless and powerless beside that. I do love you so much.'

He put his arms around her and hugged her tightly. She planted her kiss with the greatest intimacy – a kiss on his lips would have been artificial and betrayed their understanding – on his flushed forehead. It communicated more than the constancy of her love. It proved her determination to remain physically loyal to him in his terrible sickness. He held her almost so tight that she became breathless, and then he drew back and looked at her from a distance with instinctive gratitude, recognizing the loaded meaning of her kiss. Silently, gazing with an expression of distant helplessness past the side of her head, he folded her again in his arms and she began to shake with tears.

'What we've got to do above all is to remind ourselves that life is full of wonders to set against all this grimness,' Jerome said, relapsing into the kind of Californian sentimentality and perception of joy against which he had before so firmly set his face. 'The shrink said that all his patients who face the possibility of death discover that.'

'What's been the reaction of his other patients? Have they cracked up?'

'I asked him, but he was a bit evasive. Apparently one or two have already committed suicide, they just couldn't live with the moral stigma or the uncertainty or the pain, or all three. Most of them are soldiering on, their morale fluctuates pretty much out of control. Quite a few lose their libido completely. One guy, it seems, got so fed up with the anxiety that he decided there were better things to be anxious about than anxiety itself, so he set up a new business and diverted his stress into that. Some have retreated into a shell, others are out there pretending nothing's happened, making brittle jokes about AIDS while they're dying inside. And the families are getting crucified in various ways. Then there are horrific problems between lovers, one of whom may be infected and the other not. Some of them have found the incredible strength to stick together and just hope the healthy one stays that way. But I know of other cases where the sick one's been thrown out, all his clothes and possessions dumped in the street; years of love and loyalty destroyed by the fear of death. And then there are the dedicated mega-clones who've so devoted their lives to sex that when they find out they're infected, they just can't stop, they know the risks, but if they die or infect other people, that's preferable to abstaining from sex. In fact they'd rather kill people, putting it at its worst, than stop. In a way I can understand. It's a kind of terrible despair, the sort of plague mentality that made people deliberately expose themselves to epidemics and infected corpses in the Middle Ages, a sort of defiant, last-ditch bravado. And the shrinks tell me that, when they're faced with an unimaginable crisis, most people turn to what's familiar for reassurance, and in the case of these guys, it's sex. I can understand, but I still think it's really wrong. It's a kind of murder. OK, they're prepared to die rather than give up sex, but they don't seem to care how many people they take with them.'

'Stop, stop!' she cried. 'Let's not complicate things so much with a whole set of moral reflections. I know it's fascinating to speculate about what it *means*, what feelings we can have about it. But the important thing is to learn to confront it. To devise some kind of response, some strategy that'll allow us to adjust to it; you're too inclined to analyse, to see things as if they were stories you'd read in books.'

'That's one of the most useful defences I've got,' he said. 'Don't try and turn me into a hard-headed pragmatist. I *need* to look at this in a distancing kind of way. And anyway, I've got the security that you can deal with the practicalities, tell me what to eat, bathe my sweaty brow, ward off the curiosity our friends are bound to feel. I think in some strange way this whole thing could enrich us, teach us more about ourselves and about life. The kind of things we've always been too sophisticated to confront with any sincerity.'

'It's a particularly tough route to self-discovery,' she replied. 'I think it's a bit dangerous to think like that. We'll end up being *grateful* for AIDS. Loving the tragedy that's hit us.'

3

Clinical Attentions

He spent increasing amounts of time in hospital, submitting to blood-tests and skin-tests, providing urine and sperm specimens, offering cysts, mollusca and throat infections for scrutiny. He had begun to collect wrist-tags, scrawled with his name by busy nurses, to remind himself of the number of times he'd been in the special ward, measuring out his life not with coffee spoons, but with these circlets of disease. Few of the individual exercises were painful or traumatic in themselves. The strain and surfeit came from their accumulation, the growing impression that he was now condemned to lurk in neon corridors and examination rooms, wondering what his doctors would find under the apparent sleekness of his exterior. An hour and a half passed as he sat outside a room holding an X-ray plate. Another hour dragged by before a grim Korean nurse inserted a glass rod into the tip of his urethra and then dismissed him. Two manics yelled compulsively at one another in the waiting-room, 'Fucking shit man don't you fucking well do that to me d'you hear me I don't fucking care no one can fucking touch me,' in a language that seemed to deny all possibility of communication; Jerome meekly waited for his appointment with a psychologist, associated and bracketed now with these mad casualties of the gap between self and others.

In the course of this current visit, he had begun the morning feeling exceptionally irascible on account of the ferocious enema that had kept him fully evacuated throughout the preceding day. Dr Durkheim had discovered an inflammation of the tissue of his bowel, a tumour maybe, or gay bowel syndrome, AIDS-related by presumption. A biopsy on it had proved inconclusive, and so a barium enema was demanded. Jerome dutifully drank the laxative that made his entrails heave and explode, leaving constellations of shit scattered like grape-shot on the lavatory bowl. Six times he had discharged. Now he was empty, clean and luminous pink inside, as he went down the stairs to the X-ray unit.

Victorian architecture beneath ground-level has the opposite spiritual effect to the elation produced by the soaring pinnacles and castellations it so triumphantly displays above ground. Jerome's mood of self-righteousness and cleanliness – appropriate enough in this Victorian frame – succumbed to the deadening encroachment of the dark walls tinged with grime, whose dadoes seemed to press inwards with the weight of the complaining earth they restrained. He found himself in a series of long corridors so featureless and dim that even the signboards couldn't illuminate their meaning. He walked onwards with a sense of purpose he didn't feel; and the faint light-headedness produced by his fast propelled him through the tunnels as if he were a simple cork bobbing in a current. A dark-green colour predominated, suggesting strained cabbage – an image magically materialized, less for his sense of sight than of smell, as he passed a swing-door to the kitchen, still flapping after the exit of a vast aluminium trolley. The passage hummed with a motorized roar that came from the tubular cluster above his head, as multiple as a small intestine or the innards of an old battleship. With the roar came the faint sense of vibration that disorientated Jerome's step.

Outside a staff canteen, a union meeting was being held; and the disaffected members spilled into the corridor, smoking and talking disconnectedly, blocking Jerome's path. They grumbled as he edged through politely, turned sideways to make his body a thin sheet of glass that would slide past imperceptibly. His self-effacement always met the same coarse grossness, the grace and speed of his movements rebuffed by the elephantiasis of mankind. Especially now, he felt, couldn't they have understood his plight and smoothed his path a little? But the resentful thought was driven out immediately by his awareness that he was hoping for something unrealizable: that each man's predicament should be temporarily visible to his fellows and that they should be well enough disposed towards him to want to alleviate his suffering. Forget it, Jerome addressed the idea dismissively, and slouched further along the infinite ramifications of the corridors.

His natural politeness surfaced as he spoke to the the nurse who directed him to a small cubicle. He undressed and sat in a slovenly heap on top of his clothes, clad only in a robe that tied at the back and left his buttocks exposed, reminding him of better, freer times. He sat there bunched up, occasionally drawing his knees right up to his chest, silent, miserable, shivering slightly whenever the rubber door let in a draught of antiseptic air. No one spoke to him for an hour. He was on the point of leaving in a blaze of temper when a nurse came in and persuaded him that it was silly to waste the elaborate preparations he had made.

'I'm afraid we're working very late today. There are a lot of ill people who need a lot of care.'

'For Christ's sake,' Jerome exploded, 'aren't I ill? Do you think I've come along because I like it here?'

But, of course, she didn't know how ill he was. His doom was not revealed on his outside, not like the sickness of the old men who shuffled glassy-eyed and grey towards the examination table before slowly falling on to their sides like punctured sacks of coal. What was more, conceivably these nurses were not allowed to know how ill he was for fear that they would abandon their posts and refuse to examine him. He was being discreetly steered by his doctor through the shoals of public hysteria and could not therefore make use for his own comfort of the information being concealed so that he could be treated at all. His temper subsided and he was led into a room by the nurse for the final humiliating stage of this operation.

As the instruments were placed in position he remembered how he had behaved a few days earlier when, in exactly the same posture, he had succumbed to the agonizing probing of a sigmoidoscope as it sought out the infected tissue in his rectum and the higher bowel. The doctor had been new, one of the apparently limitless team of researchers who viewed his case with the eager detachment of science. The pain was at its most intense as Jerome looked reproachfully, not quite tearfully, over his shoulder at the stern figure of his tormentor, and suddenly remembered the answer to the question which had, in a different vein, also been tormenting him. 'I know,' he murmured. 'It's Virginia Woolf! You look just like Virginia Woolf!' He was going to add 'in the year of her suicide', but managed, uncharacteristically, to check the flood of his sentence. 'Really?' she had answered, but all her concentration was in the exploration of his ass.

Today, however, he could not achieve that same dissociation of self. Everything that happened had a raw immediacy. This was a day given to sacrifice and forbearance; neither his intellectual imagination, nor his memory and humour could blot out the pain. The only reflection he had was a question, Julien Sorel's in *Le Rouge et le Noir*, an achingly immediate, *'Pourquoi suis-je moi?'* Why am I this particular bundle of idiosyncrasies, afflicted with terror and condemned to die? There was no answer. Stolidly he was reminded that it was his own destiny that he confronted. Inescapably. Inexplicably. The only Pascalian fact was that he was a frail reed, subject to pain and nearly broken – *flectas non frangas* – yet a thinking reed. At other times, it was as if he were somebody else, some dramatic hero caught in a web of fatality which he, Jerome, was curiously observing through a telescope. His antics and feelings looked bright in the distance. But now he and they were reunited in some terrible celebration of suffering. It was inconceivable that the strain of illness would ever leave him alone. It was there with him now, like a humpback grafted on to him. Quietly he railed to himself against its inescapability: 'Christ, can't it leave me in peace for just a day?' and tears began to congregate round his eyes. 'Just one day, let me forget this bloody thing, it's so fucking unfair.' But the nurse carried on flapping about with her photographic plates, the walls of the huge cubic room were as imperious as Egyptian temple slabs, and the searing in his deepest gut burned like ice.

An effort of will propelled him out of the darkened room, and its workings were visible in the springy lightness with

371

which he tried to vanquish the lumpishness of his over-taxed body. He got dressed again, this time with more neatness and sang-froid, carefully folding the discarded surgical robe. After retracing his steps through the labyrinth – no golden thread needed for someone with an exemplary bump of direction – he crossed the street to revive himself first with frothing cappuccino and a Turkish bun. He then, having whetted his appetite, satisfied its deep craving by wolfing down a prawn salad with wild rice, a thick slab of fetta, four slices of fine-grain sourdough bread and a chocolate florentine. The first stage of the ordeal was over.

It was not long before he had to return to the hospital, this time to the research clinic where AIDS hung heavy in the worried air. It coated the leaves of the cheese-plant and lay in wait behind the brittle gaudiness of a Klimt poster. If he pressed and opened the studded mosaic tesserae in the brocade robe of the picture, would it release a torrent of antigens like a fatally primed Advent calendar? He had enough time, as he waited again, to feel hunted and victimized, to see himself as, for the doctor, a mildly inconvenient specimen on a conveyor belt, yet conscious that to him his case was paramount, a matter of grim survival. He tried not to look too directly at the evasive eyes of the two other patients, big men in early middle age whose cultivated muscular physique seemed dwarfed by their self-doubt, their caved-in morale. This was not a waiting-room in which you could exchange friendly inquiries about troublesome symptoms, chatter about aches and pains.

In an effort to lessen the embarrassment, Jerome turned to the magazines in front of him. Some were clearly AIDS-clinic designer-rags especially for the distraction of gays, full of black models in tuxedos and reviews of Montemezzi revivals in Santa Fe. But Jerome eschewed this familar material to concentrate on the medical journals, with their brazen advertisements for drugs (it seemed the pictorial possibilities were limited to portraying the cured recipient wreathed in idiot smiles). He settled down to leaf through *Morbidity and Mortality Monthly*.

As the waiting time drew on, he lost interest and began to dwell again on the idea of his being not himself but another.

A syllogism of Nabokov's floated in and out, an apparently conclusive proof of his own immortality. 'Other men die; but I am not another; therefore I'll not die.' Could he, the one living under a botched death-sentence, be the one who paradoxically survived? Could a philosophical sleight hold the secret of eternity? It wasn't possible really to understand it; anyway, for the second term of the syllogism you could substitute its antithesis, somebody else's idea that '*Je est un autre*' and thereby make nonsense of the whole thing. He must ask his Buddhist friend to interpret this conundrum.

He was ushered into a small room by the friendly male nurse who smiled nonchalantly, as if he was running a night-club rather than a waiting-room for death. A panel of spectacularly unsmiling doctors and dermatologists failed to greet him and proceeded unceremoniously to the minute examination of his naked body. They scoured every milli-metre of flesh, especially his feet, searching, presumably, for the sinister lesion of Kaposi's sarcoma.

'You've got a mole between your second and third toes,' one of the doctors murmured inconsequentially.

'Have I?' Jerome replied. 'You tell me. Not even my lovers know me that intimately.'

He was found to be free of suspicious symptoms. Some stray spots, mollusca, were frozen off with nitrogen. He was then returned to the waiting-room and summoned, an hour later, by his own doctor.

'John,' he wanted to say, 'you're my doctor, my friend, for Christ's sake. How can you let them treat me like this? I feel like a laboratory rat.'

He was conscious of the doctor's reddening face, the tightening of his facial muscles as he relayed the strain and tension inspired by the grim team. Would his humanity burst through and bring him to protest at his colleagues' cruelty?

'You're looking well,' the doctor said infuriatingly. 'Just you wait until we've finished with you. You'll be like a pincushion.'

Submissively, without looking to left or right, Jerome followed him into the examination. Ten phials of blood were taken and labelled with cryptic orange stickers to warn the laboratory technicians of their lethality. The blood gushed and bubbled out of Jerome's arm as the nurse changed phials, inserting each into the syringe with practised ease. Then, as Jerome staunched the puncture with an alcohol-soaked gauze, the nurse fiddled around with the implements for the next phase. This time it was more painful as he pricked, then scraped the skin of his forearm, injecting first TB, then *Candida albicans*, then *Cryptococcus neoformans*.

'If you get a reaction to any of these, you'll have to report it back to me,' the nurse said. Then, sitting down, he took a printed sheet and settled down to ticking off the answers to a questionnaire. Were his headaches severe, moderate or light? The tick went in the severe box. Where were they located? 'In my head, for Christ's sake,' Jerome answered; but then, after he indicated the exact area with his hand, the nurse wrote 'Occipital'.

The familiar catalogue of unspecific symptoms propagated itself in the melancholy list: malaise, night sweats, swollen lymph-nodes (three got drawn on to a diagram of his neck). Only the question on weight loss gave grounds for comfort, the one category in which he could register a negative. It all seemed like a complicated form of guesswork, masquerading as clinical diagnosis. He could have said, 'I feel lousy,' and been just as informative. There was such a problem describing pain. Dull, sharp, throbbing, constant? Well, sometimes it was dull, sometimes it felt as if your lungs were being cauterized, what could one say?

The doctor came back into the room with a sheaf of records on Jerome's illness. He had amassed all this information – immunological screenings, T4 helper cells, T8 suppressor cells, bilirubin levels, albumen, platelets, lymphocytes, eosinphils, haemoglobin, blood sugar, liver function – in the comparatively short interval since the first ominous diagnosis. Jerome remembered wryly how, in an easier time pre-AIDS, he'd been rather proud to discover that the records of his sexual history were so extensive that they'd been transferred on to microfiche. Now he hoped the symptoms could be pulped, shredded, clipped, erased, lost from the computer memory.

'You do realize, don't you, how important the interaction is between your physical condition and your mental attitude?' the doctor said, as if he were embarking on the enunciation of a new religion. The earnestness of what he had to say was undermined by the snapping sound of the nurse's plastic gloves being removed. 'All the indications are that the best way you can help yourself is by minimizing the stress so as to allow your immune system to stabilize and let the T-helper cells re-establish themselves. Keeping calm and steady, regular in your habits.'

'That's exactly what's so terrible about AIDS, though. It's a vicious catch since it attacks both your body and your mind so ruthlessly, so insidiously and efficiently that you can't use either one in an act of will to rescue the other. Even if you decide you're going to defeat the physical ravages of the virus, your mind is so sapped that it can't carry that through effectively. It gets you with a deadly double-pronged attack like some inevitable chess-move. The cause and effect of it so difficult to understand – whether one brings on physical attacks by anxiety or whether anxiety is produced by being ill. It seems like the nervous system gets affected, there's even the spectre of dementia, everything's connected. All one's defences are put out of action. You're often so weak that you can't effectively control the anxiety. And yet, if you let it, it'll kill you.'

'I've got to admit you're right. I've always been honest with you. I'm not sure why. Perhaps I respect you too much to pretend. It is a terrible struggle. We've got to face the fact that you're in a rather high-risk category. All the recurrent symptoms probably mean you're in greater danger of contracting AIDS than the other sero-positives – lots of them are completely asymptomatic. But, at all events, you have to stop thinking of yourself as an AIDS patient. You haven't got AIDS, and you've got a good chance of things staying that way.'

'Sure,' Jerome said, without conviction, 'I know you think it's maybe only about 10 per cent who go on to get AIDS. But on what experience are you basing that prediction? Has anyone had exactly my medical history? How long is the incubation period? What happens if I'm exposed to the virus again? There are too many imponderables and mysteries, too many hypotheses. That's the terrible thing, no certainty. I almost envy the people with terminal cancer or multiple sclerosis. At least they know what's happening, what to expect, how to cope with it.'

The doctor looked at his watch. There was a layer of harassed satiety behind his friendliness. 'You're doing very well, Jerome. Some of the others have just packed up and decided they're going to die. You're too intelligent to do that. I've seen a lot of courage in you, and it's all the more impressive because I don't think you're naturally brave. You must hang on to that courage. And you've got the intellectual lucidity to understand what's happening. Just think what it'd be like if you were too stupid or frightened to confront it all.'

'It doesn't help at all if you're clever, and you know that. Maybe it's helped me to the extent that I've known roughly what to do, what action to take. As you know, I've pushed and hassled like crazy to get treated by you. I've got to recognize that you represent my best chance for survival. Yes, I do feel compassion for the uneducated guy who's too terrified even to find out if he's ill. But the problem for a strung-up intellectual like me is just as great, but different. It's the constant analysis, the introspection, the hard time I give myself, all mixed up with a particularly unhelpful kind of residual Catholic guilt. A lethal cocktail. There's that thing in Pascal about man being the only species that knows it's dying. It feels as if I've got that knowledge reduplicated over and over; and it's no consolation that every man has to confront his own mortality. Mine seems to have been brought forward with unfair haste. Anyway, I know you've got a lot of patients to see. I'll let you get on. I really don't know how you can do this work full-time. I can't tell you how much I admire you – and how much I personally appreciate you.'

'I do it because it's the most pressing need the medical profession has faced for decades,' Dr Durkheim said with a passion that transformed the idea's primness. 'Sometimes I do wonder whether it's all worth it. There's a terrific amount of strain involved. Even my family suffers when I get so caught up in my research and in looking after my patients. But I've got to do it. I feel so strongly that this disease is a tremendous threat: and I want to be in the forefront of the fight against it. It's more of a privilege than a duty.'

'Well, I just can't say how important your contribution is. Let's hope there'll be a Nobel prize in it for you.'

Dr Durkheim smiled self-deprecatingly. 'There are bigger fish in this pond than me. Anyway,' he rose from his chair, 'I'm glad to see you're your old combative, sharp self. I'm sorry it's been such a terrible day. If it's any consolation, it's a lot worse for some of the others. You seem pretty resilient and we can only hope your condition remains stable. I'm fairly convinced it will.'

'Thanks. I need all the reassurance going. Venetia's sometimes a little brisk in her approach. Either that or she succumbs to despair too easily, and I begin to feel that her problems are greater than mine. She sends her love.'

'You're a lucky man to have her,' Dr Durkheim said, with real seriousness in his voice. 'If anyone can get you through, she can. I think she's magnificent. My only problem is that she makes me aware of the terrible solitude of many of the others, the ones who don't have such support, men or women.'

Jerome took stock of the day, a *billet du jour*, as he made his way home on the racing-bike that, with its fleet ergonomics, helped to convince him he was well. He was elated and relieved now. '*La mia salute infiorira*,' he hummed as he waited at a red traffic-light; and he smiled broadly at a passing civil servant. He had come through, he'd obeyed the rules and done everything within his power that day to keep vigilant surveillance over his health. He'd suppressed his irascibility – in the end – and found some reserves of *apathia*, resignation, the willingness to leave things that were unchangeable unchanged. At least the probing and treatment he'd been subject to had the aim of marking his progress, a positive investigation in his own interest. There was some ironic satisfaction in realizing that those same operations had been used in antiquity for the simple, brutal punishment of homosexuality. The Emperor Justinian had perfected the technique of inserting sharp reeds into the pores and tubes of most *exquisite* sensitivity. How benevolent the nurse's horrid ministrations seemed by contrast!

There seemed no point now in giving in to misery and despair. He had proved to himself how he could submit to pain and how he could keep his natural anxiety at bay, controlled by an act of will. The bright sunlight encouraged this optimism, drawing out his inner strength as his gaze fell on a bank of fat, succulent cherries arranged on a market stall.

After all, he was not alone in confronting death. The person he saw walking along could have a wife who lay screaming with the pain of cancer in a hospital bed. He could be an extraordinary surgeon whose career had been shattered by some sexual peccadillo. That woman over by the news-stand might be on her way to a road accident that would leave her disembowelled, screaming voicelessly as she sat in the gutter and felt her entrails flowing out on to the tarmac. So many private tragedies, such fortitude, the suffering patiently and invisibly borne. So many lives blighted and stricken by what the theologians inexplicably called providence but which was better defined by Shakespeare as 'the spite of fortune'. In this communality of disaster Jerome counted for little. His life was his own; his recovery and survival depended substantially on his will; he might outlive them all and remember this small crisis as a mere historical incident, a setback, shocking certainly, but one over which he had triumphed.

Finding no one at home, he executed a familiar dance with the cat; it lumbered clumsily in response to his lateral dives, and beat the air with a half-comprehending and unrhythmic paw. He talked to it as they danced in much detail about AIDS and what it could do to you. Perhaps, it occurred to him, one day he could put Lanfranc on TV as the first cat who could talk and was moreover an expert on AIDS. He listened to an opera by Rossini, that best ever anti-depressant. All those impetuous semi-quavers and breathless grace-notes. One short burst of 'Di tanti polpiti' easily out-performed clomipramine hydrochloride.

Venetia could scarcely believe his composure and strength on her return. They celebrated this slap in the face of adversity by hugging one another till it hurt; and when she looked hard into his blue eyes, she saw only the fire of resolution, the courage of a hero.

4

Democritus *v.* Heraclitus

'I refuse to look at it morally. I just don't feel any guilt. But I've got to face the fact that the world does see it as a moral thing.'

'But they're *wrong*,' Venetia insisted at his hospital bed. 'That idiotic wrath-of-God brigade, bigots who think AIDS is some sort of divine retribution. They're not just crazy, they're illogical and inconsistent. What about leprosy? Is that some kind of punishment? Or any epidemic, come to that, anything that hits the innocent and the sinful indiscriminately. You really shouldn't even *listen* to all that stuff. They're stupid, prejudiced, wrong. And what about lesbians? They're at the absolute bottom of the pile as far as the risk of AIDS goes. Does that make them God's chosen people?'

'I know that, dearest, and I love you for saying it all. Of course it makes it better, just knowing we can share even these painful secrets. I don't think I could bear it on my own. Imagine if I was one of those solitary queens – and I probably would have been one if it weren't for you and David – it would just be too much to face on one's own, not being able to talk about it or pour out the anger and terror, but nurturing all the feelings of bitterness, letting them corrode inside. God only knows what I'd do without you. Meanwhile it doesn't make it any easier to accept the fact that these great armies of moral majorities are massing against me. Let's face it, most people, if they knew about my illness, would *want* me to die, somehow I've deserved it in their eyes.

'The thing is that I'm the worst kind of person for this to happen to. I've never been stable, you know what my mood-changes can be like. And on top of that, in common with a lot of superficially happy people, I've got a tragic sense of life, I'm overwhelmed by the terribleness of things, the forces of evil. Now that I'm probably going to die, it's come home to me even harder, it's happening to me now, not just the world being torn apart by envy and hatred. I was thinking about that last night, about the way the world divides into people who accept the dreadfulness of life, are hardly even affected by it, and those who agonize and feel each sadness and evil like a knife-thrust. I think it's just a matter of philosophical conditioning, the dividing of the world into people who, when they are confronted by the torment of life, either follow Democritus and laugh at its absurdity or, like Heraclitus, weep bitter tears. There's an extraordinary passage in a seventeenth-century allegorical novel, *The Critic*, by Gracián. There are two people, one, Andrenio, a simple, instinctive creature who reacts innocently and uninstructedly to everything. The other, Critilo, is a disabused and cynical old man who reinterprets everything for Andrenio and reveals to him what things actually are, the reality beneath the surface. They travel around and have lots of discussions, and then they come to a market-place where a cord has been stretched between two houses and an elephant is dancing on the tight-rope. All around there are people laughing at this grotesque and ridiculous spectacle. And Andrenio joins in the laughter. Then Critilo stops him and explains at great length how wrong such a reaction is, how the elephant, far from being a ludicrous pantomime, is a living allegory of a terrible truth, the precariousness of daily life, and we ourselves are all like that clumsy creature trying to balance delicately as we negotiate the pitfalls of life.

'There's another extraordinary story about the divine retribution angle. A female disco singer, whose entire career's been created and sustained by her gay public, sings endless high-energy disco-trash. The kind that gay clubs have an insatiable appetite for. Anyway, she is riding high on the crest of her gay-funded wave when suddenly she announces she's become a born-again Christian and, on

380

the strength of her conversion, feels impelled to make various pronouncements on major moral issues. One of these dicta is that "AIDS is the retribution inflicted by God to show us His hatred of sinners" (notice she says "sinners", not "sin"). Well, you can imagine how the gays react, they just can't believe it. And all over southern California they set up dustbins outside the record-stores and all the queens come from miles around to dump her albums in the communal trash-cans. God, it must've been satisfying! Let's hope it finished her career. Maybe it made her wonder whether the gays' action mightn't have been a kind of retribution too!

'I can't feel guilty about getting infected in the first place. After all, AIDS was just a distant rumour at the time when my sex life was at its most uninhibited. I can't blame myself – or *be* blamed, although I will be – for not heeding the consequences of actions. In those days, sex was entirely free of all hazards except things like gonorrhea from which you could get cured easily. So the accusation that I *knew* what I was letting myself in for just won't stick. It'll be a different matter now. Ignorance is no excuse, and anyone who goes in for promiscuous sex should recognize it for an act of supreme defiance.

'The other aspect I thought might involve guilt was that I'd somehow imported AIDS from America, like some horrible gift on the lines of tobacco. But that's not true either. OK, I've been one of the first British cases, but I've been utterly scrupulous about not passing on the infection, you know that.

'I think the only reason these two things make me feel I *ought* to feel guilty is that I'm anticipating the reactions of silly, unreasonable people who might fasten on to these things and use them as ammunition. You know, "you can't put your hand into the fire without expecting to come away burned", crap like that. I *must*, I have *got* to stop this habit of adopting the views of idiots as if they should be my own. The Catholic Church might think me guilty of showing "invincible ignorance" in not understanding the moral implications of homosexuality. Quite honestly, I'm beyond caring. I'll continue to think of myself as an unfortunate victim, caught in the first strike of an unknown sickness. I'm *determined* not to feel guilty. Anyway, it'd only set back my recovery by undermining my belief in myself. In AIDS, with this terrible organic connection between physical strength and spiritual confidence, the nervous system actually *affecting* the course of the disease, you've just got to cast aside all the negative emotions.

'Sorry if I sound like a pop psychologist, but it's true. I *know* it's true. It's the excuse they always looked for to justify homophobia. Now they've got a real weapon, and it's really difficult to be unaffected by that mass hostility, the feeling that they *want* me to die, then there'd be one less lethal carrier. God, it's so terrible.'

He turned over and faced the wall. Although he lay still, the whole slant of his body emanated a restless despair, and Venetia stared helplessly at her beloved friend. Reaching out an arm, she stroked the nape of his neck at the point where the triangle of hair pointed down at his sinuous back. He moved slightly, then remained quiescent, letting her loving fingers calm and absorb his hopeless torment.

'I feel I've been singled out for an appalling fate,' he said after a while, though without yet turning to face her. 'Perhaps it's justice after all, God compensating for the incredible happiness of our life together. Sharing out the misery like poisoned sweets. That's one of the worst things about being fatally ill, it's not just you who suffers. You can't do it alone. You bring a whole lot of people down with you. I wish I could think of some way to insulate you and David from it all.'

He turned back to confront her, his face marked with impotent despair.

'You don't understand, darling,' she offered. 'We're both here to help you through it, to make it bearable. We *want* to help you, that's what love is for. We can only be happy if we know that we share everything with you, even the awful things. Of course it makes us unhappy, nothing can ever be as wonderful as it was. There's a huge great shadow cast over our lives. But the love, the climbing back together out of this trough is what'll make me survive. You'll see, darling, we can beat this nightmare, you and I and our little boy.'

There was a tremulous defiance in her voice as she moved into the positive, constructive part of what she had to say.

She had not noticed, but the knuckles of her fingers whitened as she twisted the handkerchief in her hands. She got up and began to realign the objects on the bedside table: a vase of irises, cartons of sour cherry and apple juice, huge unread historical biographies, boxes of opera tapes, a box of wooden spatulas labelled 'Tongue Depressors' (Jesus, did even tongues get depressed?), as if the restoration of order could somehow encompass the bringing of health. Although she acted like an efficient First World War nurse ministering and imposing calm, there was a hint of latent chaos in her actions that would have disqualified her from active service the moment she was spotted by a sharp-eyed matron. Instead of clinical detachment and self-control, her movements showed, to Jerome at least, a boiling inner turmoil perhaps even less under control than his own.

'And as for the question of moral justice, all anybody sensible is interested in is whether people are good or bad. You're the best person I've ever known, full of kindness and love and feeling. And it's all the more extraordinary for you because you're not naturally virtuous, not one of those dull people who live correctly because that's the way they are and they've never had to make a decision about moral priorities in their lives. They get up in the morning and everything's mapped out in cosy mediocrity, like a suburban housing-estate. You've had to struggle, there's been no easy conventional category for you to fall into and feel comfortable, you're just a *good man*, and I love you for your weakness and backsliding as much as for any boring old virtue. It's unbelievable that an allegedly just God should have done this to you. I've never understood that thing about the ennobling power of pain. How on earth can it be ennobling to suffer, for disgusting things to happen to your body? It's never seemed to me that it can be part of an efficient divine plan. And the priests can't tell you the answer, all they ever say is that it's a mystery and you have to accept it with faith. Well, I don't, and I hope you don't, because we're much more likely to conquer this by fighting it rather than lying down meekly in its path and letting it steamroller over us.'

He smiled in appreciation and motioned her to move closer

as he said, 'It's probably going to take us a long time to work out what we really feel about this calamity. We're both still shocked and confused. I don't think we should strain too hard to analyse everything and understand it all. The problem is that that's what we both like doing best, and we've had so much practice at it. Maybe it'd be easier if I was just strong and suffering, with a mute, inarticulate strength. After all, that's how most heterosexual men would probably act.'

'What a pointless comparison. All that bottled-up emotion, they'd be dead tomorrow. Heaven knows, I wouldn't be remotely interested in you if you were like that. And we've *got* to talk about it, endlessly, even if it's painful and we go round in everlasting circles and never reach a solution. But we'll have a rest now, why don't you try and sleep?'

When the nurse came in she found them in a close, silent embrace. She could not understand such love, a love transcending animal compatibility. But the nurses were great, a source of terrific strength, fearlessly cleaning wounds and administering enemas with all the aplomb of Queen Marie of Romania.

'Temperature, Jerome. Put that under your tongue.' After sticking the thermometer in his mouth, she went on: 'What have you eaten today? You know I have to write it all down.' Realizing he could not answer, she took his pulse instead and smiled at Venetia as she half-looked at the watch on her breast.

'You're not dressed as frighteningly as I thought you'd be,' Venetia said to her. 'I sort of expected some kind of astronaut encased in protective clothing. It's quite simple really. Just that plastic apron and gloves, you look like a hygienic vet.'

'When I went to the dentist last week,' Jerome said, 'I thought I'd landed on Mars.'

'No, it's not so bad as all that. Everyone thinks we must be terrified working on these wards. But it's not so awful really. My boy friend's a little unhappy about it, but I know how to reassure him. Anyway, this is the most exciting thing that's happened in medicine for years, and I feel really proud to be part of it. I've learned so much and I feel I can really help.'

'Mmmm . . .' Jerome protested, and the nurse retrieved

the thermometer. 'A hundred and one,' she said and took down the chart to mark it. 'All this fluctuation up and down, can't you stay constant for a moment?'

Jerome liked his nurses like this, upfront and no-nonsense, unaffected by sentimentality and given to direct statement, barking out bulletins and prognoses and the polysyllabic names of pills. Venetia, on the other hand, was vaguely jealous and felt she could do so much better – bring a grave, calming dignity. Much to Jerome's annoyance (however much he concealed this reaction), Venetia kept repeating her desire to be with him and nurse him constantly, as if somehow her physical proximity alone could make him well. This was, indeed, her answer to all problems, especially mental anguish, a universal panacea that calmed her with its cosy comfortableness. Jerome had tried, diplomatically though with no hope of success, to explain to her that, great as his love for her was, he needed vast tracts of time on his own to come to terms with his condition and resign himself philosophically to his possible death.

'I'm taking David to the movies tonight. There's a sort of Californian cartoon about a woman who metamorphoses at night and grows fur and then, depending on whether the sun's out or it's cloudy, she becomes a lion or a polar bear. Heaven knows what happens if it's merely overcast. I suppose she compromises with being a polar lion. Anyway, I'm sure he'll love it and it'll remind him of home.'

'I wish I could come. You know how I love lions. The bigger the cat the better! Come back tomorrow if you can. I won't have any news except for bedpans and proctoscopes, maybe a bronchoscopy if you're really lucky.'

Their cheerfulness always reasserted itself at parting to try and alleviate the stress of the intervals between meeting. But their smiles and laughter were overbright, their panic present beneath the shallow surface. Even as they promised to do their utmost to carry on as normal, to pretend nothing much had happened, they each began an inexorable slump into parallel troughs of pain.

'Try and sleep now, my dearest love,' she said (what nightmares await you!), 'David and I will be thinking of you' (as you lie here dying). 'Keep on fighting, you've got to for our sake.' (Without you we're lost.)

'I'll be out soon and we'll have some fun, maybe go to Greece.' (This bed, this ward will probably be my final prison.) 'Everything will be all right.' (Nothing will ever again even be bearable.)

They hugged with all their strength until Venetia began to quake with the silent heavings of tears. Their heads, so close that not even a sheet of paper could have passed between them, united their loving, grieving souls. And then, before Jerome had time to lie back against his pillows, Venetia left.

5

God's Gift to Bigots

The storm broke in England early in 1984. All at once the press went berserk, gripped by the lucrative potential of a terrifying epidemic. AIDS was perfect, an ideal target. Not only did it provide appalling and complicated ways to die, but it was linked in the cynical minds of the press-barons with a moral stigma and the irresistible notion of a scourge spread largely by sexual promiscuity. In full cry, journalists hunted down their victims, heedless of the misery, despair and confusion they so prodigally diffused.

Under the guise of objective reportage, they dug out stories to confirm the fears of a misinformed public. They suppressed scientific evidence for the comparatively low infectivity of AIDS and concentrated on fanning the ill-founded anxiety of closed heterosexual minds. It seemed as if there was a conspiracy between the seediest reporters and their most prejudiced readers to disseminate the idea that a sinister group of homosexuals, heedless of their threat to others and seemingly incapable of sexual self-restraint, were breathing pestilential plagues over innocent prey by all kinds of fanciful transmissions: touch, aerosol, the kiss of Judas. You could contract the disease, apparently, by the most distant, tenuous exposure. Their accounts seemed to be based on the assumption that homosexuals represented a minefield of contagion within society and that it would be in everyone's best interests to corral them in some kind of leprous quarantine. A Brazilian newspaper advocated the extermination of gays and lesbians (even though the latter was the lowest-risk-group in the entire world) to arrest the spread of AIDS (using, presumably, their already conveniently formed death squads). Harassed and committed doctors issued corrective rebuttals till they collapsed with exhaustion from repeating *ad nauseam* that AIDS could only be transmitted through blood or semen, that the panic was more infectious than the disease could ever be. The press reacted by reiterating the baseless convictions, amassing adjectives and headlines to whip up a frenzy of fear and ignorant contempt.

They lurked in hospital corridors and sneaked photographs of AIDS victims, with their pitiful Belsenic thinness and disfiguring lesions. The defenceless, wasted faces of helpless victims stared grimly out from their photographs, their privacy and dignity irrevocably invaded, their despair trivialized. They lay in wait for relatives and cruelly compounded their distress. A gay prison chaplain, a man of transparent decency and honour, died of AIDS amid hysteria and antagonism, his memory heaped with the excrement of prurient hypocrisy. Nothing, it seemed, had been learnt from the American experience, from the head-start that San Francisco and New York had in dealing with the crisis, dispelling myths and defusing the fear. It was as if the British public were being deliberately plunged head-first into the slough of a medieval pestilence.

Jerome was too intelligent to be seriously affected by all the madness. Or so he believed, till one day he discovered himself actually buying a copy of one of the most notorious tabloids to read its sensational recital of half-truths. This signal that he was not as invulnerable as he imagined led him to try and cultivate a detached and cynical inviolability, but he could not sustain it and found himself increasingly affected by an obsessional curiosity and appetite. He ransacked the popular press for mention of AIDS, almost like a murderer seeking reports of his crime (though there was no clear guilt in his search). Venetia tried to curb this self-defeating mania, arranging for Jerome to be busy when the television carried reports of AIDS and confiscating copies of the lurid Sunday papers which uncharacteristically cluttered their kitchen. She also managed to head off the overtures of a gutter journalist who had traced Jerome, God knew how. The telephone had rung and Venetia had heard the woman's unctuous, questioning voice: 'Hullo, um, I'm an old friend of Jerome's from way back. I was trying to get in touch with him again.'

'What did you say your name was?'

'I didn't. You won't know me. Do you think I could talk to him? I heard he wasn't very well.'

Suspicion darkened in Venetia's mind. 'Look, why don't you give me your number and I'll get him to ring you back?' she suggested. As she said it, the conviction formed that she needed to protect Jerome from this importunate call, a conviction based on instinct and experience. But then, as the woman's blustering answer seemed to incriminate her further, Venetia lost her temper and shouted down the telephone: 'Who the hell are you?'

'We just wondered whether he might like to tell us about his illness. It would, of course, be very well worth his while.'

The truth had emerged, and Venetia exploded: 'You fucking bitch, what fucking right do you think you've got to come sniffing around other people's lives like some shit-smelling dog? God, how can you claim to be a member of the human race? Don't you have any fucking feelings, Christ, I could kill you, you squalid fucking parasite. I hope your life is torn apart, I hope you die of the most painful cancer, I hope . . .' But the telephone had gone dead.

Venetia kept this incident from Jerome; yet it festered inside her.

Some of the lunacy came from reality, things that were actually said and done, not just bored or ignorant reportings of them. Small-minded trade-unionists puffed themselves up with self-importance and demanded protection from gays for their workforce. Self-righteous social workers expostulated about the contamination of children in their charge. Nobody tried to understand, but ignorance provided no excuse.

In suburban Essex, hatted ladies boycotted holy communion for fear that the chalice might be polluted. The residents of a co-operative building in New York rose as one to enforce the expulsion of a psychological counsellor whose clients with AIDS, wide-eyed and haggard, cluttered up their lobby so distressingly. A pregnant Zambian woman with AIDS, ill, frightened and disorientated, was left stranded in Melbourne; no airline would carry her, and even if they had, she would have probably been refused readmission to her homeland. Rumours grew of whole tribes decimated in the African bush, of mass death among the child prostitutes of São Paulo, of Hollywood stars on the verge of breaking silence. And all over the world, in the loneliness of New York, London and San Francisco, men began to despair, some deciding to end their lives before sickness claimed them, their histories of grief long and searing in their own eyes but obscure and unfathomable to posterity.

Jerome was at a loss to make sense of the welter of information and misinformation. He was torn by conflicting reactions as again and again his face was forced against the distorting glass of his sickness. On the rational level, at least, he knew that it was essential he should maintain a reserved distance between himself and the wave that threatened to engulf him. Self-preservation dictated that he should remain detached, but even self-preservation was an ambivalent quantity for him, not an instinct on which he could entirely rely. Sometimes, when he tried to see the purpose of his life, he could not quite do so, and he felt in an odd way that illness gave him a reason for living, if that wasn't too absurd a contradiction. There was something thrilling, crazy as it sounded, in being one of the first victims, a pioneer martyr. He felt singled out, less in the grim Calvinistic sense of pre-elected damnation than in his capacity as a brave conscript in the front-line, exposed to unparalleled adventure. He enjoyed a secret knowledge, belonged to a sect of doomed initiates, faced death in its imminence each hour of the day. All of this conferred a kind of specialness, an apartness which nourished itself on his natural alienation.

As the reports on AIDS increased, a number of questions preyed on his mind, new questions which had the nature of philosophical exam questions. They were absurd, he knew, like the problems of formal logic or the angelic wrangling of the scholastics. But the new climate of half-informed fear made them answerable. I know I'm infected with AIDS, the argument ran. It does not show – yet – and may never do so. What if this person, that person, those friends, that anonymous crowd, also, impossibly, were to know too? If there were some way of momentarily displaying his condition to the public, would he cut a swathe through the crowds as they rushed, panic-stricken, to avoid his path (a useful tactic in the rush-hour tube, he reflected sardonically). Would they rise as one and drive him out of a restaurant, a church, a school? Could he clear a bus? What if he was hijacked on a flight to Greece? Would he tell his captors, and, if he did, would they execute him peremptorily on the spot or would they believe their own preservation lay in promptly releasing him? Might the authorities on frontiers begin to refuse him entry, try to enforce an unenforceable *cordon sanitaire* against the foreign plague? Being more than a little of a danger-queen he would – in theory and in part – have loved to put these ideas to the test.

What would happen if he were bitten by mosquitoes and sandflies on the beach? Would they stagger back to their lairs and keel over with AIDS after first groggily infecting a few more tourists?

All these questions, and many others, wound themselves into the skeins of his mind. The ordinary tenor of life disappeared under the weight of these new and complex lines of questioning. Increasingly he perceived the meaning of his life through a veil of unnecessary hypotheses, teased out and wrangled with, till, relentlessly and with complete predictability, they yielded no answers.

The special viewpoint he'd involuntarily acquired affected everything he saw. Ironically aware of his separateness, he looked obliquely at his experience with a privileged indirection more acute even than that which had characterized his sight as a mere homosexual. The most harmless pop song assumed the lineaments of a tragic threnody for his lost sexuality: 'I can't control my needs,' sang some tigress in what she intended as a simple expression of lust. The line recurred to him unannounced, apropos of nothing, as he stood by the biscuit counter at Marks & Spencer. Overcome by a fit of silent weeping, he fell to the ground, mortified by the realization of his imposed celibacy (a cause he could hardly reveal to the staff worker who rescued him and comforted him with tissues and sweet tea). 'I have to stop this!' he told himself firmly. 'The bloody disease is beginning to control me. I'm seeing everything in relation to it. There must be life beyond AIDS – Oh no, God, that's exactly what there isn't!' Another verbal conceit struck him and took the place of real, considered thought. However hard he tried, it seemed as if he was never actually going to be able to understand what illness meant to him, to Venetia and as a general abstraction. It was somehow too fascinating, too enveloping a concept. There seemed to be an unbridgeable divide between the reflections it prompted and his own real, felt suffering. And when the suffering became too intense, he lost all control, all capacity for thought, and these literary speculations evaporated into nothingness, revealing themselves for the evanescent self-indulgent caprices they actually were.

And so it went on. Had he been unmasked at a football match, would he have been torn limb from limb? Which of his friends would flinch at the idea of touching him? Which of his enemies would seize the chance to eliminate him and rid the world of a terrible threat? What if he were mugged? And told the mugger he had AIDS? Would it cause him to back off or would it goad him to further aggression? He settled for the fact that it would be unwise to test out the hypothesis. The little old lady who smiled benignly at him when their eyes met at the chamber-music recital – how her face would drain of friendship and contort with sudden fear!

Killing time (dreadful phrase) once when he arrived early to meet David from his play school, he sat disconsolately on a park bench and allowed the gloom to settle on him, welcoming it almost, like a dark battlement accommodating a flock of ravens. As the world passed by, he looked into its inexpressive eyes, and beseeched it to know about his sickness, and then, with equal fervour, prayed that it should not. 'I'm infected with AIDS,' he tried to make his body express the idea. 'Look at me, can't you see what's happening inside me? Surely it shows? See, see, the tainted blood that streams in the firmament.' Neither self-pity nor self-advertisement underlay the charade so much as a feeling of outrage that he was not on equal terms with the rest of the world, that his illness was wrapped in a pall of opacity and secrecy, even its name a shibboleth of shame, four scarlet letters which, once declared, would win him only acrimony and hatred. What had happened to the ministration of the sick, the kindness he deserved? They had abandoned him, swallowed up by the advancing ocean of bigotry, receding into an embattled corner in which lay his only hope of uncensorious care.

His impulses were less and less within his control now. Irrationality, infused with fatalism, pulled him in the most harrowing directions. Even as he sat at that moment in an apparent pool of lucidity, performing an utterly ordinary domestic task, his head filled with tents and dry mountains as he began to plan to rush away and work among famine victims until he himself died, equal with the dispossessed, indistinguishable from them in death. The project was absurd, he knew and recognized, yet somehow it gave shape to his desire to be released from the thrall of his own contagion. And furthermore, he reflected, it made more sense than some of the schemes which flashed through the fevered minds of the other victims of AIDS. He had spoken recently to one zealot who roundly stated that, were AIDS to be eventually diagnosed, he would take it as a sentence of death and, despairing of his own life, haemorrhaging or not, he would become a kamikaze assassin and eliminate his bugbear, the egregious Mrs Thatcher. His plan stopped short, though, of infecting her by the most immediate course.

He took a book out of his pocket, *Marius the Epicurean*. He had hoped to find consolation there, maybe a ready-made comprehensive philosophical guide and panacea to reduce his terror to intelligible calm. But he discovered, as so often in these dark blighted days, that he could not read. He knew why it was; for he had conscientiously worked to discover the cause. The reason was that nothing, no narrative, either fictional or real, could possibly seem as interesting as what was now happening to him. The only conceivable book was the one that wrote itself inside his head.

David came out of school and Jerome emerged from his futile reverie. They smiled and embraced, Jerome clinging to the child a little harder and longer than was customary. He made an effort to match David's buoyant jollity as they set off home. It was always worth doing. The emotional input you invested in him was always repaid with compound interest. They laughed and chattered and recounted their lives at the points where they met. After a while, Jerome's former pessimism seemed dispelled not so much by an actual act of will as by the purifying breeze of David's happiness. A child has achieved what a sick adult could not, he mused speciously (for the impression was only apparent – his own will had been the agent). How strong this boy is, how resilient! Jerome had been watching David for signs of awareness of his plunge into illness. Not observing any, he had felt the prickings of resentment, even disappointment. But these selfish reactions were soon ousted by the vicarious carefreeness he felt on the boy's behalf.

They walked on in the sunlight cast through the lacy filter of the yellowing plane-trees. It was a rich, swollen, late-summer day with the faintest foretaste of winter. Around them were idling, contented groups of people, shopping, visiting, walking with half-smiles of benignity on faces warmed by the late-afternoon sun. Colour burst from the stalls of a greengrocer, and the houses were warm and friendly, beaming with a kind of gracious elderliness through shabby façades, 'Love from Lorraine!' yelled a clumsily spray-canned graffito in Caribbean script. Wow, Jerome thought, if that's the only way she can express love, then really my problems are pretty minuscule. Lorraine had only some cosmic anonymity to take as her lover. He was swaddled and loved like a precious hole-in-heart baby. The little boy beside him, marching in semi-militaristic step, glancing up periodically at his face, was the guarantee of his deservingness.

It happened very fast, all the more so for its unexpectedness. Two utterly nondescript women, remarkable for nothing save their slavish adherence to a working-class model, pushed prams with dogged steps towards Jerome and David. One of the pram-wheels squeaked, a detail that Hitchcock might have exploited filmically. Cigarette ash dropped from the mothers in grey abundance. As they approached, their animated conversation ceased and, according to some tacit pact, they fixed their scrutiny on the two passing innocents. Out for blood (who knew from what irrational fears or disappointments), they simultaneously cast Jerome in the role of their victim. They absorbed the signals of his appearance, the subtle characteristics that gave away his sexual vulnerability, and as he drew nearer, hand in hand with David, secure in his loving protectiveness, they spat out their venom: 'Fucking queer, who're you trying to fool? Shouldn't be allowed, touching an innocent child like that. Filthy AIDS-carrier, go and spread your dirty germs somewhere else!'

It hit him somewhere deep in the pit of his stomach. Here was what the world really thought. These two hideous vulgarians with their doomed brats were the real opposition. Hatred prevailed, and in the process you could even teach your children how to hate. It hurt more, was infinitely more damaging than the time he'd been physically assaulted in St Martin's Lane by four skinhead queer-bashers, who had punched and kicked him mercilessly in their search for masculinity and reassurance. He had managed to wriggle free and then, in an effort to exorcize his delayed shock, had reflected ruefully on the cowardice of majorities, the age-old brutality that originated in fear. Now, however, his pain was deeper. He felt sick, and came near to vomiting. The sickly stench of mankind's cruelty all but overwhelmed him. But he made no answer. Anxiety about David's reaction prevailed over his spontaneous anger and the affront he felt to his humanity. He walked on with a kind of pained gravity as if the taunts had been so much smoke; although David looked back over his shoulder and wore a puzzled frown. He got out of step with Jerome, and took little skipping steps to keep up, craning back to look at the oddly triumphant faces of the women, who had stopped to enjoy the effects of their cruelty. One of them had folded her arms in an attitude of smug defiance; the other pointed jeeringly with her cigarette.

'Come along, Davido,' he said encouragingly, using the bogus Italian he kept for affection under stress. 'They're just some stupid women, nothing to worry about.' And

David followed meekly, thankfully asking no questions, but still revealing confusion on his furrowed forehead. 'Thank God for you,' Jerome murmured. But for David and Jerome's anxiety over the boy's reaction, the knife the women had inserted in his innermost being would have twisted and torn at his entrails, wrenched away at his heart. His hand gripped the little boy's tighter and he hurried him on towards home. There was both strength and courage in his measured resilience. He had refused to give in to the battering, not now just of fate alone, but from the fellow human beings who, he had previously fondly believed, preserved kindness inside them, human warmth in their veins rather than the poisonous vitriol that now so unexpectedly and shockingly leaked.

'Hey, you two, you're never going to believe it!' No sooner had they gone in through the front door than Venetia came running heavily downstairs, breathless with effusive news. 'Wait a second, come in here.' She gestured towards the kitchen, dragging David by his playfully reluctant hand. 'I want to save up the excitement.'

They sat, dutiful and obedient to the operatic mood that had descended on her. Jerome even sneaked a conspiratorial smile with David that communicated their loving indulgence of Venetia's familiar excesses. They toyed with the food she'd prepared and listened to the story she could no longer repress.

'You know I had to do that dreary wireless programme this morning, the *Critics' Forum* thing. Well, it was all going OK, the recording was pretty uneventful until we got on to the subject of the revaluation of Italian Renaissance painting. The others were absolutely predictable. They said all sorts of solid and worthy things, especially old Roland Longjumeau, he was almost pedantic he was so reliable. And then this absolute idiot, Marcelle Whitetower, launched into an attack on Bernard Berenson and said he was a dangerous, fraudulent old capitalist who'd single-handedly rearranged the value of Italian pictures to suit his own collection, and she ended up by saying, "There he was in that beautiful villa, that tough, selfish old man surrounded by Italian paintings one would give one's eyes for." Of course none of us dared to point out the absurdity, that if you gave your eyes you wouldn't even be able to see the bloody things; but I got the feeling she half-knew immediately afterwards that she'd said something particularly crass. Ooh, it was fun! She looked all bewildered and crestfallen.'

Somehow, mainly through Venetia's courage, they were managing to preserve themselves as a family. The love and humour that bound them still kept up its buoyancy. The shadows in Venetia's mind were well-concealed, and her histrionic humanity seemed to be surviving the sidelong blow dealt it by fate.

6

The Condition of Virtue

What had he learned? How had he changed? Should he, anyway, consider his life as a kind of balance-sheet of profit and loss? His freshly heightened perception of mortality didn't seem to have afforded any great new insights. Its only effect seemed to be that he saw life much as he might see a film that he didn't quite understand and whose ending he simply couldn't guess, try as he might. There was apparently some portentous but elusive underlying message embedded in the script; and it was probable that each event, each line, each juxtaposition of images, had a precise part to play in the allegory that held the key to everything. Yet he remained tantalizingly distant from that key, estranged and frustrated, partly through his inability to see it with any clarity, partly because he was too frightened fully to confront it. No, what he really sensed was a sequence of banalities, paradoxes and ironies that would have passed unnoticed in the minds of the healthy. When he tried to look at his soul, he saw nothing. Such intangible entities paled into evanescence against the solid data of his bodily decline. To examine his soul was to try and see Australia through a curved telescope.

At all events he tried to make the ground he stood on more solid. When sickness threatens to overwhelm one, he told himself, there is a terrible danger of indulging in fatiguing, fatigued introspection *à la* Bloomsbury. He could produce infinite strings of sentences that illusionistically might appear to describe his feelings and put all his sensations into the semblance of order. But that would be false. His responsibility was to recognize the chaos for what it was and simply muddle through as best he could. Lacking a central vision, Buddhism maybe, or mystic Catholicism, he should not even try to place a coherent structure over his experience, like a child's piece of tracing-paper. It had to be allowed to unfold, confusingly, maddeningly and with no sense of revelation, in all its triumphant fatefulness. No amount of analysis would help. What he really needed was courage, tenacity and the ability to transcend setbacks.

He turned now and then to literature to discover whether it could offer consolation or guidance (while knowing, *à l'avance*, that the experience of others, fictional or real, could do little to illuminate his own). He began with Fritz Zom's *Mars*, blurbed as 'the chronicle of a lucid mind observing its body's relentless deterioriation'; but he was so repelled by the vindictive and supercilious narrator that he soon flung the book angrily against the wall. Then there was Thomas Mann's *The Magic Mountain*, A.E. Ellis's *The Rack*, Gide's *L'Immoraliste*, Hermann Hesse's *Klingsor's Last Summer* . . . He wearied of the paraphernalia of sanatoria, the chronicles of temperature graphs and probings, the lugubrious analyses of physicians and metaphysicians.

'Perhaps you really ought to try and find someone you can safely have sex with. I can't bear to see you prowling around with that hunted look on your face. Darling, I think we've *got* to talk about sex. I know you don't want to. But it's always been such a fantastically big thing in your life, we can't just ignore the fact that it's suddenly disappeared.'

'What makes you think it's important?' Jerome had snapped. 'Why do you have to assume my problems are automatically sexual? Anyway, *you* should know, I don't know why you should need to ask *me* about chastity.'

Venetia started with anger. 'How dare you be so foul, you'd never have said anything so cheap in the old days. What's happened to you? You've got to fight against this terrible temper. I hate to see you like this.'

'OK, OK, I'm really sorry. I didn't mean it. I guess I just can't face up to the fact that I don't know *what* to make of it. The loss of my sexuality, I mean. It's absolute hell, and I freely admit it. They might as well have amputated my cock. I expect they will in due course . . .'

'I suppose it's just irritating if people go on about subli-mation or priests and look at those wonderful nuns who save millions of lives in India, *they* don't let sex get in the way. It can't be any help to realize that celibacy isn't a problem for lots of people.'

'It sure isn't. The great difference is that on the whole they've been able to take a voluntary decision. They've calculated the meaning of the relative parts of their lives and decided that sex is dispensable in the end. Especially if, in their work, they need extra large doses of spirituality which can only come from denial of the flesh. Whereas for me, well, sex has had a pretty high priority. God, it's hard, I realize it all the more when I talk about it.'

'That's why I wanted to *make* you talk about it, don't you see? You've got to face up to it, decide what it means, get it into some kind of perspective. What *does* it feel like, I mean at a deep level? I don't suppose it's just like a child having a toy snatched out of his hands.'

'Judging from the fuss David makes sometimes, I'd say that could be a pretty deep sense of loss! Remember the sable cat? Seriously though, I just haven't yet worked out what it means to me, how much it contributes to this bloody irritability that you're so good about.' He half-smiled in appreciation. 'One thing I *do* know – and it wouldn't have taken Voltaire to find it out – is that there's a huge irony in the fact that when I get into my worst moods, the one thing I need to get me out of them is the one thing I can't have – sex.'

'I've noticed. That's one of the reasons why I really do think you ought to try and find somebody who'll do that safe sex thing you told me about. I know it's embarrassing, it must seem like a desperate kind of half-measure, a parody even. But surely it would be therapeutic, at least you'd have some kind of physical contact.'

At this point Jerome realized that he could not reveal to Venetia the deserts of loneliness into which the withdrawal of sex had plunged him. He longed, with a hunger that clawed and clawed at him, like the eagle that fed continuously on Prometheus's liver, for the physicality of another, for the joinedness of two people, the simplicity and reassurance of touch. He ached for the exploration of another man's body, for the hardness of his muscle, the rise and fall of his breast as he lay beside him. His secret smell, his strength and solidity, the near-dying passion that he could arouse and that could be aroused in him.

'I'll try and find some way round it,' he promised. 'Because you're right, you're always right. I'm withering up inside. The odd thing is that I veer from crying out for sexual fulfilment to almost believing that I've conquered it. If you look at it dispassionately, from the outside, what I've had to do is devise a life-style that's appropriate for a man twice my age. Bringing the menopause forward by about thirty years. I'm half-way to persuading myself that I've achieved that; even though, when I'm asked about it, I'm not even sure that that's what I actually want. But I think you *can* just abandon your sexuality, even if your libido remains intact.'

He flushed imperceptibly at the recurrent sense that so much of what he was saying related ironically to Venetia's own emotional life.

'My libido certainly fluctuates more than it ever used to,' he went on. 'I suppose I've subconsciously realized that I just can't *afford* to get as sexually aroused as I once did. I only have to dam it up again, and that's worse than not having felt it in the first place. Sometimes I almost believe that one morning I'll wake up and realize that sex is something *other* people do. Like speaking American or loving shopping or blackening your lungs with tar. And maybe celibacy isn't so very difficult, after all. Practice makes perfect. It's as if my psychosexual self is coming to the rescue and saving me from disappointment and frustration.'

'At least I haven't needed to put bromide in your tea or saltpetre in your food. They do that to poor Brazilian teenagers in the refectories of their boarding-schools.'

Venetia's inconsequential red herring temporarily made him lose sight of his own argument.

'Yes, I read that novel too. In fact, if you remember, I introduced you to the Literature of the South American Tormented Adolescent. So anyway, it's all a bit of a delicate balancing act. In fact recently I've been trying to add up all the advantages of a life entirely devoid of sex, just to cheer myself up.'

Again he wondered momentarily whether he should really go on.

'There are a few advantages and compensations,' he continued. 'I even made a list of them, you know how I need to get things down in writing. Hang on, I'll get it for you,' he said, turning to go upstairs and look.

As he ransacked a pile of books, papers and photographs beside his bed, he felt increasingly concerned at the tactfulness of what he was doing. Would Venetia take it all as a sinister underhand attack on her chosen celibacy? No, he thought, correcting his fears. It is she who's prompted this conversation. She genuinely wants to know how I'm making out without sex. It's just a little unfortunate that most of my answers apply wholesale to her own predicament.

'Here it is,' he shouted. Holding the paper close to his face to decipher its scrawled messages, each written in different inks and at different times, he read out as he slowly descended:

'1. I can still be charming, attractive, someone they want to have around. None of that seems to depend on my sexual availability or activity.
2. Have discovered the beauty of things I've hitherto been virtually blind to. The rhythm of the country day. Wild flowers.
3. Novels which previously made no sense now do.
4. I must learn more things, practical things, because I'm gradually convincing myself that I *will* survive; I must prepare for the post-AIDS phase of my life.
5. Have discovered more compassion for people struggling under handicaps.
6. Am definitely less superficial and brittle.
7. Have got a new opportunity for experimenting with my looks, inasmuch as I am no longer obliged to conform to clonedom since the whole point – sexual conquest – has gone out of it.
8. I think I have a clearer understanding of what Venetia's life is like. [Here his voice faltered.]
9. I'm no longer prey to the fear that I'm somehow at the mercy of sex, controlled by it, dominated. Like some

people are dominated by their invalid father, by being fat, by being stupid or by their fear of damnation. The only drawback is that possibly that domination by sex has only been lifted to be replaced by domination by AIDS.'

There were others too, but they were illegible.

'What do you make of that?' he asked with the eagerness of a spaniel.

'Well, if you really want to know, I think it's probably one of the worst cases of self-deception in human history. Part of me is moved by it. I know you mean some of those things sincerely, I've seen them in action. But the mere fact that you've written them down seems to me to demonstrate an amazing capacity for self-delusion. I'm afraid it only confirms my view that you've really *got* to face up to this sexuality thing more seriously. You can't just reduce it to a list of clichés like a schoolgirl's catalogue of crushes.'

'All right, if you insist, I admit it *is* pretty hellish doing without sex. I try and kid myself it isn't, but it is. One of the worst things is that the whole element of adventure's disappeared. We both know that my grasp of reality is rather limited, that I tend to live rather on the fringes of things. Sex was the avenue that forced me to live a little more intensely, to bump up against life and other people's lives and make me aware that human experience isn't just a matter of the odd unrepresentative impressions that slurp around in my own mind. *That's* what's been hard to sacrifice, in the end. A bit like taking away an intoxicant from an addict. Because then you discover that life is essentially humdrum, everyone's much like everyone else, the patterns are so banal, so predictable . . .'

'I think I understand,' she had volunteered.

'No, you don't. I could have said that last sentence entirely in the negative and you'd still have agreed. I don't think I understand it myself.'

Like Forster's heroes who'd been liberated from their puritanism by Italy and by love, Jerome's spirit had been freed by California and sex. Yet now he was being re-enveloped by a monkish self-abnegation, climbing back into a spiritual closet, and when he came seriously to examine his own feelings, he found he resented being condemned to the role of spectator, a passive and disengaged observer.

He could not see his emasculation as anything other than a severe loss. The story of Abelard made him smile wryly. Castrated as a punishment for his seduction of Heloïse, he'd been able, in later years, to write to her of God's mercy paradoxically manifest in this trauma; for, since then, his love had been necessarily spiritualized and directed towards the eternal truths. Jerome, of course, had no such sense of transcendent absolutes. God, in his divine wisdom, had not chosen to reveal himself to this errant and inveterate sinner. Lacking any such revelation, Jerome saw no alternative vessel into which to pour the accumulated force of *eros* that had before been expended in sex.

As the continence settled inexorably on him, he remembered his sexual past with increasing confusion. It receded into a shimmer of fiction. Each day made it harder for him to associate his present self with the licentious acrobat *d'antan*, the princeling satyr *de nos jours*. Had he really writhed, coiled and lunged with such abandon? And abandon to what? He had nearly forgotten the impetus of sex, the imperative to which the willing body surrendered over and over again.

He could barely recapture the ecstatic and uncomplicated pleasure he had earlier found. Looking back at his own image as it cavorted and fainted in swooning abandon, it was as if he were observing someone utterly other, on film perhaps; and the writhing seemed oddly purposeless to his newly puritanical perception. He was veering towards a harsh stance, one of outright disapproval; and he had to remind himself that celibacy, his own or anyone's, was itself a pathological and unnatural state. All of this had an internal logic and inevitability. But superimposed on the retrospective alienation, he discovered he had unconsciously reached a *moral* as well as a *psychological* distance. He had grown to despise his former self, and to believe that his frenetic promiscuity, dedicated as it had been to the sating of his pricking body, had in effect been responsible for destroying him. Destroyed his creativity. Banished his ambition. Suppressed all his faculties and capacities, all burned out on the sacrificial altar of Priapus. This genital sexuality was what had defined him.

Now that his physical needs were forcibly controlled, he found that such desire as remained was of a new kind. The old indiscriminate inflammability had dampened down, giving way to mere flashes of unfamiliar, redirected urgency. One day he saw how old and sick and *different* he had become when he found himself lusting after a young, downy boy with the slender limbs of a Cretan saint. Paedophilia had never before had any meaning for Jerome. But now he watched the boy lasciviously, longing to defile a body that in itself was devoid of sexual power but so transparently free of disease that it assumed, through that fact alone, the desirability of an Aphrodite seen through torn veils. *Déchiré* veils, like the sensations in his loins and heart. The lust of old was turning into a benign desire for wholeness and life, a protective yearning for clean blood, a transference of this innocent child on to his own faded, tainted self. Something of Aschenbach in *Death in Venice* had crept over him, the sad hopelessness of that last toilette, the running of the hair-dye and the smudging of the rouge, the doomed casting of his terminal, tired self on to the suttee of Tadzio's white flames. How much lust informed this feeling he could not be sure; he was, he knew, merely so accustomed to ascribing all desire and passion to that one source alone.

Where he had before sought to assume, for the duration of an hour or more, the beauty and strength of another man, buckling on his armour, shining with the same metallic brilliance, he now, shyly watching this unsullied boy, wished only for a transfusion of uncorruptedness. If he could only, with one momentarily agonizing vampiric lunge at the boy's white neck, suck out the pure blood that mocked his own!

How far this new obsession could lead him was a question on which he speculated, often less than seriously. Was it just a matter of time before he would develop an irresistible taste for sixteen-stoners (whose girth was such a cast-iron alibi from the ravages of AIDS)?

In spite of the fact that he couldn't exactly quantify the sense of loss, he was certain that the withdrawal of sex was slowly damaging him, changing him inexorably into another, different creature. Perhaps he was losing his Reichian energy; the drying up of the vital fluids was altering the balance of his nervous system, causing chemical blockages, emotional sterility and heaven knew what withering of the inner self. Empirically, at least, he could see that an inexorable cause and effect had produced a new seriousness in him, an almost pedantic, almost pompous earnestness which, he felt instinctively, was inseparable from the fact that he could not release his other, frenzied, Dionysiac self in the arms of a man. For a man of his kind, imprisoned in his intellectual self and unable to communicate through his barrier of diffidence, sex had been the most effective alternative medium of direct intercourse. He'd suffered all his life from that most terrible of all kinds of loneliness, the inability to project his thoughts. He'd been locked inside his differentness, crippled by fastidiousness and perfectionism, fettered by an amazing mind. Only sex had had the power to release him. And now that most accessible of freedoms was denied him by the virus that lingered perpetually in his body.

He was more and more sedentary and disinclined to go out. He had various specific fears, primarily the dread of finding himself in the midst of a discussion about AIDS. It would be an ignorant, ill-informed and sensationalist farrago. He would have to sit there, his emotions just below the surface, and either remain silent or – the infinitely braver alternative – launch into the argument and dispassionately, revealing no personal involvement, correct misapprehensions and reinstate the truth.

But still there were other, more general and shapeless terrors to restrict his movement.

7

Blood of Life, Blood of Death

Months passed. Nothing seemed to change. He believed he detected a gradual and progressive deterioration, but the symptoms were so imprecise he could not be sure.

His life – Venetia's too – became increasingly empty of incident. The days limped apathetically along, irritable and dull, with the halting gait Jerome himself felt appropriate for a cripple and leper. Only David seemed to have any vitality left.

One evening in high summer, Jerome lay naked on his bed at home. His nostrils filled with the smell of the old but clean cotton of the patchwork quilt; it was somehow headily nostalgic, redolent of the bright days of health before his collapse. He looked down at his cock as it lolled against his groin. What changes had been wrought in it by the months of disuse? It seemed relentlessly flaccid, bloated even, and the definition of its veins seemed more marked than he remembered. A childlike pinkness suffused its malleable girth and it looked wholly innocent, as if restored to its pristine state. But there was no life or movement in it.

Ordinarily the combination of the sprawl of his body, the enervating hour of the day and the suffocating city heat would have produced in him an erotic languor. Lazy sexual pictures would have floated into his hot brain and gradually taken on the coherence of a masturbatory fantasy. Now, however, he was conscious only that this natural sequence was no longer taking place, or not at least in the way that it should. The idea of it had formed in his brain; but it was being undermined and spoiled at some point before it could reach full expression. In common with all humanity, his capacity for composing narrative was most powerful during erotic reverie. But the story wouldn't cohere, it was fragmentary and jagged, each detail lost in a morass of *non sequiturs* and irrelevancies. Try as he might, he found it impossible to sustain the forward thrust, to co-ordinate the *dramatis personae*. His mind wandered helplessly through meaningless pictures as if lost in a monstrous art gallery. No effort, no assumed stillness, no fearful concentration could effectively piece together the strands of the story as they separated and spread their looseness. His body lay quiescent, unresponsive to any of the stimuli he mentally applied to it. Soon he abandoned the sequence and forced himself to blank out the pointless images that could only mock him with their half-formed edges and their refusal to materialize. There was no sex left in him. Perhaps in compensation for his newly enforced continence, the impulse itself had been withdrawn. He looked away from his own body, condemning it to oblivion, imagining perhaps that its troublesome actions would disappear once he no longer had it in his sight. He pushed his arms wearily under the pillow that supported his head. A tear welled up in his eye and fell fatly, slowly down his cheek.

I have to stop this endless grieving for my sexuality, he told himself in his mind with some firmness. It's gone. I have to decide which is more important to me. Sticking to my resolution to be celibate and being able to live with myself and my conscience. Or giving in to the demands of sex. Risking it all on one brief encounter . . .

His gaze shifted down again from the ceiling, this time towards his hands that lay flaccid and useless beside his wasting torso. They seemed unnaturally dry, as if they'd been sterilized in harsh alcohol; and the skin was so slow in its elasticity, when he pinched it, that it had the consistency of a decayed marshmallow. Around the base of each fingernail was a stiff cuticle, itself deprived of all moisture, that stuck out painfully and peeled off in strips and ribbons, interspersed with deeper cuts where the flesh beneath was exposed in those places where it was not caked in dried blood.

He pulled idly at first, then with increasing vigour, at a parched hangnail on his thumb. It seemed to have reached the point where half of its length had been rejected by the body, left to die without the sustenance of human juices, a futile and already condemned tissue of a body itself moribund. Gritting his teeth against the not inconsiderable pain, with two fingernails of the other hand he tore carefully downwards until the detached part was once more organically attached to the flesh, a feeling, sentient layer of skin that reacted to the attack on it by smarting sharply and bleeding a copious effusion of blood as if in condemnation of the perpetrator of the self-inflicted torture. The blood welled up, spurted over the glistening nail. (Why was it that the nails of AIDS sufferers were so magnificent, the only part of the tormented body to flourish? Oh yes, and there was snot, which formed itself into hard finger-friendly portions.) Then the blood trickled down the criss-cross drainage canals of the skin's microscopic surface towards the thumb-joint, thinner there in consistency than where the angry weal he had exposed glared in scarlet reproach.

Look at you, you foul fucking liquid, he thought in return to himself. To all appearances you're healthy and rich, thick with life-giving cells and perfectly aerated, blood, the staff of life. And yet you're bloody teeming with death. Slowly converting into a stream of liquid as fatal as a Borgia poison. Make thick my blood! Who else but me could even look at you without shuddering? I alone can confront you with equanimity. The damage is done, the mortal process begun and now I'm invulnerable to any further emotional harm from you. While any other person would see in you a terrifying and new risk of dying, a concoction that would threaten to flood their bloodstream with fatal, slow-acting poison . . .

With these morbid and circular reflections, he suddenly jammed his thumb into his mouth and sucked vigorously, anxious to ingest as much of the blood as he could. He alone in all the world could do this (he knew this to be medically incorrect, but he felt it none the less). It was a kind of sacralization of his blood, to drink it in defiant sacrifice of his own life – not as in the Eucharist, where it was a symbol of resurrected life, but as one of imminent death, death for which he felt so careless and resigned. The taste of the blood clung to his tongue, the tainted, pullulating blood, the blood that bled with its own blood . . .

He wished Venetia would come back and talk him through this craziness. Why had she chosen today to disappear on a shopping expedition in Kensington High Street?

The pain he'd inflicted on himself came back to reassert its immediacy, its dominance over the vagaries of amateur metaphysics. He licked at the wound like a determinedly calm cat, in slow, deliberate strokes, and then left the thumb stuck into his mouth in what looked like nothing so much as an attempt to recapture the classic serenity of secure childhood. This was how he must have appeared to his mother as she gazed at him with the ferocious love of all motherhood. Except that now his eyes were cold, sad and distant, imprinted with despair and far from the innocent hopefulness of childhood. However much he smiled today, however much he tried to radiate a kind of tranquillity, his expression betrayed the deepest wound of his sentence of death. Now, lying prostrate, with his gaze on the ceiling and beyond, his thumb placed immovably in his mouth, Jerome somehow emblematized the spirit of Disease. He was declining towards the cancers and pneumonias that would destroy him, sliding towards death, dragged unerringly and without recourse along the *via crucis* towards the Golgotha of the isolation ward.

Venetia eventually returned and came into his room with womanly bustle. She drew back the heavy curtains. Sunlight flooded the rich reds and aquamarine of the Turkey rug. She gave Jerome a big hug, there where he lay, distracted and motionless on the bed. Feebly as he responded, she remained determinedly cheerful. An only partially forced smile played on her lips; and there was no hint in her expression of the misery that afflicted her as inescapably as it did Jerome. She sat on the bed, projecting a cosy jollity, ready for a chat, anything that might distract them from the destroyed core of their lives.

'Listen, Venetia,' Jerome said wearily. 'I know you won't want to hear this. I can sense how you've come in here to help me along. But I've just got to say it. Half of me is reminding myself that dwelling on pessimistic thoughts makes things worse. But I can't be intellectually dishonest, I can't ignore the truth. Please listen.'

Venetia nervously shifted her position on the bed and placed her hands solicitously on her lap. This was indeed not what she wanted to hear. But he had so effectively pre-empted her objections.

'You know this terrible gloomy tendency I have of making lists of problems when I'm down? Well, I think this one is the most comprehensive yet. It's not self-pity that's produced it. Just that I'm looking at things with a peculiarly stark intensity. Don't worry too much, it'll pass as it always does. Don't interrupt me, I need to say it all in sequence; it's prepared inside my head and I don't want it to take a different or unexpected direction.'

She smiled tenderly. No more was needed to reassure him.

'Well, this is it. What I've got to face – and you, too, of course. First, I'm going to have to spend the rest of my life' (he would have said 'what remains to me of life', but that did smack of self-pity) 'in and out of hospital. Having treatment, radiation, drugs. I'm going to have to look on helplessly as the cancer spreads through my body. My illness will be increasingly apparent to everyone, you, me, the outside world. I have no sex life. None of that extraordinary white-heat intensity of feeling. I can't even have the solace of a drink. I shall never fall in love' (and a certain embarrassment came into his voice as he said this to the woman he loved). 'Nobody will ever fall in love with me. Of course the love that we have means that that doesn't matter so much as it would to others. But it's a horrible fact none the less, an awful limitation *of life*.' He paused momentarily, then gazed at her intently. 'I have very little money of my own. I shall have even less in the future now that I'm not able to work. I'm always going to live at the edge of life. I have no future.'

He had intended to elaborate on what he meant by that last despairing utterance, but he saw now that, in doing so, he would only lessen its impact on Venetia.

8

Mute Preference

His eyes bulged slightly, exophthalmically, more with madness than any mere thyroid imbalance. They were large and round, unsubtle and inexpressive. Their focus seemed infinite. Venetia found herself incapable of understanding whether they rested on her (and the brain behind them was therefore taking her in) or whether she was just the first in a set of theatrical flats stacked behind her in series. It was eerie not to know whether you were a part of regular, empirical optics or an element of a never-seen experiment in perspective and relativity. The uncertainty left the question of Jerome's inert state of mind unresolved, insoluble, in effect – especially since he had descended into a flamboyant and terrifying mutism. Venetia had found him lying in bed crooning, croaking in a feeble voice *'Col sorriso d'innocenza'*, the mad scene from *Il Pirata* to the accompaniment, unheard by Venetia, of his Walkman. The tears poured silently down his sunken cheeks, a watery descant to the plangent dirge of madness.

His decline had begun several days before. It had not seemed to have a physical cause. Indeed, he'd remained relatively free of the malaise and fevers of lymphadenopathy, and Venetia had allowed herself to imagine that he was battling successfully against the persistence of the virus. He had seemed to succumb more to a restless dullness of spirit. Many of the things Venetia said to him met only with a blank response, all the more alarming as he had been a man of such conversational energy. The slump in him was like the gradual deflation of a vital, liberated creature of the air; and Venetia found herself to be helpless in the face of this collapse. His counsellor, still ill at ease with and confused by Jerome's intelligence, had warned him that he seemed to be verging on clinical depression, and Jerome, apathetically, agreed.

'There doesn't seem to be much I can do about it,' he said, and smiled without humour. 'I feel so inert, so incapable of helping myself. The harder Venetia tries, the worse it gets. I just want to curl up, and let it happen.'

'But you're normally so combative,' Dr Carr insisted. 'You've got all these reasons to get you through. You know as well as I do that this is probably just a trough, an ordeal, a *stage* in the whole thing which you'll get through.'

'Yes, I know that,' Jerome said, with such lassitude that it seemed as if he were only answering in order to humour and deflect an importunate helper. 'And one day I'll look back on this and wonder how I could have let myself succumb so weakly. It'll be like a past, historical episode in a long story. I can *see* that, and I can see too that I'm heading for a really rough time. One I'm giving *myself*. But I just can't *act* on that knowledge. My will has packed up. I'm not sure I want to survive. Sometimes I think that dying of AIDS would be a kind of solution, or a release, a convenient, exact resolution of my rather messy life. I think if I were an animal, I'd have just given up by now and turned to the wall and died.'

He relapsed into a wide-eyed silence. Dr Carr, disconcerted, uncountenanced by his gaze and by the direct, unfiltered expression of his despair, wondered whether he should dispense some kind of chemical anti-depressant. Tentatively he described to Jerome the effects of a tetracyclic drip; but then withdrew it as a serious proposal when Jerome obstinately refused.

'No drugs,' he said. 'I can't bear the idea of surrendering. Losing control of myself.'

Yet that was exactly the process that had already begun, as he himself would have acknowledged with his customary lucidity. His will was sliding away, not imperceptibly, but clamorously, almost proclaiming its independence from him. It was the quantity which most recurred in his self-analyses at this time; and he chose to ascribe his undeniable worsening to its abandonment of him.

Already in these sessions with Dr Carr, Jerome had begun to reveal secondary, symbolic indications of real depression. His sentences had become shorter, and seemed to be uttered with difficulty, breathed out with shallow and irregular stress in a tone of voice that was uncharacteristically quiet. He had stopped looking at his interlocutor (except when he became too conscious of his wayward, despairing focus and deliberately forced himself into a compensatory stare). His body seemed to have become angular and awkward, only finding its natural disposition when spreadeagled loosely on a bed. He was becoming clumsy and abstracted, not noticing details which his novelist's mind would otherwise have absorbed and digested. Sleep claimed him more and more.

Venetia's usual remedies seemed fatuous even to her. Jerome had gone beyond the point when he could be cajoled into normality by agreeable treats and domestic homilies. She found herself looking furtively at her lover. Often, on the point of mouthing some inadequate sentence of reassurance, she would rein herself in, only to wonder despairingly whether *something*, however crass, was better than nothing, the mere act of comfort more important than its unconvincing words.

Now, lying on a sofa surrounded by discarded distractions – a book of architectural drawings, a bowl of pistachios, two coloured pens, a volume of Balzac's *Études philosophiques* – he had reached a plateau of supreme desolation. He was utterly disconnected from outer reality, as if someone had cut a power-bearing cable between him and the sensory world. His hands desultorily smoothed the pages of the drawings, but his eyes saw nothing of what they portrayed. It was as if he was trying to recapture a sense of belonging to the world of phenomena only to be frustrated in his attempt by fastidious, determined impostors plucking at his sleeve to pull him back into vacancy. After a while he bowed his head and, propelling his body forwards and upwards, as if he might otherwise have remained forever sitting, he rose and departed slowly and deliberately for the greater security of his bedroom.

Venetia at first decided to leave him to his own solitude. Not only was that probably the best therapy, but she was beginning to feel annoyed, both with Jerome and with herself, on account of the fact that, however hard she tried, she could not even glimpse an escape. The present state of affairs could only either continue or deteriorate. Her imagination had provided her with no new approach, no insight into Jerome's predicament, and she resented these limitations, forced, as she was, to recognize her ineffectuality. She sat at her desk and finished a letter. The mechanical routine of writing the envelope and searching for a stamp began to replace and drive out her anguish. She telephoned a friend and arranged to go to an exhibition. Jerome, she persuaded herself, would be grateful that she seemed determined to organize her own life and not make artificial, cloying allowance for his special dependence.

He did not emerge from his bedroom for the rest of the day, but remained there, lying back against his ruffled pillows, his eyes the only points of light in the darkened prison. Had he been normally conscious, his mind would have ranged over the literary echoes of his condition, drawing in the asthmatic Proust and the consumptive Violetta, the Seven Sleepers of Ephesus, Our Lady of the Dormition. Instead, he was conscious only that he seemed to be unconscious, incapable even of the most reflex of actions. He couldn't decide whether, if he were to move the appropriate muscles, send the necessary nerve-signal, a finger or a toe might move in response. He was too inert even to make the test and arrive at a simple physical proof. Nothing seemed to work any longer, neither his brain nor his body: a great heavy night had fallen on him. If I'm going to die anyway, he thought, why not let it happen now? I'm just not enjoying the run-up to it, and if it's going to hit me finally, *anything* would be better than this present state of waiting.

There had been times, in earlier, less clouded moments, when he'd been able to articulate his feelings about despair. He'd even remembered passages of literature which floated in and out of his mind and seemed more or less directed at his own predicament. 'Not, I'll not, carrion comfort, Despair, not feast on thee' had circled reassuringly, only to be driven out by the black-edged 'Comforter, where, where is your comforting?' and 'No worst, there is none. Pitched past pitch of grief . . .' But when this had happened he knew with great clarity that he was observing his own despair, studying it as he would some specimen, and that it had yet to envelop the impotent helpless him who now suffered as much from the void caused by these departing, useless words as by the terror itself. And he could find no words of his own to describe his grief. High Victorian bombast was all that occurred to him: heavy solid words that built a wall about him and, ironically, hid his misery from his own sight.

9

Scena

The chandeliers looked a little dustier, the red plush much balder and the gilding shabbier than he remembered, although his previous visit had been less than two weeks before. Opera houses really show their age, he mused, meaning it more in the sense that they revealed the general symptoms of the current epoch than that they fought a losing battle against time. Even in the precinct of a building theoretically divorced from reality's circumambient squalor, Covent Garden was undeniably a creature of the mid-eighties Britain that throbbed and seethed sullenly outside. The old polarity between the opera house and the cheerfully proletarian vegetable market alongside had been replaced by a gradual inseeping of drab colourlessness which Jerome approved as an egalitarian innovation but scorned as an aesthetic blight.

He was enjoying a period of remission, an asymptomatic phase during which he could almost forget the sword of Damocles, suspended by the slenderest thread, which hung above his tormented head. The signs of illness had receded, except that now there were insistent night-sweats and a periodic ballooning of glands that made it near impossible for him to keep his arms parallel with his side and locked his neck and shoulders in a knotted vice. He had nearly forgotten the small specks of blackish blood in his sputum and the rich dark seams of blood that veined his marbled shit. To all outward appearances, he once again radiated health and energy, a thrusting purposefulness that Venetia thought she could easily grow tired of, accustomed as she now was to the gratifying role of nurse, confidante and friend. In celebration of the relative improvement – what some doctors apparently called the 'flight into health' – they came to thrill to the newest Sicilian prodigy in her role as *Lucia di Lammermoor*.

The first interval they used less to discuss the opera than to absorb the mood of their fellows and get their bearings in this heterogeneous throng. All around them the subsidized fat-cats, bank-rolled by corporations, looked self-confident, although somehow precariously so, beside the committed opera-lovers, distinguishable by the poverty of their dress, the encyclopaedic, metalinguistic sweep of their comments and an air of melancholia around the eyes to suggest that, ironies of fate apart, their own lives were less satisfactorily conducted to climaxes and resolutions than the action of the preposterous libretti they so empathetically followed. So powerful was their obsession with this artistic construct which largely elbowed aside their own real experience, that they were barely conscious of the stolid merchant bankers and real-life Marschallins who invaded their numbers and beamed blankly through concealed boredom, reliant on the authority bestowed by status alone.

The performance so far had failed to catch fire. The combination of business entertainment and restive tourist attraction that characterized the summer season was producing a flat, unimpassioned atmosphere. What it *really* needed, Venetia reflected, was a block of subsidized seats for knowledgeable queens. *They* would soon galvanize the Sicilian canary, they alone could generate the rapport and the excitement in the human voice the singers needed, a claque of catalytic faggots. There *had* been cries of enthusiasm from the amphitheatre, determined, assertive cries of approval. But these emanated from impoverished queens, dotted ineffectually around the cheaper side-seats, too far from the stage to counter the flaccid response of the dim bourgeoisie, most of whom knew no Italian, could barely distinguish between a tenor and a baritone and thought that fioritura was some kind of Milanese jam, or perhaps something to do with flower-arranging.

Jerome, for his part, had begun to surrender to the music. He allowed it to sing with its own voice, unmixed with his critical reflections. It struck him with great force, soothing, startling, soaring, moving him with its simple and unashamed emotivity. His turmoil of passion was returned to him, made sense of, rendered coherent by the formal conventions of Donizetti. Certainly it was a passion tamed, domesticated until it fitted those conventions; but none the less it had the pulse and core of emotional suffering that he recognized as his own. He found himself wondering why he had reacted in this unusual way. Normally, as he knew so well, he remained detached and critical, his scepticism carrying all before it. Listening to opera, he would worry over a slight someone may or may not have given him two days earlier, or whether Lucia had a Morningside accent; or if that butter mountain of a Delilah really had had such execrable taste in curtains; or how on earth anyone could fall for a pathetic, self-effacing dumbo like Mimi (a Sphinxian riddle answerable only by heterosexuals); or how Violetta managed to disguise the ravages of consumption and keep her clients interested (for clients they undoubtedly were). He was ashamed at such questions. They showed him how earthbound he was, how literal-minded and obsessed with tail-chasing mundanities, while the world was able to yield itself, uplifted by the music to an ecstatic elation that obliterated banal concerns. It was, then, with some pleasure that Jerome found himself uncharacteristically moved, reduced to the simple receptivity of a child. He thrilled to the warlike *Cabaletta*, felt anger at the brother's unreasonableness and succumbed to the pathos of the heroine as she swooned and implored understanding from the implacable forces of honour.

But the agreeable trance was not to last. During the second interval, Jerome found himself battered and hemmed in beside the double staircase of the Crush Bar and brought back to the reality of his irritable, impatient self. His temper rose. He became again a candidate for dying. More than that, he quickly lost sight of the artistic purification he'd come through; and his mind filled up again with images of sickness and frustration. In effect, the cleansing by the music had been so thorough that the return of his daily concerns had an especial force and shocked him. Had they become so utterly inescapable that even opera could not dispel them? God, all that circular argument, the dreaded impasse again! He clutched on to a banister and waited for Venetia to arrive with a refreshing glass of white wine.

He had time, though, before her return, to reflect on the events of the previous evening. At Venetia's insistence they'd gone to dinner with some old and intimate friends. It was important, she felt – and he agreed – for him to maintain such contacts and remind himself of the realities of ordinary life. There would be no question of tension, for the friends knew of Jerome's secret.

Up to a memorable point in the evening, the beneficial resocialization of Jerome had forged ahead. They had talked benignly of holidays and children, books and plays, discussed the absurdities of friends' relationships, enjoyed the rich but somehow astringent sauce that smothered the tender chicken. He hadn't suspected at any point that the subject of his illness was being tactfully avoided and that, paradoxically, it therefore figured very large in their minds, like some great volcano they were sidestepping, eyes averted, slyly pretending it wasn't there. A benevolent neutrality reigned. Then, unexpectedly, Sarah had asked: 'When might you go back to San Francisco?'

'We don't have any plans yet,' he answered. 'It depends on various things. David's getting rather firmly entrenched in his school here and it seems like a good reason for staying on a while. Anyway, I'm not feeling that wonderful at the moment, and it would be a terrific upheaval going back to California. It's hard for us to make plans, the future's so uncertain, I might not even be around to go back.'

Jesus, why had he *said* that? Couldn't he have stopped two harmless sentences back? No, he had subliminally wanted her to understand the precariousness of his life, then compounded his error by revealing it in pseudo-flippant breezy phrasing that seemed to make light of death. The throwaway delivery had misfired, drawn even more attention to itself than if he'd indulged genuine fears.

Sarah, always impatient with nonsense and self-pity, said quietly: 'Jerome, that martyred tone really doesn't suit you'; and he'd screamed inside, as he now, unexpectedly,

420

screamed out loud to Venetia as she innocently handed him his glass in the crowded bar: 'How the fuck would *she* feel if she was coughing up blood and had blood pouring out of her arse? How *dare* she?'

Nervously Venetia looked around to see the consternation on the faces of Jerome's immediate neighbours. One woman stood, her glass frozen at a point not far from her lips; her eyes were round and questioning, horror-struck but still discreet. Her companion, trying not to look, furtively, manfully plunged one hand into a pocket to extract a muffling, distracting handkerchief. All around were embarrassed movements, a reorientation of heads, a drawing away from this outburst, so inexplicable and obtrusive for lacking any kind of preamble save inside Jerome's own mind. Had it something to do with the action on stage? Was it some hysterical reaction to Lucia's distress at being made to marry a man she did not love?

In her embarrassment, Venetia spilt her own glass and clumsily, confusedly pulled Jerome to one side. This irritated him further, and he glowered at her as if it had been she who'd made the original wounding attack.

'Darling,' she began, 'surely we had all this out last night. I don't see any point in going all over it again. I'm sorry it happened, I can understand how much it upset you. But there *are* going to be things that upset you, things people say or do. And you've just got to be strong enough to surmount them.'

'Don't be so fucking magnanimous, Venetia.' His face was dark and bitter, and his eyes strayed from hers. His anger lurked in the tigerish mask, the lips which quivered with suppressed venom. This, Venetia recognized, was the Mr Hyde of him, the triumphant creation of his AIDS demon. He was transformed into a creature of darkness and festering terror, transformed by a sickness that had invaded his mind in its mission to kill. No gentleness or civility overlaid his expression, for it was reduced now to its rawest elementality. Venetia, accustomed to a loved and familiar face she could no longer see, was forcibly reminded that there was indeed a new dualism in Jerome. The two facets of his personality could not coalesce, but only spring apart in a violent fission.

He had lost, permanently now it seemed, his singular, unified charm.

'I'll never forgive her,' he said. 'Never. How *dare* she accuse me of being martyred, how *dare* she? My God, if she had *half* my symptoms she'd be screaming her head off! Cow, I hope she gets it; *then* we could put her to the test.'

'Don't, darling, please don't,' Venetia entreated. She didn't dare to follow her instinct and stroke his forehead and hair, wiping away the aggressive sweaty frown disfiguring his brow. He had so utterly withdrawn from her, so clearly lumped her among the uncomprehending forces that swelled humanity at large. She had become a hostile traitor, allied with the world which believed he should be stripped, humiliated, sequestered, quarantined, annihilated. There was nothing she could do to regain her ascendancy, only stay there and not abandon him, not let the rancour infect them both, show that, however hurtful and miscalculated the ill-expressed feelings of the world, she would remain as a bastion of love.

'I just don't *need* that kind of thing,' he went on. 'That pretence of concern, that pseudo-liberal benevolence, that terrible nannying in her voice, like some bloody ward-sister. Shit!' He turned away and watched the embarrassed bystanders dispersing, seeking the safer ground from this maddened rabid animal with its blood obsession. His eyes dismissed them from under his lowering brow like a disgraced general in defeat counting off deserting soldiers. He often underestimated how fiercely formidable he could be; on this occasion, though, he was exploring his capacity to the maximum.

'I'm sick of being brave. I'm sick of being so understanding. I don't want to *have* to see things from other people's points of view. I'm no hero, all I want to do is be able to live for *five minutes* without having to think about AIDS!'

Calculating that his mood could not last, Venetia waited and projected a semblance of calm as she too watched the crowd over the rim of her glass. Her eyes were thoughtful and vigilant, and there was something defensive in the posture she adopted, one hand clasping the elbow of the arm that held the glass. It was not that she seemed to be disowning Jerome;

422

she merely appeared to have risen above the embarrassing scene and to have reached a stage of sophisticated detachment from so unimportant a manifestation of his spirited temper. It was as if it was his right to give voice to such anger, the natural expression of sincere emotion unencumbered by the attenuated niceties of the opera.

'Come on, darling, you'll have forgotten all about it in a few days' time,' she said, at the point when it seemed as if the thunder of his mood had definitively begun to pass by and become a distant rumbling memory. She calculated, with great precision, the exact moment at which, by her contribution, she could accelerate the difficult process of mollification. 'I know it seems terrible and unforgivable right now; I *do* understand. But you've got to look at it positively, maybe as a chance to show exactly how strong and detached you can be. Please try, darling.'

The bell rang for the final act. Their conversation was curtailed at that moment when a useful truce might have reduced the tension between them. Had it continued, she felt, they might have thrashed out the issue of Jerome's inordinately bruisable sensitivity to some lasting effect. But part of her was simultaneously relieved that she did not now have to find the resources to carry out this purpose.

The volatility of his temper brought about in Jerome a return to the acute emotional and aesthetic receptivity he'd experienced during the first act. He knew, from countless listenings to *Lucia*, that it was at this point that Donizetti took his most blatant risk. With the utmost cruelty, it seemed, he now forced the tenor to sing a farewell aria even as the audience's memories were fresh with the extraordinary bravura of Lucia's mad scene. It imposed an almost unbearable strain on the tenor, who now, in a cavatina of limpid simplicity, had to dispel the odious comparisons with Lucia's pyrotechnic roulades – a hard act to follow. Jerome sat back to observe the performance with the practised, arrogant refinement of an Imperial spectator at a gladiatorial combat.

The tenor was fat and gauche in his movements. Through the penumbrous lighting and the swirl of dry ice in the graveyard one could just discern the sombre shabbiness

of his tattered velvet cloak, a prop with which he made
great play, muffling, tossing, swishing with his clumsy
and ill-co-ordinated arm-gestures. He strode mechanically
through the towering tombstones, stopping periodically to
face the audience head-on and communicate, with almost
incredible unsubtlety, his mood of outrage and despair. He
tottered rather than moved, his legs emerged like graceless
sticks from under his billowing breeches, and a clockwork
aimlessness drove him from this side to that. But then, in
a voice of celestial sweetness, he began to sing. He sang of
the cursèd family to which he was condemned to belong, the
crimes of honour which ran like a bloody vein through their
dynastic past; and of the appalling betrayal of Lucia, who
had so cruelly abandoned him for the husband chosen by
her inhuman brother. His voice soared and floated through
the undecorated legato melodic line, a kind of indefinite
sostenuto that promised to break into a passionate climax.
Jerome had, at the moment when Edgardo's voice rose
above the accompaniment, lost all consciousness of his
own predicament, his own conduct, his own history, his
own self. His breathing grew shallow and tense and he
started forward to absorb every nuance of the aria. Again
his critical faculties were in abeyance; he didn't care in the
slightest degree that the orchestral resources were limited,
the harmonization of the most elementary, the phrasing just a
complacent intensification of Neapolitan clichés. Perhaps, he
reflected later, this was the state of limbo, the transcendence
of the purely rational, the leaving behind of tired old
perceptions, as claimed by the mystical religions. It was a
weightless elevation, a hovering above the plane of truth,
a vision of the realm of beauty uncloyed by the shapes and
sounds of base earth. The human turmoil of passion, self-pity
and acrimony had flown out of his mind. Venetia, who sat
beside him and watched him every now and then, sensed
the unreserved change in his spirit and uttered, not for the
first time, a prayer of gratitude, not specifically to St Cecilia,
but to some amorphous agglomerate god of music, for the
consoling transports that pacified the human breast.

At the mid-point of the aria, its mood changed brusquely
as a shadowy file of mourners crossed the stage and sang

of Lucia's tragic end. Edgardo, heroicized now and rising above the physical handicaps which had made him a creature all too earthly, sang of his incredulous horror and, in a recitative of halting phrases, articulated his growing sense of the implications of her death. She was instantaneously transformed into a suffering, innocent creature whose soul now soared heavenward, spreading angelic wings into eternity. Edgardo's voice throbbed and swelled and made sudden, stricken pauses; he stabbed brutally at the tragic sentiments, using a brazen rubato to squeeze out the effects of his paean of ill-destined love. Venetia realized that the audience was recoiling, finding the Italianate excess too shallow, too contrived in its technical manipulation of sentiment. But Jerome was lost, his head propped in his arms as he leaned intently forward, craning to imbibe the last ebbing waters of feeling. Had a Romantic caricaturist observed him in that posture, he would have portrayed the figures of a departing cloud of demons emanating from Jerome's etherealized mind. He had been evacuated by illness, it had withdrawn defeated in mortal conflict with the healing forces of art. Its blackened battalions retreated before the transparent, crystalline purity of his unsullied spirit. Battle had been joined and won. No festering bitterness remained and he was triumphantly arrayed with the trophies of victory for his further, arduous onslaughts against death.

10

Fly-swatting

While the empty days stretched ahead and he persuaded himself that he was merely waiting to die, the winter months closed in and oppressed the spirit further with their cold embrace. One afternoon, staring moodily out of the window at a grey curtain of polluted drizzle, he made a resolution to discover for himself how others afflicted in the same way were reacting, what tactics they were adopting to keep the terror at bay. He hoped, as he sprang purposefully off the window-seat, to find courage, ingenuity, resourcefulness, even humour. But not a solution, for he could never discover that outside himself. Only he could heal his spirit, though the others might inspire him with different ideas.

At first it seemed as if the gay London world had reacted with disbelief. The American statistics had not sunk in. Then, as details of casualties leaked out, organizations were formed: helplines and self-help groups, embryonic counselling services in the hospitals. Yet it was still an oddly disjointed and unrealistic response. One of the stories which most symbolized its inadequacy for Jerome was of an AIDS benefit night, a discotheque organized to raise money for victims. It had turned into an orgy. A roomful of men having sex. No one had seemed aware of the crass and tragic irony. A party wasn't a party unless . . .

But then, insidiously, like a whisper of war, the serious rumours began and there became evident, if not consternation, a kind of dull panic, a sense that an unspoken executioner had taken up his station and obstinately, remorselessly was poised to cut down his victims. Few spoke

426

about it openly; those who did were considered alarmists, drama-queens, prophets of doom allied with fundamentalist crazies. Yet the apprehension was palpable; and could only intensify as the dire casualties emerged.

Jerome, after his own shocking diagnosis, was eventually able to revisit his old haunts. He wished partly to keep a foothold in a world from which he was in effect permanently severed, and partly to observe, unobserved, what was the major thrust of reaction. Having himself been forced entirely to rethink the politics of homosexuality, now that its central prop of free sexual expression was so brutally knocked away, he was interested to see what other thinking gays were up to.

After an absence of several months, during which he'd felt unable to go back to this world, keeping himself sadly but resolutely in the category of 'non-scene queen', he really didn't know what to expect. In melodramatic moods he persuaded himself that it would have become a ghost-town inhabited only by the wraiths of memory. Perhaps there would be a defiant clique determined to dance and chatter and make love as if nothing had happened, a heedless Pompeiian band of imminent corpses. He dreaded the latter sight, for he wouldn't be able to detach it from his cataclysmic vision of a future in which homosexuality itself might be buried, like those very Pompeiian figures, in the ashes of history.

In fact little had changed, in effect, at least to the naked eye. The same tight world survived, the same subjects of conversation. The same assignations were made, with the same overt priapic gestures and sexual body-language. Sharon and Doreen were intact in a thousand production-models.

But Jerome's trained antennae detected deeper signs of unease. He watched and made mental notes in the intervals when he could lose sight of his nervousness that he might meet his old habitués, Doreen and Sharon even, who would look at him with that searing look that meant, 'Your absence has been noticed, speculated about, interpreted. How long have you got?' Swallowing hard in an effort to purge his own fear, he wondered first what had happened to sex.

How could he know? It looked as if it had survived and

would survive – which was more than could be said of many of its participants. Men were obviously still going to bed with each other. But there were almost imperceptible inklings that they *had* absorbed the warning and that their sexual habits were modified, attenuated. The transactions that took place late in the evening seemed a little more complex than before. They were as likely as not to end in frowning, shaking of the head, apologetic half-smiles. More people seemed to be tired, or to suffer from headaches or to have jealous lovers. Many of the guys who dressed up and hung around the bar were manifestly only going through the motions; and far from cruising with serious intent, they were simply enriching their imaginations to colour their solitary, cautious and safe masturbation. Probably they made love to their video-recorders.

There was a distinctly old-fashioned air of monogamy around, of dating and wooing, of permanency newly thought of as a virtue. Many of the men Jerome spoke to had decided, sorrowfully, to cut their losses, shack up with a regular guy and lie low till the going was clear. The race was on to find a partner before you got sick. This seemed entirely reasonable to Jerome (though a decade at least looked like a reasonable estimate for the medical breakthrough and the return to normal). It was, after all, in essence exactly the same as the course of action he'd adopted. It echoed, in his mind, a story of Renaissance Florence. After the death of the ferocious moral reformer Savonarola, Benvenuto del Bianco, a laid-back member of the Council of Ten, turned languidly to a colleague and said with unconcealed relief: 'And now we can practise sodomy again.' The hope was that the scourge of AIDS would one day be burned out as finally as Savonarola's body had been by the fires of justice and that the old familiar sexual licence would gracefully return. AIDS would then be a mere hiccough in the hard-fought struggle in which sexual promiscuity was accepted as a philosophical ideal. But there were other stories to show how there could never be a concerted, neat and rational response to the reconsideration of sex and its sinister link with death. A sensitive friend of Jerome's, happily ensconced in an open relationship, was curtly told by his lover that, if he discovered any sexual infidelity in the future, he would withhold his sexual favours in a parody of Lysistrata. Love and lives were being eaten into by the new canker, the worm that eats the bud.

The sickness was closing in. It was forcing changes, prising friends and lovers apart, destroying, killing.

Conversations which Jerome had seemed to show that there was no longer an automatic assumption that to approach someone was necessarily to declare a sexual interest. He, of course, had a specific and, to him, insoluble problem. A hazard of moving around in these familiar circles. How was he to remain approachable without revealing that he had no choice but to bow out of the sexual game? In a frivolous moment, pretending fascination with a blank wall to deflect the importunate glances of a lost-eyed soldier, he hit on the idea that he could counter by murmuring something like: '*Moi, je ne fais pas l'amour.*' It had everything – self-centred pigheadedness, a wimpish euphemism for sex, and, above all, the supreme antaphrodisiac of French, a language that rated zero on the modern gay-based cruisometer. Surely that would work! He was sick of arousing, involuntarily but fatally, the desire of another and then stalking off, not even bothering to invent an adequate excuse, the man of mystery. He hadn't as yet got far with evolving a strategy for dealing with sexual invitations, the kind that still fluttered thickly at his feet as he dazzled his way through the bars. He'd run out of explanations, and generally now fell back on the cliché of suffering from a headache. Because of that, it was distinctly easier to avoid gay places altogether; for they merely reminded him of his incapacity. He felt marginalized among the already marginalized; doubly stigmatized.

But he had to check this melancholia about his own prospects in the interest of his anthropological study. It was no good being over-sensitive to his own hazards if he was going to arrive at an understanding of the overall picture. Of course there were times when the two so overlapped that he was not able to separate one reaction, the personal, anguished aspect, from the other more disinterested one. Once he found himself in a huge dark room furnished only with scaffolding. Here was the familiar orgiastic scenario from the irresponsible days before AIDS: men crushed against the walls and groaning with pleasure. Christ, Jerome screamed internally, what do I have to do to get them to stop? He wanted to jump up on to a table and harangue them. No hellfire preacher could have matched his hysteria at that moment. He was possessed, racked with anger and despair. Not so much dismayed at the frailty of mankind as enraged to have himself belong to it. He just could not bear to contemplate the survival of backroom sex. It induced a kind of revulsion half-way between moralistic apoplexy and tender, resigned sadness.

The only course of action was to leave the scene of his conflict, to distance himself as fast as he could from these dire relics of the old sexuality. He passed quickly into another room, and astonished himself by the ease with which he expelled the distressing images. He'd thought it would be difficult even to move physically from where he stood, that his feet would be nailed to the floor by impotent rage, that he would be condemned to stay a spectator of these last gasps of morrowless lust. But he recognized now that he had by this stage acquired a new strength, a new capacity for detachment that allowed him, by the simple expedient of walking away, to leave behind these resurgences of hedonism and the insatiate creators of death.

His contact with victims of AIDS continued apace, giving him fresh insights, confirming certain views and overturning others. Out of so many different, private, complex tragedies he came away impressed, as he had expected to be, by the indomitable courage of the sufferers. They had little guidance, save what they could give one another. Their fears went unanswered. The sickness had no precedent. No one knew what to do. No one had ever before confronted the possibility of so many infections invading a terminally weakened system. A catalogue of atypical tuberculosis, pneumonia, cancerous sores, and meningo-encephalitis was commonplace, a day-to-day *via crucis* to be suffered with equanimity born of the fatalistic acceptance of the certainty that death would complete the list.

Buddhism had spread like wildfire in the stricken gay community, or so it seemed to Jerome. There was something

430

tempestuous and irresistible about the fervour with which it was adopted. Gay men whose lives seemed previously to have been dedicated to materialism and self-gratification now gave their allegiance with equal singlemindedness to the teachings of the Bodhisattvas.

Out went the Cuisinart and the Philip Core pornographic prints, the ruched drapes and the Magistretti chairs. In came an extreme austerity, a clean simplicity of line and design that mirrored the Japanese style. Shrines were built, elegant, calming cupboards with silvered surfaces, the symbolic cranes and the offerings of vegetable life. The efficacy of their ritual chanting was secure. They chanted regularly, together and alone, the same symbolic words which brought out their inner wisdom, rehearsed their desire for enlightenment and the revelation of inner truth, the law of life. Problems and uncertainties evaporated to be replaced by knowledge, faith and insight. The final purpose was that the deluded world should secure the same enlightenment and aspire to the great state of universal peace. In consecrating themselves to these ends, the gays utterly threw over the apparatus of their misguided pasts, the 'trappings of the pursuit of power, wealth and meaningless directionless indulgence. It was a formidable process of spiritualization, made easier, for many, by the lurking spectre of death that hung over their old, abandoned selves.

It was easy to understand the attraction of Buddhism. Jerome himself was innately drawn to the vague idea that physical reality was in effect a kind of illusion or error. His illness confirmed him in this feeling, though he never articulated it precisely, content to deny the significance of his body and its dramatic collapse and hope for the prospect of some ill-defined Platonic sphere of divinity. They rattled on about cause and effect, that sure link which underlay everything we experience. Yet it was precisely that issue which most estranged Jerome. Once he had rejected the one cause that was – to many people – most plausibly responsible for his condition, he could discover no alternative. Yet he could never subscribe wholeheartedly to a religious system, however exactly it coincided with his own undeveloped speculations. And besides, as his illness progressed and he discovered his own strength, he was more and more convinced of the notion that one had to confront the awfulness and unfairness of existence on one's own, without recourse to the consoling blandishments of religions devised by other minds – more wise, perhaps, than his, but still other.

The new world into which he now penetrated was one where gay men, infected or not, fervently embraced this ancient system of belief that seemed so peculiarly well adapted to their idiosyncratic needs. Austerity, renunciation, the seeking of enlightenment beyond the body, the maximization of one's assets, all these were injunctions effectively imposed on them by AIDS. But Jerome's intellect could not, would not subject itself to the consolation of a fixed religious system. His integrity demanded that he faced all the unknowables as they were – unknowable, uncertain, never reducible to methodical exploration. It was uncomfortable and unconsoling; but it was also honest. Buddhism worked. It helped. It explained. And yet he could not sacrifice the intellectual rigour which, he told himself, would cut down its certainties like a scythe. In a vain attempt to cure his intellectuality, he read countless pamphlets and textbooks, tangled himself up in Sanskrit mysteries and paragraphs of seductive poetic prose. He read a textbook, Lévy-Bruhl's *La Mentalité primitive*, to try and discover the nature of pre-logical thought. Perhaps if he reverted to the clarity of a savage he would at last see the divine truth. It was characteristic of him to read a book in order to find out how not to be bookish.

But his brain was growing tired. The Buddhists pressurized him, gently but insistently. For each of them Buddhism had provided a solution. The simple equation was that all that was needed was an infinite multiplication of each adherent's certainties and the world would finally understand itself and live in pacific harmony. It was so transparently obvious, so unarguable, that they found his hesitation not so much obtuse as utterly inexplicable.

In answering them, he again found his innate politeness surfacing and preventing him from saying what he actually wished to say. He had no desire to undermine the faith of these sincere, well-meaning converts. Their system was effective and impressive; it could, for all he knew, indeed be based on the revelation of truth. How, then, was he to argue against it, present his objections and reservations, without upsetting their sensibilities and destroying, through doubt, the firm foundations which their shaken lives now seemed to have acquired.

For his attachment was, before anything, to the certainty that nothing was certain. All answers were inadequate, all systems over-simplified. He never wished to suggest that they were a kind of self-delusion; but he insisted, to himself (faced with the impossibility of explaining this to devotees), that the more honest response, the one that mirrored man's condition most precisely was to acknowledge that there were many things one could never know. Life was infinitely untidy, fraught with paradoxes, events some of which seemed to prove the existence of God and others to disprove it. In which, with the existentialists, one had to diagnose this sickness and then, heroically or anti-heroically, live with it, or explain it away, pretend it didn't exist or ascribe it to some elusive divine programme.

He allowed himself to stray into illogicality, confusing providence with the apparent malevolence of God (like Thomas Hardy). His resentful exasperation was like Gloucester's in *Lear*: 'As flies to wanton boys are we to the gods; / They kill us for their sport.' He felt as if he had been arbitrarily marked out for dying, but not before his wings had been pulled off slowly, leaving gaping sockets streaming with blood on which the vengeful God could gorge. Spirituality could help you to confront it, to attempt an interpretation of the chaos. But, in the end, the bravest, truest course was to accept its impenetrability.

Emotionally, too, he found his intellectual reservations confirmed. Adherence to a system seemed to close one off from the extraordinary variety of life. He would never be able to number the phenomena which engaged his lively interest. Even in his periods of sickness, by an immense effort of will he could turn his imagination away, outside, towards some further extraordinariness of life. His Buddhist friends, on the other hand, while much of their talk was of the

433

wonder of creation, seemed cramped by their own formulas. Whatever they spoke of, their views seemed predictable and pre-fashioned. They might be eloquent, persuasive, inspired, yet he found their world-view confined by their dogma and the *ex cathedra* statements of their teachers. In the end, he had to admit, he was bored by it. Bored by the pious patterned statements, bored by the gentle and oh-so-not-judgemental belief in their monopoly of truth. He could not, of course, argue with them using the terms he was used to. The accusation came back that he allowed importance only to his cerebral mind and was suppressing all other faculties of perception; that he was arrogant in listening only to his own lost reason. Unable, then, to engage in debate, unwilling to offend their genuine convictions and their moving desire to offer him succour, he gradually disentangled himself from their tempting meshes and faced again his own solitude and confusion.

Then a Catholic had drawn him aside and spoken to him seriously as if arranging tentatively for his reconversion. 'What we've got to do,' he urged, 'is care for one another, love one another in our sickness, go out and minister to the sick, even help them to die. It's like the plague in Alexandria, the one in the third century, when St Dionysius records how the pestilence brought out all the fraternal love in the townspeople. They came out of their houses to help the sick, to embrace them and care for them, so that they too often contracted the plague. But their mutual love was so strong that they lost sight of their own self-interest, their own prospects of death. Incredible, that anyone could feel such passionate fervour. It could only have been divinely inspired. *That's* what we've got to find, that love of brothers in adversity, the spark of love that mirrors God's own overwhelming love. And pray to St Roch; the saint who helps us overcome the plague.'

Jerome found he couldn't respond adequately. Again he was defeated by the language of fanaticism, of a certainty enviable in itself, yet utterly remote from his own perception. The Buddhists at least seemed to have a romantic truthfulness about them, an intangible, exotic and smiling vision. But the Christian God of mercy and forgiveness had come to look

434

entirely irrelevant. It occurred to him that it would have been easier, in his present circumstances, to believe in some dreadful pagan god, Baal or Dagon, the God of the Midianites, some vengeful, unappeasable god who smote and struck down the weak and the unrighteous. A god who demanded sacrifices, human sacrifices, the systemically destroyed cadavers of men heaped before a bloody altar. That made sense of a sort.

Interested and competent as Jerome was in comparative theology, he couldn't really understand religion. There had been times when he thought he might have had a religious experience, but he couldn't be sure that was an accurate description of its nature. A vague pantheism, a sense of the omnipresence of some kind of regulating force, had once overwhelmed him as he looked out to sea from a Tuscan hillside. The flecks of sea-foam had seemed co-ordinated by an unseen pattern, the leaves of the olive-tree beside him infinite in the intricate design of their veins and sappy fronds, a miraculous matrix of something beyond and outside itself. The feeling was uncannily akin to the revelations of mescalin. He ascribed it, in retrospect, to some sort of natural high, an uncharacteristic impulse which a less critical spirit might have taken for divine afflatus. And then, having gone through that crucial stage of rational rejection, he'd thought that he himself was anyway just a reincarnation of that natural Greek spirit, that anthropomorphism which saw gods in the forms of created things, nymphs in the twisted branches of laurels, nereids in the spumy ridges of breaking waves. It had little to do with religion and belief. Its significance, if it had any, was more a question of mystic paganism and a desire that things should be more interesting than they probably were.

'But don't you *sometimes* think how beautiful the world is?' Venetia had asked feebly. 'Something akin to religious feeling at least? A sense of wonder at the beauty of things.'

'You must be joking, Venetia. Do me a favour. I'm lying here with my world in ruins around me, overwhelmed by feelings of injustice and despair and the utter awfulness of everything, and you expect me to imagine a pretty cow in a field and realize that everything's all right after all! Come *on!'*

He had been forcing and deluding himself into a false religiosity, disillusioned and sceptical as he was about the claims of organized religion. He had wanted to feel that he was not ordinary, not hidebound by the dull and liternal pragmatism of humanism, but susceptible to the extraordinary visions granted to those who opened their spirit to the cosmos. The effort involved in this pretence had cancelled out its efficacy.

At all events, religious belief now receded farther and farther from his mind, filled as it was with the bitterness of injustice. He was close, without acknowledging it, to a kind of Jansenism. Homosexuality, superimposed with AIDS, had a quality of predestination, the inescapable moulding of one's destiny by an external and malevolent magician; and against it nothing, not the strongest assertion of freedom of the will, could prevail. A stern God must have had foreknowledge of the straitjacket he'd slipped so carelessly on to his child-victims; later it burgeoned with illusory sequins, yet its constriction could not be counteracted, only disguised. It cloaked its victims with the fiery poison of Nessus's tunic. And then you died.

The theology of Augustine, dire rumblings of inevitability, combined for Jerome with the incipient puritanism which now accompanied his enforced chastity. The inexplicable purpose and preordained strategy of this avenging God had demanded the sacrifice of his body. It had become useless, dead, a thing of decay. He had lost interest in it. It no longer served its purpose; and he punished it with neglect. He was – though his perception of this was only intermittent – becoming a creature of spirit, hating the gross physicality of his past. Perhaps he was undergoing a real conversion, like Augustine himself, and he would soon thunder with the righteous denunciations of Tertullian against the sins of the flesh. But this, this was the dichotomy. For he clung to the pagan Epicureanism of old in the very depths of his being. This new puritanism had come from afar and battened on to him, eaten into him. It was a little like the AIDS virus itself. It had descended to inhabit his body and

436

then, from within, to destroy the freedom of his spirit, its lightness and philosophical clarity, before replacing it with a dark, incomprehensible fearfulness, a tempest of obscure patristic warnings, ominous inscriptions which told of the implacability of man's arbitrator, concupiscence.

11

Scribble, Scribble

'I've written a letter, a kind of open letter for the gay press. I don't really know why. I get so steamed up about things that I thought it might be helpful to put something down in writing. It's about my reactions to AIDS and the way I think others should respond to it.'

'That's a marvellous idea. You're always so articulate and honest about the things you've been going through; I'm sure you could help people to sort out what they ought to do and think. That sounds a bit patronizing, but I really believe they need guidance from someone who's actually experiencing it. I know I do, I wouldn't have the faintest idea what to make of AIDS if I didn't have such privileged access to you. Though sometimes you make it so complicated. I spoke to Mark Carr the other day. He told me that sometimes he comes out of your counselling sessions with his head reeling, it feels as if you'd bludgeoned him with ideas which may be brilliant and fluent but don't really *solve* anything.'

'There aren't any solutions, don't be dumb. All we can do is terrier away at the problem and try and look at it head-on. Too many people are just lying down and saying, "I just can't understand what's happening to me," and letting AIDS walk all over them for lack of courage and thoughtfulness. Anyway, you wouldn't expect me to abandon my usual cerebral habits when I get struck down by illness, would you? Quite the opposite. Apparently when TB was such a plague there was a theory that the intellectually gifted were the most likely to contract the disease, and what's more, that the consumptive fire which wasted their bodies also made their minds burn with a certain added light. I'm certainly aware that I've never been so intellectually alert as now. So many ideas flood and pour in and out of my brain, except when the pain's too great and that's all I can think about.'

'So what's in this letter? I can't wait to see.'

'Here it is.' He stretched across and picked up two foolscap pages covered with scrawls and erasures. 'I've tried to make it fairly accessible.'

She read though the sheets slowly, nodding occasionally or looking up to meet his gaze as he stared back, anxious for her approval. The text ran:

Oh God, not another article telling us what to do, another dire warning from some gloom-pedlar cranking on about AIDS! Why on earth can't they just let us get on with our lives and enjoy the freedom it's taken centuries for us to win?

Let's not kid ourselves. This is a terrible time. And things have got to change. Our survival, both as individuals and collectively, depends on our taking drastic defensive action. At least during the transitional period until medical research finally conquers – as it certainly *will* conquer – the terrible scourge of AIDS. The gay life-style we've struggled so painfully to defend just isn't practicable any more. It depended on free indulgence in sex, the miraculous liberating, all-consuming power of our bodies. But now, every time you have sex, you could be signing your own death-warrant. Or someone else's. In many circumstances, casual sex can be tantamount to murder. Do we value sexual gratification over and above life itself?

I don't say any of this out of a feeling of hostility or moralizing puritanism. AIDS has not made sex wrong. It hasn't affected its moral status. What it *has* done is to make sex dangerous. If you make love, you may die . . .

I used to believe unquestioningly in the right of everyone to free sexual expression (provided it hurt no one); I know that sex can bring excitement, reassurance, warmth, ecstasy, a sense of purpose, even love. It can express the love we feel for one another. But it has now become inextricably linked to dying. None of us can ever know or understand why this has happened. But we have to recognize that it *has* happened; and that only by abstaining from casual, promiscuous sex can we contain the bringer of death. There's a line in Rochester, the seventeenth-century poet, that expresses this very well, asking the same question about syphilis, which was as fatal as AIDS in his time: 'Is it just that with death cruel love should conspire?' We are facing exactly that same terrible injustice.

I'm relatively lucky. I belong to the last generation for whom promiscuity was a pursuable target, a going concern. You could indulge in it with impunity. I can now temporarily sacrifice my sexual career secure in the knowledge that I've explored the limits of sexuality. I feel great sympathy for younger men, the generation blighted by the shadow of AIDS. For them it's not possible to enjoy such uncomplicated freedom. Often I try and imagine what it must be like for gay young boys. No sooner are they learning to accept their sexuality than they have to face this appalling extra obstacle.

I've been infected with the HTLV-III virus for some time now and have survived OK up to the present. Maybe it's easier for me to practise abstinence and self-control than it is for someone not yet infected. Simply because I don't really have a choice. But my present life of fear, anxiety and pain is not one to which I should allow others to consign themselves without my registering some kind of protest, some warning, without urging the need for caution, understanding and a concern for one another's survival.

Once this is all over we *may*, just *may*, be able to revert to our former lives. Let's hope so. And in the interim it'll be interesting to see how successfully we can redirect the energies we've previously channelled into sex, often to the exclusion of every other aspect of our personalities. And re-examine our attitudes to sexuality as a whole.

What I'm suggesting for the present is that we should either stop having sexual contact (unless we're 100 per cent sure of one another's health) or practise the safe sex that

440

minimizes the risk of cross-infection. For some people – and I'm one of them – it's easier to give things up altogether than to mess around with half-measures. But the important thing is to change, to take account of the new climate, to prove how much you can contribute to the containment of AIDS while the research doctors continue to labour on our behalf. It's a necessary holding-operation, a period of self-sacrifice, until the clouds of illness have cleared.

We're experiencing a trauma, a period of nervous and panicky self-questioning, the erosion of our old free-and-easy values. Splits are beginning to appear in our community, splits which could easily become deep and irreconcilable as those of us who react responsibly to AIDS separate and distance ourselves from those who do not. It may be that a time will come when promiscuous gays are stigmatized and spurned as much by other gays as by the censorious straight world. We *can* prevent this, we *must* prevent it. By doing so we can also prevent the onset of the already vicious heterosexual response to us by proving our ability to modify our habits in the light of a terrible new phenomenon – one which may well eventually hit them with equal force. This crisis has undermined the delicate, easily assailable structure of our sexuality. What we have to do is avoid the punitive, repressive measures which many people would like to see implemented against us. By proving that we will help ourselves, and the wider world, to survive – by our own efforts, listening to our consciences, co-operating, loving one another in the deepest part of our being.

I realize that these feelings will alienate some people. They'll dismiss me as an alarmist and a crypto-straight. With friends like me, who needs enemies? I too find myself surprised by the conclusions I've been forced to adopt. All my adult life I've believed in the natural uninhibited expression of our sexuality. And committed myself to the love of men.

I am ill and may easily die. This has, of course, cleared my mind wonderfully. I have to look at death with equanimity and good sense. Sadly all of us, whether we're healthy or ill, now have to do the same. People are dying out there. Slowly, painfully, abandoned, in a state of complete demoralization. Going blind. Fungus growing inside their heads. Their brains scarring over and decaying. Their lungs searing with pain. This time next year some, maybe several, of your friends may be dead. Thousands will have to die, needlessly, tragically. There is no cure. No vaccine.

From my hospital bed it all seems so blindingly obvious. If there is a way of avoiding ending up like this, sick, frightened and in near-despair, inflicting pain equal to my own on my family and friends, then surely you owe it to yourself to follow that course.

This collective act of self-restraint could be extraordinary. Even if it fails it will have been an experiment worth making. It could show the depth of love, spiritual rather than physical, that gays can have for one another and for humanity at large. Their concern for the future of the human race.

This is a grim ordeal. Let's listen to our consciences and take the necessary steps to confront it. Before it's too late, before it destroys us all.

Venetia read the manuscript through a second time, then handed it back.

'Admirable,' she said. 'It's really good. I agree with every word.'

'But do you think the gays will like it? It's addressed to them, it's their reaction that matters.'

'I think the sensible ones will see the point. I just think anyway it's an irrefutable argument. Anyone can see that something's got to be done. Short of something medical that will actually stop AIDS, the only thing is to take action to control its spread, of course it is.'

'But there's a whole pressure group which goes on about the rights of promiscuous gays. It claims that even *advising* them to practise self-restraint is a kind of discrimination and a denial of their human rights. They even used the word racism, meaning anti-promiscuism, a fabulously inexact usage. They're a really powerful lobby, they could easily stop my letter from being published.'

'You've just got to steel yourself and recognize that they are wrong, it's a kind of crazy extremism, completely untenable. I know you hate to have to admit that anyone's wrong, but if anyone is, *they* are.'

'So you don't think I should change any of it? Is it written in a clear enough way?'

'Yes, it's fine. I can tell that because the first time I read it I began by wondering what style you were adopting, noticing the fact that you'd conscientiously used short sentences and made some slightly feeble concessions to a "proletarian" idiom. But then I got so caught up in the issues of what you were actually saying that I forgot all about the presentation. That must mean it's reasonably coherent and forceful. And I think you've managed to keep the element of condescension out of it. And it doesn't sound too moralizing, just a sensible, unhysterical set of simple proposals. Give it back to me, I'll send it off for you.'

'Hang on a moment, there's another one.'

'My, we *have* been busy. You're going to need me as an amanuensis at this rate.'

'Don't worry, it's only when my blood boils or when I think the pompous pricks need putting down. This one's for *The Times*, a *very* different proposition.'

She took his further offering, a script altogether cleaner and more careful, in deference to its intended recipient.

Dear Sir, I was dismayed by your decision to publish a letter on AIDS (Thursday, March 1st) from a correspondent who revealed himself to be prejudiced, complacent and thoroughly lacking in compassion. My distress was, however, enormously tempered by my pleasure on seeing that his address – Croydon – had been misprinted as Corydon, the name of the celebrated homosexual shepherd in Virgil's *Eclogues*. ('*Formosum pastor Corydon ardebat Alexim* . . .' The Alexis he adored was altogether too unambiguously masculine a lover to be played by Joan Collins. Yours sincerely.

'Now *that* one's got a cat in hell's chance of getting

published,' said Venetia, laughing. 'Really, I sometimes wonder if you're completely sane. You take pleasure in such amazingly perverse things. And what's that?' She pointed at a substantial pile of papers.

'Ah, that's a secret,' he replied. 'Well, not really. I've decided to write some thoughts down, feelings I'm having, things like that. It won't amount to anything. But maybe it'll help me to make sense of the pattern.'

'I guess that's one of the best things you can do.'

She swept aside a coil of hair that hung over her forehead. Such actions helped to punctuate the intensity of their deep discussions, these interchanges so unlike the frivolous banter of the past.

'One thing,' she went on remorselessly, 'is that I'm only just beginning to understand what it means to be gay. Remember how I used to think it was just a negligible deviation, an almost anatomical preference? *Now*, though, I can see how it colours your whole life. I think one's whole identity is determined by it, it precedes everything else. But it's taken this extra dimension, this ghastly crisis, to make me see it. I've been *forced* to think about it seriously whereas before I just let things slide and thanked God that all seemed to go so swimmingly. It's hard for straight people to understand what it's like for gays, from the *inside*, I mean. It's easy maybe the other way round. If you're gay, you're constantly transposing everything because everything you see, every model of behaviour, is conceived in a straight language, all the stereotypes are straight. So it's no longer an act of imagination to understand what it means to be straight, it becomes a knee-jerk reflex. But straight people never have to make that alignment in reverse. So they never do.'

'That's absolutely right. Us gays get a little too much practice at transposition, duplicity. Sometimes I think we're in danger of developing permanent double vision. It's a kind of bilingualism, with all the confusion that entails – and as you know, *that* can send children mad. There are compensations, of course. We're forcibly trained to see things from more than one perspective, our instincts get sharpened, our sensitivity finely honed. And then we have an insight into the minds of women which many straight men never acquire. There's an American writer who once said that only a gay could go into a room and know how *all* the people in it were feeling, men and women.'

'You've certainly demonstrated that in our life together. I've known all along that nobody could understand my feelings, almost feel them before I did, better than you. It's been the safest and the loveliest thing in our life. I never felt betrayed by you, never, even when I didn't see you for days. And my trust came from the knowledge that you knew me and loved me inside out. Oh, my darling, what'll happen if something goes wrong, if I'm left alone with David? I'll be like half a person, a shadow, darling, how shall I be able to face it?'

'One day we'll try and face that,' he said gently. 'Of course there will always be David and your duty to him to pull you through. But not now, don't let's panic. The more positively and optimistically we look at this bugger, the more likely it is to go away, or at least stay dormant.'

He smiled at her and leaned over to wipe away a tear that had swollen in the corner of her eye. Her forehead was furrowed, half with anxiety, half with the brave effort to forestall anxiety. Her smile struggled back at him. She felt proud, secure, protected, basking in his masculinity – a true, deep, manly quality that made nonsense of the assumptions of sexual prejudice.

'One thing we must never do,' he continued, 'is let ourselves grow apart. Sometimes I get used to the solitude of illness and that intensifies my isolation. At my worst I feel that no one else can possibly understand. Donne said something like that: "As sickness is the greatest misery, so the greatest misery of sickness is solitude." But then, of course, I can always resurrect myself by the knowledge that you do, that you understand things even while they're happening to *me* – not you. If I show any signs of prising myself apart from you – and let's face it, I might do, all my actions and thoughts are a little erratic – you must bring me back to the fold. I know it's difficult, we both of us know you've already had some hard times trying to do just that. You'll have to persevere and be patient with me, love me even when I'm unlovable, help me over the stony ground.

I know you will, you're the one with the strength and the courage.'

He knew that he had originally been destined to be alone. He was so extraordinary, so perverse. So easily bored, so frustrated by the stupidity of others. His curiosity about them was a thing of seconds, a momentary flicker, and, once satisfied, it dissipated entirely. Had he accepted this as an unalterable fact about his disposition, he'd have resigned himself to a life of solitude in which he would only sporadically touch upon the lives of others, happier, in the last analysis, to lead a life of intense imagination inside his own head, safe from the inroads of vulgarity and the idiocy of life. A barricade erected around him to ward off the importunate world. Only Venetia's love had changed this destiny of extremism.

After she had gone, he returned in mind to the questions he'd raised in his heartfelt letter. He had little doubt that it expressed with some precision the feelings and ethical reflections he'd experienced. Were it ever to be published, it was hardly likely to stir up much controversy. But, he reminded himself, it's human nature to believe one's own opinion to be correct, that one has the monopoly on truth; and he needed to think critically, conscientiously about the implications of what he had said.

The impulse of his letter had come from his idea that the advent of AIDS necessitated a reversion of attitudes to sexuality. This was an opportunity, one which could be seized positively and constructively, for questioning the old indulgent morality that defined men almost exclusively by their genital prowess, by their bodies alone. Once that opportunity had been seized, he felt, the moral miasma surrounding AIDS might be dispelled a little. The homosexual world could take stock of itself and its future, and emerge with some reviving ideas about the balance between body and spirit.

All the same, Jerome wished with all his heart to deflect the moral attack being mounted on homosexuality itself. It was true that hostile critics could use this new disease as ammunition, by means of distorting, false logic and slogans that sounded convincing but reinforced stupidity. Jerome was determined that these attacks should fall away like the blunt arrows they were. It was not homosexuality itself which had to be reviewed, it was homosexuality seen in the light of a deadly illness to which it could fatally contribute. The ethics of the case must arise from the sickness itself. If any moral conclusions were to be drawn, they must originate in the connection between AIDS and a particular form of homosexual behaviour. The morality of AIDS needed to be teleological, the rightness or wrongness of the case determined by the goodness or badness of *consequences*, rather than an ontological one, according to which there were self-substantiating, self-evident axioms of truth (this or that is right, whatever happens subsequently). What was needed was an ethical response that would leave homosexuality inviolate, and yet would prick the consciences of those whose actions most aggravated the epidemic. An inveterate respecter of personal freedom, Jerome baulked at the idea of *regulating* behaviour, whether through legislation, duress or any semi-official force. He found most criminal sanctions fairly rebarbative. But *conscience*, that loving but critical companion that accompanies everyone in all their actions, conscience *could* be activated and could make everyone see clearly that what we do does have both moral and practical consequences; and that those consequences should determine our view of the action itself. The more he thought about it, the more obvious it became. And yet his temperament was such that he hesitated to propagate his theory, doubting his right to impose it even as an issue for debate. It was a matter less of cowardice than of politeness.

'Politeness, in the context of AIDS!' he cried out to himself. 'I must be crazy! All this thoughtful heartsearching and meditation, and then I destroy it by being scared it might be *rude* to join battle. Wee, cowering, timorous beastie! . . .'

With his thoughts proceeding on these self-critical lines, he began to regain his convictions. Whatever consequences the letter might have, he was prepared to argue his position. Not openly; he was not yet ready to declare his own illness and have his privacy as a patient intruded upon (and the positions of Venetia and David, to whom he owed his

447

primary duty, jeopardized). But he would wield his pen with courage and conscience.

Others might take upon themselves the role of Spokesman. Men who could inspire and change the minds of their listeners. He, a mere intellectual humanitarian, could not aspire to such a role. It was better left to the charismatic, the men of eloquence. His modesty would not allow him to see himself in that heroic mould. Were he to propose himself as a public spokesman on AIDS, he would incur all sorts of justified, and unjustified, attacks. He had the wrong kind of mind. His sentences were too convoluted. He belonged to the wrong class. He wasn't a proper gay. He had no positive message of hope. He had the wrong voice. He was dying.

He must, then, leave the arena to those qualified to take up arms. His gifts, such as they were, belonged to his pen alone in the silent privacy of his isolation.

This honest self-appraisal was painful to him. He might have achieved historic stature, saved lives, bettered humanity, had his talents been differently disposed. But his was a small, tormented voice, confused further by sickness and the fear of dying. He owed it to himself to keep his distance.

12

Unwelcome Guest

He had, in fact, been amazed and delighted by the ready affection with which people treated him during his illness (although, at the same time, he recognized the irony in the fact that he needed to be surprised by this reaction). They had gone out of their way to make him feel loved, made a point of kissing and touching him, asked discreetly and sensibly about his state of health. With some of them, it was true, Jerome nourished the suspicion that they acted out of dubious motives. There was a voyeuristic element in their concern. Occasionally they showed that their attitude was in some degree an excuse for demonstrating their charitable bleeding-heart liberalism, and that his sickness was an ideal focus for their undirected and underused curiosity and solicitousness. AIDS's sensational nature provided them with a frisson of excitement as they proved, to themselves and to one another, their capacity for embracing the leper. Like holy hermits, they clasped his body to their own, less out of unaffected pity than for some obscure personal purpose.

His illness had such literary cachet to these observers that he could readily excuse their mixture of voyeurism, detachment and shock. The impression he had of their temperate, sensible concern was one that he could easily imagine growing from their incomplete vision of his condition. They, of course, viewed it only momentarily; he lived with it for twenty-four hours a day. They could absorb it as an astonishing new hazard of contemporary life; he felt it growing and spreading through his defenceless body.

'No one can do my worrying for me – although sometimes

449

I think you're doing your level best,' he had said to Venetia.

The limits to vicarious feeling made him feel his isolation all the more acutely. Some friends came close to an understanding of the utter blackness; but, unlike Venetia, they could not plunge headlong into his affliction and experience it as if it were their own.

Once he had understood this, he was better able to cast off his scepticism and see that the gentle charitableness of his friends was as much as they could ever offer for his consolation. One couldn't go on being a cause for ever. There were earthquakes and Ethiopian famines to worry about. The distress he aroused was a limited commodity; and it was really too painful to be reminded of his faint chances of survival.

He had lost, in addition, his former role as the token gay who knew everything and anyway wasn't really gay, otherwise why would he hang around with Venetia? In the past, this had been a considerable meal-ticket. He had a function, a social niche, which depended on his apparently 'safe' homosexuality, somewhere half-way between a court jester, a walker and an encyclopaedia (if such an unusual triangle existed). Now, though, he was preceded by a distress signal, a mark of Cain that flared in front of him, and he could no longer provide the effervescent froth to which his friends customarily believed themselves entitled. Even though there was little discussion of sickness, it still hung like an undissipated cloud over their conversations. Given this inescapability, it was easier, they reckoned, simply not to expose themselves to this kind of pressure.

For AIDS had become the ultimate embarrassment. It seemed irrelevant to civilized society. It was ill-mannered and disruptive. It thrust its gaunt, lesioned face in through the lighted window behind which the world held its party.

13

Unwanted Visitor

After a month – more than a month – in hospital, his resistance had crumbled and he found himself speaking in a hoarse croaky register lower than any he had heard in a raven. It was the only sign of weakness he allowed himself. One of his strengths – for Jerome, despite his compliant exterior, had infinite mental resources – was to accept the blows dealt by a malign fortune and shoulder them as they struck one by one, time after time, until the heap of them, taken *en masse*, would have seemed impossible to sustain. There was, he admitted, something of the pit-pony in his mentality. He would not have gone so far as to state that he was ennobled, improved or sinew-stiffened by adversity. That would have been too redolent of the England he half-despised. But there was in him a definite unreadiness to acquiesce, and a willingness proudly to defeat his adversaries, whether they came in the form of queer-bashing skins or protein-coated retro-viruses. Yet now even Jerome was forced to concede a margin of defeat. So much had been done to him, so much said to him, so relentless was the work of the wrecker that lived inside his body.

It had been some time before he felt able to tell Dr Durkheim about the spot on his leg. Anyone as prone to moles as Jerome had always been might have been justified in attaching no importance to a small, round brown mark as insignificant as the birthmark that lay several inches away. With the peculiar sensitivity that accompanied his enforced self-awareness, however, he was gradually less able to ignore the presence of something unmistakably sinister. First he observed that it was not in fact one spot, but two, a larger one with an appendage, and that they lay together with the exact topography of the pretty Greek islands of Naxos and Paros. However much he pressed the spot, it emitted no pain or soreness; it was merely as if it had taken up residence as an unobtrusive squatting neighbour, inoffensive but disturbing – especially to an inmate invalid who knew what he was looking for. He stroked away the curling hair around it to expose its full configuration and, bending down intently, looked hopefully for the blood-vessels that would define it as a mere vasculitis, or even a simple mole such as the one Venetia so uncomplainingly wore on her shoulder-blade. He peered at the hardness that ended at its circumference and seemed to denote foreignness, a possible malignity, something that meant more than what it was. Around it there was no inflammation. The greenness of his veins throbbing beneath the skin seemed unaffected; and he looked in vain for signs of bruising. No, it was just an odd spot, an apparition which at this stage almost gave more grounds for concern to his narcissism than to his hypochondria.

'Nothing to worry about, I'm sure,' said the reassuring voice of Dr Durkheim. 'Although I think you were absolutely right to bring it for me to look at. No problem, no problem at all.' He squeezed the flesh around the spot and looked at it from all angles. 'Though I think, to be *absolutely* safe, we ought to take a biopsy and send it to the lab for analysis. I *know* they'll just come back with something like a non-specific vasculitis, it happens all the time. But just in *case*, just to be *absolutely* sure. And you needn't worry about it hurting, we just inject a little local anaesthetic and whip it out clean as a whistle. Hardly even bleeds. OK?'

Jerome was forced, as so often, to interpret the breezy terms of a diagnosis. In a world where one was 'popped into' a brain-scanner and 'whirled off' to a cancer ward, where the phrase 'you might have a few problems' meant 'you might easily die', you needed to be careful to interpret the private language of medico-optimism as rigorously as if it had been an obscure Pali text. For a man who normally spoke and conversed at great speed, Jerome's reactions were uncharacteristically slow as he weighed up the absurdly reassuring words. Conversing with doctors had come, in his experience, to resemble ordinary dialogue as little as classicism resembled romanticism. In the first place, you needed to enter in on it with a fixed and stolid agenda, the definite sense of your own illness (even if, by chance, you happened to feel rather well that day). There was the need to challenge the first duplicitous term. Without it the session turned into a mutual clucking of contented hens happy to confront nothing deeper than their scratched-up feed. Then one had to stick defiantly to one's point as the doctor trailed off into specialism and obsessions, diagnoses he had made years earlier, the state of research at the centres for disease control, or the similarities between your neuralgia and his wife's hangovers. A strict catalogue had to be written carefully inside one's head, symptoms and questions, each one to be ticked off through the doctor's blustering replies and tangents. But it was above all important to remain sceptical about the deformation of language that went into the practised smile and the unshockable gaze. The truth lay concealed several layers under the padding of an acquired manner, an innate benevolence, or even (and in Dr Durkheim's case, Jerome suspected this certainly to be so) a carefully disguised terror of mortality. An AIDS patient needed, after all, to view his incipient illness with the utmost possible calm. The delicate and unexplained relationship between the nervous system, the psyche and the cells of the bloodstream was one in which the patient had to force the first two to generate the health of the latter by an act of will. It was no cause for surprise, then, that the doctors who cared for him should use terminology such as one might otherwise keep for the nursery. They were also, it had to be said, more than a little terrified of so formidable a patient. If they had ever been tempted to think securely that their province of medicine was a matter of inarticulate, alienated derelicts, one paragraph of Jerome's forceful self-analysis was enough to disabuse them. His habitual politeness and restraint did not extend to those who were entrusted with his life.

The biopsy was indeed painless, and the friendly warmth of the male nurse who held his hand made it pass off as a mere pinprick. Jerome was astonished at this, having worked himself up into a storm of fear. He had based his assessment of what a biopsy was on his own experience, four years before, of two liver biopsies – operations that had left him rigid with pain and the sensation that his body was a mere collection of butcher's offal to be pushed and sloshed at will into new and agonizing conjunctions. Now, however, he bounced vigorously off the bed, feeling only a cold numbness around the spot. All that remained was to cultivate a steely indifference to the outcome.

He would have bicycled home that day, only his ass had been so painful recently that he couldn't trust it to the motion of a saddle on London's pitted streets. Blood was still marble-veining his shit and trails of cloudy mucus clung to its dark mass. Each time he forced himself to undergo the agony of shitting he found that its passage down the rectum was interrupted by raw areas of bleeding that made him gasp and contract his sphincter. Dr Durkheim was obliged to hand Jerome over to a surgeon for this new symptom. When he himself tried to prise apart the anus with gloved fingers and insert the terrible proctoscope, Jerome uncharacteristically gave way to tears and screamed at him to stop. The surgeon fared little better, despite smearing a freezing jelly as liberally as possible; and he was forced to conclude that the examination, let alone the treatment for what was probably a rectal fissure, would have to be carried out under a general anaesthetic. Jerome, conscious that the pain barrier had undeniably been reached, then passed, resigned himself to a further stay in hospital, a further waste of his accidental life, many, many more days spent staring at the stained anglepoise, the pea-soup walls and the departing bottom of an Irish nurse.

Unlike the wretched geriatrics he often saw patiently awaiting their fate and their operation in the clinic, Jerome was admitted for surgery soon after his abortive examination, and with the usual fine but oddly futile moral scruples from which he suffered, he felt guilt at his preferential treatment. Venetia urged him to cast these feelings to one side and to be grateful that his appalling general condition qualified him for urgent attention.

'For Christ's sake, grab the opportunity with both hands. Your hanging back isn't going to help anyone – it's not as if you're keeping someone else out of a hospital bed. God, Jerome, when will you learn that you have to seize opportunities when they present themselves? You're so busy weighing up options and finding ambiguities and wondering what's going to happen to everyone else. You'll end up dying of altruism.'

'The truth is, Venetia, that I just *might* be a little scared of going in for surgery. I could be covering up that fear by fooling myself that I'm genuinely worried about the justice of waiting-lists. I really am scared. Heaven knows what they're going to find. On top of which, there will be the bloody biopsy result, I can't bear even to think about it. AIDS sure gives you a lot to occupy your mind. If I'm not panicking about scarlet pools in my shit, I'm fretting about whether or not some grim and unheard-of tumour is forming in my body. How would *you* feel?'

'I'd have given up months ago, darling, you know that. I think you're being fabulously brave. All I'm saying is that you ought to be honest with yourself and face up to things directly. It's *your* life we're talking about; only you can do what it takes to save it. David and I are right behind you, we love you and admire you, but we can't fight your battles for you.'

A slight nagging quality had crept into her voice, the tone that she knew he most disliked. It was, she reminded herself, so easy for sensible concern to topple into sly admonition. She curbed herself deliberately and, in compensation for the unnecessary pressure she'd brought to bear, took David and Jerome to a film, an adaptation of an Edwardian novel that left them all purring with delight at the grand design of England's sunset.

En route, three days later, to the hospital, they passed a Cypriot wedding. The guests were spilling out on to the pavement and excitedly greeting one another, laughing and gesticulating. Their evident joy did not, as it might have under different circumstances, cause Jerome to withdraw cynically into his own hardened shell. He felt genuinely pleased to see that the world still celebrated its own happiness and that the rituals of renewal continued uninterrupted like the harvesting of corn. And yet this pleasure could not change the fact that he was in for another interminable stretch of dead days, the limbo of hospital in which the outside world stopped and impinged on life only inasmuch as it sent its periodic emissaries into the microcosmic sickroom.

On the morning of the second day, he was beginning to feel a little calmer. Venetia had installed him with all her natural solicitousness and he was surrounded by reminders of their irregular lives together. She had even brought a photograph of herself, Jerome and David posing lunatically on the waterfront at Sausalito. *Oh les beaux jours!* He had ample supplies to take the place of the dire hospital food, the mashed potato and swede that tasted exclusively of salt, the custard that had congealed into the texture of old paint. He had slept well and without dreaming under the influence of a new kind of pill. Given that he really had no choice in the matter, it was undeniable that lying in bed, insulated from the world, was quite a comfortable and comforting thing. He listened happily to a burst of Vivaldi on his headphones.

When the door opened, he half-expected a deputation of specialists and students to file in and hang around in a sheepish group, as had so often happened in the past. There they had stood and been half-apologetically introduced by the consultant, watching intently (yet with an attempt at self-effacement) as Jerome's eyelids were prised apart and torches shone into his retina. This time, however, there were only two of them, Dr Durkheim and Mark Carr. Knowing, as he did, that the biopsy analysis must be delivered at any moment, his mind immediately froze in the certainty that their joint presence meant bad news. Mark Carr's forehead wore its familiar frown of concern (how much misery he had shouldered in his career) and Dr Durkheim smiled less than usual as he greeted Jerome, a tight pucker of seriousness forming at the corners of his mouth. From a near-by ward came a sudden scream of pain.

'I'm afraid it is Kaposi's sarcoma,' Dr Durkheim said.

Nothing that Jerome had considered in advance had really

prepared him for the actual impact of this blow. It was the virtual certainty of death that now stared him in the face. Sooner or later he would be dead. Smiling with his reflex politeness, eager to show his resilience and his appreciation of their difficult task, he interrupted what promised to be a long account of the medical implications.

'I thought it probably was. Somehow I felt sure from the outset that that spot couldn't be innocent. Instinct, really, like you know when there's something wrong with an animal. Well, I suppose you ought to tell me what this really means.'

As so often in his intercourse, Jerome had subtly adopted the upper hand so that it was he who orchestrated the embarrassing and distressing event.

'It's not at all good news.' This time it was Mark Carr who spoke. The lines on his forehead had deepened and the focus of his paternal gaze didn't waver from Jerome's scared eyes. He was sitting behind, rather than beside his colleague as if on a narrow bus, so that his role as backing support was clearly delineated.

'As you know – and it's rare you have to explain anything to Jerome' (he smiled conspiratorially at Dr Durkheim) – 'it's a kind of cancer that shows up in this form, purple blotches on the skin-surface. It's multi-focal, which is to say it doesn't spread but generally breaks out at several points. Eventually some of the lesions do coalesce. It's pretty fatal . . .' He toyed with a pencil to defuse his sentence. 'Most people die, 70 per cent. Though we don't really know what the classic course of the illness is likely to be. What is *crucially* important is *your* attitude to it. Some of our patients have lived with KS for three or four years and they're functioning fairly normally. There's no pain associated with it. All it needs is mental control to prevent it from intensifying and spreading. And we know from past experience that that is something you have in abundance.'

'You wouldn't say that if you'd seen me wide-awake at four o'clock in the morning wondering how soon I was going to die,' Jerome said reproachfully. With the fingers of one hand he toyed nervously with a cassette case. His feet seemed to have become very heavy and an intense throbbing filled his temples. 'OK, just let's get this absolutely straight. I *could* remain absolutely stable, and, to all intents and purposes, healthy enough. And even if it does get worse, there'll be periods of remission, is that right?'

Both men nodded assent.

'But let's face it, I've now *got* AIDS, haven't I?'

'Yes, you have. I'm afraid there's no escaping it. You'll have to cope with that as best you can. Mark tells me you've prepared yourself pretty well for the possibility.'

'The problem is, of course, that if you prepare yourself for the worst you almost end up by inducing it,' Jerome murmured. 'I've sort of known all along that I'd get it. But, don't worry' – he looked at their crestfallen faces, that seemed to show guilt as if it was they who'd allowed his illness to develop – 'I'll do whatever I can to keep things under control.' It sounded as if it was for their sake rather than his own. 'I've got Venetia and David to help me. You couldn't ask for better nursing-staff. They won't let me die.'

It felt as if there were still some questions hanging in the air, some unresolved aspects of his new condition. Neither doctor seemed ready to leave yet; and relief at the discharging of their duty had not yet expressed itself on their faces. Jerome, sensing this hiatus, plunged in with his cutomary directness: 'And what if the scenario isn't quite such a good one? What if it *does* spread? What happens then?'

Dr Durkheim cleared his throat and delivered what seemed, judged from a prejudiced angle, to be a prepared speech of warning, only its preparedness was counteracted by a distinctly nervous delivery. 'There are patients,' he began, 'who seem to give up and let the cancer run its course. In those cases there are all sorts of associated problems' (again those *problems!*) – 'problems with the gut, the nervous system, sometimes meningitis. Lots of things can go wrong. And sometimes the sarcoma itself spreads in an uncontrolled way' (like wildfire, Jerome thought) – 'although in itself it's relatively benign. But let's not consider that yet. All in all, benign is the word. You're at the benign end of the AIDS spectrum, and let's try and keep it that way. We'll do everything we can to help you, but the onus for the whole thing rests on you.'

'Does that mean we go ahead with the operation on my ass?'

'Oh, yes, that's not affected by any of this. But we're giving you a day to rest and let things sink in. Just try and rest and not let things worry you too much. Everything'll be OK.'

Up to a point, Lord Copper, thought Jerome, after they'd gone. You've just laid out one of the worst prognoses anyone could ask for. I'm a gonner, 100 per cent mortality. From now on I've got to live day by day with the virtual certainty that I'm on the way to dying and it's going to be a painful path getting there. Suffering from a disease that's highly stigmatized, and most people feel little sympathy for. I only hope Venetia can cope with it all. That's one of the dreadful things about being ill, you can't just be ill on your own, you drag other people down with you. She loves me and would never abandon me, I know, but it's going to be so grim for her watching my ill-tempered face as I slide inexorably down. I must remember to try and smile. Even if I feel lousy and my glands are swollen and my head is creaking and the cancer's spreading. Open a new window, open a new door.

The trouble was that however many times you repeated such homely guidelines to yourself, they never really seemed to mean very much; and it was never quite the same as when they were belted out by a chorus-line of 500 girls in riding-breeches doing high-kicks.

The pink and grey aquilegias flowered above their curly grey stalks. They were written all over with Venetia's love; her delicacy and tact. Jerome stared at the flowers through half-closed eyes and dreamed a dream.

14

Dental Dilemma

Waiting for the anaesthetist to come in to administer the pre-med, Jerome stood unsteadily in front of the mirror examing the tiny warts that were spreading over his face. They were insignificant in themselves; but paradoxically they upset him more than some of the more major symptoms. Christ, he thought, I'm going to end up like Oliver Cromwell. Or that hideous old woman in the picture in the National Gallery, sprouting hairs from thick, crusty warts. God, and then maybe the Kaposi's will hit my face too and it'll be like a patchwork quilt, purple patches contrasting with brown warts. But he consoled himself with the realization that the texture and feel and *his* preoccupation with these excrescences was worse than their actual appearance – so far. Touching them, stroking his fingertips around their protuberances, gave him an unnatural sense of their prominence. With great self-restraint, then, he left them alone with a sigh of resignation, and turned his attention to the more pressing problem of his teeth.

It had to be faced, this question of his teeth. They were degenerating fast. The dentist, a kind figure whose kindness was defined by his willingness to treat Jerome, had said there was little he could do, that he would just have to learn to live with it. A persistent inflammation affected the base of each tooth at the meeting with the gum. There was a constant, low-level ache which intensified to real pain whenever he drank hot tea or bit into too sweet a nectarine. He could now see white shining translucently through the flimsy gum, apparently reduced to no more than a membrane, below each tooth. His efforts to combat all of this were obsessive – five scrupulous cleanings a day, repeated sluicings with antiseptic, a vigorous poking of impregnated sticks between each irregular tooth. More important still was the ritual he observed for protecting his teeth: swirling hot tea away from the danger-zone, allowing time to elapse before exposing a cavity to a further attack, sucking with his rough tongue on the edges of a linear fissure that invariably harboured the skin of plums and the most sugary strands of yoghurt.

He contented himself with a fluoride rinse that seemed to placate combat-zone top right but left a stinging pain in the triangular cavity – abscess – top left. As the dentist said, he'd just have to live with it. As with all the wearing symptoms of AIDS. No point in over-exerting himself in self-defence. The great thing about AIDS was that you had to husband your resources, calculate your strength and capacity. If you crossed the room, then you were distinctly less likely to be able to feed the cat a little later. If you got outside the house (which in itself was more than some AIDS-sufferers managed, a heftily conditional conditional clause), then it was fairly improbable you'd be able to cope with the long-distance call on your return without letting the fatigue creep into your voice and slow down your delivery to a meaningless drawl.

A black and white television flickered in the corner, its sound muted. A man and a woman seemed to be preoccupied with a piece of rotten timber alive with woodlice. Jerome had wanted to make it across the room to turn up the sound, but this distrait butterflying of his mind had not encouraged him. He'd even thought of trying to keep the surgeons at bay by hanging a notice on the door saying, 'Hang on. First things first. Loretta Young's strutting her stuff.'

461

15

Bearing Gifts of Love

What was Venetia to do? Everything depended on her ability to sustain Jerome with all her heart.

She came in at intervals to bring him yoghurt, cheese, pale tea like the juice of flowers. She set the offerings on the table and gently persuaded him to take them. She sat on his bed, close up against the tight angle where his body bent in two for foetal security. Realizing how useless and superfluous it would be to coax him into speech, she spoke to him, in a low, soft voice, words of love and solace, and she stroked his forehead and caressed his ears and neck. Had he been able to speak, he might have said; 'I long so much to speak to you, to explain what I am feeling, to show you how I'm fighting against despair. But I just can't. There's no power in me. I know I'm making it worse by allowing myself to get like this. But it's almost as if I'd split into two, the blank, flaccid creature you see in front of you, and another person helplessly observing that feeble cypher. My own self is slipping into another and I cannot control it. Yet strangely it doesn't seem to matter to me; I'm content to let it slide. There's a kind of peace in that. Just emptiness. Don't try and change it. Perhaps it's healthy, a kind of draining so that afterwards I can recover my forces. Leave me to drift through this ether, just the concreteness of your physical presence outside me is enough. Don't judge me too harshly and accuse me of not trying to respond to you. It's not that I don't want to. It's just that I cannot. This has never happened to me before. Stay with me, even if the pain is as great for you as for me. Hold me, look at me, help me, love me, help me.'

But, paradoxically, he could not say any of these things. Perhaps they had not been even formulated in his mind, let alone blocked at the point of articulation. His strange state had declined from its earlier stillness, a creeping aphasia that had overwhelmed him, to its present irreversibility. Now it had become a kind of catatonic trance. No muscles moved and his eyes looked unseeingly out of their sockets. From time to time his hands fluttered, but only with the spasmodic contractions of a dying animal. The black hole was claiming him, swallowing him up in its infernal maw.

Once, visiting the hospital, Venetia had caught a glimpse though an observation window of a hollow-eyed, emaciated patient who lay staring out of eyes devoid of life. Solitude streamed from him. Later she asked Jerome about the other patients in the ward. 'Doesn't anybody organize visitors for them? How awful, no wonder they decline so fast.'

Jerome repressed his anger at her naïve question and rejoined, 'Just think about it, Venetia. These are people who've been rejected for most of their lives, dumped on by bigots for a mere accident of fate. And now they're facing death. Do you honestly think they'd want to be visited by some bountiful lady from a charitable organization?'

Now she tried to interpret everything. Perhaps his hands were trying to reciprocate her own, to reach out and touch her. Was he so emotionally exhausted that all his faculties were disabled? Why was he staring at her like that? Had his lips moved, maybe just a little, trying to say something? Perhaps if she waited a tiny bit longer he would find himself again. There was something very bleak in the fact that none of these questions had answers. They were condemned to hang unspoken, unacknowledged, unresolved in the air between them, just as Jerome's inner thoughts had failed to struggle into life beyond the threshold of his mind. This kind of guess-work could not but upset her, used as she was to long and detailed explanations. Jerome's descriptions, more like nineteenth-century paragraphs than mere sentences, now withheld themselves and left her to flounder in ignorance.

She took his hand with tender pressure and raised it to her lips, kissing it with fervour as she looked fretfully at his face. Then she looked down again, defeated by the unimaginable depths of his eyes. They repeated to her something she already knew: that you can die of despair.

His eyes had seemed to close, but as she made to move again, she saw that they had merely narrowed to a less tormented samurai slit, and now they opened wide again, great grey-blue orbs with an uncharacteristic expanse of sclerotic above and around the iris. Behind them – although she could not know this – lay a dread of sleep, sleep no longer a blessed oblivion but a turbulence of phantasms and terror. Each time he drifted into sleep, it seemed that an army of shades picked up his body and transported him, already in the attitude of a corpse on its bier, into regions of sulphurous torment. And then, as he gradually lost perception of his physical body and its violent seizure, he would turn to mirages of Saturnalian sex, the unbridled fetishes and excesses which he himself had made material in his healthy past, in that time before the great curtain descended.

He would find himself in the midst of a frantic, convoluted orgy, crowded by nameless organs like a paladin encircled by some flailing, polycephalic monster, orifices being pumped with colossal, futuristic pistons glistening with spent slime. And the orgasm transformed itself, as suddenly as it had come into being, into the outpourings of disease: cotton-like fungus spewed out of mouths silent with unvoiced screams, muscular copper-coloured chests began to craze like antique shards and blister into bright tumours, the angry, swollen, phallic veins burst in purple oedemas, the limbs bubbled, ulcerated and turned greenish with mildew. The smiles of sexual climax contorted into the rictus of death, the aphrodisiacs of sweat and pliable flesh were poisonous with foul-spreading buboes and the exhalations of tainted faecal blood. Tight-fitting sexual partners fell away to leave him in shivering, naked isolation, heaped all around with the stench of death, like an abandoned warrior at Gallipoli or Passchendaele. Fields of stick insects strapped into hospital beds, kicking and writhing under their restraints, stretched into the distance. A neon cloud swung down towards him, bearing the dread acronym AIDS. His feet rummaged around in the piled corpses, seeking a foothold to climb out of the pit; and then he saw that the pooling purulence had already seeped into his own feet, was climbing upwards acidifying and rending his limbs, prising the flesh off his bones in peeling, caked strips and the soles of his feet were stuck remorselessly to the glutinous ribbons of cadaverous greenness. '*Zu Hilfe, zu Hilfe!*' his brain yelled, seizing on the cry of Tamino as he tried to escape the coiling, enmeshing dragon. But he was treading impotently on the blotched members, coal-black scrota, which spawned in the mire and thrust upwards like the burnt sticks of a Flanders battlefield, and the images were becoming less distinct, perhaps like the confusion of death itself. A nurse glided past with scythes on the wheels of her feet. Her hands bore, not the stigmata or the Easter lilies, but heat-treated plasma, strips of flesh that bled with the palest lymph. '*Gott, wie dunkel ist hier,*' his entrails cried, and his hair streamed out in the viscid Catherine wheels of ooze. A blurred shadow spread across his dissolving head and the blackness of clotted blood climbed upwards until it covered the surface of his eyes.

16

From the Black Notebook

J. periodically scribbles in a book. But what is the point? Hasn't his brain already embarked on the degeneration inseparable from the virus?

Just as a detective was forced compulsively to question and weigh evidence, to turn over, as in a never-ending nightmare, sequences of events he had witnessed or heard reported, Jerome was unable to view experience except through a great stream of words, obliquely filtered by the obscuring screen. Torment of words. Since he was not a writer, nor did he wish to be one, there was a peculiar suffering in this endlessly fragmentary fashioning of words and sentences, forms which would never be resolved and reliably made sense of in the clarity of writing.

A British wartime army report: homosexuals 'form a foreign body in the social macrocosm'. Metaphor from *warfare*, but also from biochemistry.

Anglo-Saxons could not in practice come to terms with this innocent revision of sex. The leap into the prescribed guilt-free mode was too traumatic; and the darkness of their nature kept surfacing to spread its pathological stain over their recollection of lust. Jerome himself knew that it would be utterly vain to aspire to the deguilting of sex.

J. began to care about things he'd previously dismissed as

banal and predictable. He felt delight in the lengthening days as winter ceded its dark grip to spring. He savoured the pleasures of food which in his impatient, impulsive, headlong past had been mere fuel, a source of energy, and had seemed to be an obsession of people otherwise too unimaginative to see its importance.

The sense of otherness was inescapable. Just as those who lived on islands could not forget that they lived on islands, could not ignore the sea that separated them from terra firma.

Swallowing a telescope (fibre-optic). I bet Nelson was never asked to swallow his telescope.

There goes the neighbourhood.

Even a poster advertising a production of *Aïda* was enough to stop him in his tracks. And his heart gave a leap when he caught sight of a lorry bearing the legend 'Lucozade Aids Recovery'. Was this some kind of mobile field ambulance?

Televisioning himself to death.

Olivia de Havilland, dewy-eyed and Gioconda-smile.

Suddenly life would split up into six simultaneous frames with marcelled chorus-girls swooning on a couch in one room, doing a tap-routine in another, splashing in a marble bubble-bath in another (their swimming-caps made from scalloped rubber), fixing one another's maquillage in the boudoir, trying on frocks down below, mixing old-fashioneds at a mirrored and chrome bar.

How was he to cruise this one? Pull a gardenia through his teeth and murmur: 'Looking for your Shanghai Lil?' (*Footlight Parade*)

'Wait until we walk into the lobby of the Honeymoon Hotel.'

467

Dick Powell (*Footlight Parade*) to Ruby Keeler. Atlantic City. 'Getting friendly with that blonde mam'zell?' (R.K. to D.P.)

Endlessly staring out of the window at the back rooms of houses like the wheelchair-bound James Stewart in *Rear Window* – only there was nothing to see, no Raymond Burr limbering up for a murder with a butcher's knife, a small saw and a length of rope.

Dementia: it makes you a secret celebrity.

And those mosquitoes that had tormented his nights in San Sebastián de Arbuto, buzzing thinly into the silence, then cutting out their engines like doodlebugs, as he waited fearfully for their prick and slapped irritably at his face in the hope of randomly nailing one of the bastards. If they sucked his blood. Ha-ha-ha, he thought, with the triumphant rancour of Eliza Doolittle, 'Just you wait, Henry Higgins, just you wait.' Approach at your peril! Suck it and see! With me it's a suicide mission.

Would he end up covered with the myriad corpses of mosquitoes as high on antibody as the Austrian wine drinkers had been on anti-freeze?

But the song from *My Fair Lady* was so compulsive that it jostled aside the question of the unsuspecting mosquitoes' ultimate fate:

> While I, I'll be famous, I'll be proper and prim,
> Go to St James so often I will call it St Jim.

How come while I'm asleep I'm capable of constructing fantastic narratives full of thrilling, elegant dialogue, convincing characters and extraordinary incidents, and in my conscious state my imagination dries up and life is reduced to a drearily familiar story, nudged around with banal words and repetitive feeling? If only I could *unlock* my unconscious mind, release its secrets. There must be some sort of catalyst. No wonder I'm asleep half the time, it's just a lot more fun!

Dreams – disease. Often a dream might give hints of the condition of the body. Galen recorded how beneficently they had intervened in his own case. Patient should sleep within the precincts of a temple dedicated to Aesculapius (for Christians, pray to Sts Cosmas and Damian) to receive the subliminal message.

He wasted hours of sleep while his mind was besieged with slights, both imagined and real, for which he invented laborious rejoinders and elaborate revenges. His prickly sensibility, naturally Cancerian and quick to take offence, was now heightened by his sense of injustice, the bloody *unfairness* of things.

AIDS makes you feel like a fraud, because of the impossibility of acknowledging it. Every meeting, every conversation, has an edge of deceit.

Watching a group of deaf-mutes, he wondered how you talked about AIDS in sign-language.

Like the Holocaust. Impossible to reconcile Providence with AIDS.

He often found himself sitting impotently apart as a conversation about AIDS raged around him that pushed back the frontiers of crassness to undreamed-of limits. Now that he understood the sickness from its tragic inside, he was peculiarly struck not just by the stupidity of these, but by their heartless flippancy. In moments of strength, he was able to see how this concealed, masked and anaesthetized fear; but mostly it cut him to the quick, for the reminder of the world's indifference had no limits to its power to wound.

It was a cross – a cross shouldered to be borne and suffered – between flu and a hangover.

The current orthodoxy about the disease was that we should fight like crazy against it, and be seen and heard to do so.

Flex one's mental muscles, and beat off the insidious attack by dint of will. Jerome was unsatisfied with this. In his confused mind, it seemed better to try and understand the onslaught, even partially to capitulate.

He felt like a Dickens heroine whose only heroic action was to die.

V.'s bid for suicide, cf. Lily Bart in *The House of Mirth*. Half a death-wish at the disappointment, injustice and imperfection of life, half an accident with chloral.

How had Jerome made V.'s suicide attempt so remorselessly frivolous? Had he meant by this stratagem to demean himself, to understress his own importance to her? To show that their love had never really amounted to anything and should be seen as a passing, incomplete infatuation which, once destroyed, might release her for the real business of living?

It would have been less than human not to respond negatively to his promiscuity. But she countered her reaction by telling herself that some women *needed* love without sex, and that she was being more honest than others in acknowledging this and in so arranging her life as to accommodate it without embarrassment or self-reproach.

She ardently wished to know what other women whose lives had embraced homosexuals had thought about homosexuality itself. Ann Fleming, Syrie Maugham, Tallulah Bankhead. It was striking that none of them had really recorded their feelings.

One day he might wake up with a new and horrifying set of characteristics: the teeth of a Greek crone, the visual sense of the Irish, the sense of humour of Nathaniel Hawthorne.
    Life did seem to be a dream, in the sense that it was random and undisciplined. But where was the justification for the belief that we would wake up from it?
    He'd been put in the invidious position of viewing life

from a special vantage-point. He must ensure that this did not colour and vitiate his objectivity. His most desperate longing was to see life as others saw it – a desire that relied on the illusory notion that there was such a thing as 'real life'. He inspected his feet before getting into bed. One day, one day, and soon, they would bear the marks of Kaposi's sarcoma, the mottled purple lesions that proclaimed the imminence of death. His skin would blotch in clusters of sores. Glory be to God for dappled things.

Their arrival was so sudden. One morning you searched your body and there they were. But their permanence couldn't be avoided. They were there to stay, badges of martyrdom, stigmata of suffering

Oh God, don't let it get to his face. He really cared about the way he looked, and the idea of presenting a face to the world that was covered in hard purple lesions filled him with dread. Shame reared up shame that this might be vanity. Would it be vanity, the classic gay's Achilles' heel, that would be his downfall? But it was more substantial than that. It was perhaps an Englishness, a fear that people might be embarrassed by looking at him.

V.: 'You mustn't get so upset, you'll have to evolve some *physical* techniques for keeping calm. I remember my tutor at the Courtauld, the one who taught Renaissance iconography, he used to get incredibly wound up by what he was saying and then managed to calm down by squatting down on the floor and fondling a brick he kept on the carpet.'

Ferdinand VII's lying-in-state in the Royal Palace, Madrid (October 1833). 'There we behold the beloved.' Ferdinand VII dead and dressed in full uniform with a cocked hat on his head; and his stick in his hand; 'his face, hideous in life, now purple like a ripe fig, was fearful to behold' (Richard Ford). In Ford's picture the king is sitting up, in uniform, under two great canopies, one inside the other, bedclothes spread, from waist downwards, like an elaborate dress.

One Filipino nurse in particular infuriated him. Grinning and leering, her greasy hair piled up in a topknot, she cheerfully bumped into his bed and slopped his Brown Windsor soup. Once he had been sitting on the bedpan and she had opened the panel in the door which he'd left in the 'Do not disturb' position. Had he had a revolver, he'd happily have shot her through the glass.

Death must surely be so simple. 'Mistah Jerome – he dead' (*Heart of Darkness*).

There would be no cure for years. Or maybe Sylvester Stallone would burst in one day and say, 'You're the disease, and I'm the cure' (shoots his victim).

It had allowed him to prove himself. For what had he amounted to in the past? An undisciplined photographer who worked erratically, redeemed only by his fierce love for a woman and a child. Now he was the courageous battler, endowed with all the moral psychological strength that could be expected from weak humanity.

'Da-da,' said David.
    'Oh my God, he's going to be an art-critic,' Jerome said with a sneery moue.

Lanfranc bumping his arse, swivelling on casters.

*

After Jerome discovers the small spot which is confirmed as a Kaposi's sarcoma, he deteriorates rapidly and dies.
    Venetia and David grieve for him. Venetia is so shattered that her mental equilibrium is severely affected.
    In a mental institution, as an old lady, she is reading his account of his life (the first part of the book, the version in which he dies in Madrid). She struggles vainly to understand the disparity between this (semi-fictional) version and what really happened (his slow death from AIDS).

472